The Last Hayride

John Maginnis

GRIS GRIS PRESS • BATON ROUGE, LOUISIANA

*Library of Congress Card Catalog Number: 84-080875
ISBN 0-9614138-1-6*

*Published by Gris Gris Press
Edited by Barbara Phillips
Designed by Lorna Stolzle
Typesetting by Louisiana Graphics*

*First Printing, 1984
Second Printing, 1984
Third Printing, 1985
Fourth Printing, 1985*

Printed in the United States of America

What makes Louisiana America's banana republic?

Who is its Godfather and its Elmer Gantry?

Why was the sheriff's manhood in question?

How does Edwin Edwards get away with it?

Not since Huey Long has any politician so dominated Louisiana politics as has Edwin Edwards. A man of rogue energy and vaulting ambition, the Cajun governor ran the state for eight years with equal parts charm and savvy while leading a personal life as freewheeling and uninhibited as his politics.

At the start of his comeback in 1983, he said all that could keep him from the Governor's Mansion would be his getting caught in bed with "a dead girl or a live boy." Instead he would have to contend with a pair of investigating U.S. attorneys, a Republican truth squad out to expose his lies and tawdry deals, and the shifting political currents of a state facing a troubling and uncertain future.

The state's political landscape is filled in by a wild and improbable supporting cast ranging from flashy rich oil barons to streetwise black ward bosses, from the free-thinking Pentecostal preacher who unlocks the moral mystery of Edwin Edwards to the not-so-good ol' boy country shriff whose manhood becomes a raging campaign issue. Meet the Rodney Dangerfield of Louisiana politics, the Luca Brasi of the bayou, the Spider of New Orleans and the Elmer Gantry of Baton Rouge.

The roving bands of pols and players, reporters and reformers, bodyguards and bagmen all share a date with destiny: a Louisiana election in which reigning dynasties are shattered, strange alliances forged and a ton of money made. They all meet at the crossroads to embark on an American political odyssey, Louisiana's Last Hayride.

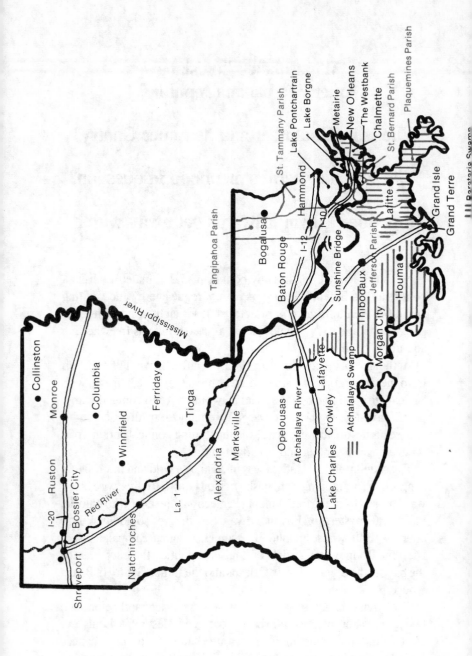

CONTENTS

To my partners Jodie and Steve,
to my Mother, and to Janelle.

We have to be responseful to the public, all the public, even the nuts.
In short, this is kind of a kissass business, to put it bluntly.

—Natchitoches Parish Sheriff's Deputy Manual

1. The Pirate King

Like the nozzle of a giant garden hose on the loose, the Mississippi River for centuries fanned left, fanned right and spewed its silty waters over its lower delta, creating at its mouth a swampy, boggy netherworld, half land, half sea: a teeming estuary for the trappers and fishermen who would live off its inlets, coves and bayous, but also a sinister, dangerous labyrinth for sinister, dangerous men who would need a safe place to hide near the open sea. Today, the wild swampland of Barataria, below New Orleans, provides drug smugglers the same port of entry first used nearly 200 years ago by Jean Lafitte, the Pirate King.

Don't call the old boy a pirate without expecting an argument. One of the few shadowy facts most natives know of the state's history was that Lafitte was no pirate, but a privateer, operating with letters of marque from the South American port of Cartagena to prey on the merchant vessels of Spain. The semantics, however, were lost on his victims. Jean Lafitte and his brother Pierre, with their fleet of fast ships and trained seamen, were smugglers on a grand scale, pioneers in the annals of American organized crime and an affront to the newly installed U.S. government in New Orleans.

Governor William Claiborne was having a hard enough time winning the hearts and minds of the hostile, suspicious, French-speaking subjects who had just been sold down the river for $15 million cash by their emperor and protector Bonaparte. The last thing the American governor needed was an independent, well-armed rival fleet exercising its own foreign policy for profit just offshore. There wasn't much, however, Claiborne could do about the pirate force. Locating the banditti's base in Barataria wasn't easy; engaging the expert marksmen in swamp guerrilla warfare just meant more dead Americans. But what galled Claiborne even more than the elusiveness of Lafitte was his broad-based popular support in the city of New Orleans. He couldn't catch him in the swamp and he couldn't touch him in the city. There the strikingly handsome, impeccably dressed, glib and flirtatious Lafitte was a favorite among the French leaders and ladies. So confident was Lafitte in his popular support that he could openly make fools of the American authorities. When Claiborne just could not tolerate the presence of the privateer any longer and put a $500 price on Lafitte's head, there appeared in the Place d'Armes that night another poster offering a $1,500 reward for the capture and delivery of the American governor to Lafitte at Grand Terre.

The proper, humorless American governor was amazed that the French and Creole citizens of the new territory would readily accept a man so clearly outside the bounds of law and good government. But it wasn't his glamor or charm or even the French tolerance for rascality that made Lafitte a local hero and stymied any American moves against him. French New Orleans revered Jean Lafitte because he gave these struggling pioneers something the brave new democracy of the United States could not: a European-style standard of living made possible through his smuggling trade.

New Orleanians would make regular trips into Barataria along one narrow finger of dry land to advertised auctions at The Temple, Louisiana's first discount shopping center, built on an island of shells where two bayous emptied into Little Lake near the present town of Lafitte. There they could buy the finest European merchandise that the victimized Spanish fleet could offer, from lace to furniture to slaves, at prices far below the exorbitant rates charged by merchants in the city. Lafitte's low, low overhead—he didn't get it wholesale, he got it free— helped create for the new settlers a standard of living far above what they could otherwise expect to scratch out in this lonely, hostile, far-flung outpost of European civilization.

Lafitte was Louisiana's first Robin Hood. He stole treasure from the Spanish, snuck it past the Americans and sold it cheap to the French. So important was Lafitte to the economic lives of the first settlers that if the Congress were to have allowed free elections in the newly acquired territory, the American Claiborne would have had a hard time holding onto his job against the wealthy French privateer.

Despite his playfully condescending attitude toward the American governor, it was Jean Lafitte's patriotism rather than his merchandising that has secured his place in Louisiana mythology. When British forces threatened New Orleans in 1815, the city's newly arrived defender, General Andrew Jackson, needed only two weeks to realize the Battle of New Orleans could not be won without Lafitte's fleet, cannon and artillerymen. The general and the pirate linked forces in one of the great upsets in American history, even if it did take place after the war was settled by treaty. In the afterglow of the shocking victory, President Madison pardoned Lafitte, who resumed business as usual. But the mores of the new country were taking hold in the old city, where the founding French families who had endured so much were steadily being overrun by the Americans. Soon not even New Orleanians distinguished between pirates and privateers, especially since Spain was now an ally against the hated British. Lafitte transferred his operations to Galveston. But soon, after one of Lafitte's captains sank an American vessel, the game was up even there. When an American warship appeared off the Texas coast, Lafitte outfitted his best ship, picked a crew of his most loyal men and set sail into the mists of history.

Though he never returned, his legend endured. Lafitte is revered and remembered as a patriot, a romantic rogue and the purveyor of the good life, which he so grandly expropriated from the foreign colonialists. To the French settlers, far from their homeland and betrayed by Napoleon, Lafitte was a bridge between cultures, as he could deliver the everyday comforts that made life in the New World more bearable. He fulfilled the people's wishes and when he was no longer needed, he disappeared as mysteriously as he first came.

It would be a long time before anyone would again share the wealth on such a grand scale. The reason is that without a cooperatively hapless Spanish navy to pick on, there wasn't much wealth to share. For the balance of the 19th century, Louisiana fell into the long poor line of Southern states dominated by rich planters and city merchants who engineered a low tax, low service state government that allowed them to keep their stranglehold on the state's economy. Louisiana, like other states, had a flash of populist fervor at century's end, but it was stamped out in Louisiana even more viciously than elsewhere, mainly because of the ruthless style of politics that had taken hold. Meeting the challenge of

3

a grassroots populist rebellion of white and black farmers in the 1896 gubernatorial election, the Democratic oligarchy was forced to great lengths to preserve the way of life it held dear. Historian William Ivy Hair quotes a North Louisiana Democratic daily newspaper sounding the call to arms: "It is the religious duty of Democrats to rob Populists and Republicans of their votes whenever and wherever the opportunity presents itself and any failure to do so will be a violation of true Louisiana Democratic teaching. The Populists and the Republicans are our legitimate political prey. Rob them? You bet! What are we here for?" Observing those tenets of "true Louisiana Democratic teaching," the planters and merchants, known as the Bourbons, reversed a troublesome liberal trend toward Negro suffrage, brought populist farmers to heel and managed to keep a lock on power and wealth in Louisiana for another generation.

It took another accident of geography and exploitation by a new colonial power to bring the poor state a new economic savior. Huey Long's populist demagoguery could not have gone as far as it did unless he had other people's money to spend. Like Lafitte, Long preyed on a new colonial power, John D. Rockefeller's Standard Oil, which was tapping and refining the newly discovered oceans of fossil fuels beneath the swampy soil. Huey came out of the piney hills the avenging demagogue and, having seized hold of state government and slapped a one cent a barrel severance tax on "the Standard," he unleashed a torrent of public works and created a powerful central government that smashed forever the tax-nothing, do-nothing Bourbon mindset.

More than wealth was pouring out of the ground. With it came enormous power for Huey Long. With oil money he remade state government in his image, forging a benevolent and ruthless dictatorship that provided a full range of state services for the people—from modern roads to free hospitals and old age pensions—and an overflowing trough for his legions of good friends and soldiers. The more oil money that came in, the grander Huey's schemes to spend it, the larger and more beneficent state government grew, the louder the cries Long was creating a socialist welfare state in this former backwater bastion of Bourbonism. Huey was indeed the modern-day Robin Hood: the greater his power, the wider his ambition, the more outrageous his public behavior. He was playing to his audience, the teeming masses of poor folk, in this state and across the country, who took special delight not only in his taxing the rich but in his thumbing his nose at the genteel sensibilities of the privileged class.

Huey Long revolutionized Louisiana politics by taking from the rich, keeping some for himself and his friends and giving more to the poor than government ever had before. Whatever national threat Huey posed to the Established Order passed with his assassination. But in Louisiana, Huey the Martyr set in motion a tradition of populism, power and public works—for as long as there would be other people's money to pay for it.

Huey set the standard for his successors to govern by: a massive, centralized government powered by oil, a wealth-sharing plan for politicians and cronies and high political theater for the people. Sometimes Louisianians would get too much of a good thing. After the Kingfish died, no strong central figure could keep the rascality within acceptable bounds, the U.S. Justice Department could no longer look the other way, and the Louisiana scandals of 1939 forced Governor Dick Leche to resign in disgrace, sent the president of LSU to jail and caused the oil-fueled binge, so amply documented in Harnett B. Kane's *Louisiana Hayride*, to crash and burn. From those ashes rose a few fitful attempts at reform, but with the rise to power of Earl Long in 1948 a new hayride was hitched up.

The basic form remained the same: high state services led by charity hospitals and free school lunches; low governmental efficiency marked by favoritism, waste and a manageable degree of corruption; and ribald political theater. Uncle Earl was no Kingfish but he was twice the showman his older brother had been. Earl could say and do the darnedest things, and when Miz Blanche finally had the state police cart him off to a mental hospital, only to have the old buzzard fire the director of hospitals and set himself free to go on a recuperative gambling fling through the Western states and Mexico, the rest of the country was predictably shocked and repulsed. *There goes Louisiana politics again: how can those poor people stand it?*

The one who took the trouble to find out, the great A. J. Liebling in *The Earl of Louisiana*, had one hell of a good time and left with the firm conviction that Earl Long was the most effective liberal in the South and one of the leading American statesmen of his time. He saw Louisiana as a misplaced Mediterranean state, an American Lebanon with its diverse and conflicting religious and ethnic factions. He saw this diversity giving the gumbo of Louisiana politics its flavor, but the body, said Liebling, was oil. Liebling's book, as close as anyone's come to explaining the phenomenon, became the primer for any outside journalist visiting the state, as they do each election year to get a taste of *joie de vivre* and to gawk at high-priced, theatrical political campaigns. The general story line they come away with is *Louisianians love their politics like they do their gumbo, hot and spicy, and they applaud chicanery and corruption as good political theater.* It's an easy story to write. About two dozen of them, basically the same, were written and broadcast during this last election. But it misses an important point, the why part.

Not even the best political sideshow could play in this state if there wasn't a good economic reason for it. Louisiana keeps electing colorful, populist rogues because it can afford them, or, perhaps, can't afford to do without them. Louisiana government is based on high services, low efficiency and colorful theater for two basic reasons: 1) a built-in constituency for populism, that is, lots of poor folks, and 2) a middle class that doesn't have to pay the bill. The oil companies do.

Louisiana's individual citizens are among the least taxed in the country. The state income tax is negligible, the residential property tax is laughable. A family who owns a $75,000 home outside the city limits of Baton Rouge pays zero in local and state property taxes. Families with $125,000 homes pay less tax in one year than a similar family in Houston pays in one month. Severance taxes in Louisiana historically pay from one-third to two-fifths of the total state bill, depending on what kind of year they had in the oil patch. And there's no state sales tax on food and drugs.

The middle class, in effect, has been bought off. Since the average taxpayer pays hardly any taxes except on sales, what does he or she care what the politicians do with the money? So the state is first provider of many services that don't even exist in other states. So the public schools are underfunded, the roads inadequate and there are more people on the state payroll doing nothing than are employed by other states three and four times the size of Louisiana. So waste is rampant and sweetheart contracts and consulting fees are dished out to friends and contributors. The Louisiana middle class, the same people who in other states stage periodic tax rebellions and crucify any politician brushed with scandal, feel no reason to complain. And so they don't.

The great myth, nurtured by Liebling, is that Louisiana people, as a group, love their politics and gossip about it incessantly in political cafes on every street corner. The truth is, the vast majority of people in this state don't give a damn about politics. They neither pay for it nor care much for it—it's rampant apathy, not interest, that gives politicians the free rein they have to perform as outrageously as they do. Even the underclass, the recipients of the more liberal state services, take them for granted. The people who do care about politics are the politicians and their symbiotic allies, the businessmen-contributors. The political contributor in Louisiana approaches politics as he would any investment. With the accepted rule of politics being to do business with one's friends in any way legally or otherwise possible, it pays to make friends with the right people. That's the accepted rule anywhere, except that in Louisiana, with most folks not even paying attention, there's more latitude in what's possible. And there is no more important friend (read: investment opportunity) to cultivate than someone who may one day be governor.

Since the oil money flows directly into the state treasury instead of to local taxing bodies, power is centralized in the state capital to a greater degree than in any other state. Within the state capital, the power of the governor dwarfs all others'. In terms of the powers vested in chief executives in other states, the governor of Louisiana has no peer. He directly controls 1,340 appointments, including cabinet secretaries and undersecretaries and the members of 135 boards and commissions regulating everything from mineral production on public lands to cosmetologists and embalmers. Through these boards and his own fiats, the governor can influence private industry and directly steer massive construction jobs and lucrative professional contracts to his friends. Earning the friendship of the governor can pay big dividends, perfectly legal and legitimate, in the form of highly profitable supply contracts (sure, there is a bid law, but bid specifications can be massaged), state leases, emergency requisitions, architect and engineer selections, issuance of tax-free bonds for private investment, nonbid professional services and friendly decisions and inside information from regulatory boards— to name just a few favors a governor can bestow on his friends.

There is no real balance of power with the Legislature, a body for many years regarded as nothing more than a debating society set in place to conform to the mandates of the U.S. Constitution. On paper, the Legislature has power, but the real power of the purse is held by the governor. In order to get in the local projects they need for reelection, legislators tend to cooperate with the governor on the total package. Whom he can't control with the carrot he can always beat with the stick—the ultimate power of the veto. The governor can line item veto, that is, excise any single appropriation important to an individual legislator or delegation. The mere threat of a governor's veto on the right project can bring almost any legislator to heel on another issue. Practically, there is no overriding a governor's veto. Sure, if you can get two-thirds majorities in both houses you can override a governor's veto. Not to say it couldn't happen, it's just that it hasn't in this century. That's one hell of a stick.

Louisiana elects more statewide officials than does any other state. But there is little sharing the power because of the governor's control of the budget—everyone's budget. Say some brave attorney general wants to launch an investigation of the Mineral Board. He may find, at the start of the new fiscal year, that funds for investigators, nay, even attorneys, have been cut from his budget.

The state bureaucracy is massive. In 1900, a group photo of the employees at the Old State Capitol contained 30 faces. In 1983, 125,000 people, including schoolteachers, worked for the state. Another 12,000 employees of local governments, from firemen to deputy sheriffs, received state supplemental pay. And though most of them are civil service employees, immune to the spoils system, they nevertheless know who's boss, for the Legislature only grants pay increases when the governor says so.

That's the primary reason why so much is spent in state elections, because so much is at stake. State government is big business in Louisiana. Doing business means having friends, and in this business, friends don't come cheap.

Louisiana government is built around the banana republic principle of one strong man, accountable only to the vote of the people and unfettered by the checks and balances found in established democracies. The system appears to invite more corruption but in another way controls it. Louisianians learned a hard lesson from the horrendous scandals of 1939. In the four years after the death of the Kingfish, the pigs at the trough got out of control, and the U.S. Justice Department had to finally step in. There were too many small-time operators tapping into the unguarded state treasury. Huey was wise enough and strong enough to see that no one stole too much. Knowing full well if there's government there will be graft, a prudent citizenry demands a strong governor to broker the deals, contain corruption to acceptable levels and in general keep everything running smoothly.

There's another reason—as much psychological as economic—why Louisianians don't mind vesting that kind of power in one strong politician-king. The lessons of the Civil War weren't lost on Louisiana. Keeping the Union whole meant keeping the South down. Today, as then, the South, with its abundant natural resources, continues to be an economic vassal of the industrialized East. More jobs may be coming to the Sunbelt but the profits from the giant refineries and petrochemical plants continue to go back north, if not overseas. Louisiana is as much an economic colony of New York today as it was when owned outright by Spain and by France. The severance tax on the state's extracted natural resources is all the tribute that can be exacted from the new colonialists. Louisiana embraced Huey Long and tolerated his excesses for the same reason it did Jean Lafitte: not just because they enhanced the quality of life but because they took a piece from the colonialists' purse to do it. Since then, Louisiana continues to look to one strong man who can keep straight the business of politics at home and exact some tribute from the outside interests that ultimately control the state's destiny.

The rest of the country may sneer at Louisiana politics, but Louisianians can at least be comforted knowing that those critics of this political system are footing a large part of the bill for all its wonderful excesses. It's as close as they can come to revenge.

2. Un de Nous Autres

Eighty miles north of Baton Rouge, you don't expect to hear French spoken in the bar at the edge of the courthouse square. This far north of Baton Rouge, you wouldn't expect to find a bar on the edge of the courthouse square. Though the area is actually in Central Louisiana, to South Louisianians, impatient with geographic subtleties, Central Louisiana is to North Louisiana as Central America is to South America: foreign soil. In a state divided in culture, custom and cuisine between north and south, anything beyond a 30-minute drive above U.S. 190 is North Louisiana, land of Baptists, hills and cotton.

But that doesn't explain the old men, joking and cursing in French, drinking at a bar that is closer to the courthouse steps than is the First Baptist Church. But this is Marksville, in Avoyelles Parish, an exception to the Louisiana line of demarcation. Geographically it is the buttonhole of the state, the center point where the Red River and the hills of the north meet the Atchafalaya and the plains of the south. Agriculturally, its soybean and cotton fields belong to the north, while culturally and historically it is French Louisiana, the northernmost tip of the Cajun Triangle, which abruptly ends at the banks of the Red River. That's the line. Within Avoyelles Parish, one is defined by being from either the "Cajun side" or the "Redneck side" of that river.

Safely on the Cajun side, in the bar on the courthouse square, the visitor, lulled by the first beer of the hot, humid afternoon and the soft Cajun patois filling the room, is jarred by a foreign sound—spoken English. The young bearded fellow at the bar is breaking the house language, but the substance of his remarks seems to fit the atmosphere. "Yeah, I ran six or seven shady deals with a clean face, so I had

10

to grow this beard to run a few more."

The old boys laugh in appreciation at the ingenuity, and a few more patrons sidle up to the bar. A bigger crowd than usual for a weekday. But it's not your every day in Marksville—tonight its favorite son is coming home.

The daylight is fading just enough so you don't have to squint, once outside the bar. A city cop directs traffic at the corner, rerouting cars away from the closed street behind the courthouse. A country western band (from the redneck side of the Red) on the courthouse steps wails out "I Can't Stop Loving You" as farmers and townsfolk, parking their cars and pickup trucks, begin to fill up the paved yard of the courthouse. Some older citizens are settling down on the courthouse lawn as volunteers dish out hotdogs and Cokes to all takers. "The square couldn't hold the crowd for Earl," an old-timer reflects, "but this ain't bad." No, it isn't, for a hot summer evening, with the sun just about to set, and nothing to bring out the crowd of well over 1,000 from their air conditioning and prime time TV but some free hotdogs, a redneck band and Edwin Edwards.

At just past seven o'clock, there is a stir on the edge of the crowd. Edwin Edwards has materialized across the street and is shaking hands with about a dozen blacks, who, conditioned by their age and the way things used to be, feel more comfortable on the far side of the street.

The band plays on as Edwards, followed by his usual entourage of driver, aides, a few reporters, local supporters and, in a rare campaign appearance, his son Steven, crosses the street and presses into the crowd, which quickly engulfs him. Edwards doesn't glide through this crowd as smoothly as he does elsewhere on the campaign trail. He's less the snappy, urbane, self-assured man of power he is before most strangers on the trail—today he's the Edwards boy come home to the people who watched him grow up. He looks into each face to jog his memory of a name of someone he grew up with, or worked with, 30 years ago.

"Remember me?" quizzes the old fellow.

Edwards reaches back. "Sure, you used to run the cleaners next to the Western Auto."

"Still do."

Some he's never seen before but knows exactly who they are. "You're Shirley Gremillion's daughter." He points to the pretty teenager.

"I'd know those eyes anywhere."

Some Marksvillians have set up their folding chairs on the lawn nearest the building, waiting for their old playmate to pass their way. "The last thing we thought he would be was governor," says one. "Sure, he said it, we just didn't believe him." Even his reputation as a ladies' man is lost on these who knew him first. According to Ellen Moulard, "We used to chase him and try to kiss him. But he'd get under the house and stick his tongue out at us. Oh, if we'd have caught him, we'd have eaten him up."

The entourage seems to be snaking aimlessly through the crowd, but by the time he mounts the steps, he has covered the entire square and shaken every outstretched hand. Now he stands before the crowd with his arm around a man in a shortsleeve shirt, who, with thinning dark hair and deeply tanned, weatherbeaten face, appears to be older than Edwards. Yet the two are close in age and linked by a searing childhood experience that forms the subject of this evening's opening parable. "Many of you already know this man, Glen Dunlap. I met him many years ago when his father paddled across the river in the night and came to our family's store and knocked on the door. There with him was this seven-year-old whose fingers had just been crushed by a falling pile of logs. I remember staying up all night with my mother, soaking Glen's hands in warm water to ease his pain. We didn't send for the doctor because it was the middle of the night, we were sharecroppers and you just didn't do that. I remember thinking how important it was to help people, that my mother was always there to help, that people, no matter who they were, should be able to get help when they need it." A fitting parable, the perfect jumping-off point to attack the incumbent governor, an uncaring man, the crowd is told, who reduced the state allowance to senior citizens in nursing homes from $50 a month to $40. With his hand on Glen Dunlap's shoulder he swears, "I would rather my arm wither and fall off before I cut the little spending money that poor widows have who just want to live out their twilight years in peace and dignity." He sees so many Louisianians who need help and can't get it. "They can't find a job and can't find anyone to talk to. Have any of you ever called Dave Treen? Go ahead and try it and see if he calls you back. By the time you hear from him again, I'll be in the Mansion answering the phone."

His words aren't new but the context is fresh, as though the memory of the boy with the crushed fingers has inspired his impromptu riff on the importance of a governor who cares. The crowd in the darkness of the courthouse lawn is with him, enthusiastic and involved. His words cut back through the years and the money and the power and all that separates him from his backwater beginnings, striking that chord with his old neighbors, reminding them what it was like growing up—together—at the bottom of the social order. They remember. No matter that Edwin Edwards now belongs to a different world of power and money—he came from theirs. One of the senior bar patrons who has worked his way up to the front of the crowd raises his Falstaff in salute: "Un de nous autres." *He's one of us.* It wasn't the first time I had heard that phrase, in French or in English, while following Edwin Edwards across the state. Every candidate strives for that kinship, whether pitching rednecks or Eskimos. Edwin Edwards' special gift is that it comes not only because of his nature but because of his background. For in Marksville, where north meets south, where divergent cultures, languages and values converge and coexist, to be one of us is to cover a lot of ground. The paradoxes of Louisiana are commonplace in Avoyelles Parish, nowhere more so than in the house Boboy Edwards built on the banks of the Red River.

Edwin Edwards calls Marksville his hometown, but that was merely the location of the nearest post office. Edwards was born in the little community of Johnson, in an area which, fitting the vague and shifting geography of the upland delta region, in earlier days, at different times took the names of the nearby communities of Catville and a place called Riddle.

His mother, Agnes Brouillette, was pure Cajun French. She married Clarence Edwards, whose mother was Cajun but whose father came from Welsh stock by way of the Kentucky and Tennessee migration into North Louisiana's hill country three generations before. The five Edwards children—Audrey, Allen, Edwin, Marion and Nolan—are three parts Cajun and one important part Redneck.

There were three class distinctions in the country: sharecropper, farmer and merchant. Clarence Edwards, "Boboy" to his friends, at one time or another was all three. When his second son Edwin was born in 1927, he was strictly sharecropping cotton. But he inherited a few acres, bought a few more and finally built a small one-room general

13

store that traded with other sharecroppers.

Boboy only had a third grade education because, as the second child of eight, he had to quit school at 13 when his father died and his mother delivered twins two months later. Yet as an avid reader of dictionaries and encyclopedias, he could firmly articulate his rock-hard beliefs. Edwin Edwards credits his father's eloquence and outspokenness for his own talent for public speaking, though Boboy did hold a particularly dim view of politicians.

From his isolated farm he watched his sons grow up to be worldly men—late in life he satisfied his own urge to see what lay beyond the Red River. "In the mid-'50s sometime," recalls his son Edwin, "he got up one morning and told our mother that he was going to take a trip. Mother asked him where he was going and he said he didn't know. When was he coming back? Couldn't say. He just left one day. He bought a bus ticket and went out to California and up to Oregon and Washington and down through the west. Sometimes he rode the bus, other times he hitchhiked. We didn't hear from him until two or three months later when he came home."

Agnes Edwards was a woman country people came to for help, whether for first aid emergencies for children or midwifing babies. By her count, she helped deliver 1,800 infants, often holding a lantern as she reassured a nervous expectant father as he rowed her across the Red River to meet the doctor. Farm life was a grind for Agnes. Through most of her child-rearing years she worked over a wood stove in a house with no electricity or running water.

There wasn't much for a kid in Johnson to do but farm chores. Edwin, the middle child, developed an odd quirk for a farm boy, an obsession with cleanliness, one that he keeps to this day. His sister Audrey remembers Edwin would not let anyone else clean his own plate and utensils. Once when the family visited neighbors and the hostess began to dish out ice cream, Edwin pulled out his own cup and spoon and ordered, "Just put it in here." His abhorrence for getting his hands dirty pushed him to get out of the cotton fields at the first chance and into the city for a job at the Western Auto store after school. As he would later tell approving farm audiences during campaigns: "I wasn't very smart, but I knew as a six-year-old I didn't want to farm. You have to work too hard. I wanted to be a politician and a lawyer so I wouldn't have to work."

Education was revered in the Edwards home. "Anything less than a B on a report card meant a whipping from my father," says Marion. Edwin and Marion rarely fell below the mark and graduated as valedictorians of their classes at Marksville High. They were as adept at getting along with their schoolmates. Neither Edwin nor Marion remembers ever getting in a fight with other children.

Though half Cajun himself and in many ways a freethinker who encouraged the children to make their own decisions, Boboy's redneck side commanded an absolute intolerance of alcohol or tobacco. Once he caught the three younger boys smoking a pipe one Sunday behind the barn. They were severely whipped and sent into the fields to pick 100 pounds of cotton—and no throwing a watermelon in the sack to make the weight. Edwin got the point. Though he would later embrace the live-for-the-moment *joie de vivre* of the Cajuns, his abstinence from intoxicating substances remains as hard-shell as any Baptist's.

On that Cajun side of the Red River, Catholicism was practically the state religion. Not in the Edwards household. Agnes, of course, was devoutly Catholic. Boboy was officially Presbyterian, but, more to the point, anti-Catholic. And though he allowed the priest to baptize the children, he wasn't silent about his hatred for the Church of Rome. As brother Marion remembers, "The only bitter arguments in our household were over religion." That split within the family, along with the natural curiosity of farm children with nothing better to do, drew Audrey, Edwin and Marion to the makeshift church that Nazarene missionaries set up across the road. "We went because it was there, because it was something to do," says Marion. "I remember thinking it was the greatest thing in the world when they gave me a little 15-cent Bible." The children were regulars at the Nazarene services and as teens even preached at brush arbor revivals, which provided young Edwin his first audiences. Miss Agnes was very upset and cried to the priest, who said the children were committing mortal sins. But she got no support from her husband, who delighted in and encouraged his offspring's desertion of the One True Faith.

He remembers as a child gravitating toward the courthouse, where he saw all elements of parish life pass through the doors, but mostly the lawyers and the politicians, people who made their living talking, dealing, negotiating—not picking cotton or even stacking car filters in the Western Auto. He decided what he wanted to be, and his girlfriend Elaine Schwartzenberg was the first person he told: "I'll be governor one day."

Since ambition that large was hard to nurture in a little town like Marksville, a teenaged Edwin got his first crack at politics at Pelican Boys State in the summer of 1943. The annual summer training camp at LSU gave young leaders of tomorrow their first intoxicating whiff of power. "You can't believe the power trip," one former child politico confided, "of blowing a whistle and seeing 500 16-year-olds cross the street." Edwin cut his political teeth not as a candidate but as campaign manager for a skinny kid from Baker named Ossie Brown, who, with the help of his energetic, fast-talking bilingual manager, was elected governor. (Edwards likes to point out that Ossie would not win another election until 1972, when as governor he helped his old friend get elected district attorney of East Baton Rouge Parish.)

After LSU and law school and marriage to Elaine, he moved from Marksville—no new fortunes to be made there—south to Crowley, where his married sister Audrey lived. He hung up his shingle and he prospered. He quickly made friends around the courthouse, especially with an equally smooth-talking young attorney named Edmund Reggie, whose taste for politics and the good life matched Edwin's. Edwards started his unbroken string of winning elections with a city council post in Crowley. In 1964, he entered the state Senate, where he impressed Governor John McKeithen, who tapped the 36-year-old Cajun as an administration floorleader. When Seventh District Congressman T. A. Thompson died in a car accident, young Senator Edwards, with McKeithen's help, won the special election and was on his way to Washington in 1965.

Edwin Edwards didn't pretend to be interested in the painfully slow workings of the Congress: he introduced few bills, skipped most debates and racked up one of the worst attendance records on the Hill. But he learned fast how the power game was played in Washington and how very much clout rested with the seniority-heavy Louisiana delegation. Clout that could help him achieve his own goals. The only real way an ambitious congressman could get any political mileage back home was to deliver some plum project that would boost his district's economy. Edwards had no seniority, and no pull in the bureaucracy or in the White

16

House. All Edwards had going for him was the friendship of the rest of the delegation. But what friends to have. Senator Allen Ellender of Houma, who delighted in conversing exclusively in French with the freshman congressman, chaired the Agriculture Committee and was the second ranking Democrat on the all-important Appropriations Committee. Senator Russell Long, chairing the Senate Finance Committee, had the last word on all foreign trade legislation. In the House, Otto Passman chaired the foreign aid subcommittee of Appropriations while Hale Boggs on the Ways and Means Committee had the ear and total confidence of its chairman Wilbur Mills. They had been just drinking buddies to T. A. Thompson, but to Edwin Edwards, whose special gift was in knowing how to use the power of others to help himself, they were giants who, with some cultivation and imagination, could give the young congressman the necessary political boost.

What the Seventh District needed most was a new market for its rice, which was stacking up in the mills as its price steadily dropped. South Korea bought a lot of rice, primarily from the closer California ports. It also bought a lot of airplanes, bombs and guns for its military arsenal. President Park Chung Hee had sent a young businessman named Tongsun Park to Washington to persuade American congressmen, by whatever means necessary, to better appreciate South Korea's needs. Park became good friends with Edwin Edwards, as well as with Otto Passman, whose subcommittee was so vitally important to Park's mission. Park was more than happy to broker the rice deal to please his friends. With the help of the other powerful Louisiana congressmen, all the right skids were greased with foreign aid, foreign trade and appropriations. All that was needed was for the Agriculture Department to approve a $31 million long-term, low interest loan for the purchase. Dealing with the bureaucrats was tricky, but Passman knew just where to push. He went to the White House to ask his friend Richard Nixon a favor. As Nixon picked up the phone to call the Agriculture Department, the President thought he was accommodating his good friend Otto Passman, not realizing how much he was in on the making of the next Louisiana governor.

In 1971, all over Acadiana, rice mills emptied and ships filled up at the Port of Lake Charles bound for Seoul. As the price of rice shot up, Louisiana rice farmers, on the brink of a disastrous year, made record profits. Their congressman had come through for them when they needed help and they felt strongly they owed him a debt of gratitude. So did their bankers, investors and suppliers. The young congressman had just ingratiated himself with most people with money in Southwest Louisiana. And he already knew how they could return the favor.

History will judge John McKeithen one of the state's greatest governors. Too bad he didn't end that way with the voters. He was the pivotal governor who broke state politics with the hidebound first half of the 20th century and lit a new industrial fire under a lagging economy. In the view of business leader Ed Steimel, McKeithen was the "all-time greatest industry hunter" whose overwhelmingly persuasive salesmanship and promise of cheap natural gas attracted scores of the great petrochemical plants that transformed the stretch of river between Baton Rouge and New Orleans into the Little Ruhr Valley of America.

McKeithen contributed even more to the state as a racial peacemaker. He started out mouthing "separate but equal" but ended up presiding over the peaceful integration of Louisiana public schools and colleges. As a politician, he earned his place in the state hall of fame by lulling voters into approving a two-term constitutional amendment to allow governors to succeed themselves.

Big John was, still is, a big man, with an overpowering personality and an ego that wouldn't quit. He thought big. And he didn't shrink from a fight. Finally, those two qualities and the nature of Louisiana politics did him in. By the end of John's second term, the state was tiring of his bigness. His Superdome was causing super financial and political headaches. The Legislature was balking at the spate of taxes he shoved through it. And the people were just a little embarrassed by John's vice presidential ambitions and the way he skulked off from the 1968 Democratic convention when those dreams were summarily dashed in Chicago. McKeithen's diminished popularity was finished off by a devastating *Life Magazine* article tracing links between McKeithen's staff and Mafia boss Carlos Marcello.

McKeithen, in many ways a reform governor when he entered office in 1964, was leaving with the people calling out for more reform. McKeithen blazed many trails but he wasn't able to break the jinx of governors who left office less popular than when they came in.

Louisiana never saw a field of candidates like the menagerie lined up for the 1971 race. The 17 qualifiers included:

—former governor and country western star Jimmie Davis, the favorite of the sheriffs and the former race-baiting sweetheart of the rednecks, whose greatest contributions to the state in his two prior terms were the infamous Sunshine Bridge that spanned the Mississippi and dead-ended in a canefield and a graceless, antebellum style Governor's Mansion built on the Interstate;

—two cousins of Huey Long, Congressman Speedy Long and Gillis Long, who had run a heartbreakingly close third in 1963 and was about to do it again;

—grocery store magnate John Schwegmann, who used his grocery bags for political advertising;

—highly popular Lieutenant Governor Taddy Aycock, who should have never dared to test the Peter Principle;

—gadfly raconteur Puggy Moity, widely assumed to be paid by Gillis Long to pull black and Cajun votes away from Edwin Edwards by saying terrible things about him (Puggy's weekly half hour live TV spots were hilarious bad taste—his tagging Edwards "Tweety Bird" got Edwards' goat more than anything else said about him);

—*Life Magazine* writer David Chandler of Mafia expose´ fame, running for governor to write a book about it;

—and two self-labeled reform candidates, the moderate, good government state senator from Shreveport, J. Bennett Johnston; and the French-speaking congressman from Acadiana, who was supposed to be good at raising money.

It would be the most free-spending election in Louisiana history, especially with the new feeder at the election trough, TV advertising. Edwards would claim to have spent $1.5 million on the whole election—an astronomical sum at the time. But as there were no campaign finance reporting laws, who knows how much was spent? Certainly not Edwards or his brother Marion, who conducted fund raising from his suite in the Monteleone in New Orleans. As Edwards would recall in the midst of a future investigation, "We sat in that hotel room and raised thousands of dollars in the morning and gave it away that afternoon and the next day I couldn't tell you where half of it came from or went."

Yet plenty of contributors counted on his remembering. According to his campaign sidekick Clyde Vidrine in his salacious memoirs, *Just Takin' Orders,* Edwards was outright promising specific state positions to contributors. Edwards would later dispute the amounts, but the promises, he said, were not illegal. As far as a political campaign went, very little was illegal in 1971.

Bennett Johnston, with his established business and oil support, had good financial backing, but more than that, he had the appeal of the dynamic new urban conservative, an articulate and progressive North Louisianian not strapped with a hick accent and a neanderthal view of race relations. The emerging middle class saw in Bennett a break with the old way of politics in this state, a decent guy who wasn't in with the courthouse gangs and their backroom deals, and folks liked that. Bennett was pure. He represented the fiscal conservative and good government ideals espoused by Republicans without having to carry that Republican baggage with him.

When the smoke cleared, and there was a lot of that, the two reform candidates led the field, Edwards with 23 percent of the vote, Johnston with 19. Bennett—otherwise known as "Bennett Who?" on election night—had the momentum going for him. Not only did he carry North Louisiana but did surprisingly well with white voters in New Orleans and Baton Rouge. But his strength was also his problem. Not only did he present the image of being unsullied by bargaining with courthouse gangs, it was a true image. Bennett couldn't or wouldn't cross over and get in the back door and deal with Jimmie Davis' sheriffs or offer to help pay Gillis Long's campaign debts or make any of the traditional second primary moves by which winning coalitions are formed.

Edwin Edwards was not so handicapped. No sooner had Johnston turned off some sheriff or potential contributor than Edwards was camped out at the door. Not only did he offer to help pay Gillis' campaign debts but promised to gerrymander a congressional district to fit Long's black voting strength. Edwards was the labor candidate, the country candidate, the Cajun candidate, the Catholic candidate (he kept the Nazarene connection very quiet in South Louisiana) and the favorite of the blacks. But it took more than that to beat back the emerging white middle class conservative vote. Edwards' secret was that he could use his assets without being trapped by them.

20

Though a French-speaking candidate, with an English surname he could plug for votes in many North Louisiana towns where an Edwin Brouillette best not even stop.

Though the Catholic candidate, he could preach in piney woods revival tents.

Though the sharecropper's son espousing populism in rural parishes, he could champion the oil and gas industry and reassure any Chamber of Commerce group that he was here "to comfort the afflicted but not to afflict the comfortable."

Though he could cut his deals with the sheriffs and black bosses, he could go on TV promising reform and an "era of excellence."

When it came right down to it, he got his vote out and Bennett didn't. Edwards did well where he was supposed to, plus he cut into North Louisiana just enough to eke out a 4,500 vote win, a margin of less than one-half of one percent or about one vote per precinct.

No sooner had he put away the Republicans' draft candidate named Dave Treen in the general election than Edwin Edwards moved to take hold of the levers of power like they had never been gripped in 40 years. He had called for reform in government, so had Johnston, but Edwards' idea of reform was to remold the whole structure and form of state government to meet the modern needs of government as well as his own.

The people wanted a new constitution—a convention was at work within a year. Publicly, he gave that body plenty of leeway but behind the scenes he tightly controlled it through the substantial number of appointments he made to the convention. His talent was in achieving the semblance of good government reform that at the same time enhanced his already considerable power. In rearranging the mire of 258 state agencies into a cabinet form of government, he didn't eliminate any jobs but concentrated his own power by creating a new top level of bureaucracy under the governor's exclusive control. He won a critical showdown in clipping the prosecutorial wings of the state attorney general on local criminal matters. The move enormously increased the power of the district attorneys, who could keep the state attorney general out of local criminal investigations unless he could get a judge to sign an order. In the past, local corrupt politicians had nothing to worry about as long as the attorney general was your Jack P. F. Gremillion-type (of whom Uncle Earl once said, "If you want to hide something from Jack

Gremillion, put it in a law book"). But this key clause, personally lobbied by Edwards, effectively limited the damage an aggressive and ambitious attorney general—like this new guy Billy Guste, who had just been elected—could do if seized by some frenzied Watergate reform spirit. Nowhere was local jurisdiction more important than in the seat of state government, now the turf of Edwards' old friend from Pelican Boys State, newly elected Baton Rouge DA Ossie Brown.

Structure was great, but what Edwards needed was money for pay raises, roads and bridges. Concrete is the currency of power, the carrot of legislative leadership. To be the kind of powerful and benevolent governor of his self-image, he'd need lots of money. The obvious place to go was the oil companies. Every populist governor thinks of that, but the oil lobby makes every penny per barrel of severance tax squeezed from them a bloody battle. Instead of nickel and diming around with the severance tax, Edwards moved to change the flat tax of 18 to 26 cents per barrel to 12.5 percent of value. Initially, the oil companies put up a vicious fight, but when Edwards turned the full weight of his office against them, they scattered before him. And as the post-Arab embargo price of oil shot through the roof, so did severance tax receipts. Even with the production of oil beginning its long-term decline in the '70s, the value tax became a revenue gusher that fueled an exponential, unprecedented leap in the size of state government. In Edwards' first year in office, the state spent less than $1.9 billion. At the end of his second term, the budget topped $4.5 billion.

The volume to value switch was a master political stroke and the most important economic legacy of Edwards' tenure, the most effective revenue raiser in the history of the state—as well as the most politically acceptable. It enabled Edwards to eliminate the state property tax and the state sales tax on food and drugs. In his first year in office, he was responsible for both the largest tax increase and the largest tax decrease in state history. The oil companies passed the tax along to customers, the consumers in the 49 other states, forcing the rest of the United States to involuntarily bankroll a massive program of public spending by Edwin Edwards. Huey Long would have approved. And Jean Lafitte, wherever he was, would have been proud.

Edwards took to power easily, almost casually. No early riser, the longer into his term, the less time he spent at the Fourth Floor office at the Capitol, increasingly conducting the state's business from his den in the Mansion. He delegated huge chunks of authority, primarily to Commissioner of Administration Charlie Roemer, the sly and ambitious North Louisiana plantation master and computer king, a man who knew how to run things. Impatient with details, the governor wanted his options spelled out on one sheet of paper, "a half page if you can do it." He made up his mind fast or he would do nothing. He knew what he was doing.

The den in the Mansion wasn't as impressive and imposing as the high-ceilinged, dark-paneled office at the Capitol, but it was far more efficient. Instead of having to deal with one appointment at a time, at the Mansion he could scatter the petitioners in several rooms around the first floor, make rounds like a doctor and then have everyone to lunch in the dining room.

Rather than adopt John McKeithen's dynamic LBJ-approach to power—the governor who would sniff out controversy, dive into the middle of it, bust heads, twist arms and force a consensus—Edwards, the boy who had never been in a fight, would go a long way to avoid an argument. When a problem had to be resolved, Edwards put the disagreeing parties in one room, told them how he felt about it but stressed it was their decision to make and then left them to slug it out.

The governor's most enviable power is to say yes. Edwards used that power a lot. His style was to agree to just about any reasonable request and then to send it through the bureaucracy where, if the plan was found to be unfeasible, there would be someone else to say no. Edwards got the credit or some flunky got the blame.

He was criticized for delegating so much authority to people he could not always control, mainly Charlie Roemer, whose ambition and ego rivaled the governor's. The commissioner of administration had his own personal agenda and with his broad powers over awarding professional contracts, writing friendly bid specifications and hiring, Roemer began clutching for power that Edwards did not even know about. An Edwards aide remembers the governor in a rage over the newest Roemer scam to hit the press. "I can't believe that sonofabitch did that," Edwards would say, but when the reporters called, Edwards backed his man up. Instead of reining in Roemer, Edwards gave him more rope and finally Charlie hung himself in the federal government sting operation called

Brilab. When the news broke that Roemer was on tape accepting a bribe from an undercover FBI agent posing as an insurance executive, Governor Edwards claimed to be as surprised as anyone and was just as much in the clear. In delegating such broad powers he was also distancing himself from those appointees who eventually self-destructed.

He made decisions fast. Sometimes, it seemed, too fast. He once told an aide, "Half my decisions are right, a quarter could go either way and a quarter are wrong. But you can adjust them later. The important thing is to keep things moving." Sometimes the decision was not to decide. Even when he knew what had to be done, he delayed until his own sense of "the tides," the timing of current events and public opinion, told him it was okay to proceed.

Throughout his first two terms, Edwards was fond of telling reporters, "There is a big difference between what's illegal and what causes you people to raise your eyebrows." The eyebrows started rising in his first year when he proudly announced he had an interest in something called TEL Enterprises, owned by his aide Clyde Vidrine and his Highway Board chairman Lewis Johnson, who were proposing to build a 62-story New Orleans office tower to be called One Edwards Square. Edwards saw nothing unusual about a governor playing a role in a speculative real estate venture but as the press scrutiny continued and the TEL deal looked shakier, Edwards treated the press to some of his finest broken field explaining. He denied he owned part of TEL or ever did, clarifying his "interest" in TEL as merely the interest of a friend in another's success.

Edwards brushed off the TEL fiasco but he began distancing himself from his old friend, who had signed on very early in Edwards' rise to power. With TEL crumbling, Vidrine resigned as the governor's aide. As his financial problems mounted, Clyde found he could not even get his old friend Edwin on the phone. He was being cut off. In his anger, Clyde committed a political sin worse than incompetence, worse than dishonesty, worse than even getting caught. He talked.

He started with New Orleans investigative reporter Bill Lynch, and then went on to the FBI. Clyde Vidrine was piercing the vital veil, secrecy, and the public was scandalized and titillated by what they read: that Edwards had sold top state positions to old cronies and high bidders, that cash prices had been fixed on state positions and that you could get anything done in government for a price. Anything. The dirtier the more expensive, claimed Clyde, who said permits for hazardous waste dumping were especially lucrative rake-offs.

A federal grand jury in Baton Rouge began investigating Vidrine's allegations amid a flurry of rumors of Edwards' pending indictment. (Ossie Brown even empaneled a parish grand jury, for what that was worth.) A dinner guest at the Mansion in October 1974 witnessed an uneasy Edwards waiting for word from the federal courthouse while delaying his departure to cut the ribbon to open the Baton Rouge State Fair. Picking at his food, Edwards wondered aloud to aides and family how he could publicly discredit Vidrine. Edwards knew that Vidrine, an admitted reformed alcoholic, had been hitting the bottle again under the pressure of his failed business deals and the investigation. If Edwards could just find a competent, respected source to say that. An aide reminded the governor he had recently appointed Clyde's brother Ramson coroner of Evangeline Parish. "That's it." Edwards snapped at the old Mafia technique of turning your opponent's brother against him. "Anyone would believe the guy's brother, right?" he said, passing the suggestion around the table. At about that time, an aide reported that the grand jury had dismissed Vidrine and adjourned for the day without taking any action. Edwards smiled, getting up from the table. "Well, let's go dedicate that fair."

During the next week, state policemen delivered to TV stations copies of a letter from Dr. Ramson Vidrine calling for his brother's commitment and claiming Clyde's "alcohol-soaked brain" was the cause of his delusions. Obstruction of justice questions were raised but not pursued over how the governor was involved in the coroner's attack on his brother.

The federal investigation wound on but eventually stalled on Vidrine's credibility problems. It would be a pattern that would pull Edwards through other scrapes. In a showdown of one person's word against Edwards', the governor's practice of only dealing with people shadier than himself paid off.

Edwards had the last word on Clyde's reputation, but Clyde would get back with a last word of his own. His book, *Just Takin' Orders*, caused a great sensation when published in 1977. Not only did it describe Edwards' fund-raising techniques, it also richly detailed

25

Edwards' gambling escapades and extramarital flings. Clyde said it was all true, Edwin said it was all lies, and Louisianians flocked to the bookstores. More than anything for Edwards, the book was an embarrassment, a lingering one at that. When *60 Minutes* made their first phone calls here in 1983 for leads in researching the planned segment on Edwards, a daily newspaper reporter suggested they begin with *Just Takin' Orders.*

Edwards' other first term eyebrow raiser followed press reports the IRS was investigating his gambling trips to Las Vegas. This was the kind of scandal Edwards could handle, for gambling was his vice removed. He could cavort in Las Vegas or Reno casinos or those near his Lake Tahoe condominium without any snooping reporters. "I don't think the people where I come from care if I get into a dice game or a poker game once in a while." They didn't even seem to mind press reports that he used a plane leased to a state agency for one trip, that a plane from Harrah's picked him up for another or that the IRS investigated both his winnings and reports someone else had paid off $200,000 of his losses. He denied ever losing more than $8,000 at one time or winning more than $6,000. "I don't make a living off gambling and no one makes a living off me gambling." When a reporter met him at the airport on a trip home from Nevada, he answered the reporter's queries on his trip succinctly. "That's none of your goddam business. Print it just like that: none of your goddam business." When the Shreveport *Journal* asked its readers if they approved of Edwards accepting free plane trips and hotel rooms from casino owners, a resounding 51 percent of respondents in this queen city of the Bible Belt said yes with such comments as "It is much better than congressmen spending the taxpayers' money to take trips all over Europe" and "No public official should be required to become a father image."

Controversies that would flatten other politicians seemed to roll off his back as easily as his nonapologetic quips about them rolled off his tongue. Governor Dick Leche of *Louisiana Hayride* fame was fond of saying, "When I took the oath of office, I didn't take a vow of poverty." The same would go for Edwards and vows of chastity. Once again he was the beneficiary of good timing. Just as Edwin Edwards was popping up on the state scene in 1971, the '60s were just hitting Baton Rouge. The drug culture and the sexual revolution were stripping away some of society's pretenses and relaxing the pressure on public officials to lead exemplary private lives. Which was fine for Edwin Edwards, because the stories had been circulating since the campaign—not just stories but eyewitness, firsthand accounts—of women who had been propositioned by Edwards, straight on and out of the blue. As candidate and then governor, he had the perfect vantage point for meeting women all over the state, and just as many contributors were promised appointments, so were potential girlfriends offered state jobs. Those who weren't looking for work might receive a color TV or jewelry the next day instead of roses. His former aide and constant companion Clyde Vidrine would later write of Edwards' insatiable sexual appetite and his use of the state payroll to build a harem within close reach.

When not able to make the advance himself, the governor would use aides, friends and state troopers to approach different women. *Say, Governor Edwards would like to meet you. He can pick you up at your apartment at eight tonight.* The trysts were brief—aides and troopers did not have to wait long in motel parking lots for him to come and go, refreshed and rejuvenated and ready to go speak to some Rotary Club or the League of Women Voters. Aides and friends came to accept his appetite. "He enjoys the game, of setting it up, of sort of sneaking around to arrange a rendezvous. I think that part has as much to do with it as the sex." His busy schedule normally prevented any longer interludes, but when he could get away for a weekend with a girlfriend, he could, observed one traveling companion, "spend 18 hours a day in the sack."

His was such a public game that he had fun implicating others, turning to a legislator upon meeting his wife to say, "I didn't know you were married." Or poking at other politicians' carefully preserved images of righteousness, once casually telling a group of reporters that he knew for a fact that a respected state politician had a mistress.

"You're telling us," a reporter asked, "that he cheats on his wife?"

"He's not as good at it as I am," answered Edwards, "but he does."

When he tired of the secretarial pool, there was always the campus. Sorority Row was a favorite cruising ground. A young woman remembers standing on the front porch of her sorority house when a white Oldsmobile rolled to a stop, the back window rolled down and Edwards asked her if she wanted to go out. She went back in.

Rejection didn't faze him. After all, he once told a legislator, two out of ten women are dying to go to bed with you, but you have to ask the other eight in order to find the two. His material was not very original—how could it be after a while? On more than one occasion he gave a woman he was pursuing a pair of expensive sunglasses and told her, "Your eyes are too beautiful to look into if I can't have you." When he did take no for an answer there was often another question. A female reporter was once heard to say on the phone, "Edwin Edwards, I told you I don't fuck politicians." She hung up shaking her head. "Can you believe he said, 'Then how about a blow job?'"

He was fortunate not to suffer any embarrassing public scenes or paternity suits from his affairs. Perhaps because "affair" is too permanent a term. "Encounter" may be a better description, brief ones at that. No one held the center spot as the other woman for more than a few days. Some encounters became running encounters that went on for months or longer. Some turned into friendships. He's watched over the careers of past lovers with the loyalty he's extended to good contributors. Roughly in his mind they equated, as when he commented on stories that Tongsun Park often supplied congressmen with women, "I'm unaware of that, but it's certainly better than cash."

Philandering is a habit normally associated with politicians, but so is hypocritical puritanism. Edwards never fell into that trap. You could say or write what you wanted of his personal life but you didn't call him a hypocrite—how could you? His passes have became so well known that women, from waitresses to society matrons, all but came to expect them, were even at times disappointed not to have the chance to say no, or yes. Far from trying to dampen the rumors, Edwards fanned them with his own double entendres and self-incriminating asides. Asked by reporters outside a federal courthouse if he thought his phone was tapped, he said no but added, "Except by jealous husbands." His image and his resulting immunity were so firmly established by the end of his first term that he could tell a reporter the only personal scandal that could hurt him would have him "caught in bed with either a dead girl or a live boy."

The larger question was not why the voters accepted it but why his wife took it. That's a private question for Elaine Edwards in her very public life. Surely when he told her when they were teenagers that he would be governor she had no idea it would come to this. The politician's family's life in the fishbowl is strain enough. Elaine Edwards, a private person, has had to endure so much more.

It's another of the paradoxes of Edwin Edwards: his open promiscuity and his tight family bonds. From brothers to mother to children, the Edwards family has presented a highly visible united front and a strong campaign force. Elaine has been the key—through everything, above everything, public scandal or behind the back whispers, she stuck by his side. Still, there have been the uneasy moments, even in public. Women who have greeted the governor, even if being introduced to Edwards for the first time, have reported feeling a burning hole in the head coming from the direction of Elaine's stares. It's not, friends would say, that Mrs. Edwards felt any competition. "Elaine is not at all threatened by those women. She regards them with contempt, but it's more like disgust, knowing they will be out in tomorrow's trash."

A reporter noted as Edwin Edwards was sworn in for his second term that the governor appeared bored and listless. Having passed a new constitution, reformed the state tax structure and survived Clyde Vidrine, what more excitement could he expect? But looming on the horizon was the spectre of Koreans bearing gifts, which would be his closest brush yet with the U.S. Justice Department.

Tongsun Park had been very, very good to Edwin Edwards. The rice deal he helped broker propelled Edwards into the Mansion. Tongsun made friends all over Capitol Hill, so many in fact that the U.S. Justice Department would later indict Park on 36 counts of federal corruption charges. When the Washington *Post* reported in 1975 that Justice was investigating a $20,000 campaign contribution from the Korean, Edwards bitterly denied the allegations as more witch-hunting and said he received nothing from Tongsun Park. But the *Post* reports persisted into the next year, as did the federal investigation, until Edwards, following an acrimonious, drawn-out cat and mouse exchange with reporters, finally said, "Look, do you want to know what really happened?"

"Why do you think we've been asking you questions for 45 minutes?"

Then Edwards offered perhaps his most bizarre explanation ever. Park had given him nothing, as he had always maintained, although the Korean did give his wife Elaine $10,000 cash to buy gifts for herself and her daughters. Elaine didn't even tell him about it, he said, until a couple of years later, but he never thought much of it. After all, he told the press conference, to a person of his means, $10,000 was not that great a sum and it would only be important "to a reporter." Asked what his wife did with the money he replied, "My daughters are trying to find that out now." A year later, another admission, this time that an employee of Park's gave $10,000 to Edwards' 1971 campaign. When reporters asked why it took so long to tell the whole story, he said, "Nobody in this press corps has ever asked me, 'Did any other Korean make a contribution to you?'" The federal grand jury indicted Congressman Otto Passman, who was later acquitted, but it did not indict Edwards since it could find no actions on his part to return Park's favors.

The Park affair, however, marked a low point in Edwards' relationship with the press. Press conferences turned into increasingly bitter battles of attrition with the truth. In the heat of persistent questioning, Edwards' pique showed and sometimes his mouth got out of control. After one Mansion press conference, while showing reporters the $1,000 Korean table inlaid with mother-of-pearl given the family by Park, the governor said he saw nothing wrong with current press reports of American businessmen bribing foreign officials. "The present supermoralistic attitude that you shouldn't be making these payments has cheated American businessmen of the right to compete in foreign countries." The headline writers had a field day with such screamers as:

GOV. EDWARDS IN FAVOR OF BUSINESS BRIBES

Edwards later recanted the statement but the damage was done. The combination of his Korean semantics and the bribe quotes did not sit well with a public that thought it had heard just about everything from Edwin Edwards. At a 1976 campaign stop with Jimmy Carter in New Orleans, Edwards was roundly booed and met with shouts of "Give back the table."

For all he had been through in two terms, Edwards' popularity was only dented. A 1977 poll showed Edwards' approval rating slipping to an all-time low: 55 percent. Out-of-state reporters were astounded at his resilience. He went hard against the grain of post-Watergate morality, the new political purity in vogue everywhere else, but his attitude of *laissez les bons temps rouler* perfectly expressed the spirit of the times at home. These were the go-go years of unprecedented industrial expansion and personal income growth in Louisiana. Everyone was making money and no one seemed to mind that Edwards and his friends were doing very well too, or that the state budget had more than doubled during his eight years. Why should they mind? Personal taxes had gone down. And so what if the governor gambled and chased women? Suffocating Southern puritanism had never taken strong hold in South Louisiana anyway. And now a new anything-goes spirit was sweeping away the confining strictures in business and personal life. Edwin Edwards was not only in step with the times in Louisiana, he symbolized them. Here was a man who talked fast, lived fast and made things happen, for himself and for others. The '70s were great years for Louisianians straight across the economic scale. Whatever Edwin Edwards was doing to help things along, folks didn't want him to stop.

Toward the end of his second term, it was apparent Edwin Edwards would achieve what no other governor, save Huey Long, had: to leave office more popular than when he came in. All that was left was to ensure in 1983 he could come back.

He kicked off massive construction projects with every dollar he could raise or borrow. They included the long-awaited North-South highway, a Mississippi River bridge at Luling, a second downtown bridge for New Orleans and overflowing pork barrels of lesser projects. He took credit for announcing the projects while leaving the next governor to pay for and build them, which should take just enough time so that Edwards could be back in office to cut the ribbon. He took care of some long-waiting constituencies, finally endorsing the flagging Equal Rights Amendment in his last year, after having refused to push it in his first seven. He shocked good government advocates by enacting several good government reforms, most of which would not go into effect until he left office. These included disbanding the gubernatorially appointed Budget Committee in favor of more legislative control on appropriations, tightening the state procurement code and decreasing the size of the Mineral Board. It took Edwards eight years to implement these reforms that would limit the power of the governor, especially the next governor. In the name of reform, he transferred some appointive positions to civil service, but in effect he was cementing his own people in sensitive posts all over government and the next governor would not be able to root them out. These new civil servants also formed the nucleus of Edwards' superb intelligence network for the next four years. In his final days in office, he even started the clock ticking on several time bombs he knew would detonate sooner or later. Asked why he named Pam Harris chairman of the Parole Board, Edwards said that she was "the kind of Republican who will give Dave Treen trouble."

He was even getting along better with the press, bouncing back from an all-time nadir during Koreagate. That thaw was put to the test in the 1978 Capitol Correspondents' Gridiron Show, which had unusually good material to work with after the publication of Vidrine's *Just Takin' Orders*. There was no lack of bad taste that night on the part of the reporters as they reenacted spicier tales from the book. The governor sat through the show poker-faced as usual, but his wife appeared far less amused. They were surprised she didn't walk out in the middle of some skits. But she was saving her response for the end. At the close of the show, when Edwards took the mike for the governor's traditional rebuttal, he pulled out a copy of Clyde's book and said there was someone with even more to say, inviting Elaine onstage.

Audience and cast held their breath as a stern Elaine Edwards faced the audience, took Clyde's book from her husband and said that since so much of the show was lifted from this book, she would like to point out some obvious factual errors. Then she read the passage about a party in a motel where Edwin made a point of stopping at Clyde's door five times to show off each one of the girls he was taking to his room.

"Well, of course, that's untrue," said Elaine to a stunned audience. "Anyone who knows my husband knows he would have been asleep after the first one."

Audible gasp. Then cast and audience spontaneously broke into applause and rose in standing ovation as Edwin stood by beaming proudly. *That's my girl.*

3. The Reluctant Leader

May 16, 1932. Governor Huey Long dedicates his majestic new State Capitol, the towering 25-story edifice that symbolizes Huey's grand vision of dynamism, strength and prosperity through a centralized state government. Huey's Capitol was not constructed like other state buildings—this one came in ahead of schedule and under budget. Long did that on purpose so he'd have a million to blow on artwork, which included massive sculptures, stone carvings, frescos and gold leaf on the ceiling of the great hall, plus beautiful Italian marble imported for the finishing touch. Louisianians turned out to gawk at the extravagance and feel uplifted by how the magnificence of this building—*their building*—defied the Great Depression gripping the state.

Among the sightseers in the crowd was Mrs. Elizabeth Treen, who brought along her four-year-old son David. For the past year and a half, from their home up by the tracks, they had watched the skyscraper being built. After the ceremony and after touring the great building, mother and son were about to go home when suddenly someone snatched Mrs. Treen's purse and disappeared into the crowd. The incident left a searing impression of injustice on the boy. And 50 years later, when the state trooper every workday morning would wheel the governor's car into his parking spot by the back entrance, very near where the theft occurred, Dave Treen would recall his first impression of state government: what a rip-off it was.

David Conner Treen was born in the North Baton Rouge neighborhood of Standard Heights, named for Mr. Rockefeller's refinery nearby. But he wasn't there long. Young Dave grew up passing through many neighborhoods, along the graceful tree-lined streets of uptown New Orleans, in bucolic suburban Metairie, on his grandparents' farm in Collinston near Monroe, even for a few brief months in Los Angeles, where a talent scout thought eight-year-old Dave was a potential child star. The Treens did not agree.

The Treen roots go far beyond Louisiana—to the English town in Cornwall of the same name ("treen" means trees in Old English) whence Treen's forebears emigrated to Boston to prosper at making shoes. Treen's grandfather, John Wesley Treen, was the mover in the family, a doctor, an ardent Democratic supporter of William Jennings Bryan and a bronchitis sufferer who moved south for the pine forest air of south Mississippi. Dave Treen's father Paul, who began his career in Baton Rouge as a housebuilder, was an inveterate tinkerer who turned his curiosity into inventions. He made his fortune on the invention of a souped-up bicycle, the Simplex, a light motorbike adapted for street travel. Simplex could have become a household name had it not been for Honda. But in the 1940s, with sales rolling, the family moved into a mansion on St. Charles Avenue, a quantum leap from Standard Heights. Paul Treen built up a fortune and such a reputation for making things happen that a group of the city's conservative civic leaders asked him to run for mayor of New Orleans, a suggestion he realistically laughed off.

The most complete account of Dave Treen's youth comes from the official biography commissioned by the Treen campaign in 1979. *Dave Treen of Louisiana* by Grover Rees III, compiled mostly from anecdotes supplied by the Treen family, paints a picture of young Dave too good to be true:

—Dave competing in a contest to sell the most opera tickets, losing by two tickets to an orphan schoolmate, after refusing his father's check for 10 tickets because that would have taken "unfair advantage of a boy without a dad";

—the good athlete who quit the Fortier High football team because a coach advised players on how to injure opponents without getting caught;

—the college student, trying to choose between law and politics and the Methodist ministry, visiting his pastor who told him that more good ministers were needed, but deeply religious, honest statesmen were needed more.

The boy who would rather play fair than win. Too good to be true. Certainly too good to be a Louisiana politician. It could be because young Dave inherited such a strong sense of Puritan reserve and Yankee industry from his Boston ancestors that the more flexible Mediterranean mores of the family's adopted state never rubbed off. In fact, he never seemed able to plant roots anywhere because the family was always moving and Dave was constantly enrolling in new schools, sometimes at midterm. Once as a lark with high school buddies trying to meet girls in Biloxi, Dave tried to enroll at Biloxi High. Instead the police showed up and ran him off the Gulf Coast.

Perhaps because he was always the new kid, Dave Treen got in his share of fights as a boy. His last, he remembers, was in a college bar, when, after a few beers, he challenged a fellow "to keep his big mouth shut" and the two went at it. Treen landed a lucky left and sent the guy to the hospital, but the victor had his lip busted in turn by the bar's bouncer. "That's why my lower lip droops to this day." Despite all that rascality, Treen was a good student while remaining something of a live wire at Tulane, your basic hard-working, hard-playing Kappa Sig. He excelled in law school, during which he courted Dodie Brisbi and married her after graduation.

Dave's real political career didn't start until almost a decade later— and he would get off on the wrong foot. Disillusioned by both Republicans and Democrats and the growing centralization of power by the federal government, young Treen embraced the principles of the States' Rights party. It was an idealistic plunge, but one taken in bad company, for most members of the States' Rights party weren't nearly so concerned with the principle of encroaching federalism as they were with keeping the coloreds down. Treen wasn't a States' Righter for long, but future opponents would delight in dredging up his early party membership.

He built a career as a successful insurance attorney, though not always employing the most orthodox means. He persuaded his clients to fight any unjust claim, even to defend small claims that would have been cheaper to settle. His efforts resulted in one landmark decision that reversed decades of Louisiana tort law. Another case, however, that of the Fly in the Strawberry Pie, showed how Dave could carry his principles too far. A customer at a downtown lunch counter sued because she found a fly in her strawberry pie. Treen, representing the insurer, brushed off the chance to settle for $100, fought the case in district court, lost, and was preparing to file the appeal when the insurance company said enough's enough and settled.

Treen's penchant for fighting the odds inspired him to yeoman labor in the fledgling state Republican party. In those old phone booth days (as the old joke goes, all the space needed to hold the state party convention), anyone exhibiting any dynamism and energy was drafted to run, like it or not. Dave Treen didn't like it. Billy Nungesser, a friend of Treen's since high school and another lonely Republican activist, remembers, "We had to talk till we were blue in the face to get Treen to run every time." A reluctant candidate, Treen warmed to the battle, thrice challenging House Whip Hale Boggs in the '60s, closing the gap more and more until the Democrats reapportioned Treen's Metairie neighborhood out of Boggs' district.

Dave Treen only ran for governor because he couldn't be a judge. The critical turning point occurred at the Republican National Convention in Miami in 1968, at which Treen chaired the state delegation. Treen went uncommitted, leaning toward Nixon, but stayed up all night before the vote thinking through the election and emerged convinced Ronald Reagan could and should win. In the Nixon camp Bob Haldeman was furious and sent word through a party official that Treen would get no national help in his upcoming congressional campaign unless he abandoned Reagan and fell in behind Nixon. Another delegate witnessing the confrontation thought for a minute that "Dave was going to punch the guy" but he restrained himself. Dave Treen emerged again the man of principle, he campaigned hard for Nixon and came closer than ever before to beating Hale Boggs. But his vote of principle would come back to haunt him. When a vacancy for a federal judgeship in New Orleans opened up, state Republican leaders sent Dave Treen's name at the top of the list to the Justice Department. But on the White House political ledger, there was still a black mark by Dave Treen's name, signifying traitor. Dave Treen was passed over. The rejection was a "stunning blow," remembers Dodie Treen, a roadblock on the natural course of Dave Treen's career. He really wanted to be a judge. He was suited and destined for it by his temperament and training. He had offered up his toils in the barren fields of state Republican politics as his dues to make it to the federal bench. Instead, it was those politics that both brought him so close and kept him so far away. As with the 1971 rice deal favor, which paved Edwin Edwards' way to the Governor's Mansion, it was the unwitting hand of the Nixon White House that banished Dave Treen back to state politics and set him on the road to its highest office.

Dave Treen tried his best to resist the siren's call of the 1971 gubernatorial election. But when the search committee couldn't come up with an acceptable, viable candidate, the party fathers came back to Treen. And he gave in. Relented. *Okay, I'll do it.* A radically different motivation from that of the man who was then scheming, politicking, arm-bending, doing everything to win the Democratic nomination, Edwin Edwards. The two met in several forums of all 17 Democrats and the lone Republican. Other candidates remember the hilarious and uncharitable comments Edwards, with cupped hands, would make behind Treen's back as the Republican spoke.

After surviving two hard primaries, Edwards was the expected shoo-in in the general election against Treen in early 1972. Edwards did win in a landslide of 14 percentage points, but Treen carried most of North Louisiana and split New Orleans-Jefferson. Maybe because he was the fresh face or benefited from the embittered Bennett Johnston supporters, but Treen polled more votes than any Republican candidate before him. As consolation, a vacant congressional seat in the Third District was Treen's for the asking. Instead of his asking, of course, his Republican friends had to once again ask, implore, beg Treen to run. He relented and he won.

Washington was a strange experience for Dave Treen. Issues he took to with relish. He pushed for legislation that mattered deeply to him, introducing anti-abortion and balanced budget constitutional amendments, voting for strong military budgets on the Armed Services Committee. Yet the most pressing concerns of other ambitious young congressmen, constituent service and hometown publicity, were lower priorities for Dave Treen. Yes, he pursued his constituents' legitimate requests, but he did not gear the operation of his office to make things happen that would help Dave Treen.

A laudable sentiment. But in Machiavelliville, one who doesn't use others ends up being used himself. For instance, Dave Treen hit Washington just as Nixon's administration was coming apart. Yet he was impressed when Vice President Spiro Agnew made a special plea for the young congressman to go on record supporting Agnew's request that his impending bribery case be tried in the House of Representatives instead of in federal court. Taken with the vice president's sincerity, Treen placed a speech in the *Congressional Record* supporting Agnew's request on the very day that Spiro came clean and pleaded *nolo contendere* in court.

With each of the three terms he served in Congress, Treen grew more disillusioned. The hard-working Treen couldn't abide the loose attitudes of congressmen rarely in the chamber for debate and who voted the straight party line when summoned for quorum calls. In his final term, he would write a plan for new rules of Congress that among other things linked pay to attendance. It was good government. It was ignored. But that mattered less now. He had given up on changing Congress—his ambitions turned to changing Louisiana.

Republican prospects never looked better than in 1979, primarily as a result of a new law which had been intended to obliterate the Republican party in Louisiana.

From all appearances, Edwin Edwards was out to finish off the feeble GOP in 1975 when he rammed the Open Primary Law through the Legislature, over the protesting but ineffectual howls of state Republican leaders. But like the compulsive tinkerer who ignored the proverb "If it ain't broke, don't fix it," Edwin Edwards and his Open Primary Law, instead of smothering the Republican party, brought it to life, making it, for the first time in 100 years, a viable political organization.

It started back in 1972. Edwin Edwards, having just scratched and clawed his way through two Democratic primaries, had to raise more money to subdue the well-financed Republican challenger, Dave Treen, in the general election. Even after his landslide victory, he complained it was unfair for Democrats to kill off each other in the party's two primaries and still have to face a fresh, well-bankrolled Republican in the general election. Never mind that there were only 12,000 registered Republicans in the entire state in 1971 and that they hadn't elected a Republican governor since Reconstruction. It was the principle of the thing, along with two disquieting Republican congressional victories in New Orleans and Baton Rouge over Democratic opponents worn out and undone by party fratricide. For the first time, Louisiana had two

Republican congressmen and Edwin Edwards had enough. In 1975, he passed, over the handwringing objections of Republican party leaders, Louisiana's unique Open Primary Law. Party primaries were thrown out. Under the new law, all candidates—Democrats, Republicans and come-what-may—run in one open primary. If no one wins an outright majority, the top two votegetters meet in the general election. The bald intent, of course, was that with an overwhelming Democratic registration, the top two votegetters would almost always be Democrats and the Republicans would be shut out before the race really began. The Democrats could save time and money while maintaining their political dominance in the state.

But it didn't work out that way. The Open Primary Law made the Republican party instead of destroying it. It brought the Republicans into the main arena of state politics instead of shunting them off into their own irrelevant primaries. If you were a registered Republican before 1975, you couldn't vote in the Democratic primaries, which, everyone knew, was where the real action was. Registered Republicans had been as effectively disenfranchised as blacks in deepest, whitest pre-1964 Mississippi. But that changed overnight. Sleek and overconfident Democratic bosses soon discovered that it wasn't their power, popularity or philosophy that kept them in power; rather it was their monopoly. The Louisiana Democratic party was like the air—you weren't really aware of it, but you sure weren't going to try breathing anything else. With the Open Primary Law, you could be Republican and still vote with regular, decent people. Republican registration zoomed from less than 40,000 in 1975 to over 170,000 in 1983. Even more dramatic has been the surge in elected Republican officials, who numbered about 40 in 1975 and stood at 225 eight years later. The Democrats still outnumbered the Republicans 10 to 1, but the new law took away the unifying consensus of the old two-primary party nomination process.

In a long hard-fought campaign against five serious Democratic candidates, Treen got the Republicans and the Democratic right wing to lead with 23 percent of the vote while Louis Lambert got most of the black and the labor vote to edge into the runoff. The four moderate Democrats in the center polled 57 percent of the total vote, but were knocked out by the conservative Republican and the most liberal Democrat. Democratic leaders woke the next morning to a revolting predicament—of the five Democrats in the race the one who made the runoff was the only one Dave Treen could beat.

Just about everything went wrong for Louis Lambert and the party leaders. Lambert was pinned down the first two weeks of the runoff by a divisive election fraud suit from Jimmy Fitzmorris, who had coasted along in second place in the polls all election only to lose to Lambert by an eyelash or maybe, as his devastating suit suggested, voting irregularities. Worse still, the four eliminated Democratic candidates—Fitzmorris, Paul Hardy, Bubba Henry and Sonny Mouton—endorsed Dave Treen, an unprecedented outrage upon the party that would haunt the defectors for the rest of their dim political careers. But it did prove helpful for all of them in retiring their massive campaign debts and getting high-paying jobs with good retirement benefits in the Treen administration. Though Treen led Lambert by 21 percentage points three weeks before the election in one poll, Lambert finished strong, with Treen's massive lead in the polls evaporating to an 8,500 vote margin election night.

Despite the best laid plans and even the endorsement of Edwin Edwards, the Democrats lost the Mansion to the party that was not supposed to be heard from again. So you might say Edwin Edwards' open primary scheme backfired.

You might.

But you might also put appearances and public statements aside and delve into the Machiavellian mind of Edwin Edwards. Whom else would he rather be running against in 1983 than Republican Dave Treen, the man he so soundly beat in 1972? You can picture Edwin Edwards in his first day in the Mansion in 1972, looking out over Capitol Lake from the bay windows in his den/office and asking himself, "How do I get back in here in 1984?"

"Simple," the little voice in the back of his mind says. "See that Dave Treen gets elected in 1979."

"Yes," says Edwards, "but I'll have to make it look like I'm trying to destroy him instead."

"Of course," answers the voice. "Have you ever thought of an open primary law?"

It just would not have done for a Democrat to succeed Edwards. Especially one who could have forged a consensus through two

Democratic primaries and consolidated patronage around him. Edwards might still have been favored coming back against a Democratic incumbent, but it would have been a messy, bloody, expensive fight. How much neater it would be to wipe out all five Democratic pretenders and to lead an avenging Democratic party into the 1983 election against an isolated Republican. Just as Richard Nixon, through his dirty tricks against Muskie, helped engineer the nomination of George McGovern in 1972, the weakest possible opponent, so did Edwin Edwards, intentionally or not, fix things so that he'd have the best shot at a 1983 comeback.

Maybe it was necessary for Edwards to sacrifice a throne room full of heirs apparent in order to set up his own return. But turning over that power and patronage, even for four years, was a tricky gamble. Who knows. If the Republicans, with less than 10 percent of the registered voters, could win the Mansion, with some good organization and fund raising, with some luck and maybe even the help of a Republican president and U.S. attorney about to take office, they might find a way to keep it. But even should Treen and party lose the election ahead, it won't be back to the phone booth. Win or lose, the Republicans should erect a statue in the garden next to Huey Long's to honor the real Father of Their Party, Edwin Washington Edwards.

The young legislative staff member had learned all the hard-boiled ways of Capitol politics during the Edwards years. He knew how the game was played in the Legislature, he grudgingly admired the skill of Edwards and his floorleaders at getting their way having to crush hardly anyone. He was raised on small-town politics and inspired as a college student by the rough and tumble idealism of the Kennedy years. He understood how state government worked but he knew it could work better. He was no dreamer. Yet he couldn't help but allow the flickering flame of latent idealism to burn brighter as the Treen administration prepared to take office. "I'm excited about Treen," said the lifelong Democrat polishing off a hamburger and beer at Ruby's. "With Bubba [Henry] in the Division [of Administration], Treen can turn things around. Good government may have a chance." He knew state government was still riddled with the friends of Edwin Edwards and that the outgoing governor's old ally, Senate President Michael O'Keefe, was moving already to expand his own power. But a strong governor could make all the difference. And never before, in this hard-nosed idealist's life, was an incoming governor as committed to the basic reform of state government.

He ordered another beer. He felt good. He could even laugh over his run-in today with O'Keefe. Seems O'Keefe had detected a troublesome air of independence in the young attorney and decided to take him down a notch or two by directing his henchman/secretary Sylvia Duke to yank the staffer's parking place behind the Capitol. Next to your own secretary, your own parking place is the ultimate staff status symbol. Relishing the retelling, the staffer describes walking into the Senate committee hearing room, crouching down behind O'Keefe's chair and asking him what the chickenshit deal was for. No incident, no raised voices. O'Keefe swiveled in his chair and leaned over and in his gentle, quiet voice that masked his ruthless will told the staffer he would do real well if he played ball with the right team but that if he didn't want to cooperate he was going to get crushed. The two stared silently for a moment and "I told him to take his parking place and shove it."

Three months later a reporter finds the young staffer sitting listlessly behind his desk in the Capitol, with the embittered, betrayed look of a survivor of the Bay of Pigs, stranded on the beach, waiting for the air cover that never came. "It's like he hasn't even taken office yet," he said of the governor who had been inaugurated two months before. "I knew he wasn't going to play partisan politics but this is ridiculous. He's letting the power slip through his fingers. He has no idea of rewarding his friends or punishing his enemies. He's appointing people who were never with him and never will be." The appointments the governor is making, that is. The staffer is dumbfounded at how slow Dave Treen is moving, how crucial patronage positions are sitting vacant or with Edwards appointees still on the job. "I don't even think he's aware of the power he has," he sighed in disgust and stared out the window, a far, faraway look, perhaps to where his car was parked.

When the Treen administration came to work on the Fourth Floor of the Capitol on the morning after the Inauguration, they didn't find much to work with. Empty file cabinets, unreconstructed records, not even lists of upcoming appointments to be filled. The new staff would point to a lack of cooperation from the outgoing Edwards administration, but the real culprit was within its own team. In fact, was at the top.

Dave Treen did not move decisively to fill the power vacuum created in the transition. He didn't move at all, setting up his transition office in Metairie instead of Baton Rouge. It was convenient for the governor-elect but a plague on his transition staff, most of whom had to commute from Baton Rouge each day. The transition staff itself was another problem. Instead of building from a core group, Treen grafted the Bubba Henry and the Jimmy Fitzmorris people onto his own organization with few clear-cut lines of authority. "Everyone had a hand in it and nothing worked," recalls a survivor. Tasks were apportioned to teams led by people with precious little experience at running an executive department. If someone didn't like the task assigned him, he just didn't do it.

The governor-elect took a textbook approach to appointments but he must have missed a few chapters. He began, logically, filling the important top jobs, the cabinet secretaries and main boards. But he paid scant attention to the most important positions in any administration— the inner circle. So intent was Treen on building the foundation of good government that he forgot about the cornerstone, that small cadre of staff immediately around the governor that controls the information coming in and directs the orders going out. Treen had his trusted top advisors but he did not have in place a functioning office that took care of the little, critical things: answering mail, returning phone calls, office supplies, transportation. "People say we didn't answer our mail," says one aide of the transition. "Hell, we didn't open our mail."

Dave Treen is not an easy guy to work for. He is not a rude or overbearing person but he is picky and demanding to the point that he intimidates anyone who works for him. He drove off a couple of secretaries with his constant and critical attention to detail, his purple pen slashing through letters that did not follow the exact typing format he prescribed. And you did not bring him a briefing book unless it was a black, three-ring, letter-size, vinyl binder labeled on the spine. His relationship with aides and advisors wasn't much better. "People were afraid to disagree with Dave Treen to his face," says a staff member. "He would look at you over those glasses and scare you to death. He was the judge and he was always passing sentence."

Treen's stuffy, severe manner, the one the public saw most, contrasted strongly with the personable, warm Dave Treen away from the office. Though stern and wooden before an audience or at a press conference, Treen was personally delightful in a casual party setting, putting even strangers at ease with his self-effacing humor and genuine attentiveness. His off-camera behavior was exactly the opposite of Edwin Edwards', who, though always charming, was ever onstage and on guard, whether talking to one person or one thousand. Dave and Dodie frequently threw parties at the Mansion and stayed until the wee hours when the last guests left, while Edwin and Elaine rarely entertained and hardly ever stayed around more than a half hour. Treen would have a scotch and relax with anyone, Edwards would sip tea and size up all who came near him. The ultimate good sport, Treen went all out for the annual press party at the Mansion, dressing up one year as Santa Claus, another year as the Great Carnack, divining the questions to answers to tease each reporter. As friendly and entertaining as he could be in these moments, he shut down his warm, natural, human side just at the time he needed it most, when trying to communicate with the people.

As demanding a perfectionist as he was, Governor Treen was still poorly served by a disorganized staff. It was, in part, his own fault. He was known as a stickler for detail and he was drowned in it. Information was requested and never received, orders were issued and not carried out. It was apparent from the start that of any office in state government, the governor's office was in bad need of a good ass kicking. But kicking ass was not one of Dave Treen's strengths. It's not as easy as it sounds—a leader has to know who to kick and how hard in order to make the lasting impression. Treen's style, when his frustration over staff bungling boiled over, was to blow up at the wrong person, usually whoever had the poor dumb luck to be closest at hand.

The reluctance of Dave Treen to take charge in his own office is ironic when you consider that the Louisiana governor has at his disposal as much or more power than any chief executive of any state in the Union. But therein lay the problem. Dave Treen seemed uncomfortable with, even embarrassed by the trappings of One Strong Man rule: the ever-present state troopers, the fawning legislators, the emissaries of business and labor and every group in between who want just one minute with the governor to straighten out their problems.

Even beyond the trappings, the new governor was slow to consolidate his own power with the most effective tool at his absolute command, patronage. He came into office without even a firm list of which boards, commissions and posts were due to be filled. Even the straightforward political appointments took months to decide. For instance, the governor appoints one member to the board of election supervisors in each parish. It's important for obvious reasons for the governor to have his own representatives on these boards that decide the procedures for holding elections in each parish. In a remote, rural parish, his lone appointee is the governor's one pipeline into the local courthouse, his primary official contact with that parish. And yet it took Treen five months to accomplish what should have taken five days. It was the perfect appointment for a parish Republican chairman but too often those posts went to some legislator's friend, a Democrat who was anyone's man or woman but the governor's.

The pattern was repeated over and over again in the governor's appointments. Treen had promised Republicans and conservatives who had worked so hard and suffered so long a different kind of administration. They were shocked to discover just how different Treen's idea was. Many of Treen's key supporters were expecting key appointments, or at least some input in naming them—some were looking for a return on their campaign investment, others merely wanted to see the right people in the jobs. But Treen and aide John Cade (as past and future campaign manager, the one who should have been most sensitive to the Republican troops) felt the need to use the appointments to build bridges to the Legislature in order to gain more cooperation for the governor's legislative packages.

But did he have to give away so much? Not just Republican loyalists but legislators too were shocked at the governor's bipartisan generosity. For example, the Mineral Board, with the multi-million-dollar decisions it makes on leasing government land for production and granting waivers and variances, has traditionally been the governor's exclusive domain—legislators know better than to even ask to have friends appointed. Yet Treen appointed to it the law partner of black New Orleans State Senator William Jefferson and reappointed Mike O'Keefe's law partner. Senator Nat Kiefer, one of Edwin Edwards' staunchest allies, was able to put one of his friends on the Orleans Levee Board. Treen may have appointed five of his own people for every seat he gave away, but the latter appointee was consistently more experienced and adept at influencing board decisions than the governor's own innocent and naive allies.

The nonpartisan approach had some merit, but the bridges he tried to build to the Legislature were as unstable as they were expensive. Treen was an easy mark for savvy legislators who knew when the governor needed a vote. They would approach Treen with an appointment or a project they wanted, leaving the impression they would vote his way on the issue coming up. Treen would often give the legislators what they wanted, and they in turn would leave the governor's office laughing at his naivete. After a few such costly betrayals, a disgruntled Republican wondered at the governor's strategy, "Do you make friends with a wolf by throwing it raw meat?"

Sometimes Treen did not even get credit for the appointments he did make. As a political courtesy, administration aides often called a legislator to inform him of an appointment the governor would be making in that area. Often the courtesy went too far. Instead of telling Mr. Legislator that "the governor wanted you to know that he is about to appoint so-and-so to this board," the aides were told to say, "The governor is considering appointing this person and would like to know if you have any objections." Often the legislator could think of several strong objections to that person and might tell the aide, "Okay, as long as I get to tell them," or "Okay, as long he [the potential appointee] calls me first." So the governor decides the appointment and the legislator, by breaking the good news, gets the credit. Or the appointee is humiliated by having to make peace with the legislator, often his political rival. As a result, often the governor's own appointees felt they owed their loyalty to the legislator instead of to the governor. And Treen couldn't understand why his policy-making boards often didn't vote the way he wanted.

Dave Treen did a poor job of rewarding his friends and a worse one of punishing his enemies. A governor should not be overly vindictive, but it is critical to demonstrate that there is a price to pay for consistently opposing the administration. A lobbyist felt the governor could have been a nice guy and still stepped on a few people just for effect. "Treen should have picked one guy at random, someone who was bound not to vote with him, say a James David Cain, and made an example of him. Nothing overt, just cut him off totally from any appointments or projects, even shut him out from the little things like sending a proclamation he'd requested to one of his constituents. No big deal, just let the word out that James David is a nonperson in this administration and whatever disease he has you'd better not catch." A bit extreme, perhaps, but the point is that a governor gets more done extending the carrot, but once in a while he has to show he knows how to use the stick.

It's interesting Treen felt the need to take a nonpartisan approach when he came into office carrying as much bipartisan baggage as he did. Something had to be done with and for the four unsuccessful Democratic also-rans who endorsed him in 1979. Though Treen would insist the endorsements played no part, each of the four got high level jobs in the new administration.

Former Lieutenant Governor Jimmy Fitzmorris stayed on as the state's top industrial recruiter and was even allowed to keep his old office in New Orleans—a direct snub of incoming Lieutenant Governor Bobby Freeman.

Former Secretary of State Paul Hardy, still with his eye on the Mansion, wanted the Department of Natural Resources in the worst kind of way, but not even Dave Treen was that naive. Paul did get the patronage-heavy Department of Transportation and Development and in the long run was one of the governor's most loyal and effective cabinet secretaries.

Former Senator Sonny Mouton, one of the state's most brilliant and effective legislators ever and a man who waxed more eloquent in debate and more crafty in strategy with every hit of Stolichnaya he had from the pint bottle he carried with him in the chamber, seemed a natural for the job of executive counsel and top liaison with the Legislature. Yet Treen, who vests his trust in others painfully slowly, would not give Mouton the latitude and leverage to wheel and deal, even within modest bounds, for the administration. Treen should either have utilized Mouton or fired him. Instead he just ignored him, leaving Sonny free to work quietly behind the scenes for Senate President Mike O'Keefe and labor boss Victor Bussie—while on the governor's payroll.

And then there was Bubba Henry. The former Speaker of the House had emerged from the ranks of the Young Turks in 1972 to become a leading proponent of legislative independence and a lightning rod of opposition against the Edwards administration. Henry was Mr. Clean, the Knight on a White Horse, and when named commissioner of administration, he seemed the perfect antidote to his predecessor Charlie Roemer's Prince of Darkness. Trouble with Henry, the knight never got off his high horse, as he made a graceless transition from leading legislator to leading bureaucrat, burning behind him the very bridges Treen needed most to the House.

Not to say everything Treen sent down to the Legislature returned to the Fourth Floor in little pieces. The administration suffered few real legislative setbacks and pushed through some innovative business development and criminal justice packages while reforming the overly politicized capital outlay process. Treen reformed the Racing Commission, set up the Department of Environmental Quality, established the Professional Practices Commission and instituted merit pay for schoolteachers. The workmen's compensation and unemployment compensation reforms he sponsored reversed decades of the most liberal and costly labor benefits programs in the nation.

But on the real meatgrinder issues—the two annual money bills—Treen could not engender budgetary discipline without resorting to the highly unpopular line item veto. The veto is the governor's most awesome power—especially since the Legislature has never overridden one—and must be used sparingly, lest the governor earn the reputation of a Scrooge and a double-crosser. A strong governor is one who can say no, but a smart governor is one who can get someone else to say no for him. That was Edwards, who used his control of the Senate to smother anything he didn't want to sign.

Besides that, Dave Treen was the victim of incredibly bad timing, not the least of which was the national economy going to hell shortly after he took office. Added to that, Treen badly handled the extraordinary predicament of starting his administration with too much money and ending with not enough. In 1980, Jimmy Carter signed the law deregulating the price of oil, resulting in a massive severance tax windfall that lasted into the first two years of Treen's term. It couldn't have come at a worse time. Just when politicians were managing to break the news to taxpayers that a decade-long decline in oil and gas production pointed to the need for long-term solutions, the state was rolling in unbudgeted surpluses. A legislator, groping to explain how things could be so bad when they looked so good, called it "an embarrassment of riches."

Treen wisely used some of the surplus to pay cash for construction projects but couldn't resist the old Republican temptation to give as much as he could back to the taxpayers. Though popular at the time, his state income tax cut would become one of his worst decisions, a classic case of giving away too much too soon. Though the 1980 tax cut took many low income earners completely off the tax rolls, it most helped the wealthy—a point Edwin Edwards would drive home relentlessly. The worst part is he cut long-term taxes based on a onetime windfall. The embarrassment of riches in his first two years turned into an embarrassment of deficits in his last two. Treen continued state spending and state hiring at an Edwardsian clip the first two years and had to resort to Draconian budget-cutting the final and most important two.

It led him in 1982 to propose a massive and highly misunderstood tax on oil and gas, the Coastal Wetlands Environmental Levy (CWEL)—a measure that forced rare and vitriolic opposition from two of his strongest supporters, the oil and gas lobby and the Louisiana Association of Business and Industry, led by Ed Steimel. Steimel and oil threw everything into the fray, applying their time-honored torture of calling in the major financial contributors of each targeted legislator to squeeze where it hurt most. The fervor of his traditional allies' opposition surprised the Treen administration, which had done a very poor job of building a consensus for the tax which would have been mainly passed along to out-of-state customers. The spectacle of conservatives clawing conservatives delighted Edwin Edwards, who told friends he couldn't lose: if Treen passed the massive tax, it would beat him for sure in the next election, leaving Edwards with all that money to spend.

But Treen lost his tax initiative. His major legislative setback was a double whammy in that it also soured important oil and gas contributors on his upcoming reelection campaign. As the business lobbyists danced on the tables the night the Treen tax was beaten back, a friend of the governor who had just fought the governor harder than he had fought any populist predecessor said he was confused and tired and didn't know whether he should laugh or cry.

The surest way to raise a Treen loyalist's ire that first year was to compare the Republican governor to President Jimmy Carter. The similarities were too striking to deny. Both took engineers' approaches to executive power and ran for office on the strength of being outsiders to the system. In the name of nonpartisan reform they eschewed party politics and disillusioned some of their staunchest supporters. They gave people who were stabbing them in the back the benefit of the doubt. Both were men of deep moral convictions who insisted on seeing the world as they wanted to see it instead of as it really was. Once they satisfied themselves with the answer to an issue, they felt justified in sitting back and waiting for everyone else to come around. And they didn't.

Besides his problems with the Democratic Legislature, time also was not on Dave Treen's side. As much as Edwin Edwards benefited from the booming economy of the '70s, Treen suffered from the disastrous downturn in the oil and gas and the petrochemical industries in the early '80s. Even if there is nothing the governor can do about housing starts, new car sales and the world oil glut, Louisianians have come to expect a lot from their One Strong Man ruler and to focus on him their discontent when the rigs aren't working and the boats aren't running. Treen's steady, stolid style and conservative convictions did not play well in a state accustomed to governors who could make or appear to make things happen. But that was not Dave Treen. For all his hard work and firm convictions, Treen failed as a politician to present a clear vision of what he wanted to achieve, to point the direction in which he was going and marshal resources to get the job done. The effective political leader uses the momentum of public opinion and the needs and desires of other politicians to guide problems to resolution without being sucked into the maelstrom. The description may sound very Machiavellian and not *Mr. Smith Goes to Washington,* but in trying to bring reform to Louisiana politics Dave Treen should have been forewarned by the words of *The Prince*: "There is nothing more difficult to carry out . . . nor more dangerous to handle, than to initiate a new order of things." In struggling to reverse the tide of 50 years of populist, big government politics, Treen was forced into the role of the Antikingfish, most noted for what he was not, instead of what he tried to be.

As the election year begins, Dave Treen's wooden image and his awkwardness with power, especially compared to the act he has to follow, don't make it easier to broaden his narrow and flimsy political base. Through three years of relatively scandal-free administration, Treen consistently has trailed Edwards by 15-20 percentage points in polls. And yet . . . Dave Treen is not in a bad place. Voters surveyed don't consider Treen very effective, but they think he is honest. And they like that. Treen's approval ratings in the polls are consistently in the high 70s, as high as Edwards' were. Many people respect Dave Treen for not being a traditional, successful Louisiana politician—slick, shallow and corrupt.

For all his faults, decent, earnest, hard-working Dave Treen does represent mainstream American political values that ever so slowly have been taking hold in Louisiana since Governor Claiborne's first frustrating attempts to introduce them 180 years ago. With a changing world closing in on a state's uncertain economic future, a case can be made for Dave Treen's honesty and seriousness being the proper values to meet the challenge of the '80s. But to do so will require of the candidate more forcefulness and leadership than he has shown so far as governor.

4. His Brother's Keeper

Fifteen months before the election Edwin Edwards is trying to wrap up his fund raising. With his friend and longtime supporter Roland Manuel at the wheel, Edwards has one more stop to make here in Lake Charles before getting back to his plane to fly to New Orleans. "I'll be meeting with four or five people tonight where I hope to raise $75,000." A good haul, claims Edwards, considering the source: all former supporters of Dave Treen "but not anymore."

Why?

"They can't get a phone call returned. They can't get any of the things they thought they were going to get out of Treen when they backed him in 1979. To Treen's credit, many of these people never supported a winner before, and they expected more in the way of service and involvement than he could deliver."

Won't they expect the same service from you?

"No, because I'm not their guy."

Classic Edwards fund raising: he finds contributors angry at Dave Treen and gets into their pockets before things are patched up. Edwards wants to cast his net wide. He doesn't want to get a lot of money from a small group of contributors, he wants a lot of money from a large group of contributors. He turns around in the front seat. "Here's a scoop for you. I've lined up $2.5 million in signed pledges from a group of 100 people. The money's available whenever I need it. I just have to pick up the phone." With only a small staff at his Airline Highway office in Baton Rouge, he doesn't need the money yet. He just wants to know it's there. He already has $1 million in the bank, the proceeds from his 1979 and 1981 gala fund raisers. With the pledges and the paid-for $275,000 plane, Edwards can count on $4 million for the October 1983 election.

With another million or two, he'll feel comfortable going into the election year knowing he won't have to relive the horror of last minute campaigning and fund raising at the same time. "I'm not going to have my friends overextend themselves signing notes they can't afford to repay and I won't be in the position of waking up the next morning facing the kind of debt that those Democrats faced in 1979. That's an economical and emotional burden I won't carry."

Manuel wheels into the Black Angus Restaurant parking lot. "This should just take a minute," says Edwards. We sit down to coffee with two young businessmen. Edwards goes off in the corner with one of them and comes back to the table in a few minutes ready to go. Outside he pulls the two checks out of his pocket, one for $5,000, the other for $25,000.

It's been a good day on the trail—it's been a good week. The fund raising is made easier by the latest poll he's flashing about showing him 20 points ahead of Treen. "The poll shows any credible candidate would make Treen the underdog. My analysis is that Treen couldn't win if I died tomorrow."

Edwards has seen from past experience that Treen was a lousy candidate. You can't come as close as Treen did to losing to a snakebitten politician like Louis Lambert and call yourself a good campaigner. But Edwards couldn't rule out the possibility that Treen would be a good governor, that is, a popular governor. But Treen has satisfied him on that point too. "You hear Billy Nungesser and these people saying the same things they've been saying since March 1980, that 'in the next month, just around the corner, before the end of the year, people will realize what we're doing.' The truth is, the people do realize exactly what they are doing. Treen has done a good job for only one person in this state ... me. For my own selfish interests, I'm totally satisfied with him."

Satisfied as he may be, Edwin Edwards has been running and raising money as though he were working under a more stringent deadline than the October 1983 election. At this point, Dave Treen is not the problem. Another Republican, U.S. Attorney Stan Bardwell, and his grand jury investigation into Edwards' involvement with a state employees' tax shelter program, is. Edwards has flatly declared that an indictment will not stop him from running, but it sure won't help fund raising. That's one reason he's hustled to lock up $4 million in July 1982. For a while there was another, even darker cloud on the horizon. But it has just lifted. Edwards has just learned his brother is going to live.

Edwards had already resigned himself to going through this campaign without his brother. In April 1982, Edwards was sitting in his Airline Highway office reviewing campaign plans with his secretary Ann Davenport when the call came in from Marion. The blood left Edwards' face as he hung up the phone.

"He's got liver cancer." The two sat silently for a minute until Edwards sighed, "Sure makes all this seem unimportant."

Born eleven months apart, Edwin and Marion Edwards had been extraordinarily close in Marksville. They both excelled in school and preached as teens at Nazarene revivals and tasted politics at Pelican Boys State. They double-dated in high school and when Edwin and Elaine were having a spat, Marion would pass notes between them. It was easy to mistake Marion for the older of the two brothers. Edwin favors his mother with finer French features while Marion takes after his father. Edwin's hair turned silver early, Marion's disappeared almost as fast. The striking feature they share is Boboy Edwards' eyes, dark, cold, piercing and intense—they can cut right through you without giving a hint of what lies behind. The older they grew, the more the brothers' looks changed, the more the eyes linked them. Edwin is hipper, better looking, faster talking, sharper dressing, even more youthful than his younger brother. Even as boys, Marion was the sickly child, Edwin always full of health and energy. Though their careers diverged when the older Edwin went into the Navy and then college and law school while Marion went into business, the younger brother moved his family to Crowley soon after Edwin hung his shingle there.

When Marion checked into the Houston hospital in April 1982, his older brother had to prepare himself for more than just a personal loss. Through the 13 straight elections he had won, from city councilman to governor, there was one indispensable constant: his brother, his alter ego. Edwin had the gift for politics, but Marion developed a gift as rare—a talent for raising money. With each more expensive step up the political ladder, Marion's fund raising acumen grew too. It was Marion in 1971 who sat in the Monteleone raising the thousands of dollars every morning for his brother to spend that afternoon. "If you want to raise money," a politico once said, "get an insurance man." That was Marion. Perhaps he wasn't as eloquent as his brother in front of a crowd, but he could come close when enough money was on the line. After Marion walked out of one hotel suite with $50,000 in pledges, a witness to the experience declared, "When Marion was through telling that poor guy about his brother, the fellow was reaching for his checkbook and his handkerchief at the same time."

Though it crested in victory, the 1971 campaign was an internal nightmare, racked with pressure, money problems, backbiting and power struggles among the many strategists, contributors and hangers-on vying for a piece of the action and the ear of the candidate. Through it all, Marion was the rock. He took care of more than just the money—his prime concern was his brother. Edwin could rest assured that regardless of what anybody else was trying to angle out of him, Marion Edwards at least was nobody's man but his. Marion represented stability and strength for the coming campaign. All staff jealousies, doubts about who was in charge, worries about others not pulling their load, all dissipated at Marion's door. Marion was often the only acceptable substitute when a supporter insisted on speaking to the candidate. When Marion got on the phone and stroked him, the supporter felt sure his message would get across, all special requests would be relayed. Even those who just wanted to touch the cloth knew that Marion would touch it for them.

Going through the campaign ahead without Marion bothered Edwards more than anything Dave Treen or Stan Bardwell could do. Partly for that reason Edwards sent out his first major fund raising letter in April 1982, shortly after Marion checked into the hospital. The letter worked well.

More surprisingly, so did Marion's radical, intensive chemotherapy to stymie the growth of the tumor. After three months, two trips and one operation, Marion was healthy, happy and ready for action.

"Fund raising," says Edwin Edwards, "is the most disagreeable part of politics. You are torn between two principles: there are people who don't want to fool with politics and there are those who would be offended if you don't let them make a contribution." From that, Edwards formed one principle he won't violate. "I never ask for money, I just don't do it. I raise my money by people coming to me who want to contribute. Or I may get a group of supporters together and ask them to help me put on some fund raisers around the state."

Or he'll have Marion ask for him.

After getting his real estate and insurance business affairs in order in Crowley, Marion got into the campaign full time at the beginning of March 1983. At the top of the list was to raise some more money. He knew that $5 million, though nearly as much as the record amount Dave Treen spent in 1979, was not going to be enough. On his first day in the office, he and Bob d'Hemecourt, the New Orleans coordinator, made two phone calls to New Orleans—one to chiropractor Jerry Norman and the other to Ford dealer Bill Watson. Norman gave $38,000 and Watson kicked in $45,000 and the use of four cars. Watson was a major Treen defector, one who had contributed to all of Treen's congressional races and who had chipped in $46,500 to retire the 1979 campaign debt. Watson had been named chairman of the Motor Vehicle Commission but was unable to have a hand in naming the other commission members. That and a string of unreturned phone calls and unreturned favors left Watson ripe for Edwards' picking.

Despite his initial success Marion knew he would be operating under far tighter restrictions than in wild and woolly 1971. There were no campaign finance reporting laws in those pre-Watergate days. In 1983, the name of every contributor of more than $1,000 would have to be reported, as well as every dollar spent. In addition, the candidate had his own demands. Edwards was determined this time to spread out the contributions so that no one would think they owned a piece of him, an impression that a less experienced candidate helped to foster in the 1971 race. In the runoff against Bennett Johnston, Edwards found himself behind in the polls and desperately short of cash. According to his aide and bagman at the time, Clyde Vidrine, the candidate started promising contributors the right to name board members and administration posts that he had already promised three times over. It was suitcases full of money and pockets full of promises. According to Vidrine, Edwards took $125,000 from the Benezach brothers to have their man named conservation commissioner, $75,000 from Jerome Glazer for a seat on the Mineral Board and $50,000 from Lewis Johnson to chair the Highway Board. Edwards said Vidrine exaggerated when he did not outright lie, denying that any of the contributions were that high. He said he only received $45,000 from Glazer. "I think Clyde skimmed $30,000 from the money," he would later tell *60 Minutes* matter-of-factly. Sounds downright awful, but it wasn't illegal. He even admitted accepting contributions from corporations which were barred by law in 1971 from making campaign contributions. The distinction, Edwards pointed out, was that it was illegal for them to give but not for him to receive. Those nettlesome ambiguities were cleared away when Edwards signed a law repealing the ban on corporate contributions.

Not that Edwards was totally without ethical standards raising money in 1971. He routinely "took money from people leading them to believe they were going to get something when I had no intention of doing so. I didn't want them to get angry at me during the campaign for refusing their contribution so I took the money out of circulation so they couldn't give it to someone else." After the election, he says, he refunded "$170,000 to eight or nine people." This time around, he didn't want to have any misunderstandings or to give anything back.

And he absolutely wanted no trouble. The advent of campaign finance reporting laws and the curiosity of U.S. attorneys spelled an end to some of the more outrageous fund raising practices. Such as the blatant shakedown. Politicians as a group are lucky that there is usually one among them so greedy and recklessly arrogant he stands as an object lesson in going too far. Gil Dozier is the lesson for the '80s. Shortly after his election as commissioner of agriculture in 1975, he began his financial footwork for running for governor, without noticing the world had changed. Gil would plead later in federal court that he was doing nothing more than any other hustling politician had done before, that is, shake down anyone who did business with his department. A North Louisiana banker/farmer got the Dozier treatment firsthand in 1975. Dozier called the agribusinessman's secretary, set up an appointment and flew in that afternoon. Greeting the candidate, the banker said he felt that Dozier would win and he wanted to cooperate with him (his businesses held some Ag Department contracts), but that old loyalties demanded he vote for Dozier's opponent, incumbent Dave Pearce.

Dozier growled, "I don't care who you vote for. You can vote for him three or four times for all I care. I want your money. I know exactly how much you gave Dave Pearce and if I don't get double that by tomorrow, you'll have hell to pay." The businessman restrained himself long enough to show Dozier the door. Nothing came of Dozier's threats—he made so many of them he was convicted of racketeering, then jury tampering and sentenced to 18 years at Fort Worth.

Candidates still chafe at the new campaign finance reporting law, even though the $1,000 minimum in the governor's race is the highest reporting threshold in the nation. But there are other interesting loopholes, such as the law's silence about what can be done with the money. A candidate doesn't even have to spend campaign contributions on a campaign. If a candidate raises money and decides not to run, or has no opposition, or a lot left over, he can buy a CD and keep the interest until the next time he does face opposition, if ever. Legislators and congressmen keep from a few thousand to a few hundred thousand in the bank waiting for the next hard contest that may never come. And when that last day does come, if they don't take him out feet first, the perennial candidate-fund raiser can, like a good citizen, pay taxes on what's left and keep it.

Nineteen eighty-three was a good year to have a nest egg, because any legislative candidate who didn't have his money lined up by the spring began running into barren fields picked clean by the Edwards combine. Through carefully culled fund-raising lists and networks of political friends, the tentacles of the Edwards fund-raising machine reached for every loose—and some it had to pry loose—$1,000 bill in the state. "In any community in the state, I can call 20 people on the phone and ask them to help get something together for me. The tickets are $50 to $500 or more and expenses are 10 percent of the take." In any community. He claimed a $100-a-ticket Edwards function in little Many in Sabine Parish at the end of 1982 raised $40,000. "Ten years ago I couldn't have raised a quarter there." Ten years ago, North Louisiana was alien country for Edwards and this time around the Treen folk are counting it solidly in their column. Treen may be counting on the votes. Edwards is already counting the dollars—600,000 of them raised at a $1,000-a-plate dinner at year's end. A good fund raiser does more than bring in big bucks—it shows you know how to spend them too.

It looks just like any other $1,000-a-plate buffet special, until they wheel in the mermaids. The guests are just arriving at the New Orleans Hilton for Edwin Edwards' Fun and Fund Spectacular when two bellhops roll in two tables, on which sit two attractive young blond, well, mermaids. The femme fishtails, in their tight-fitting, strapless, blue sequin-covered gowns, are hoisted onto a table already graced with delectable hors d'oeuvres, where they sit the rest of the evening, enduring just about every stupid come-on in the book. "My talent agent thought I'd be just right for this," coos one. And the money isn't bad either—$85 for three hours.

Mermaids aren't the only strange creatures on hand. Edwin Edwards, who arrives with his entourage of a dozen or so family and extended political family, greets guests of every description: liberal and conservative, labor leaders and businessmen, the indicted and the unindicted, new rich, old rich, filthy rich. Plus a lot of people who didn't have to pay for tickets, but who were given a few by big contributors who got 10 or 25 tickets to sell or give away in exchange for their contribution.

Big Bad Bill Dodd, as Earl Long used to call him, shakes his head watching the varied assemblage. "It's a long time since I've seen the hawks and the doves and the billygoats all moving in the same direction."

The Hilton has put out an enormous, spectacular spread, about the best on the campaign trail—no rubber chicken tonight. From the oyster bateaux to the trays of lobster claws, a full array of seafood delicacies are laid out, adorned by ice sculptures of the State Capitol and the Mansion. Only the best for an affair underwritten by Louis J. Roussel, a man who not only uses and enjoys his wealth but flaunts it, as his gold and diamond-encrusted oil rig tie clasp shows. In business as in politics, taste is for losers. Louis is a big winner, an oil and gas magnate, who scrapped his way up through the oil patch. He was one of the smart pioneers who started lucky and poured everything gained from his first wildcat hit back into more drilling, and then into banks and insurance companies and real estate and politicians. The Jett Rink of the Louisiana oil patch, Louis has blazed a ruthless trail in making his fortune without any of the old family connections that control the course of big business in New Orleans. For entertainment, he bought an interest in the Fair Grounds, the city's wonderful, historic racetrack, and also owned horses that raced there until Treen's Racing Commission shut that practice down. Roussel looks forward to a newly constituted Racing Commission to see things his way again. Not that it always matters. Louis and his friends have been successful at getting the Racing Commission's pesky fines and suspensions overturned in civil district court.

Now the highlight of the evening, the auction of the most extravagant symbol of the campaign, a life-sized oil painting of a contemplative Edwin Edwards, posed in his study with a book on his knee. An odd touch, since Edwin doesn't read books. Maybe it's Clyde's book. Whatever, it's a breathtaking art statement, just the perfect addition to any hangar-sized living room. The bidding begins and quickly runs up past $50,000. "Do I hear $60,000?" And sure enough, he does. Then, just to show you how tough things are in the oil patch, it takes a full 60 seconds for the price to creep up to $100,000.

The fix is in. Louis and his Fair Grounds partner, grocer Joe Dorignac, have already committed to giving $100,000—this is just the way of showcasing it. If your name is going to appear in the paper as a contributor, why not dazzle them a little and show off some. Insiders get in on the fun. George Fischer bids $96,000, why not? Edwin has a little fun with George as well, stalling Dorignac's bid, leaving George to twist there for a second, just long enough to get nervous, before Joe raises his hand.

As incentive for paying homage, Edwin promises, "Whoever buys it, we'll get it appraised for a quarter million, donate it somewhere and write it off."

Edwards knows on his own he can't find every available dollar, but that's what friends are for. Many of his $25,000 pledgors won't put up any of the money themselves but will tap their own friends and neighbors. And what are they looking for? Not work. "If they can make a contribution, they don't need a job," says Edwards. A campaign contribution is an investment in government. State government is huge business in Louisiana, easily the fastest growing industry of the past decade. The state pie grew exponentially in the '70s and early '80s, so a contribution to the 1983 winner was a bigger investment than ever.

There are rules for doing business with the state, but rules can't cover everything. Bid specifications, waivers, extensions can often be massaged by a governor's appointees or even by lower-ranking civil service bureaucrats who have nothing to lose by playing along. Even the bid process can be circumvented in an emergency (such as unexpectedly running short on certain materials and having to get more fast) and it doesn't take many emergencies to make a killing. Suppliers and contractors have been told by their state contacts not to bid on an upcoming project. "This job's going to someone else," one was told. "There will be another along soon that will be right for you."

Property owners are continually leasing office space for the continually expanding work force. The leases are done by bids, but the specs can pinpoint the location to entire blocks owned by friends of the governor. Some experienced bidders have begun winning leases and then going out to find a building to match the specs.

Professional services are a bonanza for the connected. Millions yearly go to architects and engineers who are chosen for state projects by selection boards for the most part controlled by the governor that tend, coincidentally, to name firms in good standing with the governor.

There's not even a selection board to legitimize the hiring of attorneys. Though the state has plenty of attorneys on staff, departments hire even more for specific cases. The Revenue Department may pay a lawyer $500 a month for a day a week of collections work. Public Safety hires attorneys to defend the state police against suits, and Transportation has extensive expropriation work. At the top of the lawyer ladder, the closest friends of the governor get the lucrative oil and gas cases which can bring fees in excess of $1 million.

There's a gubernatorial board to regulate nearly every state business and occupation, from plumbers to beauticians, and there is no shortage of potential contributors anxious to serve on those boards or name those who will. Consider the clout of the cosmetology board member, who decides on licensing standards for beauty parlors and beauty schools and who has inspectors empowered to shut down same. But none of the governor's 1,340 appointments are as important as the nine seats he fills on the Mineral Board. The potential influence from a Mineral Board appointment outweighs that of almost any position the governor can hand out. Though the Legislature tightened restrictions against board members dealing with state leaseholders through their oilfield service companies, the potential for taking big advantage of those positions is there. The routine granting of an extension of a due royalty payment or a variance or a waiver of a lease requirement can make millions of dollars of difference.

Ken Martin, high-flying independent oilman who struck it big rich and is almost big broke chasing the fortunes of the Tuscaloosa Trend, says influence peddling in the oil and gas business is entrenched. "Under Edwin Edwards and previous administrations, it was standard procedure for a guy to walk into your office, say he was on the Mineral Board and also in the boat supply business and that he would appreciate your business. Then he'd say stop by his office for coffee next time you're in Baton Rouge. No promises made, but that's what I call influence peddling. Anybody that didn't happen to in the '60s and '70s was not very active in the oil and gas business."

Not that Martin hasn't an axe to grind. He contributed and lent a total of $111,000 to Treen's 1979 campaign. He claims he got nothing from it—he may have done worse than that. In 1982, Martin became so seriously overextended when the demand for natural gas plummeted that he was forced into bankruptcy by a major creditor, fuel distributor Tommy Powell of Eunice. Powell's attorney: Edwin Edwards.

Some contributors aren't looking for anything from the state but just for the more intangible benefits for a businessman to be on a first name basis with the most powerful man in the state. A phone call returned or an invitation to bring a client for lunch and an audience at the Mansion can make a heavy impression. A businessman's friendship with the governor can take many forms, but it is almost always based on the financial considerations.

But the very best contributors and often the most ardent supporters are some who just want to be with a winner, like prominent New Orleans trial lawyer and $25,000 contributor Darleen Jacobs. "I'm an independent businesswoman and a lawyer. I make a lot of money and contribute to a lot of campaigns. I have more business than I can handle, and I'm not interested in political jobs. I support Edwin Edwards because he's my '11.' He's a great, charismatic man and I'll work my tail off for him."

Marion is today's squadron leader as Clifford Smith's Energy Helicopter stands by on the field across from the Baton Rouge Hilton, ready to whisk the troops off to St. Landry Parish. A campaign is not run on fund raising alone. The other half is spending the money and getting something out of it.

We set down in an airstrip in Opelousas, named for an old Indian tribe, kin to the Atakapas. As for St. Landry, I always thought that was some Cajun joke played on a mapmaker, as though the chances of there being a real St. Landry were the same as there being a St. Theriot or a St. Bourgeois. But no, St. Landry was some bishop of Paris who built insane asylums.

In town the VFW hall is filled with about 200 police jurors and aldermen and politically active citizens, of which there are a good number in this parish of 30,000 registered voters, 42 percent of whom are black. Marion imparts his message with a style that's a cross between evangelist and cheerleader. The words are evangelical, but the spirit is Knute Rockne. "What's Opelousas going to do?"

"Elect Edwin Edwards!" the crowd bellows back. And that's what Marion and his band of coordinators are here to show them how to do.

First a joke, about the 80-year-old man who goes into the confessional and tells about being picked up in the grocery store by two teenage girls and making wild, violent love to them all night.

"Are you sorry for your sins, my son?"

"No, father, I'm not even a Catholic," the octogenarian answers through the grille.

"Then why are you telling me?"

"Father, I'm telling everyone. . . . Just like I'm telling everyone," shouts Marion, "that Edwin Edwards is coming back to help this state." Now for a little music. Marion flips in the cassette and sings along to a monarchist ditty called "Bring Our Cajun King Back." Marion keeps his routine going. "We were in Napoleonville the other night and one old Cajun asked me, 'When your brother is elected, how many beers can you drink and still drive?'"

But before the celebration comes the work. Marion wants to see each parish organization do all it can without help from Baton Rouge. He calls on the people in this room to find a building suitable for a campaign headquarters in the parish—rent it, donate it, squat in it, just so long as Marion doesn't have to pay for it. They will find two, one in Opelousas and one in Eunice. Then he needs volunteers to man the headquarters and come in for phone bank work. And he needs people raising money, but he didn't say spending money. Marion spent enough time as a Catholic to know how that deal works. "Everything you get, you send to headquarters in Baton Rouge." There Stephanie Alexander will keep track of every dime to come in, along with every name and address, all of which go on Edwards' massive contributor lists, which will reach 10,000 names by campaign's end.

Marion holds up an imposing poster filled with fine print, it looks like the U.S. Constitution. "These are the rules and regulations we are running this campaign by," warns Marion. And the first commandment is: "The tax people don't allow an income tax deduction for a campaign contribution." Marion doesn't want any funny stuff with contributions or spending. "The other side has a man named John Cade and he is out to hurt us." A menacing murmur floats through the crowd. "He knows his man can't win fairly, so he will try to hurt you and disgrace you any way he can. He knows he can't carry St. Landry Parish, so he will try to embarrass you. So we must stay within the law."

Rule No. 2, which is not on the poster: "We're not involving Edwin Edwards in any election except for governor. You can get involved with your local candidates, but keep your governor candidate at the top of the list."

For brass tacks Marion calls on nuts and bolts man Paul Hayes. "Edwin Edwards looks for bumperstickers on the back of cars and you can only imagine how many we see every day all over the state. We've given out a half a million of them. But bumperstickers only do us good if they are on cars, they don't do any good on a kitchen cabinet. And they cost us 20 cents apiece." Next come the yard signs, expensive full color jobs, with EWE's likeness laminated thereon. "These are yard signs, not tree posters. We have printed up 90,000 of them. At $3 apiece, we want them in people's yards, not on the side of the road."

Marion, grabbing the mike, can't resist the temptation to evoke more partisan ogres. "There's a guy who runs the Highway Department named Paul Hardy"—derisive murmurs, scattered boos—"you might know him as Benedict Arnold. But you go start sticking these yard signs on telephone poles along the highway and his men will be laughing the whole way back to the Highway Barn as they pull our signs in and throw them away." Marion wants 5,000 signs in St. Landry Parish, in yards, not in the fiery incinerators of Paul Hardy's evil Highway Barns. The message by now should be clear: This is a Louisiana election, but with the Mansion under enemy occupation, the law for once is not on our side.

Last come the cards, postcards with poker face of Edwin on the front and the place for your message on the back. The cards are to be distributed to volunteers who write messages and address them to their friends. Then they go back to the headquarters where they are bundled up and sent to Baton Rouge for a massive mailing with more than half a million pieces (out of two million registered voters) hitting mailboxes in the final days. An excellent touch, the perfect marriage of old and new political methods—massive direct mailing with personal, handwritten messages, going from one friend and neighbor and relative to another, asking for a vote for Edwin Edwards. The Cajuns are amazed by the enormity of the picture they fit into. A half a million pieces of mail—that's more than Sears and Roebuck sends out, that's even more than Jimmy Swaggart.

The crowd quietly filters out of the hot VFW hall, nearly all of them with something, yard signs, bumperstickers, postcards and team spirit. One of Edwards' top supporters and campaign coordinators, Billy Broadhurst, is delighted with the gathering. Marion and company know they are going to beat Treen here, but they want a big turnout and a big margin from one of Edwin's Cajun parishes. Beating Treen takes organization and discipline, beating him bad takes the kind of fervor you find in revival tents and football stadiums. Says Sam LeBlanc, "They want a good fight. That's why these things are like a church revival. These people don't want to come to a business meeting. They like their politics to be contests, us against them, the good fight. They want to get psyched up."

And they are. The organizational meeting has been like a confirmation: they came as friends of Edwin Edwards, they leave as soldiers.

5. Two Friends

"I know he'd love to cut me up. Edwards hates my guts," chirps John Cade as he gets into the back seat of the Treen staff car for the ride down to Kenner, for the debate of his life.

It just sort of happened. Yet another speaking engagement, this time a debate sponsored by the Kenner Businessmen's Association. Edwin Edwards routinely accepts, hoping to get Treen in debate this early. Treen routinely declines, he's not about to let Edwards drag him into the campaign in May. But campaign manager Cade offers to debate Edwards and Edwards, when he hears of the substitution, is delighted to get the intermediary, that is, the candidate, out of the way and meet the one he considers the real force in the Treen campaign if not the Treen administration, the man who has been saying all those awful things about him, John Cade.

"He's taking a chance, like LSU playing Southern. He's supposed to be able to beat a nonpolitician. But it will look especially bad for him to lose to me." Cade may be a nonpolitician but he is hardly a nonplayer in 1983's political drama—and he's writing his own part bigger by the day. The greater the public role he plays, the more obvious it is that John Cade is a very private man, one who worked his way up to the top of the Republican party in the days when you could do that and still remain unknown. Cade was born to class but not money—his grandfather was a wealthy Lafayette Parish sugar planter and Republican legislator before going bust. John grew up a merchant's son in Alexandria, took over his father's store and built it into one of the leading businesses in Central Louisiana, the Alexandria Seed Company.

It was easier to rebuild the family fortune than to breathe life back into the state Republican party, beaten comatose by 100 years of one-party rule. A party leader by default, Cade would make the pilgrimage to Metairie every two years to help talk Dave Treen into running against Hale Boggs and would stay to help fight the good fight. He managed Treen's 1971 gubernatorial campaign against Edwards and finally had a winner with Treen for Congress the next year. He was state party chairman and Republican national committeeman in the '70s and, after managing Treen's 1979 win, commanded Reagan's troops in carrying Louisiana in 1980.

Along the way he developed the reputation as a shrewd analyst and a hard-nosed party power broker who takes to political infighting and backroom dealing with almost Democratic zest. Republicans are not supposed to enjoy politics—very bad form—and John Cade does not appear to, resembling more an English professor, tweedy and pre-occupied. On first impression, he projects a shy, gentle manner and a hint of vulnerability. You only realize when you feel the blood that he has a gut instinct for attack politics and loves to play the game.

Not the people part—leave that to the ambitious and the insecure. Cade is tuned in to the abstracts—polls, media and strategy—defining options by the numbers. He's a tough customer to deal with and to work for. He doesn't suffer fools gladly, but he disagrees with his reputation for being demanding and hard to work with. "I'm the most patient and soft-hearted guy. It's extremely difficult for me to do anything to hurt anyone. But I make an exception for Edwin Edwards."

He knew when he hung up the phone on that interview he shouldn't have said that. It wasn't the first time, it won't be the last that the cool, plotting Cade opens his mouth to his real feelings in front of a reporter. That's John's handicap in politics—for as dispassionate an operator as Cade tries to be, he is basically motivated by a deep moral spark, an outgrowth of his devout Christian Science beliefs. To John Cade, politics is a moral expression, and the politics of Edwin Edwards is a moral outrage. Only as deep-seated a feeling as that will prompt Cade to throw himself into a relentless attack throughout the campaign on the deeds and rhetoric of Edwin Edwards. "This one comes from the heart," he told the Baton Rouge Press Club at one appearance as he described sitting up the night before writing down "25 of the most recent bald-faced lies of Edwin Edwards."

Well, someone's got to do it. Cade can hardly stand by and watch as Edwin Edwards runs wild and free about the state making the most outrageous claims about his own record and Dave Treen's while Treen is too busy back at the office being governor to defend himself and set the record straight. That leaves John Cade. Had early in this campaign someone sat John Cade down with a poll that showed his attacks on Edwin Edwards were not helping Dave Treen, it's doubtful Cade would have let up. For already this has gone beyond party loyalty and personal friendship to a pressing moral question. There is the sense of urgency in John Cade's quest that seems to warn that if someone right now doesn't stand before the people and reveal the whole real ugly truth about Edwin Edwards . . . no one ever will.

If you could point to anyone in the top GOP echelon and say, "What's that Democrat doing in here?" it would be Billy Nungesser. With flushed face and red hair to match his favorite suit and a robust, wisecracking sense of humor, the chain-smoking Nungesser looks like he would be more comfortable at the Half Moon Bar handicapping Mike Roccaforte's Uptown Democratic slate than sipping chablis at some sedate uptown wine and cheese affair. But Billy doesn't hang out uptown. His world is the Westbank and the waterfront, where he built a family seafood business into a multi-million-dollar offshore catering concern. Yet even when he was sweating making the payroll he could always find the money and raise some more to back conservative if not Republican candidates in New Orleans. "I always told Ruth that electing the right kind of candidates was as important as putting money away for the kids' education." Nungesser developed into a phenomenally good money-raiser in that he opened up virgin financial territory for Republicans in the industrial parks along the Harvey Canal while avoiding the sleepy and self-congratulatory GOP finance committee meetings at the Fairmont. Always his money went down first. In 1979, Nungesser shelled out $200,000 in contributions and loans to elect his old Fortier High buddy governor.

Neither Cade nor Nungesser intended to stay long in Baton Rouge after Treen's inauguration, but the governor didn't want them to leave so fast. He had depended on them so heavily in his campaigns and now that he finally won an executive office, Treen wanted his two good friends' help in getting this brave new administration off on the right foot. Cade and Nungesser complemented each other in so many important ways, in background, personal styles, interests and abilities, and both were so personally loyal to Dave Treen that they seemed the perfect twin nuclei of a political team. Only trouble was they couldn't stand each other.

Within the hectic, non-stop, short-lived pace of a political campaign, there is plenty of room for clashing personalities to contribute without colliding. But when a campaign turns into an administration, clashes are unavoidable. The principals won't talk about their differences that much. There is likely fault on both sides that their political and personal differences would disintegrate into a polite and unspoken but unmistakable power struggle that slowly strangled unity, trust and communication at the very heart of the new administration.

Neither had any governmental experience. Yet Cade the strategist and Nungesser the fund raiser brought to the transition sharply differing ideas of how the spoils should be divided and policy made. Neither was much help to the governor-elect in setting up a tight inner circle and a smooth-running office since they were so busy fighting each other over appointments to boards and commissions. Soon the division affected the entire staff. There were Billy people and there were Cade people and you had to watch what you said to whom. Responsibilities were divided several different ways several different times so that Billy and John could stay out of each other's way but they continued to meet and to clash at Dave Treen's desk. You could count on Nungesser opposing anything Cade proposed. Plus Billy, more used to dealing with shrimp pickers, displayed little finesse or consistency in relating to the professionals in government. With a staff's energy divided and with a governor who disdained shortcuts and short answers, the process of getting anything done on the Fourth Floor slowed to a crawl.

Legislators and lobbyists, savvying the feud, found it hard to get something done even by playing one against the other. Nungesser was the more forceful but Cade was the more persistent. One lobbyist said, "I found out pretty quick that Nungesser would hear you out and you could trust he would take it to Treen, but he wouldn't push it. If Cade didn't like it, he would fight it and keep fighting it until he got his way." On the other hand, if Treen told Nungesser to do something Billy opposed, it wouldn't get off his desk. The situation complicated relations between the governor's office and the agencies. When Nungesser told an agency head to do one thing and Cade countermanded with an order to do something else, the bureaucrat routinely took the safe way out and did nothing.

Cade the strategist quickly found out he would be little help to the governor with the Legislature, as lawmakers, either because of prior dealings with Cade or because of his reputation, wanted nothing to do with him. Rather than give any real authority to an experienced Democrat like Sonny Mouton, Treen felt it better to let a relative unknown like Billy Nungesser deal with the Legislature even if he didn't know much about the process or the people who ran it.

Cade moved into his own area for which he was uniquely unqualified, political fence mending. Given Treen's own indifference to politics, Cade was not the best man to pick up the slack for him. Already he had taken much of the blame for appointments that could have easily gone to Republicans going instead to friends of Democratic legislators. Word was out that being a Republican true believer and a campaign soldier didn't open any doors in the Capitol. Not even little ones. Cade didn't help matters much by ignoring routine political maintenance. He didn't keep up with past parish chairmen and contributors to elicit their advice, keep them informed and prepared for 1983. Dealing with diffident and unapproachable John Cade made you feel it was your duty as a Republican to toil hard, shut up and not expect any thanks. And the resentment spread. Not only were contributors defecting to Edwards— that was business and nothing personal—but hard workers from 1979 were vowing to give Treen nothing more than a vote in 1983. A Shreveport regular watched one of Treen's strongest regional organizations going to seed. "We have lifelong Republicans up here who wouldn't piss on John Cade if he were on fire."

That's the other thing about John Cade—he was loyal to Dave Treen and took a lot of heat that should have gone straight to the governor. Cade let himself be used as a shield for his friend against the hot, cruel world of politics that he should have dragged him kicking and screaming into. He tried, but perhaps only Dave Treen is more stubborn than John Cade. When Cade began early pleading with him to get around the state more, to show the flag and to start preparing for 1983, "Treen would tell me often," remembers Cade, "that four years is a long time. 'I'll start politicking when I have to. First I have to build up a good record to run on. All the happy troops in the world won't help if I have a lousy record.'" Life poked along on the Fourth Floor as though there was not a political world outside.

Dave Treen was not completely blind to what was going on. He knew there was a well of resentment toward John Cade out in the field. Word was coming from contributors and workers to dump Cade or run without them. With pressure against Cade mounting, Treen moved early in the year, telling his parish chairmen that overall coordination of the campaign would belong to Don "Boysie" Bollinger, son of cabinet secretary Donald Bollinger, a huge contributor and an ally of Nungesser against Cade. The young Bollinger would deal with parish coordinators with the assistance of able detail man Larry Kinlaw. Miller Dial would serve as campaign treasurer and John Cade would handle polls, advertising and strategy. Cade, Dial and Bollinger, with Kinlaw working for Bollinger, would form a sort of triumvirate with Bollinger the more equal among equals. That's the way it was sold to the GOP chairmen, but it just didn't work out that way. Kinlaw proved to be an excellent all-around detail man who could juggle the enormous pressures of the campaign with sanity and levity. But Bollinger had neither the experience nor the unnatural, tormented political commitment to be the moving force and public face of this campaign, only gradually and slowly getting into the swing of the race.

The new structure may have relieved Cade of dealing directly with campaign workers, but instead of fading into the background as a strategist and advisor, he moved even more into the limelight as a spokesman for the governor and constant critic of Edwin Edwards.

Some Republicans would boldly suggest that John Cade was not the right man for a public role, that he was too strong to control and should be fired. Fat chance. Not only was Dave Treen petrified of firing anyone, but John Cade, for better or worse, was a political extension of himself. The two had much in common in the way their minds worked and in their views of the world and of government. Treen would often initially disagree with Cade in the Tuesday strategy sessions (for one thing the governor wanted a more positive campaign), but Treen respected Cade's logic and persistence and eventually would go along with Cade if he went along with anyone. Even in their differences they found a bond.

Dave Treen was far more interested in government than in politics, as though he had discovered some way to separate the two, and was relieved to delegate bothersome politics to one of the few people he could trust.

John Cade and Miller Dial encountered the results of three years of political neglect when they began trying to raise money for the 1983 campaign. Having spent two years retiring Treen's 1979 campaign debt, they were far behind Edwards at the bank and about to fall farther back. For many contributors, the fund-raising call marked the first time they had heard from Treen's office in three years—and often that call would mark the last time Treen's office would hear from them. Some stalwarts could be counted on, such as Secretary of Public Safety Donald Bollinger, the bigger-than-life boatbuilder from Lockport. His reason for contributing $84,000 to the Treen 1979 campaign and deficit payback: "Two words: good government. I'm 67 years old. I've been successful, I've made a lot of money. I've had all that a man can want to have, including many troubles. I'm willing to put something on the line for my country, instead of just to sit on my hands and give it all to the Communists when they take over."

But the Bollingers were few and far between—the contributor list that had produced $5.8 million for Treen in 1979 (at the time an American record) was wracked by defections to Edwards and untimely disasters, such as generous oilman Ken Martin's bankruptcy. Plus, the Republicans were not able to tap the big oil and chemical companies, still stung from Treen's attempt to tax them and not anxious to stick out their necks in Louisiana politics.

The problems raising money had a big impact on campaign strategy. The farther they went into mid-1983, the more Cade realized there would not be enough money to build up Dave Treen's image while tearing down Edwin Edwards'. There was little doubt which they would choose. According to Cade, "January 1983 dawned with people feeling Edwards was a very capable, effective leader who was not quite honest. They felt Treen was a somewhat ineffective leader but they admired his integrity. Our job was to convince the people that Dave Treen was a more effective leader and then to win on integrity. But it's difficult to repair an image in that short a period of time. You can attack in a shorter period of time with less money, but you can't repair a negative image that easily. To have convinced people that Treen was an effective leader, which I think he was, we would have had to change the image he had let himself acquire over three years' time."

Instead they felt it easier to change an image Edwin Edwards had acquired, cultivated and broadcast over 12 years' time. Yet Cade felt that Edwards had had a free ride, on account of the lack of an organized opposition or a particularly vigilant press in the past. Cade felt that with the sparkle and the glitter stripped away, Edwards' Robin Hood myth would be debunked if it could be shown that he used his powers to help himself and his friends far more than the people.

To uncover the real story of the opponent, Cade ordered comprehensive research into the politics, the friends, the deals, the life and times of Edwin Edwards. To conduct this unprecedented study, Cade hired as research director Scott Welch, a 27-year-old hereditary Republican (his great-great-grandfather Salmon P. Chase was a former secretary of the treasury, chief justice, cofounder of the GOP and the face on the $10,000 bill). Welch, though trained as a landscape architect, proved to be a relentless investigator. Within a year and a half he amassed and organized a library of every alleged scandal or shady deal associated with Edwards, his family or his friends. Welch spent days in microfilm libraries and courthouses just piecing together the record on the former governor. Nor was there any shortage of people who wanted to talk. "We've had lots of individuals come forward with information on Edwards. I get lots of rumors and innuendoes, but unless I can substantiate them, they will die with me." The calls ranged from inmates' families who claimed they paid for pardons to watchful neighbors who knew the time and place Edwards visited various girlfriends. The Treen office was even contacted by Edwards' old friends, Clyde Vidrine and Lewis Johnson. Clyde volunteered some information and sources, but Johnson wanted money and a government job for his stories. Cade declined.

Welch found the rumor mill fascinating but not very useful. "You don't need to worry about rumors and innuendoes anyway—his record is so bad as it is." In his balcony niche in the Jamestown Avenue headquarters, Welch presents the efforts of his labors, a wall of bound notebooks, stretching 15 feet, bearing such tantalizing labels as "Campaign Scandal," "Governmental Scandal," "Ethics," "Lying,"

"Bribery," "Koreagate," "DCCL." The effort to debunk the myth goes as far back as Edwards' childhood. The first page of the "Personal" file shows an affidavit from a retired Marksville rice farmer who states he knew Clarence Edwards, "more common [*sic*] known as Mr. Bo-Boy Edwards . . . who owned a plantation store . . . and would sell on credit to about 30 or 40 families . . . in-turns they would pay Mr. Bo-Boy Edwards when they harvest their crop." The affiant further stated that "the Edwards family was considered to be well-off people" and that "they were never known as sharecroppers." No log cabin bullshit is getting past Welch, fast earning his nickname Captain Fact.

For all his work, Welch's research unearthed little that had not found its way into some press report already. But the breadth of the research, better than any prior effort, reveals a composite of how Edwin Edwards wielded power to help his friends, punish his enemies and advance his career. But most of the really interesting research, especially the business dealings of Edwards and his friends, pointed to smoke but not fire. The more Welch researched Edwards, the more he grudgingly came to admire the master's craft and cunning. "He's done an extremely good job of covering his tracks," says Welch, drawing diagrams showing the relationships between Edwards and key contributors. "You can see the deals where his friends made the money, what you only rarely see is the money getting back to Edwards. There are many, many trails that disappear in the dust."

As fascinating as Welch's notebooks are, very little of the information is eventually used in the campaign. Instead of the shotgun approach, Cade and Treen decide to focus the anti-Edwards campaign on three major scams: Edwards' retirement, DCCL (the tax shelter program still under federal investigation) and pardons.

The real importance of the research was to satisfy Dave Treen's maddening insistence that every fact be tied down before shooting back at Edwards, a quirk that would cause Treen to pull a punch in a debate when Cade wanted him to go for a knockout. But with Treen safely back at the office, John Cade, armed with Scott Welch's notebooks, strides confidently into the Kenner Sheraton this May morning to expose Edwin Edwards.

Cade is poring over still more notes with Scott Welch when the worthy opponent enters the banquet hall and makes his way through the buffet line. The former governor has this rule about never getting too keyed up for a debate—he appears now only concerned with the choice between lasagna and roast beef.

Sponsors of today's face-off, the Kenner Businessmen's Association, review the rules. Awful rules, designed to numb even this audience. Candidates will answer questions on five topics, ranging from finance to education (yawn), rebut and make opening and closing statements. A little heavy to go with lasagna.

Cade wins the toss and elects to kick off. "I feel like David going up against Goliath. I am heavily outnumbered." There goes poor-mouthing John, underdog Southern taking on LSU. "Governor Treen can't be here today. He's back at the Legislature, since some of my opponent's friends are trying to sabotage the bill to create the Department of the Environment."

Cade leads off with some exciting statistical acrobatics, explaining how Treen's last budget, though nearly $2 billion higher than Edwards' last budget, actually represents a decrease in state spending. Factor in 37 percent inflation and 6 percent population growth, and Treen's 31 percent spending increase is truly a net decrease in state spending. Want more numbers? How about Edwards' increasing spending 73 percent his first term and 59 percent his second for an eight-year increase of 163 percent. Not to mention, continues Cade, as eyes in the audience begin to glaze over, Edwards increased bonded indebtedness 121 percent compared to Treen's three-year rise of only 38 percent. Then a litany of percentage spending increases for education, higher education, social services, environmental protection. Other Treen reforms include competitive bidding on insurance contracts, elimination of restrictive specifications on state bids, enterprise zones, the World's Fair and a climate for industrial development.

"You ought to feel like David, for you are entering the Valley of Death," Edwards tells Cade as he takes the mike. "And like David, your cup runneth over." Then Edwards blows away Cade's carefully constructed house of numbers with a backhand flick. "Of course, figures are all relative and I can play that game too. That's one thing we do well in public life. But what's important is the bottom line and we're broke." To demonstrate, Edwards returns the serve with his own torrent of numbers: the $550 million surplus Edwards left that's gone, the $300 million in the LIFE Fund that's gone, the unemployment compensation fund that's depleted, the 108 new programs Treen started at a yearly price tag of $188 million, the 8,000 new Treen employees . . .

As Edwards rattles on, Cade and Welch furiously flip the pages of their notebooks, pegging down misstatements, confident they've nailed him this time, in public. So busy are they in their notebooks that they're totally missing what's going on. Edwards is doing more than proving his point that numbers can say anything—he's winning the audience over by keeping them awake with a few wisecracks.

Cade can't hold back any longer by the time he gets back to the microphone. "This man is running all over the state saying whatever comes to his mind. I'm not going to call him a liar, but I've not heard one number today that is accurate." Then Cade tracks back over all Edwards' numbers, giving the right number or whole new sets of numbers no one has heard yet, that no one is hearing they're so bored. There are so many false numbers Cade can't list them all, though certainly he has tried. "Edwards harms the environment every time he speaks aloud, because he fills the air with garbage. He needs someone to come behind him to straighten him out. I have a whole page of misstatements here . . ."

This debate may not be David and Goliath, but instead the vaudeville routine of the frustrated short guy swinging furiously but unable to hit the other fellow who's holding him at arm's length.

"Mr. Cade, just so that you can take down one number from me that is an absolute fact, let me say that I am 55 years old." Then he tears back into Cade, accusing Treen of overoptimistically estimating revenues in the current and coming budgets, a reckless fiscal policy certain to cause deficits. Cade, in his turn, hotly defends Treen's budget. After all, the revenue figures come from a civil servant, he says, Ralph Perlman, over whom the governor has no control.

Edwards laughs getting up. "I wish I could hire you. You're great. You really think Ralph Perlman makes an independent revenue estimate. Man, he's got you conned. When I was the governor, Ralph would come up with any figure I'd want him to come up with. He's the lightning rod for when the Legislature gets mad on the budget. There were many times Ralph didn't want to go face them, but I'd say, 'Ralph, that's what you're paid for. I don't want to go lie to them, you go lie to them.'"

Edwards said as governor he would get Perlman to lowball the estimated revenues so that the Legislature would not overspend and so that he wouldn't have to veto projects, as Treen is forced to do again this year.

It goes on like this for most of the rest of the very long lunch hour. Were it not for the verbal fisticuffs, the business people would be snoring by now. Finally, from Cade, an offer: "Mr. Edwards, if we can prove that any of the figures you have given are inaccurate, will you get out of the race?"

"Yes, if you make the same deal. You can say no now, because that's one neither one of us can win."

Even Cade laughs as he nods his head.

Amazingly, John Cade has battled Edwards here on the issues, on the figures, but without one word about honesty and integrity, about DCCL, retirements, Brilab . . . until the very, very end, with Cade's final shot. Describing the fresh new respect people have for government, Cade closes effusively, "Gone are the days of sweetheart deals, of scams, of scandals on the Racing Commission and the Real Estate Commission, of friends and relatives having inside information on land sales. No TEL, no DCCL, no special retirement bills to aid the governor and his friends. And you won't see Dodie Treen taking $10,000 from Koreans."

Edwards and Cade shake hands and exchange a laugh. Cade nervously asks well-wishers, "No, really, how did I do?"

He didn't do badly, holding his ground and taking the fight to Edwards. Trouble was, Edwards could turn the audience around with a one-liner and have them laughing just minutes after Cade had proved conclusively, just once more and for all time, that Edwards had lied. Here was an audience of Dave Treen's friends and neighbors, laughing with, not at, Edwin Edwards. But would Edwards' flippancy have gone over as well had it been Governor Treen in John Cade's shoes? At the same time, it's hard to imagine Treen swinging nearly as hard as did John Cade today. Cade did a creditable job, he worked hard, but he still managed to get in trouble for it.

When Governor Treen later asked a reporter about Cade's performance, she gave Cade good marks but was curious about Cade's closing comment about Dodie not taking money the way the other First Lady did. As the reporter relayed the quote to the governor, Treen got red in the face and asked incredulously if Cade really said that. Treen was genuinely hot and later ordered Cade to never, under any circumstances, bring his family into this campaign. Poor John Cade: chewed up by Edwin Edwards and chewed out by Dave Treen. And all he's trying to do is win. You'd think at times he has more at stake in this than does the guy he's working for.

6. Getting the Message

As the country western band finishes the campaign theme song "On the Road Again," Marion Edwards is back before the mike, broadly clapping his hands together like cymbals, imploring the crowd of 3,000 to stand up and tell him "Who's our next governor? . . . I can't hear you."

No less than 3,000 folks are milling about in the front of the State Capitol, getting free hot dogs, popcorn and cold drinks on this balmy Sunday in May waiting for the main attraction to make his appearance.

It had to take more than free hot dogs to get 3,000 people to show up for a campaign rally five months before the election. But look past the stage and into the sunken gardens where technicians are gingerly stepping over a tangle of cables as they rush to set up the shooting of an Edwards TV commercial. Marion at the mike is now asking the crowd to move over and take their seats on the steps of the Capitol to provide the backdrop for the TV spot. How else do you get 3,000 people outside for a campaign rally than tell them they'll be on TV?

Vicki Edwards sits behind the cameraman on the boom crane which goes up, then down as Vicki passes on instructions moving the crowd this way, then that, to fill up the frame just right. A woman on the steps, perhaps thinking she would get to play a larger part in this drama or at least hoping to meet Edwin Edwards, is miffed at being herded about, but most folks are curious and patient and follow their mass stage directions.

Finally the star emerges and takes his place at the crest of the slope with the crowd at his back and his face to the gardens and Huey's statue and the camera. A reporter edges in closer to the action, but his companion doesn't want to get too close. Pointing to director Tom Buchholz she warns, "Buchholz has a horrible temper. If we get too close I know he'll start yelling at us."

Buchholz barks for action and the crane lowers to ground level, six feet below Edwards. Then as Edwards begins speaking, the camera slowly rises so that the viewer first sees only Edwards and the Capitol tower behind him, then the front line of 20 people—demographically representative—standing behind Edwards comes into view. As the candidate talks about caring for people and his hopes for the future, the rising camera reveals the masses on the steps. Edwards is making the point that he's a man of the people and he cares—if that takes sticking 3,000 people on the steps of the Capitol, fine. The point's been made. Vicki has already unofficially dubbed this commercial "the Gandhi spot."

The idea for the spot comes from Edwin Edwards, creative director of his own campaign. Statewide candidates who insist on following their own creative instincts on campaign advertising are said to have fools for clients, as the lawyers would say. Edwards may have believed that once, as he has used a variety of advertising consultants in his past races. But at the beginning of this campaign, he disappointed all the hungry agencies by announcing that his daughter Vicki's advertising firm, Edwards & Stafford, would handle his account. For one thing, since he'll be making his own creative decisions, he won't need any overblown advice from the state's great media consultants. For another, he sees no reason why that 15 percent agency commission (on a total media budget that will eventually near $3 million) shouldn't stay in the family.

Some might criticize him (some advertising executives might anyway) for not using the considered advice of objective professionals to define his image and project it through the media. But just as Edwards keeps his own counsel on strategy, so does he show little patience for advice on his image. For Edwards, creating a TV message is not a detail to be delegated. He approaches a TV spot as he does a stump speech. If he chooses his own words in talking to 100 folks on a North Louisiana courthouse lawn, he's going to have even tighter control on a TV commercial that reaches hundreds of thousands.

Edwards' decision is a reversal of a trend toward bringing in more and more prestigious and expensive outside media consultants. In 1979, candidate Bubba Henry brought in Charlie Guggenheim of Washington to produce his commercials, the centerpiece of which was a beautifully produced and largely unseen 30-minute biographical spot. Henry ran fifth. Sonny Mouton went to New York to hire the famous David Garth. Mouton finished sixth. The most renowned Louisiana agency, Weill-Strother, handled the fourth place finisher, Paul Hardy. That campaign appeared to be a classic example of the trouble Edwards may be heading toward. Hardy was an excellent media candidate and the early Weill-Strother spots were effective—Hardy was on a roll. But instead of cutting a new set of spots late in the campaign, Hardy overruled the agency and stuck with one spot he felt was so good (the one where he was for the good teachers and against the bad ones) that he ran it over and over ad nauseam and shut down his own momentum.

That's the danger for the strong-willed candidate, to be so full of himself he projects an image he likes but that turns viewers off. Edwards acknowledges that danger—he surely doesn't suffer bouts of modesty often and his snap decisions aren't always the right ones. But Edwards knows the trick of do-it-yourself media. Edwards has a nose for the camera and plays right to it—without appearing to manipulate the media. He'll ride an issue or a situation or even a gag for maximum benefit but he knows when to shut it off. There's a light meter inside him that pulls him back from overexposure. In politics, in gambling, in image making, he keeps his emotions on an even keel and a poker face on his countenance. He neither exults nor despairs. He knows himself and the voter. And he has a daughter in the business.

"He's in a terrible mood today," warns Vicki Edwards, stepping over TV cables, sound equipment and around the lights and reflectors jammed into Marion's office for today's TV shoot. "He's the worst person to do TV production for, because he's made up his mind what he's gonna do and that's it. He's the one candidate you just can't write a TV script for, because he's going to make it up as he goes along."

With the TV lights on and the air conditioning off, temperatures are rising in Marion's corner office as Edwards tells the TV crew what he wants. The political crew—Marion, Billy Broadhurst, Mike Baer—try to stay out the way while the master creates his media.

With his forehead buffed down to dull the shine, Edwards reviews with Vicki and Tom Buchholz what he wants out of the next shot. "If I don't like the way I've said something, can I cut and then you patch it together?"

Vicki: "You mean edit?"

Edwards levels the don't-tell-me-what-it's-called-just-do-it look. Daughter gets the message. "If you want to stop, just say cut."

Buchholz hasn't got the message yet. "Now, Governor, you mentioned your 'campaign blitz.' Is that the right word? Will people know what you mean?"

"What?"

"I was thinking of the word 'blitz,' is that the right word?"

"You take care of the film, I'll take care of the words."

Now Tom has the message.

Edwards has two 30-second spots to get out of the way, one in English, one in French. He stumbles twice getting the French spot started and then is interrupted by the sound of a door shutting somewhere down the hall.

"Goddam son of a bitch! Vicki, we've got 30 guys on the payroll doing nothing. Get someone to sit on the goddam doors!" As Vicki and Broadhurst bolt for the doors, Edwards' eyes turn back to the camera. A warm smile. "Mes amis . . ."

Early in 1982 the political establishment was shocked to hear Gus Weill had been retained as political consultant for the People for Dave Treen campaign. Not that it should have surprised anyone—political consultants are like lawyers: they'll represent anyone, Democrat or Republican, guilty or innocent, as long as they get paid. But Gus Weill made his reputation and his fortune handling top Democrats running for governor, including John McKeithen and Edwin Edwards. But the field was narrower this year and his old friend was already spoken for.

As with every other major political or personnel decision, the choice of Gus Weill was subject to the usual divisive struggle between John Cade and Billy Nungesser. Weill was Nungesser's idea, so Cade was predisposed not to like it. Cade preferred going back to State Representative Ron Faucheux, who had handled the media in the 1979 campaign. But Nungesser had his problems with Faucheux, not the least of which was that toward the end of the 1979 race Ron was driving around New

Orleans in his new Mercedes bought from commissions he made off the campaign Nungesser had sunk $200,000 into.

Treen heard both sides and decided to retain Weill for 1982 with no guarantees for the election year. For $7,500 a month, Weill in 1982 offered political advice which usually wasn't taken and wrote speeches that Dave Treen seldom used, but proved to be very good at ghosting jokes for the governor to deliver at banquets and Gridiron shows. At $90,000 a year, he was one hell of a gag writer.

Gus Weill was not complaining yet but he could see signs of trouble. Having developed an excellent rapport with the governor to land the account, Weill was finding his entree to Dave Treen severely limited, not by palace intrigue, though there was plenty of that, but by Treen's own jammed priorities in running his office and lack of interest in politics. Treen began to make fewer and fewer of the Tuesday strategy sessions with Cade, Nungesser and Weill. When Weill tried to call the governor, an absorbed Dave Treen would refer the call to Cade. It wasn't long before friction developed there. Weill was used to dealing with headstrong candidates, but he had never had to contend with as headstrong a campaign manager as John Cade. Word of the problems began to leak during the summer campaign. A friend of Edwards who had just spoken to Weill said, "Gus swears he'll never accept another campaign without a written contract with the candidate himself, not the campaign manager."

Limited access wasn't all that was new to Gus Weill. Though a veteran consultant, his style of operation had long been to get an account, develop a few ideas and turn the campaign over to his partner Ray Strother. But the successful team split up when Strother left Weill to go national, handling Democratic congressional and gubernatorial candidates and a longshot presidential hopeful named Gary Hart. Strother's departure left Weill to rely on the able but less experienced Roy Fletcher.

With the start of 1983 comes showdown time between Weill and Cade. Cade suggests letting Weill keep the account but wants to turn TV production over to an out-of-state firm. Gus asks for one shot to show what they can do—the result is the excellent five-minute "Integrity" spot with the happily married Dave and Dodie projecting all the right virtues of fidelity, honor and hard work and closing with a Waltonesque long shot of the Mansion as the light in the bedroom window goes out. "Integrity" is a smash hit, the Treen account is saved for Gus Weill, though Edwin Edwards can't resist his own critique. "Just running an ad showing you walking in the house at night with your own wife is hardly what's needed to convince the people that you can run the state."

The boldest move of Edwards' advertising campaign is an attempt to get out of it altogether. He appears before the Baton Rouge Press Club in February to propose a "no frills" campaign in which neither candidate would spend money on advertising, paraphernalia, parish headquarters, anything but the bare necessities for traveling the state and presenting the issues to the voters.

Treen, of course, rejects the disarmament plan out of hand, citing, as would a nuclear superpower, the difficulties of verifiability and the impossibility of controlling the spending and campaigning of third parties, such as labor unions and black groups. Besides, even if both candidates are well known to the public, as Edwards says, Treen and Cade feel that the public doesn't know enough of the right things, or wrong things, about Edwin Edwards, which they intend to expose through advertising.

Within a week of Treen's rejection, several hundred Edwards billboards spring up across the state—a showing in force. Two comments on the billboards. First, the $400,000 buy is dismissed as a massive waste of campaign money and evidence of Edwards' naivete in advertising. As John Cade points out, billboards are for building name recognition, which Edwin Edwards already has. But according to Edwards, the billboards serve a purpose having nothing to do with name identification. "It was the best way to counter the rumor Treen was spreading that I would not run. As this affected our fund raising, I decided the billboards would be the most visible statement that I was in the race to stay." Spending money so that he can raise more—from this point campaign treasurer Marion Edwards knew the planned $5 million budget was just wishful thinking.

Comment two. Okay, so Edwards has a valid reason for the massive billboard buy. But the billboard itself is not worthy of a race for police juror. Observe the small passport photo of Edwards peering expressionless from the board. A funny thing about Edwards' pictures—the more serious and statesmanlike the pose, the shadier he looks. He is a man who does not look good standing still. His most attractive pose is the exhortative, whether he is urging on the voters, the legislators or the dice. At these times, he instills a sense of confidence and involvement. When he stops moving or talking and stares straight at the camera, he instills fear. The billboard copy is no better: "Edwards . . . Now." For boards going up in February it doesn't make much sense, if indeed any real thought went into it at all. A later slogan, developed as an afterthought, is more appropriate: "Let's get Louisiana moving again." Others in the campaign are left cold by the boards, but wisely hold their tongues.

Early in the campaign year, Roy Fletcher tells his boss Gus Weill, "We can't change an image that took four years to make with one 30-second spot." That's a sentiment echoed throughout the Treen campaign and administration and the blame rests squarely back at the governor's feet. Dave Treen is about to spend millions of dollars to correct an image that he has run into the ground for free. Over and above the disorganization and divisiveness within his office, Dave Treen shows a singular lack of interest in using the media not only to improve his leadership image but to lead. How else is a governor to mobilize public opinion if not through the free media? His own cabinet officials blame Treen's biggest legislative loss, the defeat of his oil and gas tax, on the governor's failure to build a case for his program with the public before pushing it in the Legislature. It's as though he thought government should work in a vacuum apart from public opinion instead of in concert with it.

The damage this failure to communicate did to his programs was minor compared to what it did to his politics. Part of problem lies with the governor's inexperienced press office led by Billy Nungesser's niece Sally. She can only work with what she is given, yet obvious little things fall through the cracks. When Treen visited the White House and met with the president in 1981, no one saw to it that a picture was shot of Dave and Ron together. Yet the one celebrity picture that does hang prominently on the press office wall shows Dave Treen touring the Atchafalaya Basin with . . . James Watt.

The pervasive Cade-Nungesser split colors the governor's press relations as well. The press office staff is run by Billy people, the campaign office by Cade people. Needless to say, they don't cooperate.

Not that Dave Treen is oblivious to the press. On the contrary, during his term he carefully follows and comments on what is written about him and the administration more than any governor before him. About the only time the governor calls a Capitol correspondent is to point out an incorrect statement or conclusion in a newspaper story. Even editors of country weeklies receive long letters from the governor taking issue with a news story or a column in that paper. For all the attention he gives to the permanent record—by which historians will judge his administration—he rarely watches or tries to correct the TV news, a medium with far greater potential to distort the facts and to influence not historians but voters. "The governor says the most important influence in his life is religion, but I don't believe it," mutters a frustrated aide. "I think it's the editorial page of the *Times-Picayune*."

For as little as Dave Treen understands the press, Edwin Edwards knows, cultivates and manipulates it to a fault. Though he doesn't always get along with reporters and editors, he keeps the lines of access open to them. That, in return, keeps open to him his access to the public, through which he continues to enhance his image as a leader and a stand-up comic.

His approach to the press is exactly the opposite of Dave Treen's. Though Edwards has often been stung by newspaper investigative stories and critical columns, he seldom bothers to even answer stories or editorials he feels are untrue or unfair. He knows that people that read the newspapers that closely are either Republicans or well-educated professionals who aren't inclined to vote for him to start with. TV is another matter. He plays to the camera without being obvious about it. He rarely loses his cool on camera and is fast with the quip so that he can turn a hostile interviewer into a straight man for his punch lines. Though his answers don't always satisfactorily deal with the questions, his style—the self-assured casualness, the candor that passes for honesty—is compelling and effective with his TV audience. Because Edwards understands TV. "I learned a long time ago that no matter how great a speech you make, 30 minutes later people will forget what you said." That is his special oratorical gift: not what he says, but how he says it, makes him the star of the TV news.

Even with publishers and editorial writers posed against him, he keeps on good terms with individual reporters, fanatically returning phone calls and dropping what he is doing to grant an interview on the spot. He got a good break at the beginning of his first term, inheriting a young press corps inexperienced in dealing with an operator in Edwards' league. A young man who worked briefly in TV remembers, "I'd walk into an interview loaded for bear and come out feeling like a whipped puppy." A newspaper reporter knew he was in for trouble when his editor ordered him, without any documentation, to go ask Edwards if he owned stock in a hazardous waste company doing business with the state. The reporter braced himself as he floated out the question and watched Edwards swivel around in his chair, lean forward and malevolently sneer, "You're so fucking stupid."

The one reporter Edwards did not even pretend to like was the experienced and aggressive Capitol correspondent for the New Orleans *States Item* and later the *Times-Picayune*, Bill Lynch. The investigative reporter raised early questions about the governor's credibility and honesty over TEL Enterprises and the IRS investigations into his Las Vegas gambling trips. Then he broke the story of Clyde Vidrine's allegations of rampant payoffs and kickbacks. Edwards counterattacked, accusing Lynch of distorting the facts and plying Vidrine with alcohol to aid his memory, and he distributed survey results to legislators that showed low public confidence in the *Item*. Though careful not to make Lynch a martyr for the rest of the press, he clearly froze Lynch out in hopes of making an example of a path for other reporters not to take.

His hostility toward Lynch boiled over in public only once, and for a couple of hours he even regretted it. In attending the Capitol Correspondents' Gridiron Show his first year out of office, he told cast and audience after the show how surprised he was what lambs reporters had turned into for Dave Treen, especially Bill Lynch. With Lynch sitting with his wife in the audience, Edwards said: "I finally figured out that Bill Lynch is a latent ass kisser. He's just been waiting for the right ass to kiss."

Well before the 1983 campaign begins, Edwards is broadsided by a series of investigative reports that are not only uncomplimentary, they are televised. WBRZ-TV in Baton Rouge, owned by the Manship family (who also publishes the city's two dailies), airs three reports detailing Edwards' deals that helped his friends at the expense of the state. The station heavily promotes the investigative stories by reporter John

Camp, presenting them both on the news and as half-hour documentaries. The televised reports are a clear threat and dangerous precedent, the equivalent of putting Bill Lynch on camera. Soon thereafter he sends Channel 2 a message of what they can expect when he comes back to power.

Senator J. Bennett Johnston is assessing Reaganomics and El Salvador before the Baton Rouge Press Club in April when Edwin Edwards strolls in with his brother Marion and buddy Gus Mijalis in tow. Lunch is breaking up and reporters filtering out when Edwards starts going tit for tat with WBRZ assistant news director Bob Courtney. Just speaking in general, Edwards asserts he has no quarrel with investigative reporting or even adverse editorial comment. But the abuses come "from guys like John Camp who feel free to go out and dig up false and malicious stories about me just because your station owner wants to hurt me." The state needs a punitive damages law to hold in check the "Doug Manships and Hugh Shearmans who feel they can carry on a personal vendetta against public officials without fear."

Courtney interrupts him. "Manship had nothing to do with John Camp's stories. He knew nothing about it until it was produced. All he said when he saw it was, 'I can't believe you are doing this at this time.'"

"Then why didn't he stop it?" says Edwards.

Courtney: "Because he doesn't interfere with the stories we do."

Edwards: "Well, he should, because he's getting blamed for them."

Courtney: "Just to give you an example. Remember I did that story on you when you went out of office. Every reporter here thought I had gone totally overboard, that it was all glowing and there you were riding off into the sunset. Well, the only letter I got on it came from Doug Manship. He said he liked it very much."

Edwards: "He should have. It was very factual. I liked it too." The guy doesn't give an inch.

Beth George, news director on public TV, asks if it's true that Edwards has excluded Channel 2 from his first statewide media buy of the campaign.

"That's right. No ads on Channel 2 or in the *Morning Advocate.* I'm not going to feed the news media that is trying to undermine my campaign. Well, I'm not boycotting them completely. My barbecue stand still advertises. No one's writing bad things about it," he says, referring to the two Luther's Restaurant franchises he owns in Baton Rouge.

"We'll have to send John Camp out to review them," Courtney says jokingly.

"Just let me know when he's coming," Edwards says half-jokingly.

Standing behind Edwards, brother Marion and buddy Gus are exchanging nervous glances and shuffling their feet. Senator Johnston, following the proceedings with a tense smile, sees his opening, wishes everyone lots of luck and dashes for the door.

Beth George is surprised Edwards, in boycotting Channel 2, is letting his politics affect his marketing. "Isn't that cutting off your nose?"

Edwards: "It's a long nose. It won't hurt me but it'll cost you [nodding to Courtney] about $200,000 on your bottom line."

Courtney: "No it won't, all our spots are already sold out. We have to bump spots to get politicians on now."

Edwards: "Well, it will hurt you if people in Baton Rouge have to watch Channel 9 or 33 to find out what's happening in state government for the next eight years."

The smiles are off the faces now. Though voices aren't raised, the comments are lined in ice. Beth George is more surprised than mad, but that's about to change. "That just sounds so malicious and petty on your part. So if you don't like what people say about you, you just shut them out?"

And he says, "You're either not hearing what I'm saying or you're stupider than I thought. I don't care about the editorial policy, I care about the accuracy and the fairness in reporting the news."

Courtney is weighing Edwards' threat. "I'll be concerned about not having access to you. But that's not going to hurt the station."

Edwards: "It'll hurt if you have less viewers each time there's a flood or a disaster and I call Channel 9 and 33 and not you."

Courtney: "By cutting out one station, it sounds like you're trying to manage the news."

Edwards: "I'm not trying to manage the news, but I manage the vehicle that gets the news to the people. What I'm saying is that I will not let Channel 2 photograph me on the news. As long as Channel 2 continues its attitude of partiality, I will do what I have to do."

By now the conversation has degenerated into a bout of "oh yeah" and all parties just drop it at that.

The wonder is, what's Edwards gaining with these volleys. Talking about shutting out Channel 2 and getting back at Doug Manship is grand political posturing in the Kingfish tradition. But outside of the well-informed voter and certainly outside of Baton Rouge, no one really knows or cares who Doug Manship is. As much as the press ascribes subtle political motives to every Edwards move, this looks like a case of pure human spite, Edwards' need to hit back at Doug Manship in the only place he'll feel it: in the pocketbook. But Manship has a very big pocketbook that has cushioned him amply from all past advertising reprisals. Other than personal satisfaction, Edwards is gaining nothing from the no-win war he is wading into. Edwards' aides don't like it, but there isn't much they can do to stop it.

Young Marion and Edwin Edwards in Marksville.

J. F. Cado

Paul Brou

Marion Edwards

Edwin Edwards hugs his mother,
Agnes Brouillette Edwards.

John Maginnis

Danny Brown

Elaine and Edwin Edwards

Dodie and Dave Treen

Danny Brown

Billy Nungesser

Gus Weill

Sandy Hubbert

Edwin and the Edwards women: Vicki, Anna and Elaine.

Paul Brou

More than anyone, John Cade had the Governor's ear.

The candidate flanked by daughter and wife.

The Edwards billboards were up in March, to counter rumors he wouldn't run. His campaign was smooth but not perfect: this faulty board remained up for four weeks.

dwin the charmer.

Dave the charmer.

Edwin Edwards demonstrating the Jimmy Swaggart kneebend.

Mike O'Keefe

Ben Bagert

Heavy hitters: Legendary oilman Louis Roussel, Jr (left), gave and lent Edwards $250,000; Edmund Reggie (right), Edwards' longtime friend, gave nd lent the campaign over $300,000.

The many races of Peppi Bruneau: (right) masquerading as "The Rev" in the Opera; (above) and receiving recognition from the Black Caucus on the floor of the House.

Rev. Clarence D. Bates   *Don Kelly*

Edwards and U.S. Senator J. Bennett Johnston at the Pentecostal tabernacle in Tioga.

7. A Night at the Opera

His tentacles bobbing in the faint summer evening breeze, the State Insect looks silly but is at least having an easier time handing out programs than his sidekick the State Crustacean, who has to use both his claws just to hold a drink. The costume rental place couldn't come up with any representations of species that the Legislature, in its infinite boredom this session, proclaimed as State Things. Certainly the State Drink, milk, is absent tonight, as inside the American Legion hall a converted Slurpee machine gurgles frozen margaritas into salt-rimmed glasses.

The Legislature has entered its final critical week, when not only are some of the most important bills decided, but some of the best parties are thrown. Partying is integral to a legislative session. Folks back home may sneer in repulsion at the idea of Senator Jim Bob dragging into his desk in the morning after a hard night of swilling some lobbyist's bourbon and chasing committee secretaries through one bacchanalian bout after another. But, you see, that's only part of it. The parties are all but necessary to drain off some of the demagogic energy these legislators bring to Baton Rouge, all puffed up like bullfrogs about to pop. Without these parties to wear them down and lay them back a bit, legislators might begin taking their power seriously, at which point our lives and property really would be in danger.

That's a beneficial side effect but not the real reason for the fun, which is to foster communication and understanding between lawmakers, constituent groups and lobbyists of disparate and special interests. Lots of understanding occurred this session, with some of the more lavish bashes ever to add sparkle to a summer social season. Best spread had to be a tie going to the Restaurant Association party (a 200-foot serving line featuring dishes from dozens of the state's better-known restaurants) and the Retailers Association's Foods of the World extravaganza (spectacular international cuisine prepared by the hotel chefs' school in New Orleans). Galas ran the gamut from the Oilfield Contractors' swank soiree at the Camelot Club to construction lobbyist Charlie Smith's ongoing tailgate party in the Capitol parking lot on the last night of the session. Overall, the best parties are casual affairs held in the spacious courtyard of the Pentagon Barracks. There under the oak trees of the historic parade grounds, with a serene view of the Capitol over the old barracks rooftops, on any summer's night you can feast on fried shrimp and raw oysters from a contingent of Plaquemines Parish fishermen or barbecued brisket from the volunteer fire department in Welsh. Legislators, lobbyists, staff members and reporters review the day's events as the sun sets before moving the party on to someone's apartment or a hotel bar.

The partying, the getting together after adjournment, week after week, summer after summer, helps form the bond of community for the cast of characters of the legislative session. The parties are not so much for discussing business as for getting to know the people you're doing business with. They have grown to know each other pretty well, not just lobbyists and legislators, but legislators and legislators too. It's healthy to be able to cut up a colleague in a committee hearing and raise a toast with him that night. Black and white, Cajun and redneck, lawyer and farmer—the different legislators get to know each other partying together as they do working together, or against each other. Tonight they will take the communication one step farther, from self-knowledge to self-parody, with the quadrennial presentation of the Opera, written, staged and performed by the members of the Louisiana House of Representatives in spoof thereof.

The House members have done everything to put on tonight's show and party, except, of course, pay for it. As is customary, even necessary, the evening's entertainment is sponsored by a group of 31 different individual lobbyists and organizations ranging in flavor from LABI and the AFL-CIO to the Beer Industry League to the Louisiana Bankers to the Mobile Housing Association. Wherever there are legislators and whatever they are doing, there are lobbyists close by. It is all part of their investment in good government, government that is good for them.

Tonight's players have been writing and rehearsing scripts in spare moments, a few verses having even been composed during some especially dry committee hearings. This is the House's celebration. The Senate is a closed and stuffy club. The House is more an open, egalitarian, rambunctious and unpredictable debating and drinking society. But tonight it is family. One big happy one.

Partygoers mill about with margaritas in hand for this celebration on the eve of the circus leaving town. An island of tranquility in this sea of revelry is Woody Jenkins, strait-laced young libertarian once dubbed the Miniature Adult, whose only concession to the merriment is that he has taken off his coat. With tie perfectly knotted at the collar of his starched white shirt, the three-term representative sips on a Coke and quietly takes in the madness around him and, as if to classify the experience, notes, "After 12 years here I realize the more things remain the same, the more they change." Curtain time approaches, the line slackens at the margarita machine, time to grab a drink and a seat, but . . . what the hell are you talking about, Woody? *The more things remain the same.* Turnover has been on the way down in the Legislature since the first single member district elections in 1971 brought in a new wave of legislators. Most of them have stayed, growing not only more attuned to their districts but steadily more entrenched. With campaign costs continuing to increase out of control, anything more than token opposition to an incumbent is becoming the exception. Were it not for reapportionment this year and some scattered retirements, the upcoming legislative races would be shaping up to be as interesting as the elections to the Soviet Praesidium.

And yet, *the more they change.* "It's a different group of people than who came here 12 years ago," says Jenkins. Most have achieved what they set out to do or have given up their initial agendas out of practicality or embarrassment. They're less hungry for publicity, he says, less eager to take the mike for speechifying and posturing. And he's right, for the number of bills filed in the past two sessions has dropped considerably from the normal glut. "They're maturing as they're getting older," observes the 36-year-old Jenkins, "and they are also getting tireder. I can count on less than two hands the number of people I need to talk to in order to kill a bill." Woody should know, he's one of the House's all-time leading hit men. "You know we're not wrapping this session up early only because there's no money to spend. I don't think they want to spend any more time here. They want to get home to their families and their businesses."

Family and business will have to wait. Emcee Bob Israel is insulting honored guests, including the governor and the Speaker of the House. Most House members not in the cast are in the audience. After some panicked commotion backstage, King David LaTreen, King of the Lost Fairies, stumbles onstage for the opening of the Opera, "Capitolot."

I'll tell you how the state is running tonight!

Unprepared. And scared.

More elected representatives horn in on the action, stepping on the cues they don't outright blow, mixing and matching pieces of costume, singing off-key, scandalously impersonating one another. One hard-drinking legislator is portrayed as Sir Staggermore, and a legislative Lothario is called Sir Overknight. Benny Bagert as Mary Landrieu prances on in drag. The Bible Belt's Jamie Fair in makeup and tights promenades through the audience as the World's Fairie while a trendy North Louisianian is portrayed dancing onstage shaking a Coke bottle that gives off clouds of white (talcum) powder.

So what makes them so tired? They don't look like they're missing the hearth and office too badly tonight. But something more than just creeping maturity among the players has changed the spirit of these summer sessions. They just don't seem as fun as they used to be. And it's not just empty pork barrels or the recent bonecrunching business-labor battles that have been the downer. There is a feeling of something missing here. Like a governor.

At the front table, Dave Treen is getting into Bruce Lynn's portrayal of bumbling King LaTreen. Dave Treen's a good sport and is well-liked by all brands of legislator. He comes to their parties and he and Dodie throw several great bashes during every session. He believes in legislative independence. He works long hours. He does his homework. Now if he'd just start acting like a governor, maybe more of these guys would know what's going on. For over three years Dave Treen, with only limited success, has been trying something new: treating the Legislature as a co-equal branch of government, as recommended in the U.S. Constitution. Sounds great, but it just doesn't work in Louisiana, if it does still in America. Regardless of how they do it on the Potomac, in Louisiana the chief executive is expected if not to call the shots, at least to send very clear signals. The governor's presence and power in the Legislature are vital to achieving a consensus on the big issues and the budget and pushing them through. Treen awkwardly horsetraded for cooperation with the Legislature; Edwards showed that pork barrel politics is only part of it, that leadership and friendship are slowly built and cultivated by keeping the door open to legislators and knowing what they want.

That seemed somehow too wasteful a process for Treen, too much time to spend away from the careful study and deliberative analysis of issues before making up his own mind, without checking what was on the minds of the legislators. Each session the horror stories grew worse of crossed signals, mixed signals or no signals from the Fourth Floor or from the Division of Administration. The governor can't return every call, but if he doesn't at least start with the Legislature, he wastes a lot of time he thought he was saving in putting out fires or having to beat back stubborn resistance.

Not that there was daily chaos—the bulk of what Treen wanted got through. But a lot got through he didn't want and he had to either swallow a bad bill or project or make someone mad by vetoing it. Each summer brought more missed opportunities and misunderstandings. Legislators who exchanged votes for the governor's support on projects would find their pet construction projects redlined from the final package. He accomplished some innovative legislation but failed to build a consensus for the item he pushed hardest for, his tax on oil and gas passing through the state. The CWEL debacle showed that Treen was essentially powerless to push through a program without the support of LABI and the rest of the business lobbyists.

Edwards did it differently, and more successfully. He not only cultivated legislators, he wooed and seduced them. Edwards almost always got his way, but he only moved after he knew where the Legislature wanted to go.

Here's Dave Treen having a good time at the party—a time to work and time to play. With Edwards, the whole process was more fun. You couldn't tell where the work ended and the party started. The party was the power—there was the daily shuttle of legislators to the Mansion for breakfast, back for lunch, in and out of his den during the day, meeting one delegation of legislators, getting back to others on the phone. And back at the Capitol, they were always waiting on the word from the governor—what did Edwin want to do? Any legislator who wanted to play had fun keeping up with it, being in on it. When Dave Treen came in, they kept on waiting for the word from the governor. But it never came. I'll believe Woody Jenkins that his colleagues are tired of the Legislature when they stop running for reelection. The real source of their fatigue comes from having to learn new rules when it's the old game they want to play.

The Opera company is not dwelling on these themes of failed leadership and miscommunication—they're numbing enough to have to deal with by day. Tonight, we are playing on more basic and emotional topics, like race. The fun of the show is in the casting, as the black representatives are in white face playing the most conservative, reactionary legislators and vice versa.

Here's black New Orleans Representative Lee Frazier in whiteface, blinking his eyes in perfect imitation of Woody Jenkins, though in his pompadour wig he looks more like Little Richard. He's followed by Peppi Bruneau, a Lakefront Yat and intellectual ramrod of the Right (as well as the moving spirit behind the Opera), bounding onstage as ageless wonder Reverend Avery Alexander. Wearing blackface is one thing, but when white boys start throwing dialect around, it can get touchy in mixed company. But Peppi breaks up the house, first slaying the pretenders, as the Rev tells off the Johnny Jackson character. "Youse may be the chairman of the Black Caucus, but Ise its *tit-too-lar* head." Then he exposes the turncoats, like Treen supporter Charbonnet. "You looks white, you votes white, and when Frazier's bill passes, you bees white." (Frazier's bill would repeal the antiquated Louisiana law classifying anyone with 1/32 black blood as Negro.)

But the crowd and cast, black and white, cheer the racist humor. Indeed these are different people than who first came here 12 years ago. When the first black legislators outside New Orleans were elected to the Legislature in 1972, the differences between the races were no laughing matter. Each side kept to itself, a social segregation that reflected real life. Tonight this group can laugh at the raw black and white humor because they have shed some old attitudes during the past decade of working and playing together.

Voting power has even more to do with it. As black voter registration increases, more legislative districts are turning predominantly black. And in many of the other districts, blacks are the decisive bloc that white candidates must vie for. The new reality is best expressed by Ralph Miller, a dark-skinned white legislator from Norco, who steps out of character onstage to confess, "When I first ran, people in my district started rumors that I had black blood. Then after the last reapportionment, I looked at my new district and then I started those rumors again myself."

Racial harmony and racial jokes are the rage this last week of the session, climaxing in the final hour of the final night, as black legislators call Peppi Bruneau to the mike to present him with a white sheet and hood. A touched Peppi appropriately responds, "I consider this gift from my colleagues as something of an honor. It's been a long time since someone in this uniform could stand at this mike."

But back to the Opera, where the fat lady is about to sing. A bevy of committee secretaries in hoopskirts have joined the entire cast in singing "Capitolot" to Dave and Dodie and guests. Author Bruneau acknowledges cheers and catcalls: "If you were insulted by tonight's performance, it was intentional. If you weren't, go do something in the next four years." The band strikes up again, cast members leap from the stage to the bar, the World's Fairie is making advances to the governor, Benny Bagert in drag waltzes with John Hainkel, comely maidens in hoopskirts sway to the music with blacks in whiteface, and a white talcum cloud drifts through the dimly lit hall. The more things stay the same, the more they change.

Things are changing fast in the Senate too, but no one there is laughing about it. Entering the cool, marbled mausoleum, you sense nothing different—the Senate is in one of its typical funks today as debate, if you can call it that, grinds on routinely, the drone of muffled voices broken only by the occasional voting machine bell signifying yet another bill that had been debated and fought over hotly in the House has just passed the Senate 38-0. The only difference the careful observer would note is that Mike O'Keefe is no longer in his presidential perch on the third level of the dais. Instead he sits in the side gallery, talking intently with a reporter. Not that he goes unnoticed. New Orleans District Attorney Harry Connick has urgent business to discuss and Vic Bussie taps his toe nearby. But O'Keefe can't be bothered right now. No, he doesn't want the interviewer to come back later—he only wants to talk about the one subject no one else wants to bring up in his presence: Mike O'Keefe's conviction.

He's covered this ground with everyone in earshot, including the entire Senate. He's discussed in detail every nook of his legal problems, yet it's all so fresh as if with each retelling the shock of his conviction settles in anew. He is a victim, he claims, of federal persecution arising not from a mere fishing expedition but from a dredging operation by the FBI into his entire financial history. "They've looked at every check I've written since high school."

The feds' thoroughness finally paid off. In 1982, U.S. Attorney John Volz tried and convicted O'Keefe of defrauding his limited partners in a real estate deal. The trial was a bitter experience for the proud O'Keefe. Mike is not your arrogant sort and he wouldn't step on anyone who stays out of his way. As tough and ruthless a politician and businessman as he is known to be, he's exceedingly humble in person, soft-spoken, conciliatory, speaking in the reverent hushed tones of an Irish politician at the wake. The O'Keefe manner worked well on his constituents, business partners, senators. But in the face of John Volz and the complicated business dealings and an all-woman jury, O'Keefe's obsequious charm fell flat. In two separate trials, he was convicted and sentenced to 16 months for mail fraud and obstruction of justice arising out of an apartment deal in which he swindled investors.

Mike O'Keefe cannot yet accept he is going to jail—it is pretty hard to fathom that Mike O'Keefe, known in the Capitol as the Spider, would get caught in someone else's web. He stands without peer in the corridors of Capitol power while in the world of New Orleans business, his subtle, wily hand moves through every level of the city's banking, real estate and trade—strengthened in fact by his political power in Baton Rouge. Yet in the Senate, he is labor's leading ally, Vic Bussie's goal line defense against the business lobby and the governor's bright-eyed reforms. O'Keefe comes from a long line of Irish politicians and businessmen. His father was a prominent judge, his grandfather once was mayor. But Mike's power, in business and politics, has eclipsed his ancestors'. Completing his sixth term in the state Senate, which, under the terms of the new constitution, elected O'Keefe its first president, Mike O'Keefe before his resignation was easily the second most powerful public official in the state—on Dave Treen's bad days, O'Keefe, arguably, was No. 1.

His power was that of the Senate, that narrow gate through which all bills must pass. O'Keefe acquired and exercised his firm control without having to ramrod bills or crush opponents with a heavy hand. With his own autocratic powers over committee assignments and Senate rules, as well as his knowledge of parliamentary tricks, political strategy and human nature, he controlled the process without having to raise his voice, or sometimes even speak—often an arched eyebrow was enough to smother a bothersome motion in red lights.

O'Keefe disarmed his critics with his modest manner, soft inflection and touching though calculated acts of kindness. Like all the great politicians, he was an irrepressible favor granter. He treated his fellow senators in a style befitting their dignity and self-image, burrowing into the Capitol basement to build plush offices and private dining rooms. He'd do anything for a senator, as one O'Keefe aficionado told *Gambit's* Liz Galtney. "If you need a state trooper to give you a ride somewhere, he'll get it for you. If you need a bill killed in committee, he'll help you kill it. He'll do favor after favor and won't ask anything in return. But when he needs you to vote with him, and he doesn't ask often, he'll just say, 'I need you on this one.' And you may be voting against your mother when you vote with O'Keefe, but you'll go ahead and vote with him anyway." Dispensing favors with one hand, O'Keefe divided and conquered with the other. He could smell an alliance coming together to oppose the order of things and would insert just the right wedge between allies to break up pesky coalitions.

Mike O'Keefe was immensely liked but also feared: it was costly, often senseless to oppose him unless you presented a formidable phalanx of support both inside and outside the rail. But even a senator who could stand up to O'Keefe and get away with it on one issue knew that later he could be clobbered on another important bill or a project even dearer to his heart. So the Senate behaved. O'Keefe ran the upper chamber from his back pocket but he ran it well. Although some chafed under O'Keefe's reign of fear, many feared even more a Senate without him. O'Keefe deferred only to Edwin Edwards, and when Edwards left office, the Senate president didn't necessarily have to defer to Dave Treen. Treen, instead, deferred to O'Keefe, who charmed the governor—one New Orleans boy to another—into an unholy alliance. Treen flatly refused to try to develop an alternative leadership in the Senate, continuing to deal primarily with O'Keefe—who got the best of the bargaining—and publicly supporting O'Keefe's efforts to hang onto power after his conviction.

A swelling tide of newspaper editorials called for the Senate president's resignation, but the mutinous talk stopped at the Capitol steps. No one in the Senate, no one in the governor's office would dare suggest that two felony trial convictions would make an official unfit to preside over the top legislative body in the state. But on the first day of the 1983 session, Mike O'Keefe took his colleagues off the hook and laid his burden down. He stepped down from the president's dais to the lowly podium where mere senators speak and resigned his cherished office, but not before, one more time, he told his side of the story. Senators squirmed at their desks as an emotional O'Keefe, citing statutes and trial testimony, warned his peers—mostly attorneys and businessmen—the same thing could happen to them should they become the targets of an ambitious U.S. attorney with the full weight of the federal government behind him. It was a sad moment for most senators there: they genuinely liked O'Keefe and appreciated the prestige and grandeur he had attached to Senate service. But knowing Mike O'Keefe, they were less convinced of his innocence than they were shocked that he had been caught. After all, they don't call him the Spider for not stepping carefully and covering his tracks. Some of them doubted the rightness of the case the government had built against O'Keefe—instead of reacting in rage, they took it as a warning that a new order is at work in state politics, a new power from which not even the highest and the mightiest are immune. The alarm has been sounded in Louisiana politics, just as the cry went up in the French Quarter two centuries ago when word of the Louisiana Purchase broke: *The Americans are coming.*

Federal investigations into state politics are nothing new. Their success is. One only has to look at the federal court docket for the body count. The former commissioner of administration is in jail, the former agriculture commissioner is in jail, the Senate president is going to jail, even Mafia boss Carlos Marcello is in jail. This unprecedented incarceration of the state's political and criminal elite—along with various lesser lights, from councilmen to congressmen—is the work of a hard-nosed cadre of bright, young U.S. attorneys, the most successful of whom is John Volz of New Orleans. Armed with new, far-reaching racketeering statutes and aggressive sting operations like Brilab, the feds have nailed powerful state politicos for doing what has always come naturally—shaking down contributors, accepting kickbacks, using political clout and influence to pull off dubious business deals. In the past, what local DA or state judge would pursue them? Then starting in the 1970s, one of the few effective initiatives of President Jimmy Carter set the Justice Department on the trail of white collar and political criminals. The instrument of that power locally is 49-year-old U.S. Attorney John Volz. The quiet and unassuming native Orleanian, who grew up in the projects and later a boardinghouse and worked his way through Jesuit and Tulane, has had the greatest effect on state politics since the feds moved in on the Louisiana scandals in 1939. The three most important hides on John Volz's wall are: O'Keefe, Roemer, and, most impressive of all, Carlos Marcello, the Little Man, another unwary victim lured and ensnared by the Brilab sting. Many Louisianians were shocked when Marcello, a self-described humble tomato salesman, reported to Parish Prison in April 1983 to begin a seven-year sentence for racketeering. For 35 years the undisputed boss of organized crime on the Gulf Coast, Marcello had been convicted before, he had even been deported, but few believed he would ever see the inside of a prison. For Volz, it was more than a case of justice delayed, it was justice arrived. "We've had people say to us that Carlos Marcello would never spend a day in jail," Volz told *Dixie Magazine*—now he's telling those people, "There are no untouchables." The Marines have landed. The American presence gains a firmer foothold in Louisiana.

Volz and his compatriots are sending shock waves through Louisiana politics. Times are changing. Officeholders engaging in hallowed political practices are now being prosecuted. Some of the state's very biggest political fish are being hauled in. But not the biggest. Though someone's working on him too.

Mike O'Keefe is mortally wounded. But the ambitious young pols in his district aren't quick to take the vulture's roost. O'Keefe has given up his president's power but not his seat in the Senate. He announces he will seek his seventh term—to do anything else would be to admit he had done something wrong. And that point obsesses him. But during most of the coming campaign, his opponents—sensitive to the incumbent's personal popularity—will avoid mentioning O'Keefe's conviction. That's all O'Keefe will talk about. "Thanks for listening to me," he tells a *Picayune* reporter after rehashing the details of his trial at length. "I should send you a psychiatrist's bill."

The polls don't look great for O'Keefe, yet his opponents are cautious. They know O'Keefe has strengths that don't show up well in polls, such as the unified support of Mayor Dutch Morial and the leading black organizations in the district, the state and local leaders of the AFL-CIO, the New Orleans district attorney and Edwin Edwards. O'Keefe has another intangible, the Louisiana voters' ambivalence toward corruption. There's a myth that Louisiana loves to elect crooks. Not true. It all depends on what one has stolen and from whom and the politician's built-in popularity with the people. Agriculture Commissioner Gil Dozier ran for reelection when he was under indictment in 1979 and he was drubbed 2-1. Yet the same year in Baton Rouge, a state senator and the clerk of court were both reelected shortly after being convicted. And there's Potch Didier in Avoyelles Parish, who won reelection in 1975 though he had to campaign from a jail cell. So there is always hope. In fact, on the ballot this fall are two former congressmen, one who was indicted but acquitted of vote-buying and one who did time for violating federal campaign laws, who are running for their old seats in the Legislature.

Mike O'Keefe has his pluses and minuses. He's served the district 24 years, has done a lot for New Orleans and did not receive any state money in his apartment deal. *It's not our money.* But face it, the man's been convicted twice by New Orleans residents on charges arising out of a deal in which he enriched himself by $900,000. One hell of a cookie jar.

But Mike O'Keefe is not ready to concede defeat, he's not even ready to concede opposition. During the legislative session he begins quiet negotiations to keep opponents out of his race. And he almost pulls it off. "Either Mike O'Keefe is the craftiest person in the world or he is the most sincere. He almost had me psyched out," says the major potential opponent State Representative Ben Bagert. Bagert, at 38 completing his fourth term in the House, has already run a poll showing he can win. But Benny's not sure he wants it this way, if it wouldn't just be easier to sit back and wait for Mike to go to jail and then run for the seat. Sounds strange coming out of Benny Bagert, the Boy Wonder of urban electioneering and one of the scrappiest, sometimes sneakiest, infighters on the floor of the House. Bagert seems to be a natural to take on the beleaguered O'Keefe, but he has his own crisis to contend with, the mid-life crisis. Bagert, first elected to the House at age 24, fears he may have started in politics too young, before he earned the personal fortune, honestly, that would give him the freedom to concentrate on politics. He would just as soon let time and the courts take care of O'Keefe instead of having to appear overly ambitious and ruthless (two traits of Bagert's which evoke uncomplimentary comparisons to Bobby Kennedy) by snuffing out the Old Warrior's career at the polls. So Bagert in early summer puts his decision on hold and watches in amazement as O'Keefe tries to arrange a Lebanese-style political cease-fire. O'Keefe could only get Bagert to stay out of the race if he could ensure that the DA's top assistant, Terry Alarcon, wouldn't run either. But he also had to keep another state representative, who had been reapportioned into Bagert's House district, from running against Bagert by talking the other representative into running for a neighboring House seat that would be vacated if Ron Faucheux committed to run for lieutenant governor. For weeks, O'Keefe, Harry Connick and Vic Bussie would huddle on the side of the Senate chamber trying to get all the pieces to fall into place. Instead they fell apart. The DA's assistant could not be restrained, Bagert could not be assured a safe return to his reapportioned House seat. Concerned that if he sat out the Senate election, someone else would beat O'Keefe, Bagert resolved his mid-life crisis driving home with Suzanne and the kids from Grand Isle one Sunday. "Hell, I can beat them all." And he qualified the next day.

The Bagert brothers have created a new phenomenon in New Orleans politics, for decades controlled by a well-oiled labor machine, by an army of politicized city workers led by the mayor and, most recently, by overlapping black political groups. In this tightly managed political atmosphere, Ben and Brod Bagert, working on their own, have built up and fine tuned their own highly effective political machine. Except don't call it a machine. "People think of us as machine politicians. Well, here's the machine," he says, holding up an organization chart with only a dozen names. "The rest is done with volunteers and very good organization. The machine is we implement well," explains Bagert in blue jeans and work shirt on a tour of his headquarters. "Getting elected is a marketing function. You don't have to be a good legislator to be a good politician. But you have to have a plan and an organization. The rest is salesmanship and promotions."

The Bagerts are organizers and they are scavengers. Everything in the campaign is borrowed: the word processor, the copier, the refrigerator, a jukebox for envelope stuffing parties, even the headquarters building, the vacated Reuters Seed Company building on North Carrollton that the owners preferred to lend to a politician rather than leave it for neighborhood gangs' target practice.

The memory of the campaign rests in Goodwill, code name for the word processor. "I designed the program myself," says Bagert, calling up voters' names in block to block walking order. Information about each voter, who is with Bagert or is leaning or is undecided ("We just throw away the O'Keefes"), who will take a yard sign or, better yet, may contribute, is built up by a 10-person phone bank that will call every voter in the district in the next three weeks. He augments the list as he walks the district, checking off issues that concern voters. Bagert has a routine for maximizing the effectiveness of door-to-door campaigning. As he walks a neighborhood someone is running ahead, getting the next resident to come to the door. "Ben Bagert is here, he wants to see you," giving Benny the excuse to cut off one conversation and go on to the next voter. When he gets back to headquarters he turns in the sheets to Goodwill that fires back a computerized, personalized form letter geared to his chat with each voter. "I remember our conversation about flooding . . ."

The team meets later that night at the Bagerts' home on Bayou St. John, a nice place Benny was able to buy after winning a couple of big personal injury suits. The "machine" is a handful of the Bagerts' friends and neighbors, who, though not seasoned politicos, are battle-tested team players who will plug into their roles within an organized plan and do their jobs with deadly efficiency. Benny dips into the potato chips and reviews the success of the first three weeks: "For Phase 1, just filling in the organization chart and getting the yard signs up, everyone gets an A plus. Now what we have to do is to get me on the street and out of the headquarters and to have it run smoothly while I'm not there."

On the basis of one big fund-raiser and a direct mail piece, Bagert hopes to have most of his fund raising behind him, though they'll need money for more than media advertising and hi-tech electioneering. Al Jackson, Bagert's organizer in the black neighborhoods, reminds Ben that singer Irma Thomas, still the reigning queen of Louisiana R&B, is seeking donations for robes for her church's choir. "Okay," instructs the candidate, "remind me to buy a robe for the choir. No, find out how many robes she needs and we'll get them all."

The machine takes a break for a white wine refill and Bagert strolls out to his little pier on the bank of the bayou in the back yard, practices his duck call into the darkness and gets a quacking reply. Bagert says he came close to settling back to practicing law, enjoying his family and getting out of the wearisome ratrace shuttle between home and Baton Rouge. "No way I would have run for the House again. No way I could have won. I couldn't get that kind of enthusiasm from those people in there if I were just running for my House seat again. They think I should be attorney general by now. That's the problem of starting too young."

But that's not his problem now. Ben Bagert's mid-life crisis is behind him. Ahead of him lies his reckoning with the Spider and the allied and entrenched forces of organized labor, the mayor's machine, the city's most powerful black leaders and Edwin Edwards. Benny's gone and done it now. His hat in the ring, his career on the line, the Boy Wonder is not young anymore.

8. "Jesus...the Rock"

Thousands of cars, RVs and campers are already filling up the rolling acres of the United Pentecostal Church Campground outside the town of Tioga early this Monday afternoon, the Fourth of July, the first day of the weeklong revival and spiritual retreat to the woods. There is still one red, white and blue corner of Louisiana that keeps holy the national holiday—every year politicians from all over the state flock to the piney woods north of Alexandria to pledge allegiance to God and Country, and to be welcomed by thousands of believers. All sinners are welcomed to the annual Louisiana tent meeting of the United Pentecostal Church.

Pentecostals from across the state, visiting on the benches outside the main meeting hall, look up as the state police helicopter whirs over, heralding the governor's arrival. Most of the men are in suits, many polyester numbers, while most of the women wear sedate, abundantly frilly dresses that modestly cover the knees and the elbows. The young women wear their hair long, a few down to the waist. Most have their hair up in buns, with some affecting the barest hint of fashion in the tying of their buns. And, of course, no makeup.

My native guide for the occasion, a compatriot from underground newspaper days who was saved and now sells advertising, is helpful in dispelling a few myths. "The women's long hair is no rule of the church, there's no such thing, it's just a common belief by some that it's a sign of holiness." Indeed, the fashion must be fading: the shortest hair is on the preachers' wives.

We step inside the newly constructed, cavernous tabernacle, the object of the day's dedication. It's a gargantuan but wholly utilitarian structure, designed in the high school auditorium motif: half a football field long, a basketball court wide, with low slung balconies wrapping around three sides. Capacity: 10,000—it's about three quarters filled for the afternoon dedication ceremony. One of the day's many preachers is onstage reaffirming the Pentecostal belief in the Holy Trinity. "We do not deny any part of the consecutive powers of the Father the Creator, the Son the Incarnator and the Holy Ghost the Animator."

Worshippers respond to the preacher as they deem appropriate, some hold out one hand palm down while cradling their Bible in the other or stand with hands over their bowed heads as they pray aloud or silently move their lips. But most are following the service quietly, except for throwing in an occasional Amen or Praise Jesus. You can see in their eyes they are into the service, but hardly enraptured, as they sit calmly, taking their worship naturally and easily. As the spirit moves them, they get up and leave, coming and going at will. Some teens whisper and giggle in the back of the tabernacle while outside a few dozen more press in at the refreshment stand for fries, nachos and Cokes.

The Pentecostals seem oddly . . . normal. I'm not sure what I came expecting: zealots preaching from the pinetops, swinging from the balconies, cartwheeling down the aisles? My guide admonishes me for harboring the same prejudices many Pentecostals hold of Catholics. Yes, I have to admit that's true, but I was expecting something more in the way of fervor.

"You'll be back for the evening service?" he asks.

"Sure."

He smiles the believer's knowing smile. "You'll see."

The service moves on and Reverend Tom Tenney, introducing the various politicians sitting onstage, hails Dave Treen as one who has "always been a friend to the Pentecostals. He has done us no special favors, but he has been real genial to us." Real generous too, as Brother Dave commences his remarks by sharing witness to the persuasive powers of the brethren. "Last year when I spoke here I said that government can build the roads to the churches but it took the churches to get the people to come. I got a large and happy response to that and was told later the congregation interpreted my remarks to mean I was going to fix Holly Hill Road out there." And he did just that, the state Highway Department having recently completed the $204,000 resurfacing of the road to the campground.

Dave says he likes to call the Fourth of July Freedom Day and goes on to enumerate the freedoms we enjoy in this country, especially that of religion and the freedom "to have your own schools and to run them as best you can for your children without interference from the state."

Treen is touching all the right chords with this crowd:

—On abortion: "We're going to win this battle in the legal sense to stop this murder against the unborn."

—On the lottery: "Religious leaders spoke up and they defeated that bill. Don't we have the right to speak out against those things?"

"It's almost word for word the same speech he gave last year," critiques my guide, "but his delivery is getting much, much better. The first few times he came up here he didn't go over so well, he was so stiff." That makes sense, since decent Methodist Dave Treen, before his first pilgrimage to Tioga, had probably been no closer to the brush arbor than the rough on the fairway of Metairie Country Club. But he's hot with the message today as he thanks the Pentecostal leaders for their guidance on the scientific creationism issue he faced when the Legislature passed that hot potato to his desk last year. "You helped me decide. I studied over it, I prayed over it. And then the answer came to me, it was clear what I should do—I signed that bill and have been comfortable with it ever since." The congregation is clearly with him now as he closes on a rousing Falwellian note. "Some say it's interfering for church people to voice their concerns about these issues and others like school prayer, but while I steadfastly hold that the state shall not interfere with the church, I reject the argument that the church shall not interfere with the state. We're going to continue interfering. . . ." The faithful break into applause, cheers and cascading Amens.

Dave Treen, evangelist, has peaked. The times bode well for the decent man, the moral man. The more the governor acts like a candidate, the more the Treen organization seeks to highlight the comparative morality of the two candidates. All he needs are more friendly forums such as this. Up until this election year, the Pentecostals were the only white denomination to allow politicians into their churches. But that is changing in this election as already the Treen campaign has a traveling morality play headed by Reverend Videt Polk and his Bibletones Quartet.

For the Treen campaign, the morality question will be a key issue if not *the* issue in the crusade against Edwin Edwards. Treen has built a career on being decent and honest if not terribly effective. His election chances rest on appealing to the strong religious feelings in this conservative state and connecting those convictions with the Treen image as the moral leader. Treen and campaign manager John Cade are placing such stock in the moral issue that they have added a preacher and gospel quartet leader to the campaign payroll to carry Dave Treen's message into places white politicians have never gone before: white churches.

Reverend Videt Polk has been mixing preaching with politics for 20 years, since the days he and John McKeithen would barnstorm together. Videt with a gospel quartet, the Bibletones, would hit a small town, set up at the bandstand, start that gospel singing, get a crowd together and then bring on Big John. "That was the end of old-fashioned stumping," reminisces Videt, sitting in the Treen headquarters outer office one day waiting to pick up his check. Stumping may be dead, but in this campaign Polk is finding it even easier to get his message across because of a radical new development in white Protestant churches. "For the first time, I've found the doors of all churches, large and small, open to me to talk for Dave Treen." And he's finding an enormous acceptance for his candidate there. "Ninety-five percent of the church members and the preachers are for Dave Treen. I've never seen such strong church member support behind one candidate. I can tell you this," Videt raises a prophetic finger, "this time North Louisiana is going to vote and Dave Treen is going to get the Bible Belt."

Polk believes that preachers and congregations are waking up to the moral challenge facing society today. "When it gets down to a question of what is right and what is wrong, the churches should have a voice. I tell the preachers, if they don't get behind the pulpit and say it now, they'll have to get behind the pulpit and fight it later."

Polk says he keeps it simple, sticking to one issue. The Issue: morality. To compare and contrast he uses a questionnaire prepared by the Louisiana Moral and Civic Foundation and sent to the candidates, requesting their position on issues from school prayer to gambling to abortion. "Dave Treen took the time to answer each question carefully, but Edwin Edwards refused to return his. When I go into a church, I read each question, I read Dave Treen's response and I have to say that Edwards was too busy to answer. And that speaks for itself."

Videt Polk expects his pulpit campaign, unheralded as it has been, to reap huge returns for Dave Treen on election day. "I've never heard of anything like the reception we've been getting. It's really a breakthrough. There's a giant silent vote out there, a tremendous movement in the churches for Dave Treen."

So strong is this silent movement for Dave Treen (the really true believers, apparently, don't talk to pollsters) that Polk claims Treen's fundamentalist moral message is eating into Edwards' traditional strong support among the Pentecostals. "I want you to know that the biggest percentage of those preachers are with Dave Treen."

The gospel-singing, political preaching minister sits back with a confident smile. Videt is either the biggest bullshitter I've yet to meet on the campaign trail, or . . . does he know something the pollsters, the political establishment and the press corps do not?

Back at the tabernacle things are just heating up for the big evening service to wrap up the first day of this revival week. As the faithful stream into the tabernacle, the politicians are waiting backstage for the arrival of Edwin Edwards. J. Bennett Johnston has arrived, so has young Woody Jenkins, Bennett's conservative nemesis from the last Senate campaign and a favorite of the Pentecostals, as he has written controversial laws to keep the state's accrediting nose out of church schools and daycare centers. State Senator Don Kelly, the hard-working, hard-playing, street smart country lawyer who is emerging as a natural leader in the Senate, explains to a bevy of preachers' wives one of the more important pieces of family legislation he helped pass this session, a law to push back the start of deer season to after Thanksgiving Day. "I can remember even as a little boy the womenfolk all upset because they couldn't get the men back from the hunt for Thanksgiving dinner."

Finally Edwards arrives, uncharacteristically 15 minutes late. His plane was delayed taking off from Shreveport, where Edwards just hosted a "Giant Fourth of July God and Country Rally" which turned out to be a disappointing bust. With him is the usual entourage, including his pilot Gloria Holmes and his personal aide Darrell Hunt. And Darrell, on a lark, has brought a date along for the ride. The young blonde is strikingly attractive, fashionably dressed and about as out of place here at the tabernacle as the Whore of Babylon. But the Pentecostals I have met so far are extremely nonjudgmental and stay out of your face. With their own penchant for unorthodox, unrestrained worship, they've endured enough of the slings and arrows of the unctuous, sanctimonious, respectable congregations in their old-line uptown churches. They don't go looking down their noses at anyone else.

Reverend G. A. Mangun leads the politicians onstage while press and entourage sit with the preachers' wives in the side rows. My native guide materializes and nudges me with this silly Just You Wait grin on his face. The politicians take their seats on the altar meekly. I've yet to meet the politician who shies from the spotlight, but sitting on an altar in front of 10,000 Pentecostals can be an intimidating experience. The pols look like a restless pack of boys collared for Sunday School. I'm half-expecting a toad to climb out of Don Kelly's back pocket.

For a processional, the Pentecostal orchestra behind the altar is pounding out a hymn to the driving backbeat of drums, keyboard, accordians and a hot horn section. Even if you don't get into the preaching, the music is hard to resist. Interesting, no guitars, but drums? They do add a feisty, dynamic edge to church music which usually sounds wimpy if not dreary. This doesn't even sound like church music as the band whips into the next number, a song, my friend says, that has been adapted from a Jewish hymn and jazzed up some. The congregation joins right in the singing and, yes, the dancing, especially one young lady in the front row who is pogoing for Christ. The Pentecostals not only dance, they're into New Wave.

"The Bible says clap your hands," shouts Reverend Tenney, and the faithful clap. "The Bible says shout unto the Lord" and boy, do they. "Yes, worship the Lord with all your strength and soul and heart. We might even get into a little Pentecostal two-step," preaches Tenney, who quickly adds, "I'm not talking about the frenzied motor emotionalism, that crazy, fanatical radicalism we see in the youth of today. For dance first belonged to the Hebrews, before the Devil counterfeited it and made it *sex-yu-al* and lascivious. Now we're reclaiming it for the Lord. For I'd rather try to cool down a fanatic than to warm up a corpse." No problem here as the worshippers are back into more swaying and clapping and shouting out to the Lord as a new musical group, the De Quincy Pentecostal Orchestra, breaks into what sounds like an Aretha Franklin screamer—and the whole place rocks some more. After all, the theme of this camp meeting is "Jesus . . . the Rock"—which sounds like a 24-hour Pentecostal bop radio station. This joint is rockin'. Stepping out from the front row of the De Quincy Pentecostal Orchestra, a prim teenage girl, her knees and elbows covered for the Lord, her hair hanging down mid-back, leans back and wails into her sax.

This audience is red hot, and Brother Mangun's timing could not be more perfect: when he introduces Edwin Edwards, the congregation rises as one and shakes the house with an enormous secular cheer. Edwards is taken aback, just briefly, but lest there be any mistake about his intentions, he sets them straight. "I'm not here to politick, I came to worship." He revs their motor a little more as he eyes the huge banner hanging from the balcony bearing the camp meeting theme and completes the scriptural reference. "On Jesus the rock will I stand. All other ground is second sand."

No politics tonight, but he can't resist the implied analogy between the bad rap given to him and to the Pentecostals. "People say a lot of things about me. But if you're not being criticized or having them jeer at you, you're not doing something right." It's the same with Pentecostals, he says, "There are no lukewarm people in heaven." Considering the Edwards reputation, how strange that a pulpit be his natural stage—but he was into revivals well before he was into politics, one followed from the other. "I remember as a boy so many of the brush arbor meetings that we would hold in little clearings in the woods and the families would come in their horse drawn wagons. For lights my brother and I would hang lanterns that attracted the June bugs and mosquitos. We knew that if you were really involved in praying, then you wouldn't slap away the mosquitos. We'd watch the folks out of the corner of our eye. If we saw someone slapping, we knew they weren't right." The elders in the congregation smile knowingly. The prouder they feel of their beautiful new tabernacle with its 300 tons of air conditioning, the more they cherish the cross they bore. "You have the real message," preaches the candidate. "If you ever lose it, this church will come down." The roof about comes down as the faithful's clapping and cheering crest with his offering of $5,000 on behalf of himself and, motioning to the grateful gallery of candidates on the altar, "to let you Democrats off the hook."

The service goes on and I go backstage, searching, you can say, for the moral mystery of Edwin Edwards. Is it providence that I run into Reverend Clarence D. Bates, who hands me his card: "Won't you help me elect Edwin Edwards governor on Oct. 22?" What's his angle? "I'm not running for anything, except to run the Republicans out of this state."

Reverend Bates, I learn, found his vocation after a career as a state trooper and a bodyguard for Earl Long. These days the preacher from Jonesboro fashions himself as a sort of Pentecostal ward heeler, eliciting the problems of the Pentecostal and Baptist preachers in North Louisiana and working through Russell Long or Bennett Johnston or Edwin Edwards to get them worked out.

Reverend Bates is no stranger to the complex morality of political life, having been tutored by Uncle Earl. He loves to tell fellow preachers the story of Earl stumping in Colfax on a steaming hot day. Uncle Earl, in need of rejuvenation, asked C.D. for the flask of whiskey and a bottle of Coca-Cola, poured out half the Coke and replaced it with bourbon. "Then," says the reverend, "Earl went out there and delivered the damnationest anti al-kee-hall speech heard in those parts, all the while swiggin' on that bottle of Coke."

This makes Brother Bates just the man to answer the Big Question: "How can any church so intent on holiness and morality support a man like Edwin Edwards, who, though he comes from camp meeting roots himself, is known to gamble, chase women, laugh about lying and constantly be under investigation for corruption?"

The reverend regards me as though I had just checked in from another planet. "Well, he doesn't drink or smoke."

The Rev, a shrewd reader of men, seeing me stunned and off balance, moves in for the kill. "You want to talk about Dave Treen? Here's a man who gave a $4.5 million tax exemption *to the Dixie Brewery!* So we take $4.5 million away from our schools and give it to a brewery so they can make beer for our children to get drunk on and drive. Now you're gonna talk to me about morality?"

C. D. Bates, ward heeler for the Lord, rests his case triumphantly. Sure like to be there when Videt Polk and the Bibletones show up at his church.

9. The Isle of Orleans

Every night at 10:30, Bob d'Hemecourt picks up the early edition of the *Times-Picayune* at the corner of Tulane and Broad and calls Marion Edwards with the headlines. The *Picayune* swings a big club in New Orleans politics, and d'Hemecourt is just waiting for it to come down on Edwin Edwards. Whether it's true or not, city politicians, especially the labor variety, believe that if the *Picayune* is against you, sooner or later in an election it's going to step on you bad. As the New Orleans coordinator for Edwin Edwards, Bob d'Hemecourt is anticipating a major frontal offensive from the state's largest daily newspaper. What blows his mind as he reads Iris Kelso's column under the streetlight is that Edwards' mouth has just supplied the enemy with its ammunition. John Cade could not have written the headline better:

EDWIN EDWARDS ENDORSES UNLIMITED TERMS

As d'Hemecourt would later relate, "I was paranoid, I grabbed the newspaper and ran to Marion with it and told him this will be the start of many, many bad things to come: I could see the reprints of this column going out as Treen direct mail pieces, the white on white phone banks and much more from the *Times-Picayune*." D'Hemecourt could see thousands slamming the morning paper down on the breakfast table and swearing, "To hell with Edwards, now I'm voting for Treen."

Edwin Edwards has just stumbled into the hottest raging debate in the city of New Orleans, what to do with Dutch Morial. Midway through his second term, New Orleans' first black mayor is putting to the vote a change in the city charter to allow the mayor to seek unlimited terms. His bid for dynasty has caused howls in the white community, which has almost adjusted to the idea of a black mayor but cannot tolerate Dutch

114

Morial any longer. Morial is employing his usual tactics of baiting the press and stirring the racial cauldron to make this a black-white, Dutch-no Dutch civil rights crusade instead of a philosophical issue. And now Edwin Edwards has planted himself right in the middle of it, with his arm around Morial.

Edwin Edwards doesn't make a habit of stepping into local controversies, knowing there is more to lose than win by getting on one side and alienating another. Morial's unlimited terms question isn't just hot, it's radioactive, burning to the very heart of the New Orleans political psyche, exposing a tangle of racial, personal and political attitudes upon which no outsider, not even an insider, should enter.

Stay out of local politics, especially in the New Orleans area, where any controversy is a regional affair touching one-third of all the voters in the state. Though the city is more than half black, the entire metro area is 70-30 white. Many of the whites in Jefferson, St. Tammany and St. Bernard parishes moved there from New Orleans and still follow politics there in the *Picayune* and on TV. Those folks hate Morial too and are prime targets, Edwards' organizers fear, for a classic and massive racial polarization campaign by Treen and the *Picayune* which could easily cost Edwards more votes than any other single issue in the campaign.

New Orleans is a part of the rest of Louisiana on the maps only—not in the minds of its residents. The early pre-Purchase maps indicate the Isle of Orleans, formed by the crescent of the river, Lake Pontchartrain and Lake Borgne. An island it is. New Orleans is its own world, a city and a state of mind separate and apart from the rest of the country, the South, the state—especially the state. The average Orleanian will acknowledge there is a state of Louisiana, a vague, distant, desolate hinterland, somewhere "across the lake." Thousands of adult Orleanians walking the streets have never set foot outside The City, or if they have, it is recalled in the same horrified tones that Ignatius J. Reilly used about his Scenicruiser trip to Baton Rouge in *A Confederacy of Dunces*. The rest of Louisiana has this love-hate relationship with New Orleans. The farther north you go, the more likely you are to run into people who revile New Orleans as a stinking sinkhole teeming with blacks, whores, homosexuals and Catholics. Yet deep down there is the grudging recognition that without New Orleans, a vital and convenient resource for sinning and good eating, Louisiana would be no different from Mississippi.

Pedigree counts for more in New Orleans than in any other big city in the country. The Old Guard, the descendants of the first American families to settle in the city (they were very much the New Guard to the French and Creole families living in the French Quarter in the early 1800s), have shut the door tight to social acceptance. It is said that major corporations are reluctant to base operations and officers in New Orleans because their daughters can't be presented to society and the executives, no matter how big their paycheck, can't eat at the Boston Club.

The *Times-Picayune* is the voice of New Orleans' ruling class, the rich, old, powerful families who live in the elegant mansions along St. Charles Avenue. Their direct control of city politics slowly gave way to the Irish and the Italians and then to the blacks. But that's okay—as long as the elite families can control their Mardi Gras rituals and preserve their Garden District way of life, they contentedly rely on the moral weight of the *Picayune* to help guide the city's economic destiny and cultural life regardless of who's hiring down at City Hall.

New Orleans' provincial attitudes are reinforced in its politics. For years the Legislature was considered a *pro forma* sideshow, lacking in any of the relevance or glamor of service on the City Council. The state House of Representatives was the farm club where city pols sent the second stringers or the sons of assessors to get a little experience before returning to the bigs. It wasn't until the '70s that the city began taking the Legislature more seriously, sending higher caliber pols to Baton Rouge. The investment paid off as Orleanians took over the prime leadership positions in both houses, giving the mayor, the traditional *de facto* leader of the delegation, enormous clout in Baton Rouge as well as in New Orleans. That influence in the Capitol has enabled New Orleans to capture some big deals in the past two decades that have benefited the area's economy generally and the top families and business leaders specifically. There was the Superdome, built by John McKeithen (the North Louisianian was perhaps the best friend New Orleans has ever had in the Mansion) as a temple for spectator sports. Though still subsidized by the state long after it was supposed to be paying its own way, the Superdome has created jobs and attracted tourist dollars. But the real beneficiaries of the state investment have been the downtown landowners and developers whose sprouting office towers have turned

116

Poydras Street into the main drag of the Central Business District. Many of the old names and business leaders who pushed hardest for construction of the Dome have profited handsomely in developing the area around it.

Just as the heady decade of development at one end of Poydras Street is tapering off, the state and city are chipping in for an even more spectacular deal for the landowners at the other end by the river. The 1984 World's Fair in New Orleans will be the first World's Fair ever held primarily on privately owned land that has been leased to the fair operators. After the U.S., the state and the city help underwrite clearing the old warehouse district and building these magnificent pavilions and fairgrounds (as well as the city and state guaranteeing the first $5 million in losses), the land will all revert to the landowners at fair's end in November. The fairgrounds and structures will be converted into a downtown entertainment district with restaurants, hotels, nightclubs, shops and condos: a permanent tourist center for the city, a producing gold mine for the landowners and developers.

Even if the World's Fair is a total flop, it will be good in the long run for New Orleans, but it will be even better for the site's landowners. Never in 50 years could they, on their own, put together the financing and the politics to clear and rebuild the 20-block area in the warehouse district into a money-making adult playground. Fortunately the city, state and U.S. governments lent a big hand. Nothing wrong with that—it's a time-honored way of doing things in The City. As with the state-subsidized Superdome, the World's Fair will be good for New Orleans, good for the state, but best for the movers and shakers behind the scenes who quietly helped to put both big deals together.

As black voter registration grew during the '60s and more whites fled to Jefferson Parish, it was inevitable a black would be elected mayor of New Orleans. Yet Dutch Morial's victory in 1977 had as much to do with his whiteness as with his blackness. Dutch grew up in the Seventh Ward of the city, in a neighborhood populated by many of the city's Creole families, old-time New Orleans residents who can trace their lineage in the city farther back than can the "Americans" on St. Charles Avenue. The definition of "creole" is as touchy an issue as that of the future of Dutch Morial. The *Picayune* tried to define that once and

117

opened itself to a deluge of letters that are still coming in. Whatever the mixture of Spanish and French, black, white and Indian, the light-skinned Creoles are the elite in black New Orleans business, politics and society. In fact, outside New Orleans and Louisiana, many of these Creoles would not even be considered black. Morial, during his Army stint in Germany, could easily *passer pour blanc.*

When politics opened up to blacks in the city, it was the sons of these Creole families who led the way. Not only was there Dutch Morial, the first black legislator and mayor, but also Sidney Barthelemy, the state's first black senator since Reconstruction; Louis Charbonnet III, a state representative and son of the city's leading black embalmer; Civil Sheriff Paul Valteau and State Senator Hank Braden, whose father, Dr. Henry Braden, president of the prestigious International House, stands atop New Orleans black society, with a foot in the white world.

Morial won in 1977 not only because he was a rallying point for blacks but also because he did not offend whites. That changed quickly enough. Perhaps the white establishment did not expect that Morial would do just what every new mayor before him had, dispense patronage with a vengeance. Even if it should have been expected, it was still resented.

Through years of Chep Morrison and Moon Landrieu, New Orleanians had come to expect their mayor to be a suave, progressive civic booster who could present the right image for the city in circles of international trade and national politics. What they got from Morial was a throwback to the old-line city boss in the Bob Maestri mold, the city's mayor and boss in the '30s and '40s who not only ruled New Orleans with an iron fist but had a hand on the reins of state power during the giddy post-Huey hayride. Like Maestri, Dutch was less interested in image than in raw power, and he used city patronage and the electioneering strength of city workers to advance his friends and pummel his adversaries into submission. Politically and personally, Morial is a complex blend of streetwise savvy, brass-knuckled intimidation, civil rights fervor and martyred paranoia, all of which he uses to manipulate both the black and the white psyches of the city. The mayor's lashing out at reporters at a televised press conference may be offensive to whites but to blacks it is heroic. To them, Morial is their maligned black leader, taking on the white establishment, be it the press, the business community or the Mardi Gras societies. Morial's abrasive style drives a wedge between blacks and whites in New Orleans, and although he claims to be a unifying force, he uses the division to suit his own political aims.

After Morial won reelection, whites were resigned to a future of black mayors but not to any more Dutch Morial. When Morial's friends announced the proposed charter amendment to lift the limit of two terms on a mayor, opposition in the white community was immediate and deep-rooted. Dutch's heavy-handed bossism made getting rid of him a cause not just among white Orleanians but also among a critical portion of blacks who wanted a new black regime in City Hall.

So why did Edwards even come near Morial? Edwards knew the blacks were with him anyway—a link with Morial would win him no more there and would scare off thousands of whites. But Edwards, agile as he is, may not have been able to avoid Dutch, who, rumor has it, threatened to run for governor and siphon off thousands of black votes that would otherwise go to Edwards. Edwards could not let that happen, so endorsing Morial may have been the least perilous way out. Edwards knew the association would hurt him, but he did it early and downplayed it. He kept his sense of humor about the bad situation, such as when Dutch Morial bragged at a function that he would make a great running mate as lieutenant governor on a ticket with Edwards. "That's a great idea, Dutch," said Edwards. "That way no one will want to shoot me."

The polls tell Dutch Morial early on his unlimited terms proposal is in trouble—not only is the white bloc vote set against him but so are some major black rivals who feel threatened by Dutch's continued reign. With good reason. For Dutch Morial, if he can't be mayor, is still determined to be boss. If he has to leave office at the end of his term in 1986, he wants to make sure rivals for his throne will be out of office too. Like any self-respecting boss, Dutch Morial keeps careful track of his enemies, with full accounting of their sins and plans for their eventual destruction. At the top of the list is Hank Braden, who must suffer for the sins of his father. Morial and Dr. Braden have been feuding since they fell out as business partners 15 years ago. Braden's son Hank, with his name, his wealth, his political organization COUP and his state Senate seat, is primed to fill the vacuum of power if Morial cannot succeed himself. He even tried to rush that process along by endorsing Morial's white challenger, Ron Faucheux, in the 1981 mayor's race. Braden may be mayor or congressman one day, but Dutch has other plans for his second generation rival. The mayor has systematically slated challengers in the fall election for the half-dozen or so names on his get-even list, but the best has been saved for Braden, who is vulnerable in a newly reapportioned Senate district. Morial places in the race the unknown, untested but undoubtedly loyal Dennis Bagneris with promises of full moral and financial support and, more important, an army of campaigning City Hall foot soldiers.

A white politico marvels at the unfolding strategy. "Dutch is trying harder to beat Braden than he is to pass the charter change. I think it's more important to him. Say Morial beats Braden and doesn't lose on the charter change too badly. He could put the charter change back on the 1984 ballot and with Braden's hide in his trophy case, there's not a black politician in this city who will oppose him."

Morial's naked bid for undisputed bossism has more than whites and rival black officials concerned. Also feeling very nervous these days are the leaders of the black political organizations in the city. In the past 20 years these groups that go by acronyms like SOUL and BOLD and COUP have delivered the votes for the candidates they endorsed and shared in the patronage. Not only are they into power but into business too. The candidates they endorse chip in for election workers, printing and whatever other expenses the leaders like SOUL's Sherman Copelin and Don Hubbard put on the bill. Their support can be costly, but not as costly as their opposition. These groups flat control the politics in their neighborhoods, especially the neighborhoods where white politicians aren't going to go. If the candidate's name is not on the printed sample ballots handed out on election day, he will be shut out colder than if his name were Leander Perez.

In return for their clout, the black groups have controlled some city and state patronage. And like big white contributors, the black bosses' names tend to show up in corporations with service contracts with city and state agencies.

No wonder some of these bosses, who have kept peaceful relations with Morial during his reign, fear how far his dreams of empire extend. Copelin and Hubbard at SOUL must worry if Braden goes down will they be next. Could the mayor's personal vendetta against Braden be just the first step in his quest to undermine the clout of the political organizations and concentrate all power and patronage around Boss Dutch?

Even the old-line white pols down at Mike Roccaforte's Half Moon Bar must grudgingly admire Dutch's capacity for retribution, his unerring knack for going straight to the jugular. The new style of civic leader/mayors—Chep Morrison and Moon Landrieu—earned respect with the progressive image they gave the city. The throwback Dutch Morial skips the Chamber of Commerce crap and commands respect with blatant political muscle by which he rewards his friends and vanquishes his enemies. Many find Morial's tactics repugnant but the ghost of old Mayor Maestri, eating *dem ersters* at Huey's side, would cackle and approve.

Snafu time at the Treen campaign. The governor is to make an announcement in New Orleans about the World's Fair and then have lunch on a riverboat. Treen has gone in one direction, his press team in another, and two reporters are left standing at the dock, gazing idly at the sun reflecting off Big Muddy, which just keeps rolling along. So what else is there to do in The City on a morning shot to hell? Bud Rip's, of course.

Bud Rip's, at the corner of Burgundy and Piety, is New Orleans' premier political bar, as well as one of the many outstanding neighborhood establishments in Bywater. This riverfront neighborhood between the French Quarter and the Lower Ninth Ward is one of the few sections of town that looks much as it did 50 years ago, down to its corner grocery stores and bars and its old German and Irish residents coexisting with the blacks, who work on the waterfront or for the leading manufacturer in the area, the Hubig Pie plant on Dauphine.

Bud Rip's, though it's only been open 20 years, has attained the timeless grace and ambience of the great old bars. From the old pictures on the wall to the old cronies at the bar, Bud Rip's exudes the feeling of old ward-heeling New Orleans politics in a grander age.

And what luck. The proprietor himself is holding forth today, standing shirtless at the cash register counting change. Above him is his favorite relic, a photo of Bud between his two heroes, Dave Treen and

Ronald Reagan. The great traditions of Bud Rip's stop at party lines: Bud Rippoll is a staunch conservative Republican who has waged three unsuccessful campaigns for the Legislature in the old neighborhood. Most of Bywater is union and proud of it, but that has not blocked Bud's political advancement as much as have the Ninth Ward blacks who have overwhelmed the Bywater whites by voting the SOUL ticket at the polls.

Bud would have hung it up this year, except that reapportionment has taken Bywater out of the predominantly black district and thrown it in with Arabi in neighboring St. Bernard Parish. Only one-third of the district is in New Orleans, but the demographics give even a Republican a fighting chance. Bud's secret is that he doesn't come off as a stiff-necked hidebound Republican but as a regular Lower Ninth Ward bartending kind of guy. And he'd just as soon keep that secret. "I think I'll do best with the people who don't know me or what I stand for."

It's a zoo of a race in the 103rd District, the battle of the Yats, a term derived from the universal greeting of the inhabitants near the Industrial Canal: "Where y'at?"

The incumbent in the 103rd is the cheerful Eddie Bopp, who with his flowing white pompadour resembles a Louisiana Liberace. There's not much you can say against Eddie in the Legislature—he's so seldom there. Toward the end of the session in 1983, Bopp's deskmate Frank Patti rose for his routine request of Speaker of the House John Hainkel.

"Mr. Patti, why do you rise?"

"To request excused leave for Mr. Bopp for the day."

"Which day?"

Besides Bud Rip, Bopp is being challenged by the irrepressible Rick Tonry, a go-getter who started his political career winning the 103rd's seat and ended it in a federal prison cell. In between, the gutsy, hard-campaigning Tonry won an upset victory for a seat in Congress in 1976 but had to detour past the Capitol to a federal prison in Alabama, where he was incarcerated for illegal use of campaign funds. Rick's career has been a rollercoaster, but even in his hard times he's the charming Yat brimming with rogue energy. Now he's back in St. Bernard staking claim to "my seat."

An ancient customer shuffles in and before he can slide onto his regular stool, Bud has uncapped a Barq's and slid it before him.

With his new district, Bud thinks he has a real shot. So does the state

Republican party, which has targeted the 103rd and is encouraging support for Rippoll. "I gotta check da udder day from a guy in Shreveport I never hoid of." Plus, a LABI organizer and State Representative Gary Forster, Bud's cousin, are helping Bud introduce modern campaign tactics to the Lower Ninth Ward. "Me, I'm from da old school. Down to oith politics, get out and shake da hands. But dese young guys are fantastic, they've showed me more stuff about politics than I ever knew. Phone banks and direct mail, we sent out a letter from Livingston [the congressman was a Bud Rip's regular himself when he was working his way through law school]. And we have a letter goin' out to all da ladies in da district. Da women likes to see da wife campaignin'. Dookie goes out and knocks on doors wit' me. I hadda promise her I wouldn't borrow any money if I ran. Jeez, I still owe $50,000 from da last three races. Hey, whatcha think of my slogan?" He points to the banner over the entrance: "This Bud's for you." Not bad at all.

A commotion at the end of the bar interrupts the politics. The Hubig Pie man sidles onto his barstool and is goading Jimmy, Bud's gofer and the resident liar.

"Jimmy," says Pieman, "whatcha gonna do when Bud gets elected, go to Baton Rouge wit'im?"

"Naw, I'm gone to Washington with Bob Livyston, he called me da udder night at home."

"Oh yeah?"

"Yeah."

Bud pops a couple of Dixies. "I'm gonna do real good over here. Dis is a great neighborhood and it's coming back. By 1985 it'll be what it used to be." Bud recounts the problems of the new realities of Bywater and its neighborhood bars, mostly racial clashes between patrons. There was Irv at Irv's Place who was blown away with a shotgun blast by a gang he had thrown out of the bar on pool tournament night. Then there was poor Miss Pearl. "She had dis little place around da corner, she kept it going after her husband died. I went in dere one cold night about 8:30 and she was sittin' by da heater wit' her little dog at her feet like he always was. She was empty 'cept for dis one drunk at the bar. I says, 'Miss Poil, trow dis bum out and close up and go home.' She wouldn't do it. Later dat night, they come in and shot her and her little dog too." Bud looks off. "I just don't know."

Pieman is extracting more wild tales from Jimmy.

"Jimmy, whatcha cookin' tonight?"

"I'm cookin' da liver special."

"Is that what you call cirrhosis of the liver?"

"Yeah," beams Jimmy, "serosy of da liver and smashed botatas."

Bud smiles, wiping out his glass and considering the question of his political career and his barroom. "If I win, if I can't get da right help, I may lease da place. I tell ya, it'll be one helluva victory and goin' away party all at once. We'll drink up all da liquor in da house."

Bud's friends know how badly he wants to win this race and they want it for him too. But Bud Rip in Baton Rouge means no Bud Rip behind the bar. Such are the sad tradeoffs of democracy and city politics.

10. The 15 Percent Factor

The old woman backs away behind her screen door as the silver-haired white man enthusiastically bounds straight toward her across the long courtyard of the Lafitte Housing Projects. Must be election time, here come the white politicians. She waves the oncoming figure away and retreats into the doorway. The public figure hesitates as trailing campaign workers and TV crews watch in suspense: just five minutes into his blitz through the projects, will the governor have a door shut in his face? "Don't bring those cameras over here," scolds the voice from the doorway. "I'm not made up."

"Neither am I," shouts Dave Treen as he bounds up the back steps to shake her hand and press into it his brochure "Ten Reasons to Vote for Dave Treen."

The more they hear of the Treen black strategy, the less the Edwards people in New Orleans can believe it. Instead of the Treen troops using Edwards' massive black support to polarize whites against him, here's Dave Treen hustling for black votes as hard as any Democrat. Treen could have, maybe should have, done what blacks expected him to do from the start, write them off and shut them out of government. After all, blacks shut out Dave Treen 32-1 in 1979, having nothing more to go on than 100 years of ingrained suspicion, hostility and distrust against Republicans.

Democratic activists predicted that Treen's only black votes would come from conservative, middle class older blacks and upwardly mobile young professionals. But in early summer, the Treen campaign announced a major breakthrough, the endorsement of Dave Treen by the New

Orleans Voters Alliance, the tenants' association that represents the 62,000 residents of the seven housing projects in New Orleans. After meeting with representatives of both campaigns, NOVA goes with Treen and promised an all-out canvassing effort to reach the 19,000 registered voters in the projects.

SOUL leader Sherman Copelin dismisses the endorsement as bought and paid for. "Dave Treen's not gonna get any votes in the projects. We could have had 'em, it's just a matter of money." It may also be a matter of jurisdiction, as NOVA wanted to use its own people to canvass the projects at $5 an hour, not Copelin's SOUL troops. The leaders in the projects feel like they've been taken for granted by the city Housing Authority, by Morial and by the black bosses who regard the projects as political colonies, from which votes are extracted without any reinvestment. NOVA leader Crystal Jones is talking political rebellion as she promises her group will keep the SOULs and COUPs off NOVA's turf. "We run the projects." And she sounds like she means it.

NOVA looks like they mean it as two dozen t-shirted workers fan out across the long courtyard at the St. Thomas Projects when Dave Treen's van pulls up. Curious faces peek out screen doors and down from balconies as Treen walks down the center sidewalk waving hello and offering encouragement. "We're gonna help you." St. Thomas could use some help. The older project near the bridge is far more run-down and neglected than the Lafitte Projects by the Interstate. There is more glass on the playgrounds, more trash on the sidewalks, more gaping holes where windows used to be. A resident takes the governor across the hall from his apartment to one of 200 abandoned and vandalized units strewn with liquor bottles, fried chicken bones, assorted trash and rotting mattresses. "Apartments," wrote Ed Anderson in the *Picayune*, "that looked more like landfills than homes." A candidate for state representative, Paulfrey Johnson, explains the Catch-22 of the projects. "We shouldn't be boarding up apartments when we have 10,000 people on the waiting list to get in. The Housing Authority says it takes $10,000 to renovate each apartment and they don't have the money. But they won't even board these places up and they just get worse."

Dave Treen won't tolerate it. "We will have to secure this place against vandalism. This is totally unacceptable. This is a local responsibility. I want the local government to do it. We will work with them every way we can, but we're not going to let this go on." But it goes on. The projects are run by the city Housing Authority with federal dollars. There is not much constructive criticism Dutch Morial is going to take from Dave Treen unless the state sends along a check to pay for the improvements.

Dave Treen does a few chin-ups in a playground littered with broken glass as a dozen young kids gawk. He offers a little gubernatorial advice. "When I was a youngster your age I didn't think too much about school. But I regret I didn't learn everything I could. Now you should learn everything you can, study your math and your science . . ."

A middle-aged man struggles to put on his shirt as he shakes the governor's hand while a toddler plays at their feet.

"How many grandchildren do you have?" asks the governor.

"Well, I don't really know."

"Well, the schools are going to be a lot better before this one gets there."

Crossing the street, Treen greets two young men in t-shirts out taking their ghetto blasters for a stroll.

"What can I do for you?" asks the governor, raising his voice to be heard over the music.

"I need a job," says one, turning down the volume as an afterthought.

"Well, you know we have a new job-training program starting this week. It'll train you for the jobs that are available. I want you to check with the Job Service Office of the Department of Labor."

On the way between projects, NOVA organizer Anna Johnson, riding in the back seat of the press van, orders the driver to stop at the next light and commandeers the front seat.

"I saw this woman in a car give me a dirty look and I figured it out. What am I doing riding in the back of the bus?"

"I don't see the big deal," says another NOVA member. "I'm black and I was in the front seat."

"You're driving," shoots back Anna. "Plus you're half white. You're whiter than Morial. No one knows you're black. They can see me and it's not doing Dave Treen any good for folks to see me riding in the back of the bus."

The small caravan crosses the river to Algiers and the Fischer Project, where the governor's car is met by an intense, massive young man named Warren Carmouche, who, between barking orders to his NOVA minions and into his walkie-talkie, announces to no one in particular, "This is my mother-fuckin' project."

And what is Fischer Project going to do for Dave Treen on election day?

"He only got one and a half percent here in '79, but he'll get five percent this time." Five percent? Some mother-fuckin' project.

One of Treen's leading black organizers in the city, James Tipton, is more optimistic. "We can get 28 to 30 percent in here. SOUL's already pulled their workers out of here to work in other neighborhoods."

"The hardest thing," says Anna Johnson, "is convincing people that Ronald Reagan is not running." She says "a political group" had 30 people calling in the Ninth Ward last week telling people "a vote for Dave Treen is a vote for Ronald Reagan."

The governor gets another eyeful at Fischer, stopping to ask about a gaping hole at the base of the structure, caused by some plumbing repair work left unfinished. As in other projects, the governor is invited into the homes of some of his supporters for coffee and cake and words of encouragement from his projects allies. But out along the balconies, the reception is different. "Get Edwin Edwards in here," demands one woman leaning over her balcony. "That's who I want. Dave Treen ain't shit."

As Treen leads the gangling entourage into the lobby of the main Fischer building, an old fellow, smoking his cigarette, leaning on his cane, sounding exactly like Richard Pryor's Mudbone, regards the procession with scorn. "Don't know why you gwan in'ere. Ain't nuttin but niggers in'ere."

The yards between buildings at Fischer are bigger, but there's nothing in them. The governor promises playground equipment if the tenants will organize recreational supervision. "I am committed as the political leader of this state to solve the substandard housing and safety and health conditions we see. The bottom line is we are not going to let this continue."

Sounds nice. The folks in the projects have heard it before. Dave Treen has shown his sincerity and commitment to improving what he's seen here today. But as the scattered residents in front of Fischer watch the governor's caravan pull away, they know, perhaps better than he, that for all the impressive political powers of the governor, life in the projects is not going to change much, regardless of who lives in the Mansion.

You have to wonder how white Democratic leaders, in power for the past century, have demonstrated to blacks that they have their interests any more at heart than Republicans do. How is it the state party of Jim Crow laws and redneck sheriffs with bare-fanged dogs, the party of Leander Perez, Willie Rainach, "Segregation Forever" and a long string of governors whose idea of opening government to blacks was to bring down some trusties from Angola to wait on tables at the Mansion, how did that same fine old party of racists sell itself as the friend of the black man? Somehow, the fix is in that the Republicans, the party of Lincoln and Earl Warren and Louisiana's only black governor, are some wicked cabal conspiring at the country club to put blacks back in chains. Southern Democrats have done one hell of a number on their hapless GOP rivals, who, you have to admit, haven't done much to help turn their image around.

Until Dave Treen came to power and from the start opened his administration to minorities far wider than had any governor before him, appointing more blacks to high-level positions than had all previous governors put together. And he paid them far more than even the highest-paid blacks of the Edwards years. From his first appointments straight through to his campaign, Dave Treen's determination to reach and win over blacks stood out both as a sincere and high-minded commitment to fairness and as evidence of his hopeless political naivete.

Treen's burst of affirmative action wasn't all fair-mindedness and altruism. He was also trying to get reelected. In sizing up the 1983 race, Treen and Cade figured that even if they carried the white vote again by over 60 percent, the monolithic black vote would still give the election to Edwards. But if they could peel off 15 percent of the black vote without losing any white support, they could just pull it off.

Treen's other top supporters—Billy Nungesser chief among them—don't buy it. They view this unprecedented black strategy, the appointments and the campaign initiative, as both futile and dangerous. The dissenters aren't racists, just realists. They fear Treen will divide his time and energy going after a vote he's not going to get when he should be playing totally to his strengths. Even a black political consultant, one who makes a good living advising conservative white candidates on how to deal with the black vote, has already offered Treen this advice: forget it. Observes Bethel Nathan, "Treen will get the black votes he's going to get and, more importantly, far more white votes if he doesn't get into a contest with Edwin Edwards over who is the blacks' best friend. Most blacks aren't going to believe him no matter what he says, and he stands to lose a lot of conservative whites the more he goes after blacks."

Even within the administration, Dave Treen and John Cade hold the minority position on the question. They persist. Cade recognizes that the black strategy could backfire among conservative whites, but he insists that playing it safe is even more dangerous. "We're trying to win, not come close." Cade privately tells doubting supporters that even if blacks don't vote for Treen, if he can at least neutralize his Republican image, fewer blacks will feel so threatened by Treen that they'll rally to vote against him and may just stay home instead.

But perhaps the real reason Dave Treen sticks with his minority policy has less to do with practical politics than his own moral view of power: he went out of his way to embrace the principle of equal opportunity, even in political patronage. That's the nice thing about being governor. When it comes right down to it, you can overrule your own advisors, enrage your own supporters, defy conventional wisdom and risk political oblivion for no other reason than just that you think it is right.

Treen's black strategy amuses black political leaders as much as it at first surprised them. During a lull in the action on the floor of the House, Dick Turnley, running to become the first black senator from Baton Rouge, views Dave Treen's chances of pulling 15 percent of the vote in his Scotlandville district this way: "Sheee-yit."

But aren't blacks impressed by Dave Treen's minority appointments?

"The blacks he appointed are," shoots back Turnley, "but he didn't give those guys authority to hire anyone else, so how's that helping anyone but them?"

In opening up state government to blacks, Dave Treen has shut out the black leaders through whom patronage has traditionally flowed. Turnley's comment reveals that deeper down black leaders are less amused by Treen's affirmative action than they are threatened by it. No wonder the word of Dave Treen's good works did not carry far into the black community. For Treen to bite into even a piece of the black vote could do more than beat Edwin Edwards, it could unravel an elaborate, ingrained system by which white money and black power have cemented the traditional Democratic coalition for decades.

There is a myth in Louisiana politics called buying the black vote. It doesn't work as simply or directly as that. In the isolated areas of the state where individual voters actually are paid $5 to $10 each for their vote, there are as many whites in on the action as blacks. That's the accepted practice in Vernon Parish and parts of Acadiana. Edwards himself describes the Sixth Ward of Vermilion as the "Bloody Sixth" where two traditional factions are evenly split and the 200 so-called independent citizens in between put up their votes for the highest bid. Sometimes out in the country, that's what it takes to get people to travel five miles to a voting booth on a Saturday when they could be fishing. Besides, the expense is not too great.

In the city the system gets much subtler—the concept of buying votes covers a lot of ground and even gets into upper middle class white neighborhoods. According to one suburban politician in Baton Rouge, "If you're a local candidate, you buy the white vote by sponsoring Little League teams or taking out ads in high school programs. It's not a direct deal but see what happens when you say no."

In the black neighborhoods of the cities, even if you can get away with it, buying black votes retail is too costly and cumbersome, especially when someone can get them for you wholesale. Conservatives for years have harbored horrific visions of black bosses with flashy suits and diamond rings counting big wads of bills as they direct the traffic of school buses filled with voters, bought and paid for, being hauled to the polls. The times and U.S. attorneys have forced changes on the system that have made it far more sophisticated if not legitimate.

If not innocent. Many black voters who have no reason to keep up with white politicians are open to the recommendation of their minister or councilman on who is the better friend to blacks. The choice is obvious if a black is running or a notorious Republican hanging judge. The word of the minister or a major political group works best in a close race between two white Democrats equally unknown in the black community. That's where the political groups come in with their little printed sample ballots handed out at polling places. The most respected and effective groups—the SOULs, BOLDs and COUPs—are those who function year-round, not just at election time, and have built a track record of getting folks jobs and granting small favors. In other words, the same old ward heeler system perfected by big-city Irish politicians a century ago.

All that's changed is the way the job is done. Some organizations, like the major New Orleans groups, have elaborate canvassing and direct mail operations, phone banks, registration drives and transportation to the polls. Others just print up ballots to give out on election day. Though it's impossible to trace how much is spent on actual expenses and how much ends up in some boss's pocket, no doubt most of it does trickle down, for often a group's strength and respect in the community are based on how many $25- to $50-a-day campaign workers get on the gravy train. The abuses in the system were getting out of hand in Baton Rouge in 1979 when U.S. Attorney Don Beckner cracked down on some black groups' endorsement scams, sent one councilman to jail and made everyone else get more serious about itemizing expenses and signing contracts with the candidates, as required by law.

Tighter laws and more vigilant law enforcers have cleaned up some abuses, though treachery still plays a part in this business. Traditionally the groups operate in secret, not revealing their endorsements until their ballots hit the street election week. Sometimes there is more than one ballot. Some poor white devil may pay some black group to put his name on their ballots a week before the election, only to find on election day a new ballot on the streets with—whoa!—his opponent's name on it. Or, even sneakier, the paying candidate's name but next to his opponent's ballot number. Candidates burned once have resorted to the safest strategy of getting there the lastest with the mostest.

The new reporting laws have caused the expected bellyaching but they have won a surprising advocate at the Edwards headquarters. Says campaign treasurer Marion Edwards, "It takes the guesswork out of the system. In the old days you didn't know how much it would cost you to the very end or what you were getting for it. Now it's all written down and I can plan on exactly how much I need to raise."

A lot. Edwards knew he would get a massive black majority, but Treen's publicized 15 percent goal causes Edwards to redouble his efforts to line up every possible political organization, dependable or not. "We could cover New Orleans with 14 groups," says Bob d'Hemecourt, "we have 50," though some received as little as $200. Statewide, an Edwards campaign finance report in the last week listed 75 different groups and civic associations that were paid over $1,000. Not every group is pleased by the sum paid or the terms. While campaigning in New Orleans, Edwin Edwards comes upon a young black man wearing a white turban distributing crudely printed leaflets in the crowd. This is the message:

> We find it highly embarrassing how grassroots organizations are being treated with only a chosen few political organizations receiving financial means sufficient to do the job. We are against what is taking place with $200.00 budgets that Edwards is forcing on organizations to sign contracts for, which wouldn't even supply enough funding for blacks to support his candidacy. We are asking organizations that have received such a check from the Edwards campaign to take them back and re-negotiate your contract.

Edwin and Marion get a good chuckle out of it and on the way out the candidate surprises the leafleteer when he asks, "You fellas send that check back yet?"

Dave Treen is not fighting this battle alone. With good reason almost every black he appointed to a major position has been on the campaign trail with him. He got more visible support from the Ulysses Williamses and Hosea Neds and Linton Ardoins than he did from some white Republican officeholders in the state.

State Representative Louis Charbonnet of New Orleans, the only black legislator supporting Treen, doesn't mince words with his black audiences. "Let's open our eyes and not blindly lead our people to the slaughterhouse. We need to wake up and realize that we can no longer just look out for ourselves, our people need a fair share. You're not alone in this room. Blacks around the state are waking up and being educated."

Charbonnet, more than any other black supporting Treen, is putting his own career on the line—not only Edwards but Dutch Morial and organized labor have a big X by Louis' name and there are three opponents running against him. "It's a hard decision to make when you run in the black community. But I'm going to bear my cross and I'm going to walk down the street with it and I'm going to tell the truth."

Edwards will have his own share of fun with the crossbearer. "Take my friend Louis Charbonnet," the former governor tells a press conference the same week. "He got appointed to two positions in the Legislature that allowed him to take trips to Paris twice. His wife has a state job. His father is on the Embalmers Board. His wife is on the Board of Supervisors and the family leases several buildings to the state. He ought to be supporting Dave Treen. Dave Treen is supporting him."

Charbonnet burns when he hears the words, insisting that he paid his own way to Paris, that his wife is a classified civil servant, that she receives no economic benefit from serving on the LSU board and that the family has been leasing buildings to the state since Edwards was governor. Not that Charbonnet has been a complete fool about public service. "Edwin missed my cousin Bernard here," says the dapper Louis. "We got him appointed to the Levee Board."

Edwards' criticism does hit a nerve. Outside of blacks Treen has appointed to office, where is Dave Treen's black support? He will woo important black ministers such as Reverend T. J. Jemison of Baton Rouge, the president of the National Baptist Convention. Treen has appointed the Baton Rouge minister to the Superdome Commission, and Jemison in turn will say some nice things about Treen, without going so far as to endorse the Republican—a recommendation, Jemison admits, that would be very hard to sell to his congregation. Some of Edwards' top black supporters, also members of Jemison's church, aren't concerned if they hear a few good words about Dave Treen on Sunday. They know what is said from the pulpit three months before the election and what happens on the streets on election day are two different worlds.

The mark of a preacher's clout is how many white politicians show up at his church at election time to worship, to say a few words to the congregation and to leave behind the offering in the little white envelope.

Edwin Edwards has been at it all his career, speaking in hundreds of black churches around the state and being blessed and endorsed from their pulpits. The bond between the churchmen and the Democrat goes beyond that of black preachers and white politician—there is an even stronger bond between these Baptists and this fundamentalist Nazarene, who shares an appreciation of free-spirited, unrestrained worship.

Though Edwin Edwards already has a strong relationship with the black preachers, Treen's strategists feel that an administration based on honesty and morality will have to get a hearing in black churches. Especially when they have caught Edwards in a lie . . . in a black church.

"I am appalled that Edwin Edwards would desecrate the Mt. Zion Church with a blatant string of lies," blazes a Treen press release following an Edwards address to a group of black ministers in Baton Rouge. The virulent press release goes on to nail Edwards on a series of untruths about his minority hiring record versus Dave Treen's. Treen's rebuttal shows the Republican administration drubbing the Democratic in every phase of equal opportunity, from the governor's staff to state troopers. The flurry of numbers concludes that 36 percent of the state work force is now black whereas it was only 25 percent under Edwards and that 200 blacks now serve on boards and commissions compared to only 80 under Edwards. Treen finishes with a flourish. "If Edwards thinks he can continue to appear before black groups, tell them funny jokes and a pack of lies and have them follow him like a Pied Piper, he is sadly mistaken."

That remains to be seen. Edwards' discrepancies may look shabby in the press but from the pulpit he strikes a chord with congregations and preachers stronger than can any corrective press release from the People for Dave Treen. Though Treen's minority appointments are almost double those made by Edwards, Edwards can claim to be the first governor to really open state hiring to blacks. It's like criticizing Branch Rickey in 1948 for only having one black, Jackie Robinson, on the Brooklyn Dodgers. Black leaders are enjoying this debate over who has done more for minorities, knowing that the rhetoric is just upping the ante of what they can expect from the next governor.

By midsummer, John Cade feels very good about his much-maligned black strategy. Dave Treen feels even better, as it has opened a new world of campaigning for him. Coming out of one black church where he received an especially warm welcome, the governor agrees with a reporter who notes that Treen seems even more relaxed campaigning with blacks than he does with whites. "I am. I feel that they're more sincere."

It all hangs on that, doesn't it? Are they more sincere or does Treen just not know when he's being jived? It's quite natural for a black congregation to be honored and complimented by a governor, a Republican governor, who cares enough for their vote to come talk to them on Sunday. But elections are held on Saturday.

You can't fault the Republicans for being optimistic their radical strategy could work. They go overboard, however, in viewing the black community as they want to see it. At the P. B. S. Pinchback dinner honoring the memory of Louisiana's only black governor (and the last Republican before Treen), GOP State Chairman George Despot is beside himself in describing the new emerging black spirit. "If they want economic progress, blacks have to go with us," George is instructing reporters in the Capitol House lobby. "Go to any ghetto in Louisiana and you'll see that nothing has happened with all the money the Democrats have thrown at them." But you don't have to believe George. Here is a black Republican, Harvey Thompson, jumping in to criticize the Democratic philosophy of pouring revenue-sharing money into construction of huge civic centers instead of into smaller projects in depressed areas that would truly stimulate black business and black employment. George Despot is so proud of what he's hearing he breaks back in. "Can't you feel it? Can't you just feel the new spirit in what he is saying?"

Allan Pursnell of the *Advocate* has his fill for the day. "Yeah, I can feel it," he sighs, closing his notebook, "I just can't believe it."

11. "A Real Man for the Job"

The aroma of the cochon de lait drifts out over Cross Lake in Shreveport, where gathered for pork and politics are about 60 of the most important politicians in Louisiana: Edwin Edwards, Russell Long and most of the state's sheriffs. A couple of reporters snicker at the idea of a pig roast at a sheriffs' convention, but wisely keep it to themselves. With three years to go until his next election, Russell Long is making one of his infrequent political appearances this side of the Potomac. That Russell Long would come to the Louisiana Sheriffs Association convention to endorse Edwin Edwards shows his respect for this group and for this candidate who is running not only for governor but for his place in the political pantheon at the right hand of Huey's throne.

Overstuffed sheriffs lean back in folding chairs as the once and—he hopes—future chairman of the Senate Finance Committee praises Edwards' fiscal responsibility that left surpluses and his Robin Hood populism that has led to sales and property tax reductions and "such prosperity as we had never known before. And certainly not since."

Edwards beams as the sheriffs stand and cheer. He could not ask for a more potent and personally pleasing double-barreled endorsement. But let's keep things in perspective. The senator's endorsement is good for pride and fund raising; the sheriffs' endorsement is good for about a quarter of a million votes.

There was a time in this state when only two political offices really counted: governor and sheriff. Just about everyone else derived power from them or stayed out of the way. Legislators, especially, were sent to Baton Rouge by their sheriffs to do what the governor told them to do. Times have changed, but maybe not as much as people think. Legally,

137

the chief executive has had to share some power with the Legislature and local governments, though with the right man and enough imagination and will, the power of the governor is as breathtaking as ever.

The sheriffs are another matter. Out in the country, the sheriff is much more than a law enforcement officer: he is The Man, he runs the parish. His law enforcement powers alone are awesome. Not only can he run in anyone whose face he doesn't like, townsfolk and outsider alike, but when the jails are full, the sheriff decides whom he lets go. Often the DA defers to the sheriff on who gets charged and who gets off. In rural parishes, the state police use the sheriff's office, and probation and parole officers depend on him too. In areas where the mayor and the police jurors are part-time and you need something right now, the sheriff is the government. He collects the taxes. He dispenses food stamps. He sends out deputies to catch the farmer's pig that got loose.

A sheriff is as strong as his personality, especially in politics. The backing of a strong sheriff makes all the difference for local and state candidates alike. His good name is one thing, but on election day when the deputies are sent out down the back roads and bayous to bring in carloads of rural voters—blacks and whites, sharecroppers and fishermen, people who wouldn't even vote if the sheriff didn't come get them and tell them whom to vote for—that's power.

Yet even in the country, times are changing. The old-line sheriffs are being retired not by rivals but by age. The traditional sheriff who ruled by common sense (or depending on the man, the lack of it) and the seat of his pants is being replaced by more professional lawmen, trained administrators and younger politicians attuned to the changes in the state. But great traditions don't die easily, those changes don't always last. This election year, nearly a dozen old sheriffs, who had retired, been defeated or sent to jail, are making comebacks. The people may have turned out the old sheriff for a more professional, better-trained or simply better-dressed replacement, such as a former state trooper, and then find the new boy doesn't understand people or power as well or shows little interest in catching their pigs.

With Edwin Edwards crisscrossing the state to rewire the old coalition of labor, blacks and courthouse gangs, the old sheriffs' comeback trail looks better than ever. Though the candidate does not want to get directly involved in any local election, he knows it's in his best interest to have as many hot sheriffs' races going as possible. Nothing brings out the voters better than when both the old sheriff's organization and the new sheriff's organization get to working the countryside. Like the Longs before him, Edwards' strength is in the country. The only election Huey ever lost was caused by the torrential rainstorm that kept the country vote at home on election day in 1924. Edwards is determined that regardless of what kind of rainy days he'll face, there will be a heavy country turnout this time, even if that means messing with some sheriffs' politics.

In at least two parishes Edwards or his supporters worked behind the scenes to encourage former sheriffs to make their comebacks. St. Landry Parish offered the natural climate for such mischief. One of the state's more colorful parishes and the crossroads of east-west and north-south travelers, St. Landry for decades was the logical site for a thriving whorehouse industry. The sheriff in the '50s, the legendary Cat Doucet, didn't seem to mind. Asked by a *Times-Picayune* reporter why he sanctioned prostitution in the parish, Cat answered, "So what's wrong with a little pussy?" End of interview.

Even after Cat was succeeded by Adler LeDoux, several establishments, most notably The Spot just off Highway 71 south of LeBeau, prospered for years after the Chicken Ranch in Texas was shut down. The watchful, paternal Sheriff LeDoux was all for letting the good times roll but could only be pushed so far. Years later in retirement, when asked by the *Times of Acadiana* why he had tolerated prostitutes and pimps in the parish, Adler snapped, "No pimps!"

LeDoux hung up his spurs in 1979 and was succeeded by straight arrow Howard Zerangue, a former deputy so serious about presenting the correct moral image of the sheriff's office that he wears his uniform to church. Howard is a popular sheriff and an intelligent politician who appears to be on the way to winning reelection by default. But in early 1983, Adler LeDoux begins making the rounds from Krotz Springs to Eunice, saying he's running again with Edwin Edwards' and Mitch Ashey's backing. Ashey's a wealthy oilfield contractor and one of Edwards' top friends in the parish—the two are even partners in a ranch. If Mitch Ashey is giving money to Adler LeDoux, it will force Howard Zerangue into a serious and costly race—an affront and inconvenience the incumbent sheriff does not take lightly. The best place Howard

Zerangue knows to squeeze is on Edwin Edwards. As the battle lines are drawn in St. Landry Parish, the hot race, big turnout strategy almost backfires as a peeved Howard Zerangue declares his neutrality in the governor's race and even begins talking about how strong Dave Treen looks in the parish and how the race there may be closer than the Edwards people think. Within a week, Adler's spigot is turned off and he's out of the race.

A couple of months later, after addressing the service clubs in Opelousas, Edwards asks Sheriff Zerangue into a side room at Indian Hills Country Club for iced tea and fence mending. Edwards doesn't seem to mind the traveling reporters grabbing a late lunch nearby—they won't even know what's happening.

Taking his seat, the sheriff nods grimly across the table to Mitch Ashey and retains his humorless expression as Edwards, Tommy Powell and Wayne Ray start ribbing Ashey about the ranch in Eunice the four have just bought. "Ashey gets us to buy in on this thing telling us it will be a working ranch," says Edwards. "He was right, we have to keep working to pay for it."

From ranching to politics, Edwards tries to keep the mood light as he offers up Ashey for sacrifice. "Do you know how much you've cost me in promises I've had to make to Zerangue after he heard that you were giving LeDoux money?" Ashey rolls with the banter and Zerangue does too, laughing along as Edwards describes how LeDoux was going about the parish actually making people believe that Edwards was backing him. "LeDoux walks into Diesi's and puts a suitcase on the counter and says he just got all the money he needs from . . . " Edwards points a finger to his chest. "He was telling people he was getting $100,000 from me," he says, laughing at the idea of 1) giving any candidate in St. Landry Parish that kind of money three months before an election and 2) encouraging anyone to run against a great lawman and community leader such as Howard Zerangue.

"This is all your fault, Ashey," browbeats Edwin, "you started all this and dragged my name into it." The performance is not lost on Zerangue, who is getting the full treatment by Edwards, climaxing in a final mock reproach to Ashey. "All right, I'm going to say it now in front of you and Howard Zerangue that if you ever fucking double-cross either one of us again, that's it for you, sonofabitch, we'll write you off. We'll cut you out.

And we'll tell that nine-year-old girl to sign the charge." Ashey and Powell and Ray are bent over laughing and Zerangue even manages a nervous chuckle—he appears satisfied, even if he's not used to ultimatums being put quite that way.

A strange scenario, but a mission accomplished. Zerangue had to be satisfied for real or imagined threats to his incumbency, Ashey had to be reprimanded for aiding and abetting a rival, Edwards had to have his united front in St. Landry. It takes about 15 minutes and he didn't have to hurt anyone's feelings. The touch.

So what if the Edwards mischief backfires in St. Landry? There are plenty of other parishes with retired or repudiated sheriffs just aching for a comeback, with or without Edwin Edwards' encouragement.

In Rapides Parish, old sheriff Grady Kelly, who had been indicted, had resigned and got religion, is coming back against aging incumbent Marshall Capelle.

In Edwards' home parish Avoyelles, former sheriff Potch Didier had once before proven his resilience and reputation as a man of the people by getting reelected in 1975 while serving a misdemeanor sentence in his own jail. Potch retired in 1979 and was succeeded by a former state trooper, Bill Belt, a sheriff so unpolitic that he will endorse Dave Treen in this election. Here's a man just asking for opposition, and with Edwin Edwards' support, out of retirement comes old Potch, his chances looking better than ever since he will not have to campaign from jail.

Another major comeback is being staged in Tangipahoa Parish, in the heart of the wild and woolly Florida parishes, a land of beautiful piney woods, dairy cows, strawberry fields and moral contradictions. In Tangipahoa Parish, there is hard-shell Baptist country and there is the city of Independence, where gambling is a way of life and bookmakers are among the town's leading citizens. (Independence and large parts of Tangipahoa Parish were settled by Italian immigrants so they don't exactly look to Mississippi for societal role models.)

Tangipahoa Parish goes its own way and for years the rules were written by Sheriff Frank Edwards. Edwards, a shrewd political operator, fell victim to a reform zeal and growing urbanization when he was turned out of office in 1979 by young reformist Ed Layrisson. Folks got a whiff of how bad things had been in the sheriff's office when Sheriff Edwards, before leaving office, had to sell off the department's squad cars and file cabinets to eliminate the deficit for which he would have been held personally responsible. Though Layrisson was elected as a reform sheriff, not everyone could quite believe the sheriff of Tangipahoa would be above some friendly bribery. What a surprise for Frances Pecora, wife of a reputed Mafia associate, and mother of a young man being held in the Tangipahoa Parish jail on drug charges. Shortly after Layrisson was sworn in, Mrs. Pecora approached the new sheriff with an offer of $100,000 to spring her baby. What a mother won't do. Layrisson put her in jail too.

Layrisson was leaning toward supporting Dave Treen in the 1983 election. Though Edwards is popular in the parish, Edwards supporters could not allow an unfriendly sheriff a free ride back in with free time to hurt Edwin Edwards. Thus, the comeback of Frank Edwards. Many of Edwin Edwards' people in the parish were supporting Frank Edwards, but just in case anyone missed that point, Frank wrapped himself around Edwin's campaign, to the point of using the exact same colors and typefaces on his signs. He didn't even bother to use his Christian name in the ads. "Edwards for Sheriff" did just fine.

In most of these comeback tries, the hand of Edwin Edwards or his friends was obvious. Even if their candidacies weren't successful, the old sheriffs would create more interest and turnout, which would help Edwards, or they would keep busy the reform sheriffs who might dare to try to help Dave Treen. Edwards wanted to make sure any such infidel was kept very busy. But the most interesting and outrageous sheriff's race in the state had nothing to do with Edwin Edwards or Dave Treen—it was about the one issue no sheriff dare come up short on: manhood.

You can tell something's up by the first billboard on your way into Natchitoches on La. 1. The candidate's face is the caricature of the good ol' boy with his hard features, stern eye and cowboy hat cocked just so, and the message:

ELECT BILL DOWDEN
A REAL MAN FOR THE JOB

That's about the tenor of this sheriff's campaign in this northwest Louisiana parish, where the real issue has nothing to do with law enforcement, catching pigs, or even politics. The prime issue is raised in backwoods communities like Grappes Bluff and Spanish Lake whenever a certain candidate takes the mike at a political forum, points to the sheriff sitting nearby and declares, "It's time we got homosexuality out of the sheriff's office."

Norm Fletcher is not your everyday good ol' boy North Louisiana sheriff. He's not even a crisply correct former state trooper. Before putting on the badge, the closest Norm Fletcher had come to law enforcement was to read the crime news on the local radio station he owned. But when the old sheriff retired in 1979, Fletcher parlayed his media name recognition (he was best known as the Voice of the Demons for Northwestern State University football game broadcasts) and his record of community service and honesty into winning the election. In a parish evenly split between college town residents and cotton and soybean farmers, Sheriff Fletcher presented a modern, urbane image of an able professional and smart politician who didn't see the need to kick ass, chew tobacco or otherwise fit the proper comic strip image expected of a North Louisiana sheriff.

And he will pay for it. Though Fletcher has built a good record to run on, the inevitable backlash against the new image in the sheriff's department brings out a host of deputies, former deputies and deputy pretenders to oppose Norm in the 1983 election. The major opponents, former deputy Herman Birdwell and real man Bill Dowden, only talk generally about the need for a tougher crime-fighting image in the sheriff's department, but another candidate named Clarence Noel lays it right on the line. "It's time we got homosexuality out of the sheriff's office" is practically his sole campaign message. The groundless attack on Fletcher, considered in Natchitoches to be a decent, Christian widower, shocks and repels many citizens but also causes a flock of rumors to spread all over the parish. And to set some folks thinking. "Well, you know," the gas station attendant offers his opinion, "you ain't never seen the man with a woman . . . "

The accepted, almost expected, response from Fletcher to Noel's charges would be a good pistol whipping. After all, we are talking manhood. The maligned sheriff, instead, does nothing, refusing to be baited, refusing at first to even acknowledge and thereby legitimize Noel's wild charges. But not even Fletcher's dignified silence quells the rumors or shuts up Noel. When the sheriff finally accuses Noel of

143

impugning the reputation of everyone in the department, Clarence plays innocent. "I said we didn't need to elect a homosexual sheriff. I didn't say anyone in particular was a homosexual. We don't need to elect a homosexual congressman or a homosexual president. My platform is I am against drugs, alcoholism and homosexuality. Anyone who attacks my platform must be for what I am against." When the sheriff threatens Noel with criminal defamation charges, Clarence stands his ground. "If I have broken the law, it's the sheriff's duty to arrest me here and now. I can prove everything I've said, but I'll wait my day in court."

One of the many rumors about Fletcher also floating about town is that he had been arrested in Shreveport in the mid-'60s. A check of the Caddo Parish records reveals no arrest of a Norman Fletcher but does turn up an arrest record for—lordy, lordy—Clarence Noel for criminal neglect of family by intentionally failing to support two minor children. Looks like no one's going to win any merit badges in this race.

The Great Silent Issue takes precedence over all others but it doesn't crowd them out. Certainly, since the Natchitoches *Times* will not accept any queer ads or refer to the salacious stories in print, the candidates need something to talk about in their ad wars. Without its own TV station, Natchitoches candidates have to rely, as politicians did in pretube days, on ads in the newspaper to attack one another. Week by week, the copy-heavy ads become the best reading in the paper, a splashy, messy mix of intrigue, interfamily attacks and plain old character assassination.

Sheriff Fletcher's most severe critic on the record is former deputy Herman Birdwell, fired by Norm for violating the deputy's manual rule against causing "disgrace, non-trust and bad public relations for the department," or, in other words, preparing to run for sheriff while still on Norm's payroll.

In his open letter to Natchitoches Parish citizens, Herman explains his own firing and then lays into his old boss:

> The truth is I touched a sore spot with Mr. Fletcher when I criticized him, while still a member of the Sheriff's Department, for allowing Playboy Magazines in the jail and for terminating church services in the jail. A jailer, who disapproved of Playboy, invited me for a tour of the jail to see the nude pictures that were taken from the magazines and placed on the walls by the beds. Mr. Fletcher said that this was good for the men . . . that it would relax

them . . . that psychiatrists had proven it. I disagreed! I still disagree! This is not good for confined men.

Punishment can be as much an issue as crime in a sheriff's election. For although a judge may give the sentences, it's the sheriff who really sets the terms of the punishment. Folks like to see their prisoners punished, and if there aren't enough rocks for them to break in the red clay soil, they sure don't want them being coddled. The idea that church services are not allowed in the jail, but that Negro prisoners are hanging pictures of naked white women in their cells, presents a moral contradiction a "strong" and "decent" sheriff would not tolerate. Not to mention that we're talking black on white pornography here.

Norm Fletcher is doing the right thing in ignoring the attacks on his manhood, but he cannot let go insinuations that he is coddling criminals. In his own ad in the Natchitoches *Times*, he blames "FEDERAL LAW" for the prohibition on holding religious services in a jail unless there is a separate room so that heathens won't have their constitutional rights violated and further assures the readership, "WE PASS OUT BIBLES REGULARLY." Federal law, that favorite scapegoat, not only ties his hands on providing Christian worship, but also dictates that prisoners be allowed to receive and ogle *Playboy Magazines*. According to Norm:

> FEDERAL LAW: The ONLY books or magazines which we can KEEP from the jail are those dealing with HOW TO ESCAPE or HOW TO MAKE A HOME-MADE WEAPON. FEDERAL LAW: The Sheriff's Office has spent NO MONEY on shorts for inmates. But the Police Jury has purchased some short pants for inmates to wear up in 90 to 95 degree temperature cells.

Good thing he explains that. In the minds of some citizens, the combination of no religious services, *Playboy Magazines* and short pants on prisoners is conspiring to turn the Natchitoches Parish jail into a federally mandated Sodom and Gomorrah. At least they know now it's not Norm's fault.

Pressed hard to compete with issues of such magnitude and moment, Bill Dowden is trying to convince the voters he was so strong and uncorruptible that certain elements wanted to get rid of him. In a front page story and photo in the *Times*, Dowden claims he was the target of an assassination attempt when his car and then his person were fired upon on a lonely country road. The car was then set afire, obviously the work, insists Dowden, of some criminal element afraid of a real man taking over the sheriff's office and cleaning up Natchitoches Parish. But the good ol' boy is even more upset when other candidates voice the obvious suspicion that the incident was staged. Even the *Times* uses quotation marks in referring to the "assassination attempt." Talk about get no respect—once the campaign is over, Dowden will be indicted for filing a false police report.

For all the heat and bombast of *Playboy Magazines*, short pants in the jail, assassination attempts, sweetheart deals and who got fired for what, those issues are overshadowed by the Great Silent Issue, what they're saying about Norm. It's hard to imagine a candidate, whatever the details of his private life, taking as much maligning without flailing back or pulling some macho stunt. But shrewd Norm Fletcher not only disarms the public and gains its respect by his dignified silence, he also manages to take the wind out of the sails of all other issues advanced by all other candidates. "The whole campaign has centered on the rumors," says my guide, "and Norm's silence has made everyone's campaign just fizzle."

This doesn't calm nervous sheriffs in nearby parishes. Norm cleverly and early got the sheriffs in Grant and Caddo to cut radio tapes endorsing him. Then when the rumors started spreading all over the state, the sheriffs were scared, but they were sort of stuck. My friend echoes the admiration of a lot of folks in this parish who, even more than homosexuality in the sheriff's office and *Playboy*s in the jail, object to the cheap shot character assassination campaigns of his opponents. Just one more indication of the way politics is changing even in the outback. In the old days, the rumors against Norm, true or not, contested or not, could have killed a sheriff. But in 1983, these vicious rumors, and Norm's stony disciplined silence to them, are all but winning him the race. My native guide feels that Norm has met the enemy and whupped him. "Sure, there's a lot of things being said about Norm Fletcher, including what a damned smart politician he is."

12. Punish Thine Enemy

Senators Russell Long and J. Bennett Johnston have three goals on the front burner:

1) regain Democratic control of the U.S. Senate;
2) re-elect Edwin Edwards;
3) crush Dan Richey.

Who dat? As he has never had any race closer than a mild landslide since his first election to the U.S. Senate in 1948, Russell Long doesn't have to work too hard to keep up with the changing faces of the state's political hierarchy. It's doubtful he can connect the names and faces of more than a handful of even the most powerful members of the state Legislature. But both he and his colleague Johnston are keenly aware of a young North Louisiana senator named Dan Richey.

And you aren't? At age 36, Dan Richey has achieved in two short terms what few legislators can accomplish in a lifetime: the enmity of a two-term governor, both U.S. senators and a commanding two-thirds of both houses of the Legislature. Dan Richey's problem is that he is not just a conservative, but an unbending, unrelenting ideological conservative intent on winning at all costs battles he can't help but lose. Edwin Edwards has a whole Dan Richey routine, gathered from the arguments Edwards has engaged in with Richey as a matter of perverse intellectual curiosity. "Richey tells me the only legitimate function of the state is police protection. When I ask him who's going to build the roads, he says private enterprise. Yeah, sure. I asked him to find the business that would build a road between Opelousas and Baton Rouge." Edwards ceased to regard Richey as funny the day he approached him with a tax he was sure Richey would have to vote for. "'Richey,' I told him, 'you'll have to vote for this tax. It's to raise salaries for schoolteachers, such as your mother.' Richey tells me, 'Absolutely not.' 'Well,' I said, 'that's it. I have no use for anyone who would vote against his mother.'"

Dan Richey cut his conservative teeth at LSU as a Young American for Freedom and entered the House as a young sidekick of sorts to the libertarian Woody Jenkins, the lone red light on the House voting machine. But even Woody Jenkins knew where to draw the line between ideology and practicality—in light of his unionist North Baton Rouge constituency, Jenkins found a way to square his ultraconservative beliefs with an astute political vote against the Right-to-Work bill. But Dan Richey is not burdened by such practical baggage. And his district was far enough away from Baton Rouge and isolated enough politically that Dan not only survived but managed to get elected to the Senate, where he was even less tolerated and liked. The House is big enough to humor eccentrics of the Right and Left. The get-along-go-along Senate just runs them over. Not that it deters Dan Richey. In the face of just about everyone's opinion that taxes would have to be raised in 1984, Richey formed the Club of 14, representing the 14 votes needed to block any new tax in the Senate. By session's end, his Club of 14 still only had one member.

All the more reason why Russell Long would not have the slightest idea who Dan Richey was. It took Woody Jenkins' determined run for the U.S. Senate to reintroduce the state's senior senator to campaigning in Louisiana. And out on the stump he ran into Woody Jenkins' most vigorous campaigner, that is to say Russell Long's most virulent critic, young Dan Richey. Bennett Johnston got acquainted with Richey the same way in Jenkins' 1978 campaign against him. Stumping his rural North Louisiana district as though a postmaster appointment hinged on it, Dan Richey tore Russell Long up one side of Concordia Parish and down the other side of Catahoula. Richey took harder shots at Russell Long than Woody Jenkins did, causing Long and his people to deduce that Richey was in it for more than loyalty to his fellow liberty lobbyist Jenkins, but that Richey actually believed that Russell Long was indeed the imminent threat to freedom and free enterprise that his rhetoric suggested. Now Russell Long can take a political projectile or two—his hide's had 35 years of hardening in the Washington cauldron. But as much cold-eyed sincerity as he was hearing from this Richey fellow left both Long and Johnston with no choice but to crush the little bastard.

Edwin Edwards was more than happy to cooperate, as was an ambitious state representative in the area, Bill Atkins, who filed to run against Richey. Edwards, of course, was motivated by more than kinship with the senators or his aversion to politicians who don't vote the vested interests of their mothers. Edwards could not tolerate as dedicated a critic as Richey free and unopposed to roam his senatorial district blasting away at Edwin Edwards in 1983. Not that Dave Treen didn't show up a little pink himself on the rigid Richey litmus test, but he was clearly a candidate Richey could recommend over such a clear and present danger as Edwin Edwards. A cardinal rule of hardball politics is to never give an enemy a free ride at election time lest he use it to run you over. Therefore, the former governor and the two U.S. senators were heartened by the news that a fine young state representative named Bill Atkins would oppose Richey. With champions like that, Atkins was an instant hit and success on the fund-raising trail.

Richey had dragged Edwards over the coals long and hard enough, not just on the stump, but also in Richey's weekly column in the district's leading journal, the Concordia *Sentinel*. Those Richey columns raised the ire of Long and Johnston far more than Richey's work on the stump. All three politicians had implored the *Sentinel*'s highly respected publisher Sam Hanna to yank Richey's column. But Hanna, one of those rare publishers with a sense of history and a gift for writing politics, admired Richey's spunk and continued to support him. Until, that is, Richey turned on publisher Hanna in the vilest way, by starting up a competing newspaper. Politicians joked that they didn't know if Sam Hanna's face was red from anger or embarrassment but they had little pity for him. "Serves you right, Sam, you created him" was a common rejoinder in Ferriday.

If Dan Richey gets off on standing alone, here's his chance. With nearly the entire political and money establishment of the area pitted against him, Dan Richey is in for the fight of his life.

Nearly a third of the voters in the area are black, but Richey is far from shut out in that community. He has cultivated his own black preachers and leaders and had consistently pulled their votes in the past. Also, Richey has a strong following who believes that Dan Richey is ultraconservative—probably more so than most of his constituents—not just because it is politically expedient but because he really believes all of what he says. A rare quality in a politician, it has taken Dan Richey a long way. And has made him a lot of enemies.

But more than just sincere and energetic, Dan Richey is a tough political fighter from the old school. Beyond his brave new ideology, Richey employs the time-honored methods of political attack that have made Louisiana politics so rich and varied and vicious. Some of the ads he writes (and runs in Hanna's papers as well as his own) reveal his natural gift for the comparison attack. Richey's side-by-side comparison ads are some of the best of this genre I have seen all campaign. Through Dan Richey's eyes, let's compare:

DAN RICHEY	HIS OPPONENT
EDUCATION:	**EDUCATION:**
B.A. Degree, LSU	Attended Northeast State University.
Law Degree, Loyola	No Degree.
Masters Degree, Education, McNeese State	
OCCUPATION:	**OCCUPATION:**
Teacher	Owns a Pinball Machine company
Attorney	
Newspaper Publisher	
LARGEST CONTRIBUTOR:	**LARGEST CONTRIBUTOR:**
LAPAC. Goals: to promote free enterprise and good government.	Vending Machine Operators of America. Goals: to promote pinball games, jukeboxes, video games and cigarette machines.

Folks around Ferriday agree that the best thing Dan Richey has going for him in this election is Bill Atkins. The best thing, that is, next to Richey's wife, Jennie, an attractive and intelligent woman Dan met in Puerto Rico. Even if she doesn't campaign but just poses with the couple's lovely children in the *de rigueur* Family Man ad, she is an incalculable asset to the young politician. To have such a good woman at his side says that regardless what one has heard or thought of Dan Richey, what a fool he is to Edwin Edwards or a fiend to Russell Long, beneath his humorless, uptight doctrinaire exterior there is a man to be reckoned with.

Maybe.

150

Political retribution is not an exclusively white vice, as New Orleans Mayor Dutch Morial's vendetta against everyone who gets in his way amply proves. But as black power grows throughout the state, so do backbiting, low-swinging struggles between the brothers. Reapportionment has created two new predominantly black districts in the state Senate. One, in Shreveport, is becoming the scene of one of the bitterest struggles between two black politicians who had once marched together.

That Shreveport now has the opportunity to elect its first black senator—that in fact many whites will vote for the black candidate—is a testimony to advances black politicians and Shreveport have made. That the major obstacle to that first black senator is another black politician working hard for the white candidate shows how thin blood can be when money and ego get in the way.

Until now, the leading voice in black politics in Shreveport belonged to the feisty, tough Alphonse Jackson, a state representative and black kingmaker. Jackson, content to hold onto his House seat, nevertheless is determined to play the lead role in the Senate election. The natural choice is Greg Tarver, an old ally of Jackson's and a firebrand from the civil rights struggle in Shreveport. They've had their differences since, but this election provides the opportunity to put their differences behind them and send a black from Shreveport to the state Senate. But there is just one hangup. Political observers in Shreveport say that before qualifying, Tarver learns that he *must* employ Jackson's advertising agency to reach the black community. A surprised Tarver reminds Alphonse that the old advertising agency routine is reserved for white candidates, not brothers. But Alphonse Jackson is not letting mushy sentimentality get in the way of business. He runs an equal opportunity political operation. Also, Jackson is being pressured by his labor supporters to back their friend, incumbent Bill Keith. Instead of the two black leaders joining hands, the schism grows wider and Jackson moves his operation behind Keith, a hot-tempered ex-newsman whose Senate career has been split between loyalty to the AFL-CIO and Christian fundamentalism. Keith may be the only senator more unpopular than Richey and certainly more effective in that he pushed through the Senate and prevailed on the governor to sign a scientific creationism bill that mandates the balanced treatment in public schools of the origins of the universe. Legislators cursed Keith beneath their breath as they voted for the bill that would be political suicide to oppose back home. Dave Treen, after, he said, much thought and prayer, signed the bill into law, a law which has so far withstood the challenges by the ACLU and the ingrained opposition of the education establishment. The Christian voice in the heathen stronghold of the Legislature, Bill Keith is not one to turn his cheek. He challenged a visiting Arkansas legislator who called his creationism bill trash by calling the legislator trash and inviting him into the corridor to square off.

But it's a different Bill Keith who is campaigning in the largely black senatorial district, where he stresses his liberal labor record and barely mentions his fundamentalist conservatism. In his reapportioned, blacker district, Bill Keith would be about as popular as a disco in Tioga were it not for Alphonse Jackson's determination to demolish his former political brother, Greg Tarver. Tarver's refusal to pay tribute to Jackson could have been overlooked by a less resolute politician for the sake of electing a fellow black to the Senate. But brotherhood goes only so far in the hard, cold world of power, ego, politics and money. What else is Alphonse Jackson to do? A man must stick to his principles.

Ned Randolph appears to be a bundle of nerves as he paces outside the main hall of the Civic Center in Alexandria this muggy August evening. Rich, handsome and Princeton-educated, a three-term legislator with an impeccable record of pushing good government reforms, the heir apparent to Gillis Long's congressional seat and the beau of a TV soap opera star, Ned Randolph nevertheless has two very serious problems, both of whom are in the Civic Center tonight. One is Edwin Edwards. The other, much worse, is Tilly Snyder.

Ned latches onto Edwin as the former governor exits the public hearing and walks him to the door, speaking low and fast as he tries to explain that he neither asked for nor really appreciated Dave Treen's recent endorsement of him. Randolph has annoyed Edwards in the past with his pesky campaign finance reporting bills and a particularly galling recent law written by the young state senator that requires candidate Edwards to disclose the sources of his income.

Edwards assures the concerned Randolph that he doesn't hold Dave Treen or financial disclosure or anything else against Ned and that he won't be out to hurt him this election. Edwards can afford to be gracious. He doesn't have to destroy Ned Randolph. Because he knows Tilly Snyder is going to do that for him. A politician like Ned Randolph may wake in a cold sweat at night wondering what he did to deserve an opponent like Tilly Snyder. Randolph needn't wonder—he knows the mistake he made. With everything going for him in his political career, Ned tried to rush things some in 1982 when he challenged Gillis Long for Congress. Even if Ned were not successful, observers thought he would do well to run a good race and position himself as the logical replacement for Gillis, who, with his heart condition, was not expected to serve many more terms. Ned worked hard, raised an impressive war chest, made a good issue of his youth and energy and cut a dashing figure on the campaign trail with his girlfriend, TV soap star Deidre Hall (Marlena on *Days of Our Lives*), on his arm. Ned Randolph only made one mistake: he didn't win.

Gillis, the wounded bear, outraged at the amount of money he had to raise and time he had to spend in the district explaining the money he spends in Washington, resolved not to have Ned Randolph kick him around again. Wouldn't it be nice if Randolph had such a hard time getting reelected to the state Senate in 1983 that he wouldn't have the war chest, perhaps not even the political base, to bother Gillis again in 1984?

Gillis is the reputed master of using other politicians to punish his enemies. It was widely assumed in 1971 that candidate Gillis Long financed the campaign of the outrageous Puggy Moity, who spent his considerable budget on wild and hilarious weekly TV shows in which he regaled the state with unreal and imaginative attacks on Edwin Edwards, who was vying for the same segment of the vote as was Gillis.

Early in 1983, Snyder approached John Cade with the idea of the Treen campaign funding his entry in the governor's race to once again do a Puggy Moity on Edwin Edwards. Cade didn't go for the idea, coming up short on either money or imagination. But Gillis Long had plenty of both, and—so goes the story around Alexandria—encouraged Tilly to go after Ned Randolph.

John K. "Tilly" Snyder is the mayor of Alexandria and, more to the point, the scourge of anyone so unfortunate as to have to run against him. You don't have to run against Tilly to fear him—just to have him talk about you is enough. Tilly's an attacker from the Uncle Earl school—he delights in picking apart the personal foibles of his political enemies. Earl Long is the past master of personal attacks in public. Yet Earl laced his stinging barbs with brilliant humor (often turned against himself) and the rich imagery of

153

his peapatch vernacular. By his folksy delivery and populist fervor, Tilly is in ways a throwback to the Earl Long-style campaigner, but absent any subtleties, humor or wisdom. Tilly throws all his energy into the attack. When Snyder, trying to pay a compliment, introduces Edwin Edwards at a testimonial this night as someone "who's been called just about everything you can call someone," Edwards corrects him. "You haven't heard or can't imagine the worst thing you can be called until you get into a race with Tilly Snyder. It's another world." Ned Randolph is about to enter that dark and grisly world as the summer campaign unfolds.

Not that Tilly has any shortage of targets in his present position. Since his 1982 comeback to unseat an unpopular mayor, Snyder quickly fell to fighting with the City Council, city officials, the business community and anyone who doubted his wisdom or whims. To Tilly, a hardline populist and conspiracy theorist, all that ails Alexandria emanates from a complex and far-reaching cabal comprised of the *Daily Town Talk*, the Guaranty Bank, the Central Louisiana Electric Company and, of course, all their dupes and lackeys who help them to gouge the people while subsidizing the bloodsucking paper mills. A last bastion of municipal populism, Alexandria under Snyder has continued to provide long-standing city services that test the treasury's means, such as giving residents free plastic bags for garbage collection. Garbage collection was the issue last summer that touched off a Tilly tirade that brought him just the kind of state and national publicity civic leaders dread. When the City Council balked at Snyder's move to eliminate the monthly sanitation fee paid by residents, Tilly lashed out at one black councilman, calling Columbus Goodman an Uncle Tom and a chimpanzee. The story hit the wires within an hour—it looked like one of those not uncommon public gaffes that a politician lets slip and forever lives to regret. Not Tilly. Even when provided an out, Snyder responded by insulting the black leader even more.

After Councilman Goodman demanded an apology for the "crude racial insult," Snyder wrote back a letter, referenced "Monkey See, Monkey Do," and called Goodman the racist for abandoning his people and following "the dictates of the Town Talk, the big utility company and the Guaranty Bank." Tilly wrote that after speaking "to several hundred people in the black community . . . they feel about you as I do. You are no longer one of them, but in effect are a Judas goat, or as one time was said, an oreo cookie, black on the outside and white on the inside, but really with green in your eyes—the green of money. . . . Also, I have been informed by some of your former students that your classes referred to you as the 'monkey man.'" Rounding out his attack, Tilly invited Goodman to meet him in debate on this issue but added a P.S.: "Bring your own bananas."

If Snyder, elected on the strength of black support, can bait a leading black politician with impunity, what calumny can he have in store for Ned Randolph?

The chimpanzee episode thoroughly embarrassed those progressive Alexandrians who were hoping the rest of the state would not find out about their mayor. Until this latest outrage, their chances seemed good, as for the last two decades the rest of the state has paid so little heed to the capital of CENLA.

Alexandria is Louisiana's Atlantis, swept away in the shifting tides of communication and transportation. Back in the days before the television networks and the highway planners decreed that America would move from east to west, Alexandria was the geographic and political center of the state, a proud oasis of civilization for weary travelers making the arduous journey from North Louisiana to New Orleans. Then came the Interstates, and the state was split along two parallel bars of concrete, one in the north running from Shreveport to Monroe and one in the south running from Lake Charles to Baton Rouge and New Orleans. Alexandria was left high and dry in the middle, linked to these two disparate and foreign worlds only by lonely, two-lane La. 1, a poor excuse for travel and a further barrier to the commingling of North Louisiana and South Louisiana culture and commerce. Marie Cade laments the cultural isolation of her hometown: "When I was a little girl, the New Orleans symphony would come up the Red River on a steamboat to play for the city. Now not even the [Baton Rouge] *Morning Advocate* comes here."

For years Alexandria was a meeting place and melting pot of North and South Louisiana, with influences both redneck and Cajun, Baptist and Catholic, rural and urban. Alexandria and Rapides Parish were critical campaign stops for gubernatorial candidates: to capture Alexandria was to seize the center of state politics, as it struck the delicate balance of the state that had not yet swung so heavily to the fast-growing southern end. Now Alexandria, aging and isolated, is Louisiana's genteel old maid aunt, nostalgic for the glories of her youth, resentful of her isolation and irrelevance, a city with a proud culture and a sense of history, strongly rooted in Louisiana's past but cut off from its present. Alexandria is the missing link in a state that has yet to notice anything missing. But Alexandria's day will come again, as the long-awaited, long-delayed north-south interstate highway is scheduled for completion before the decade's end. When that golden yard of concrete is laid near Alexandria, the capital of CENLA will be restored to its rightful pivotal position between the two ends of a state that have lost touch with each other.

Until then, Alexandria treads the backwater of the state's consciousness, where resilient strains of populism and demagoguery combine to create a political climate where the likes of Tilly Snyder can still strut the public stage. You can sense the temptation in some Alexandrians to elect Tilly senator just to get him out of the mayor's office. But the city seems to have more concern for the image it projects than to set loose its most outrageous personality for the rest of the state to gawk at. An early poll indicates Snyder running a weak third in a field of four. Snyder's not going to win, but that hardly comforts Ned Randolph, as the black support Tilly is attracting (they either missed or agreed with his assessment of Columbus Goodman) in the past has gone to Randolph.

Snyder's campaign is built around his amazing nightly TV spots, 10-minute streams of malice that he directs not just at Ned Randolph but at the bloodsucking City Council and all the minions of the vast conspiracy committed to keeping down Tilly and the little people. Nightly Tilly appears on the independent station, with no introduction, no music, just old Tilly, dressed in a blue leisure suit, his white hair swept back, a scowl on his face. He sits at a slight angle to the camera and leans to his side with an elbow on his knee, giving the viewer the feeling of sitting on a country store porch watching Tilly chew the fat and trample reputations. He speaks slowly, looking down occasionally, seeming to carefully measure each thought as he builds each denunciation to a ringing conclusion two or three octaves higher than when he started.

The personal life of the incumbent, who is separated from his wife, is obvious fair game for Snyder. "Some candidates are coming on, showing you their wives, telling you what a good family man they are, what a good father they are. The voters are tired of this and wise to this. . . . What difference does it make what a fine bunch of children he has, what about your children?"

Just because Tilly is running for the Senate doesn't limit his attacks or his mean-spiritedness, as he shows in his comments on City Clerk John Grafton. "Here's a young punk, a grade school teacher, who has no experience in what he's doing at all, wasn't elected by you people. No one knows who John Grafton is, he lives in Pineville. Most people don't even know him, can't see anything but his eyes, he has one of these heavy hippie type beards." Or in his description of a city official, "Talk about a wimp. He had some medical problems with his legs, something or another and it warped his mentality."

When not thrashing the City Council or Ned Randolph, he sets his sights on the heinous courthouse gang: "I intend after this election to finish cleaning up the Ed Ware gang [the Rapides district attorney]. Under the dictation and domination of pinhead old Ware, your so-called district attorney, who is responsible for the crime, rape, dope, murder, thousands of people here who have been nol cased and no prossed. All kind of people making money, dragging schoolchildren into their dope ring. As I've said many times before, how can a grade school child find a dope peddler in the courthouse and them not know about it? Why don't they prosecute these people? Somebody out here wants to sell your wife lipstick or a pair of pantyhose on Sunday, they'll rush out there and arrest them and lock them up, why can't they get the dope peddlers? The marijuana peddlers. The alfalfa hay that they spray with hog tranquilizers and sell 'em to the children here in the grade schools and grammar schools. I'm gonna clean it up . . . gonna have a good time."

The mayor is unclear on why he needs to be elected to the state Senate to purge Alexandria of the alfalfa hay sprayers, but he promises not to stop there. "I'm gonna get rid of you, Mr. Columbus Goodman. You hear me, Columbus? I'm gonna get rid of you, Mr. Jay Bolen. You hear me, Jay? And I'm gonna get rid of Ed Ware at the same time. All it's gonna take is a little TV money and I know the people who said they will be happy to put it up. Ol' Mr. Pinhead Ware invented the recall system in Rapides Parish and I'm gonna show how to make it work to get rid of these three birds."

By now the story around Alexandria is that Tilly has lost sight of his original purpose of simply pulling poor, populist votes away from Randolph and now thinks he can actually win—a prospect to make even his key backer recoil. "The story on the street," advises my native guide, "is that Tilly really thinks he can win and he's mad Gillis won't stake him enough." And anyone who gets Tilly mad hears about it on TV. "Probably

Gillis needs to be out the Congress no better than he seems to be doing at this time. Sure ain't helping me any. I don't know that I want his help, his politics is twisted. Call him and tell him what I said. If he's in town he's up on Toledo Bend instead of tending to the people's business in the Congress."

After a few nights of this, Tilly finally returns to the topic at hand, the election. "Never really had time to talk to you much about my opponent. Not really nothin' to talk about, he's been in the Legislature 12 years and he's done absolutely nothing. One thing he brags about is his shoot the burglar bill and I'm gonna work to repeal it. All that's gonna do is get some innocent people killed, give some man or some woman who hates their maid the chance to shoot 'em, or it's gonna get some policemen killed. People gonna call him up, say there's a peepin' Tom, next thing you know he's down there and pow someone shot him side of the head with a shotgun. The silliest legislation I've ever heard of. It's the shoot the bull bill."

But attacking pinheads and peons can only substitute so long for Snyder's greatest nemesis, the heinous bloodsucker conspiracy. "It's time in this country we got some leadership with guts! G-U-T-S, *Town Talk*. Leaders that will look out for the interests of the people and not the interests of the major corporations as you have been doing, and as that council has for five and a half years, when they bankrupt the city, took the city employees' pay away from them to make up for their mistakes, and they went up so high on your utility bill and you couldn't pay 'em and *they cut you off,* by the hundreds, through the winter, cold and hungry, and no utilities. Yet they go up to the International Paper Company, giving them a half a million dollars a year, subsidizing that huge papermill corporation, *with your money,* costing every one of you $45 to $50 a year, to furnish them water that they weren't paying for. . . . What do we want with industry if we got to subsidize it? You mean I run out of time again? Speaking of running out, I'm about to run out of money. I need you people out there to send me a little TV money, help me keep this thing going. You tune in at 9:50 and we'll continue this line of discussion. Until then, God bless each and every one of you."

13. With a Little Help for My Friends

Ken Womack checks his apartment one more time to see that everything is just right. The place is trashed, furniture knocked around, papers strewn about, the safe wide open and more documents spilling from it. The back door has been jimmied open. The slender, silver-haired 47-year-old man looks the scene over one more time, and for a final touch drops his wallet on the floor. Everything's set. Closing the door behind him, he goes down to the parking lot to meet the taxi that takes him to the Holiday Inn on Airline. Instead of entering the motel Womack turns and walks off into the darkness. Ever since he came to Baton Rouge 12 years ago he had been involved in some big deals and with powerful men, which, combined with his own imagination and ambition, should have made him rich. Instead the last of the deals is crumbling to dust, his powerful friends are growing nervous and his creditors more persistent. Ken Womack, his back to the wall, is leaving town in the middle of the night, not to make a fresh start but to find a peaceful end. Taking his last hike in Baton Rouge in the mild January night, he can take consolation in knowing that for all the success that eluded him here, he is about to gain, *in absentia,* the most intense recognition of his life. He will become the state's most famous missing person since LSU President Jim "Jingle Pockets" Smith went on the lam in 1939. He can see the faces of the people who will be asking where is Ken Womack and what does he know? The legacy of question marks he leaves behind will frame the agenda of the election year to come and will haunt the destiny of Edwin Edwards. Reaching the waiting car in the DCCL parking lot, the thought of that fitting irony may have caused Ken Womack to chuckle—for all his bittersweet memories of the place, this troubled, mysterious figure was at least getting the last laugh on Louisiana.

During the campaign Edwin Edwards would often say that there are three types of people he could appoint to office or help get state business, "qualified friends, unqualified friends and enemies," and then add, "I'm still working on the first group." And vice versa.

Instead of "Union, Confidence and Justice," the state seal should be emblazoned with the motto "When all else is equal, take care of your friends." The beauty of that rationalization is that so much leeway is allowed in determining "when all else is equal." In the absence of provable fraud, who is to say that a friend of Edwin Edwards could not do a better job than an applicant or a consultant or a supplier who has no connections? In the absence of a viable Republican party as the loyal opposition, who's to even suggest it?

According to Edwards, therefore, being a friend of the governor is the most important qualification for anyone who wants to work for and do business with the state. State government is such a huge business that one can get rich off it without a position, without even a contract. So important is the friendship of the governor that those who enjoy it—be they realtors, attorneys, investors—will find opportunity seeks them out to get involved in projects where the dropping of a name, a well-placed phone call or a little inside knowledge can make all the difference. Most of what the governor's friendship can bring one is gained entirely legally, if not fairly. The governor's friendship need not—legally, cannot—be repaid directly, though campaign contributions or dozens of other acts of kindness can cement friendships satisfactorily for all concerned.

The friends of Edwin Edwards, and his relatives, did quite well the first two times around. Charity and friendship begin at home. Marion, the governor's loyal brother, broadened his contacts in real estate and insurance after 1972—on at least one occasion pricking the curiosity of the FBI. In 1977, the FBI investigated the possibility that Marion got part of a $100,000 brokerage fee on a $2.2 million state purchase of land for the proposed Jean Lafitte State Park below New Orleans. After directly negotiating the 556-acre sale for over a year, the sellers, just before closing the deal, inexplicably paid a $100,000 brokerage fee to little-known Arian, Inc. One of the three partners in Arian told WVUE that he didn't know who the third man was. The Edwards brothers said they cooperated fully with the investigators but refused comment to the press. Nothing ever came of the investigation.

Earlier the same year, Marion did broker the sale of 382 acres in Livingston Parish for a company called Southwest Environmental whose incorporation was handled by Nolan Edwards' law firm. After the company received permits to store hazardous wastes, it sold the permits and the land to BFI, which now operates the hazardous waste site near Denham Springs.

Three of Edwards' top supporters in Terrebonne Parish bought two parcels of land in Houma just after the 1971 election when Edwards promised to build a high-rise bridge across the Intracoastal Canal. After the Highway Department picked the site—guess where?—part of the land was sold to Nolan Edwards, who later told the Houma *Courier* that he hoped to make a "great deal of money" on the investment, whereas his partner in the deal told the paper he could not remember how he learned the land was available for sale.

When Louisiana Democrats began raising money for President Jimmy Carter's reelection campaign in 1980, the state central committee paid Vicki Edwards' advertising agency $15,000 and Edwards' secretary Ann Davenport's consulting firm $25,000.

When it comes to choosing lawyers to represent the state in suits, the governor has a free hand, which he used to steer two of the most lucrative cases during his term. Edwards' close friend from Crowley, Billy Broadhurst, earned $546,000 unsuccessfully arguing the constitutionality of the First Use Tax in 1978. Before Edwards left office, he picked an even fatter plum for his friend, the Mineral Board's multi-million-dollar case against Texaco. Arguing the case into Treen's term, Broadhurst's firm was paid over $600,000 and awaiting his disputed claim before the Mineral Board (with the eventual makeup of the Mineral Board pending the 1983 election), Broadhurst could be awarded an additional $800,000 in fees.

Up in Shreveport in 1976, Edwards' close friend and top fund-raiser Gus Mijalis offered a 15-year lease at $354,000 a year for a parking lot for the LSU Medical Center. Even though a four-acre site closer to the hospital was available for sale for $480,000, Governor Edwards threatened to scuttle the entire appropriation if the Shreveport legislative delegation did not agree to take Mijalis' deal. After a year and a half of wrangling, a compromise is struck to pay $1.42 million to buy up Mijalis' lease and another $250,000 to buy the land itself.

Edwards' major fund-raiser in Monroe, Sam Thomas, was involved in a local investigation where it was alleged that the state illegally performed drainage work on Black Bayou that later allowed Thomas to develop a shopping mall near the site. No charges resulted from that investigation.

Then there are the scores of architects, contractors, engineers, attorneys, consultants, suppliers and lessors who contributed to Edwards' campaigns and later received lucrative state contracts. Just because Edwards left office, the gravy train from his administration didn't stop. One of Edwards' favorite architectural firms, Cimini-Meric, was awarded a contract on an expansion project at Charity Hospital before Edwards left office, before the site and the size of the expansion were even decided.

It's easy to trace the trails of favors from the governor's office to his widening circle of qualified friends, but the trails going back to the governor are fewer and harder to follow. In most instances, favors are primed or repaid with handsome campaign contributions. Broadhurst, Mijalis and Thomas all contributed or lent over $50,000 to the 1983 campaign and together raised millions more from subfriends. On other occasions, Edwards was cut in on good investment opportunities. Along with Nolan, Broadhurst, George Fischer and State Senator Nat Kiefer, Edwards bought 942 acres in St. Tammany Parish in 1979 from the Catholic archdiocese on speculation that out-of-state investors would develop a Disneyland-theme park there. Edwards even promoted the concept at a news conference without mentioning his interest in the speculative venture.

Edwards said he had no dealings with his friends that could cause him trouble because he kept straight in his head all favors done and promises made and where the line of legality was drawn. "If I didn't, I would be in jail now."

The office of governor offered Edwards legitimate opportunities to help himself but also to help his friends. He loves power, he loves wealth, yet one senses that at heart he loves even more to use his own power and wealth to help his friends. Often it was a purely warmhearted ego trip. Even little things. In the midst of a heavy session of tailoring the governor's legislative package, Edwards surprised executive counsel Camille Gravel by asking him to fix a traffic ticket for a friend at LSU. No favor too small for a friend, especially a qualified friend.

Of all the favors Edwin Edwards has done for all his friends, none stands out more than what he tried to do for Jules LeBlanc. The governor claims the help he gave Jules LeBlanc was purely altruistic, "to help a friend who was struggling." Yet the lifeline thrown the drowning friend almost sank the lifeguard.

Ever on the lookout for new qualified friends, politicians are drawn to young movers and shakers looking to make their marks and their fortunes in the fast lane where business merges with politics. No one was moving faster in that lane in the early '70s than Jules LeBlanc.

Then the *enfant terrible* of Baton Rouge business, Jules LeBlanc was the scion of a respectable South Baton Rouge family and at the same time the newest of the nouveau riche. As teenagers, Jules and his brother Roger were pacesetters in a town full of rich, wild kids, leading a free-spirited, privileged joyride in their infamous green Jeep. What trouble they couldn't talk their way out of could be fixed. Jules settled down in college and breezed through law school, pouring his pent-up energy into body-building, pumping up his impressive physique, out-bench-pressing anyone on the LSU football team. He was quietly practicing law and helping raise a family in 1970 when he slipped. He slipped in a shower, crashed through the glass door and severed his right arm. He later named his second son after the doctor who saved his life at the hospital. Jules LeBlanc survived and fortunately he didn't depend on his arm to earn a living. But he did depend inordinately on his strong body for self-esteem, for a massive release of energy and satisfaction. He needed another outlet.

He found it in another kind of building, putting together a loan package through local and New York banks to enter the field of big-time real estate development—bigger than anything that had been tried before in the overgrown college and smokestack town. Pulling off the financing for bold ventures proved to be Jules' consummate skill: he knew how to talk to the guys on top. He sold himself and his dreams to the heads of the town's two biggest banks, daring these older, powerful, established men to dream as big as he could. And they did, lending him millions of dollars and going to bat for him with the New York banks to lend him millions more. He was 26 years old and hadn't so much as swung an apartment deal and here he was borrowing millions for entrepreneurship on a Houstonian scale: an office park, a mall, a hotel, a string of apartment complexes and all the raw land he could find around the newly opened Interstate corridors. As fast as the New York money flowed in, it was sunk into cement and more raw land, more apartment complexes, a helicopter and a TV station.

Through the complicated corporate paper shuffling, Jules made sure there was plenty of money available to make sizable political campaign contributions and to support himself in a handsome if not—for Baton Rouge—ostentatious splendor. Jules LeBlanc was immune to the small-town morality, just as he had been as a teenager. The green Jeep was replaced by an Excaliber and a fleet of other expensive cars, and Jules was always spinning one into trouble, either on Sorority Row or in ditches off College Drive, with young women at his side. The more money he borrowed, the more he built, the grander his swagger. Displeased at a bar patron being too friendly with his girlfriend, Jules' henchmen buddies escorted the young man outside and held him down in the parking lot while Jules worked him over.

High finance was even more fun. Little brother Roger joined Jules at the crest of the wave and together they began to battle rising interest rates and nagging cash flow problems. They bought a string of five small banks, from Jackson to Thibodaux, and were constantly shuffling checks and deposits from one to another. That helicopter came in handy. These were heady deals for two young men not yet 30, landing them in negotiations with giants like oilman and banker Louis Roussel and even Mafia boss Carlos Marcello. Not only did they play with the big boys, they played hardball. On the Brilab tapes Carlos Marcello mutters, "Those LeBlancs are bastards. They tape you." For those of us who grew up in Louisiana and understood and respected its legends, the thought of a couple of guys we went to high school with being cursed by Carlos Marcello—w ll, it kind of made you proud.

It was fun while it lasted. It lasted until 1977, when their pyramid of loans, tottering under escalating interest rates and overleveraged assets, finally all came crashing down.

Jules LeBlanc had gone bust on a scale worthy of his dreams. But bankruptcy laws being as they are, Jules and Roger didn't fare as badly as some of the creditors who were stuck. Jules continued driving his expensive cars and living in the opulent home he built in South Baton Rouge. Those assets, and his million-dollar walled compound on the coast in Biloxi, belonged to his children's trust which Jules set up in the good years.

Still the guy needed something to do. Though Jules LeBlanc could not personally borrow a dime in 1977, he was still thinking big. Now, however, there was only one older, powerful man left who could broker Jules' comeback. All the campaign contributions and personal kindnesses he had invested in his friendship with Edwin Edwards paid off when Jules got into what looked like a surefire deal—he began helping an out-of-state company that had the contract to sell a tax shelter investment plan to state employees. For Jules, it was more than some good income, it was a chance to get in on the ground floor of a low risk, high potential multi-million dollar opportunity where, for a switch, interest rates would be working for him instead of against him.

In 1977, several companies were seeking what amounted to an exclusive state franchise to sell the tax shelter plans to Louisiana state employees. A governor's commission chose a new company in the field, Deferred Compensation Corporation of America, over a more experienced company recommended by an investment consultant. DCCA was owned by a Pennsylvania man but its Louisiana operations were managed by Ken Womack. Womack's position in the investment company worried several legislators who remembered how he ran a local insurance company into the ground and wiped out the investment of its Louisiana policyholders. Auditors of one of the insurance companies recommended Womack's firing for padding his expense account and having the company pay for the apartment of a young female friend. The chairman of the board of the troubled local insurance company was Baton Rouge lawyer Rolfe McCollister, who was influential in getting American Bank to lend millions both to the failing insurance company run by Womack and to Jules LeBlanc in his go-go years. Also an Edwards friend and contributor, McCollister was instrumental in bringing together Ken Womack, Jules LeBlanc and Edwin Edwards. The two young businessmen, fresh from their recent, respective financial disasters, joined their experience, contacts and imagination, and were again in a position to run a potentially successful company into the ground. But this time they almost took the most powerful politician in the state along with them.

With the state contract, DCCL got off to a fast start as its salesmen, armed with slick brochures and a videotape presentation, began selling the benefits of the investment program to state employees. But no one benefited as much as Jules LeBlanc, who, seriously strapped for cash, began receiving monthly fees from DCCL. For what? According to LeBlanc during his bankruptcy proceedings, "When they run into a snag as far as getting in touch with a department head on making their presentation with different department employees, they get in touch with me. I try to go see the department head and make sure they tell their story, and they send me money once a month for these services." His bankruptcy records show he was paid $26,000 by DCCL in the first six months of 1978—the subsequent federal investigation will show LeBlanc, through circuitous payments to corporations owned by friends, received $200,000 from the employees' investment program.

The real door opener was Edwin Edwards, providing big help behind the scenes. DCCL appeared to be such a good deal that in 1978, Governor Edwards coguaranteed a loan with LeBlanc so Womack could buy DCCL's parent company, DCCA, with its North Carolina and Pennsylvania operations. The governor gave LeBlanc personal letters of credit totaling $400,000 (the guarantees would eventually rise to $550,000) to support Womack's acquisition loan. When Womack lost his North Carolina contract and fell behind on his $15,000-a-month note payments, Edwards, by now out of office, put up a $200,000 certificate of deposit to secure the loan.

As governor, Edwards interceded when a recalcitrant department head would not let DCCL salesmen in to pitch employees. And in 1979, before leaving office, Edwards signed an executive order adding a life insurance contract as an investment plan DCCL could offer. The insurance option was not a good deal for any employee who invested in it, but it was an excellent source of high commissions for DCCL.

And what did Edwin Edwards receive for his beneficence besides the satisfaction of seeing his young friend straighten out his life and earn some spending money? According to Edwards, "Nothing, n-o-t-h-i-n-g. I got not a watch, not a ring, not a credit card, not a leased automobile, not a Boehm bird, not a nickel, not a dollar, not a hundred dollars." But he did get a stock option for one-third of DCCL and along with Jules LeBlanc held voting proxies on all the company stock. Edwards insisted the stock option was of no value to him because he did not exercise it. However, the code of ethics for state elected officials in effect at the time Edwards received the option specified that "no official shall receive compensation of anything of economic value other than that to which he is duly entitled from the state" and then included under its definition of economic value "any option to obtain a thing of economic value, irrespective of the conditions to the exercise of such option." Edwards would say the option was not compensation but instead protection of his loan guarantee. "Look, let me tell you something. I put my name on a $500,000 indebtedness for this man [Womack] and I'm gonna tell you without any fear of concern that I did everything I could, took everything he had, covered everything that he had to make certain that if he went sour that I could keep from having to pay the note."

He was putting over a half million dollars at risk not to get anything in return, he claims, but to help his friend Jules LeBlanc. "I did not do it for Womack. I did it for Jules LeBlanc, who, when he was rich and riding high on top of the world, was very helpful to me, very supportive and paid a lot of my expenses." After the crash, said Edwards, "He was struggling to make it and I was struggling to help him survive."

Edwards stuck to his guns that the option was nothing to him because he did not exercise it. But what if he had at some time in the future?

"What if I had?" He turned the question around on John Camp in a TV interview. "Suppose three years after I got out of the governor's office and this business in North Carolina had been doing well . . . and I wanted to then consider getting into the business in North Carolina or in Louisiana or in Florida or in Pennsylvania. So what?"

Indeed, the question would not have even come up of what Edwards got out of DCCL had the employee-investors felt they got more out of it themselves. The biggest problem with the deferred compensation plan was that it was such a lousy deal. According to legislators later looking into the program, the problem was that earning high commissions (for the salesmen and the company) was put above earning high interest rates for investors. The employees could choose from three investment plans that were hardly structured to give the best deal possible. The savings account plan paid 5 to 5.5 percent interest, whereas Treen officials would later move that money into a credit union paying 12.78 percent. The biggest rip-off came from the insurance plan, which paid commissions of 100 to 110 percent of the first year's premiums. Guess what plan the salesmen pushed hardest?

They might have been less successful had they been dealing with more sophisticated investors. But the DCCL salesmen's prospects were, for the most part, low-paid state employees: secretaries, janitors, guards and maintenance workers. They later claimed to not even know they were really buying insurance until their first annual statement showed a sizable portion of what they paid in going to high front-end commissions. Dorothy McGhee, a maid at the state penitentiary, reported investing $1,552 her first year and was stunned to learn the investment had bought a life insurance policy with a $343.50 cash value. June Stringfield in the Department of Culture, Recreation and Tourism said she invested $12,320 in an annuity and was not told of the 20 percent commission charged in the first year. Only three years to retirement, Ms. Stringfield cannot even earn back what she put in before leaving the state payroll. Cecilia Breaux in Opelousas said she put in $4,800 the first year, to learn her current cash value stood at $3,450.86. "I blame the state for robbing me," she told the *Wall Street Journal*. "I was gypped and I want my money back." These cases were the extreme—most employees only failed to earn as much interest as would have been possible under a better-structured program. In the end, DCCL's poor salesmanship saved it from doing more damage—only 3,600 of the state's 80,000 employees signed up.

Womack and LeBlanc faced greater problems than customer complaints. With both the North Carolina and the Pennsylvania operations defunct and new sales in Louisiana slowed to a trickle, DCCL began to fall apart. To his horror, Jules LeBlanc could see the same forces that wiped out his empire in 1977 were at it again. The very high interest rates that he felt were his ally in this venture were rising so much, they were choking off consumer spending and bringing on another recession. Employees began worrying more about making ends meet than sheltering income, and new sales fell off drastically. Womack was having a terrible time meeting the payments at the bank. And with a Republican governor now in office, the new Commissioner of Administration Bubba Henry was making continued demands on the company to file reports and provide documentation showing it was fulfilling the obligations of its contract with the state. Another dream gone bust, on the line for a half million in debt, Womack saw only one way out. Before he closed the door on his ransacked apartment in January 1982, Womack must have realized that when that door would be opened again, the biggest secret of DCCL would be revealed. The story of DCCL was told in the papers and documents spilling from his safe and thrown around his apartment—and Edwin Edwards' name was all over them.

The disappearance of Ken Womack sent an expectant shiver through the state. Nothing was known yet of Edwin Edwards' or Jules LeBlanc's connection, but the story had all the tantalizing elements that suggested more shoes were going to drop. Investigating police saw right through Womack's flimsy abduction ruse and filed a missing persons report. The FBI moved in quickly, scooped up the evidence and took it to the U.S. attorney for the beginning of a lengthy grand jury investigation. Early spadework by Bill Lynch of the *Times-Picayune* and John Hill of Gannett News Service whetted the public's curiosity with the revelations of the loans Edwards and LeBlanc guaranteed and the stock options Edwards received while he was governor. Over the next 18 months, Lynch and Hill, tapping their sources and digging through courthouse records, piece by piece put together the major facts of the immensely complicated story. They traced the transactions leading to the formation of DCCL and DCCA, they uncovered the trail of payments back to LeBlanc, they noted the actions Edwards took to promote the company. The only missing piece was one that would more closely tie Edwards to DCCL. The press investigation was a nuisance to Edwards, who was busily raising money and assuring nervous contributors that nothing, not even an indictment, would stop him from running. "I knew somewhere there was a piece of paper," says one reporter, "that would make Edwin Edwards look very bad."

He was right—the only important piece of evidence the press did not uncover was the voting proxies by which Edwards could control the company doing business with state employees. Had that piece of information leaked out, it would have filled in the DCCL picture and Edwards' involvement in a way that would have been very damaging to the former governor. And only one reporter on press row knew what it was. In fact, she knew the entire case backward and forward—but she could not say a word about it.

The middle-aged woman cries in the high-ceilinged federal courtroom as she fills out her personal questionnaire for jury duty. With an invalid mother at home, how can she serve on a jury? Joan Duffy feels sorry for the woman sitting next to her yet realizes even the excuse of an invalid mother is not as effective a preventative from jury duty as is Duffy's occupation as a reporter. Sure, she knows that federal courts do not excuse potential jurors as readily as do state courts, but she figures that no prosecutor, defense attorney or judge wants a reporter—the UPI Capitol bureau chief, at that—sitting in the jury box for a sensitive case. When Judge John Parker, conferring with the bailiff, motions Duffy to approach the bench, she assumes this is the end of her interesting experience. It's just the beginning.

"I see here you're a news reporter," says Judge Parker.

"Yes, your honor."

"Well, you know you can't report anything that goes on in the grand jury."

Joan Duffy is too surprised to answer. When the judge looks up she swallows. "No, I guess not."

So starts the most fascinating and frustrating chapter in Joan Duffy's career, sitting in on the biggest story in the state and having to remain totally silent. Duffy's next door office neighbor, Gannett's John Hill, is stunned a couple of weeks later when he strolls into the UPI office to share the latest DCCL revelation. "I'm sorry, John," Joan cuts him off, "I can't discuss any details of the case." Hill just stares at her as it sinks in why she can't talk and soon Joan Duffy's civic duty is as hot a topic of conversation on press row as is Ken Womack's whereabouts.

"So many times I wanted to walk next door and plead with her to tell me what was going on," remembers Hill. But he didn't. Slipping away to grand jury meetings every week or two, Duffy steers clear as pressure on press row mounts to break the big story first. UPI covers the story through clipping and rewriting the dailies' stories as soon as they break. It's bizarre for her to attend press conferences and hear the reporters playing cat and mouse with Edwards, knocking about in the dark, getting hot, getting cold, trying to put together the big picture she saw only too well.

With the campaign over a year away, with the Legislature flat out of money to spend, DCCL is the only game in town. Reporters and politicians know that what happens in the grand jury will have a far greater effect on the outcome of next year's election than will anything either candidate does between now and then. The conventional wisdom is that only a grand jury indictment can knock the wind out of Edwin Edwards and melt his mounting lead in the polls. The pressure on press row intensifies as grand jury subpoenas go out in February 1982. Gannett (publishers of dailies in Shreveport and Monroe), the *Picayune* and the *Morning Advocate* are pressing hard for the story, too hard. Duffy can see the *Advocate* skating on thin ice as it breaks one story way off the mark about alleged missing money in DCCL. On the next Sunday, the *Advocate* falls straight through the ice when its lead story quotes an unidentified source who says the feds know where Womack is and that the federal investigation has broadened into other dealings of the Edwards administration. It's wrong. U.S. Attorney Stan Bardwell shoots down the story, and Edwin Edwards has his old nemesis right where he wants it. Not only is the story patently false, says Edwards, but he has proof of malice on the part of executive editor Jim Hughes. Edwards claims to have a witness to testify that he overheard Hughes in a downtown restaurant saying he would "get Edwards." The *Advocate* buckles. In an unprecedented front page statement, the paper retracts the story and apologizes for it. The *Advocate* is embarrassed but more significantly, it halts all DCCL coverage and any substantive investigative reporting on Edwards.

Edwards is pleased with the apology. Through the course of the incident, he has even gained a new perspective on editor Hughes. "I used to think that Jim Hughes was out to stick it to me. But I have found that the man has ice water in his veins and he will assassinate anyone's character, tear anyone down and ruin any reputation, no matter who they are. And you know, I respect that."

Edwards can afford to be magnanimous, if you can call it that. Wringing the apology from the *Advocate*, long an editorial foe of Edwards, marks one of his most successful victories against the press. For the rest of the DCCL adventure, one of Edwards' severest critics will be watching from the sidelines.

With the press corps slipping and sliding, the grand jury investigation

171

grinds on. Jurors meet regularly through the winter to map out the basics of the case. In March, a federal arrest warrant is issued for Ken Womack on the only charge they can find against him, making a false statement to a bank in applying for a loan. Then the grand jury meetings stop as the overworked assistant U.S. attorneys attempt to digest the mountains of paper gathered not just from Womack's apartment but from every person, bank and government agency that touched DCCL. Bardwell's office is pressed with a heavy load of major cases and hit by untimely staff resignations. He knows he's working on a political deadline but does not cut one assistant loose to concentrate on DCCL. The grand jury picks up again in the summer. Jules LeBlanc is called to testify, but pleads the Fifth Amendment, as he also does before a legislative subcommittee investigating DCCL. Edwards asks to testify before the grand jury but is not called. In July, expectations rise when Ken Womack's car is found in the Philadelphia airport parking lot, but still no sign of Womack. The FBI is not exactly scouring the East Coast for him since a missing Louisianian accused of a bank violation is not a major priority. But at this point, Womack's testimony is less important a factor than time. By October 1982, Edwards is telling friends that if he is not indicted by November he is home free because federal indictments that close to the election would appear to be politically inspired. Then early in the morning of January 13, Ken Womack's girlfriend in Philadelphia calls Ken Womack's former wife in Baton Rouge. Ken Womack is dead. For the past six months, Womack has been checking in and out of a federal hospital in Philadelphia. Edwards, who when Womack disappeared said he hoped he left "for love and not for money," now suggests that Womack may have known he was sick and left town to die quietly in peace. But hospital doctors say his cancer was diagnosed in the past six months.

The best thing Edwards has going for him on the DCCL case is how poorly he came out on the deal. He tells WBRZ's John Camp, "That doesn't mean that I was skimming or raking off or getting a kickback from him [Womack] or Jules because I was not. I have a lot of friends that I help in all kinds of situations. Some work out well and remember it. It works out good for me because it doesn't cost me anything but every now and then thinking that I'm helping friends without exposing myself I get in situations where the opposite is true. This is one of them, but that doesn't make it immoral or illegal. Might make it stupid or unwise but it's neither immoral nor illegal. If it'd been the other way around and he paid me, you understand, or I had gotten anything out of him, you might want to raise your eyebrows but listen, uh, this is one time where the politician got stuck." According to Edwards, he ends up paying $256,000 on the note he and LeBlanc guaranteed for Womack. But he makes most of that back on a family trust real estate deal Jules lets him in on. Edwards' final loss comes out to about $90,000, half of which Uncle Sam, of all people, picks up at tax time.

But Stan Bardwell and the grand jury are not through. John Hill reports that in April, Bardwell sent a draft of a four-count indictment against Edwards to Washington for top-level review. In it, the former governor is accused of conspiracy and mail fraud as part of a scheme to use his office to aid a business in which he held stock options and voting proxies. But the Justice Department won't buy it. Sources say Justice officials in Washington felt that although Bardwell had enough for an indictment, the odds of getting a conviction were not high enough, especially this close to an election. The Justice Department is said to have looked at the whole picture, including Edwards' popularity in the polls and the feds' failures to persuade Louisiana juries to convict Congressmen Otto Passman and Buddy Leach in their recent trials.

Was it bungling by Stan Bardwell, bungling by the FBI or political jitters in the Justice Department? Or was there no case to start with, only, as Edwards claims, a desperate attempt by the Republican U.S. attorney to read criminal wrongdoing into an innocent effort to help a struggling friend? But that's not the grand jury's problem. It is only charged with finding probable cause, not weighing the chances of getting a conviction or determining the effects on the coming governor's race. The jurors have studied this case for 18 months and aren't ready to drop it because someone in Washington got cold feet. At least not without comment.

When the grand jury files back into open court in July 1983, the foreman hands to Judge Parker not an indictment or a no true bill but a three-page report. Parker looks it over and returns it to foreman Michael Barr, who, hands shaking, reads it in open court.

It is an unprecedented report, the first such ever returned by a grand jury in the Middle District of Louisiana. As reporters scribble furiously,

Barr reads the jury's opinion that DCCL "was manipulated to funnel money to friends of then-Governor Edwin Edwards." The report says principals in DCCL took advantage of the program "to line their own pockets—including big chunks of money to political cronies of a governor who held a financial interest in the company." Employees, it says, lost money because the funds were invested to most benefit company officials and they weren't told of the governor's "significant personal financial interest in the success of DCCL." The bottom line, however, is: "No indictments were issued in this case because Jules LeBlanc—who received payments for his influence—was not a public official, and because Edwin Edwards—who used his public office to help DCCL—received no payments." It concludes, "This is the kind of activity a state code of ethics should protect against."

In response, Edwards says the same thing he has said when past grand juries have not indicted him. "Once again, months of investigation have been concluded to set to rest silly and repeated rumors and allegations for which there was never any substance. . . . Once again, time and inquiry have proved me right." Still one good blast deserves another, as Edwards blames the timing and wording of the report on Bardwell, calling it "the most unfair thing ever done to me in public life."

Statements tumble forth from other parties. State ethics administrator Gray Sexton says he doubts Edwards violated the ethics code in effect when he was governor. The old code was not as clear or encompassing as the state's current ethics code, which, like other reforms, was signed into law by Edwin Edwards but did not take effect until he left office.

Dave Treen gets his two cents in, calling Edwards' response "statements befitting a con man," and says the grand jury report expresses "the genuine outrage that this sleazy and unethical conduct cannot be brought to justice."

The end of the DCCL saga leaves both political camps edgy and dissatisfied. In a way, this gubernatorial campaign started 18 months ago when Ken Womack split, leaving behind a trail of paper on which would ride Dave Treen's best hope for reelection. Now Dave Treen will have to get from DCCL what he can as a campaign issue, a very difficult one to explain and understand at that. Edwin Edwards isn't much happier. Though he won't face charges, the simmering grand jury report doesn't exactly clear his good name. He will have to explain his actions, not in a court of law, but in the even trickier court of public opinion, still sitting in judgment for the next three and a half months.

14. The Honest Man

Edwin Edwards' back is to the wall—literally. He faces off with reporters at a press conference in a room too small for all the cameras and reporters that want to get at him. His first press conference after the stinging grand jury report is a minuet of mutual distrust as Edwards and reporters go round and round on what it all means and what it appears to mean.

- Wasn't it a conflict of interest for you to hold voting proxies on 50 percent of the DCCL stock and an option to purchase a third of the stock?

"I don't think it's a conflict of interest at all. I didn't do it, that's the important thing."

Do you think it gives the appearance of a conflict of interest?

"Well, I don't think the appearance is what's important."

But do you feel it does give the appearance of a conflict of interest?

"I don't know if it gives the appearance at all . . . "

The grand jury did not indict Edwards but neither did it clear him. The critical report hovers over him, the lingering cloud of a lengthy investigation he desperately wanted behind him. Instead the report just sits there, quoted and requoted in the press and in a hard-hitting Dave Treen ad on the air within a week.

Edwards has been through grand jury scrapes before and nastier press conferences than this. But not during an election, against a Mr. Clean opponent poised to take the worst and make the most out of what the grand jury had to say about him. In the past, he could have kept his mouth shut and let the bad publicity fade away. But silence now in the face of Treen's assault would imply guilt. Edwards shoots back, not with cool control, but in burning anger, perhaps the most dangerous emotion in politics. Through July if Edwards is not complaining about the low blow dealt him by the U.S. attorney, he is seething over Dave Treen's quest to seize the monopoly on honesty and integrity in this campaign.

It doesn't take much to set him off. Edwin Edwards glances below his feet as his Highland Road estate passes from view beneath Clifford Smith's helicopter whisking us across the Mississippi and into Bayou Lafourche country. The candidate is reading over press clippings from the Thibodaux *Comet*'s coverage of Treen's recent visit there when he explodes. "Look here, it's the honest fucking man again. He says in the paper, 'I will carry Lafourche and Terrebonne Parishes.' That lying sonofabitch. How's he gonna do that when he can't get over 35 percent in any poll?"

From the back seat, Houma Senator Leonard Chabert offers an explanation. "He must be smoking some of that stuff that's not on the market."

"It's fucking on the market all right and he's full of it."

Through the flight, through the day, Edwards will return to the myth of Dave Treen's honesty, the grand jury's independence and the press's impartiality. "The grand jury and Bardwell put in the goddam report that I opened doors and twisted arms and it's a goddam lie. It said I funneled money to my friends and that's a fucking lie. And the fucking press, which has been sticking it to me every chance they get, was so goddam anxious to draw the conclusion that something was improper. Let me tell you something. If the major media in this state did what they were supposed to do and did an in-depth study of state finances and reported it with the same intensity as this chickenshit DCCL thing, there would be a revolution in the streets. I wouldn't even have to campaign."

The profane Edwin Edwards is a side of him he never shows his public. The man is confident enough in his masculinity not to have to curse to convey a macho image, and he's articulate enough not to have to use expletives to make up for a shortage of adjectives in his vocabulary. And he's in control enough not to lapse in public into his more colorful vernacular. More in control than Uncle Earl, say, who, as State Senator Sixty Rayburn loves to recall, once went overboard in reviling an enemy in the Legislature. "Why, Willie Rainach ain't nothing but a little cocksucker." Five seconds later he realized what he had said and took it back. "Ladies and gentlemen, excuse me, I meant 'sapsucker.'" Edwin

Edwards, on the other hand, will swear to make a point or to show he means business, as slow-moving bureaucrats have learned when he's called to check on a pet project. Other times he'll swear playfully, to convey mock anger, or—and there's no mistaking this—when he's truly pissed. Today's torrent belongs in the last category.

Dave Treen, Honest Man, is getting under Edwards' skin in a way no opponent before has affected him. "Hell's hottest fires are reserved for hypocrites," he bristles as he straightens his coat, checks his hair and prepares to meet the public, hail old friends and cut the ribbon at his Thibodaux campaign headquarters.

As the Edwards campaign, now two years in the field, overheats on the candidate's anger, Dave Treen is just loosening up for action. This midsummer Sunday finds the governor in coastal St. Bernard Parish motoring down Bayou Loutre in a shrimp boat, waving to fishermen and families lined up in boats or under shelters onshore, celebrating the blessing of the shrimp fleet. The governor and Congressman Bob Livingston are guests of fisherman Kenny Robin, his wife and a batch of rowdy buddies practically falling overboard to attract the attention of TV crews onshore. "'Ay, getta picture of me," shouts a squat seaman wearing a t-shirt inscribed "Matcho." Captain Kenny behind the wheel tells the reporter the next governor has to do something about the twin evils facing the native St. Bernard fishermen: Alabamans and Vietnamese. The bigger boats from Mobile are spending more and more months in Louisiana, making it tougher for the smaller Louisiana boats to compete. And the Vietnamese—toward whom Kenny is quick to point out he bears no personal prejudice—are harvesting shrimp with V-shaped steel plows that are burying and smothering oysters on the sea bottom. "Yeah, we talked to him about it," nods Robin to the governor, at the bow of the boat waving to onlookers. "I think he'll help us. If . . . "

Matcho is star-struck. "'Ay, dey gonna put me on da TV. I got myself right in da picture next to Treen."

"Bullshit," admonishes Kenny. "Dey gotta way of shootin' Treen and cuttin' your ugly ass right outa da picture."

Robin eases his boat over to shore, where Dave Treen disembarks for an interview with the waiting TV reporters. The election is barely three months away but the governor would rather talk shrimp than politics.

But with his arms around the women from the boat and smiling apolitically, he accedes to the interviewer's question and slices Edwards thin with a few choice remarks about DCCL, the grand jury report and those poor, abused state employees.

Even from his shrimp boat on Bayou Loutre, Kenny Robin is not unaware of the war of words raging between Edwin Edwards and Dave Treen as to who's honest and who's not. "Ay, ain't no way Edwin Edwards is gonna make anyone believe Dave Treen's a crook. He's one to talk. You look at the papers, they say he's a crook. Some Korean gives his wife $10,000 and he says he didn't know anything about it? My wife come up with some shit like that, I'd say, 'ay, hold everything, what's goin' on here? This guy gettin' somethin' off ya?'"

Through July, Edwin Edwards does most of the talking—too much talking—as Treen coasts along gubernatorially, timing his shots and waiting for the right forum to give Edwards his best one. They finally meet in New Orleans for the Alliance for Good Government forum. Six candidates show, but other than double-wide Joe Robino's plea for "God, peace, love, sex and brotherhood" and his suggestion that Edwards and Treen rent the Superdome to mud wrestle, the evening boils down to a glaring, head-on exchange between the major candidates.

Treen touches it off, accusing Edwards of structuring and financing DCCL to help his friends more than the state employees who invested in the program.

Edwards can barely wait his turn to point his finger at the governor and dare him. "You just said and you've got dozens of ads running on television that say I financed DCCL. I'll make you this deal. You get out the race if I can prove that's not true, and I'll get out if you can prove that it is true. Now yes or no, will you take the deal?"

Treen starts to laugh as the hoots in the audience drown out any applause for Edwards. Edwards just gets madder.

"Will you take the deal?" he shouts to Treen, who gets up from his seat with an aren't-you-making-an-ass-out-of-yourself smile and retorts, "You have no right to ask me yes or no. You want to get in a debate about it now, we will. You helped buy . . . you helped finance the acquisition of stock by Womack in DCCL or DCCA and I think that's what we're saying on radio." He smiles again, to the growing cheers of the good government, uptown audience, and sits back down as Edwards pouts.

"All right, if you think that, then take the deal." He points his finger back at Treen as the moderator attempts in vain to restore decorum. "You can get me out of the race tonight. If you can show that, then I'll get out of the race tonight. If I can prove to you that I didn't, you get out the race. Now let me say that one more time . . . "

Treen, getting annoyed, doesn't need to hear any more. "I'm not going to get out of the race under any circumstances and neither are you."

Edwards unloads on Treen by accusing him of bribery in accepting a $25,000 cash contribution shortly after reappointing businessman Jerome Glazer to the Mineral Board. Treen, who was tipped in advance of the Glazer question, gives his version of the timing of the contribution and reminds Edwards that Glazer got on the board the first time after giving Edwards $75,000 in the 1971 campaign. Edwards starts losing control as he gets madder, stumbling over words and twice referring to Glazer as Jimmy Moore, another Edwards crony whose questionable past contribution to Edwards was the source of a grand jury probe.

The Alliance for Good Government votes to endorse Dave Treen, even though the Edwards contingent crows that their man backed Dave Treen down and put him in his place. The view of the audience and of journalists is that Edwards is fortunate that the forum was aired only in New Orleans, for on this night he did something he rarely does in public: he blew his cool. That wasn't lost on the young social worker outside. "Before tonight, I was definitely leaning to Edwards, but not anymore. Treen was a real gentleman, he was in control, and Edwards wasn't."

For the Treen supporters who had been getting nervous about the governor's lack of campaigning, the New Orleans forum is a rallying point, proof that their man can stand toe to toe with Edwards and come off looking more reasonable, more controlled, more gubernatorial. Less than three months before the election, Edwards is angry and on the defensive while Dave Treen, barely out of the blocks, is quickly gaining momentum.

Billy Nungesser is already talking about turning points, standing off to the side at a contractors' reception. He shadowboxes the air with a drink in one hand and a cigarette in the other as he tells where the opponent went wrong. "Edwin Edwards made his biggest mistake three years ago when he conceded Treen the honesty issue. You know when he was talking about how being an honest governor is not enough. When it gets down to people going in the booth, that may be all they really care about." Billy shifts the cigarette to his mouth so he can shake hands with a contributor. "Edwards should have never done that. Now he's scrambling to get it back but it's too late. Anything could happen, not just to him. Ossie Brown or anyone could get indicted that week and a guy goes into the booth and says, 'Goddam crooked politicians—at least I know Treen's honest.' And that's what's gonna do it."

Blackham Coliseum is a sea of blue t-shirts as 5,000 Treen teamers have been bused to Lafayette from as far away as Shreveport to officially kick off Dave Treen's campaign. It's a full two years after Edwin Edwards officially kicked off his campaign, but somehow the timing seems just right.

"Hey hey—Big Mo's on our side," bellows a hulking youth for Treen, as the pep rally atmosphere heats up. For a campaign that has been purposely subdued about being too political, today's rally is a time for letting it all come out. Even the benediction is blatantly political, as Father Nickie Trahan asks God to help Treen because "the hopes and dreams of many find their fulfillment in his honesty and integrity."

Political priests are one thing, but the real stunner is seeing Gus Weill take the stage for Treen. The political consultant, who had often counseled young account executives on the dangers of getting personally involved in a campaign they're just trying to earn a buck off of, steps over the line as he tells the cheering masses, "The question history has posed to us is this: can good, decent, honest government work in Louisiana? . . . We who were the laughing stock of the nation can now be proud that we are represented by honor, integrity and decency."

The crowd is hot for Dave Treen when the governor finally takes the mike. And he doesn't disappoint them. For once he has a well-written speech, the same he gave to the state party convention in February, and he delivers it without notes, hitting all the right rhythms and buzzwords. He's on the kind of roll he's only rarely been on before.

"Edwin Edwards talks about being a good fiscal manager. Why, he can't even manage a little company like DCCL, despite the fact that he holds 50 percent of the proxies and his friend, Jules LeBlanc, has the other 50 percent. If he wants to talk about fiscal management, then I say to him, 'Come on, Eddie, we're ready.'"

The crowd roars back as Treen describes the surplus Edwards did leave him—"14 hazardous waste dumps that we have to clean up. So if he wants to talk about the environment, then I say to him, 'Come on, Eddie, we're ready.'"

One by one he ticks them off, from integrity to education to crime. Comparing the 34 pardons he has signed to Edwards' 1,181, Treen sets the house to screaming and chanting when he says, "If he wants to talk about law enforcement, I say to him, 'Come on, Eddie, we're ready.'"

It's a golden, positive afternoon for Dave Treen. His campaign staff members, despondent and worried just one month ago, are brimming with confidence. Two different polls show Treen cutting Edwards' 20 point lead of May in half. Now the staff's beginning to understand what John Cade has been saying all along about momentum. Everything in its time. And on this first Saturday in August, momentum and time are on Dave Treen's side.

In Baton Rouge the same day, Edwin Edwards is celebrating his 56th birthday, but looks none too happy about it. Guests mingle and drink beneath the canopy and the massive oak on the lawn of Edwards' neighbors Jack and Cathy Davenport. Edwards engages in his mandatory flirtations with a bevy of hoopskirted hostesses who are on hand to lend atmosphere, but the sight of a reporter at the punchbowl pushes his "liar, liar" button. Edwards makes his way over and, stabbing at chunks of watermelon in the cascading fruit display, snarls, "The goddam press is letting that lying sonofabitch get away with murder. Why hasn't anyone followed up the Jerome Glazer contribution? It's a clear violation of the campaign law. And no one's calling him on his lying DCCL ads. He knows they're lies. He backed up like a whimpering pup when I hit him with it in the debate. He didn't want any part of that action." In deference to his guests Edwards has deleted some of his expletives, but in his heart you know he's pissed. He spears another chunk of watermelon and storms on. "His whole campaign is based on a goddam lie and the lie is that he's honest and everybody else is a crook."

Edwin rejoins his guests. His brother Nolan has just arrived, along with another sheriff or two, and Jules LeBlanc with his bride Denise. It's interesting that for all the trouble Jules has caused Edwin, the candidate has not told LeBlanc to stay out of sight. Earlier that summer, reporters going into Edwards' headquarters were shocked to find Jules LeBlanc waiting in the reception area. When asked about LeBlanc's presence, the candidate cracked, "He may have some options for me to sign." What these guys lack in good sense they make up in pure nerve.

As Edwards stalks off, his bodyguard Gene Jones sidles over. The lanky, friendly former state trooper is wearing an uncharacteristic scowl. "The goddam press, why aren't they doing anything about the Jerome Glazer deal? The sonofabitch broke the law and the press is protecting him." *Is this a recording?* Gene stomps off, but is back in a minute. "Look, I'm sorry, I didn't mean to get on you like that. I just can't stand to see that bastard Treen get away with those lies."

The bitterness is ingrained in the Edwards campaign. Edwards can turn the venom on and off, but it seems to have been running nonstop for the past week. And Gene Jones—I had never seen him as angry, especially over politics, as he was today. And wouldn't again. Gene would be dead of a heart attack in 12 hours.

15. A City Needs a Myth

Raising the beer to his lips, the guy at the bar caught sight of the soundless TV screen, and almost choked. The TV scene was devastating and unbelievable: Billy Cannon, great All-American and local legend, being led in handcuffs to the parish jail. "Are we busting poker games now?" said the fellow as the bartender rushed to turn off the stereo and up the TV volume. The news is shooting through town like a stabbing pain. Baton Rouge's only bona fide hometown hero, a storybook success and role model, has been charged with masterminding a $7 million counterfeiting scheme to bail out his own shaky finances. The arrest of Billy Cannon knocked the wind out of Baton Rouge, and the charge cut to the quick of the city not sure of itself. If Billy Cannon was manufacturing money, faking it, what did that say of the city that had idolized him, all but deified the hard-running, good-natured kid from North Baton Rouge who put LSU football—and hence Baton Rouge—on the map and then built a respectable professional career on top of his sports reputation?

The massive irony was not lost on the locals, who, beneath the bravura of the football myth, only know that they don't know this city well. Baton Rouge is Louisiana's Houston, a quick-forming, ready-mix, industrial city that sprouted from a quiet river burg a small fraction its present size a generation ago, on the way becoming as much an enigma as it is an economic success story. The city Baton Rouge is today was formed and is still largely controlled by outside forces. It was built on John D. Rockefeller's vision of an inland Gulf Coast refinery and on Huey Long's political vision of a strong and large centralized state government and premier state university. The magnetic poles of state and industry were an irresistible pull. Baton Rouge became the mecca for opportunity, far more so than New Orleans, a closed city harder to bust into. It was open to anyone—Mississippi farm boys looking for a refinery paycheck, kids from small North Louisiana towns who came to LSU and stayed, young couples fleeing the rigid caste system of New Orleans, looking for a fresh start with a state job. They flocked to Baton Rouge because it was new and it was growing, a lot of things starting, always a new ground floor to get in on. Opportunities weren't closed off here or tightly restricted—if you had any drive or common sense, you could make money even if you had no taste or real talent. The influx of so many fresh dreams and new starts smothered the quiet small town Baton Rouge had once been—the city grew so fast after World War II, it was hard to keep up with what it was. Certainly, it was a bustling, comfortable place to live and work, and of course a nice place to raise children, as the mushrooming child ranches at the city's eastern end bore witness. For many with top jobs at the plants, Baton Rouge was a prime pass-through town, a place to get your ticket punched before the next step up the career ladder. As a result, Baton Rouge developed a fast-growing but interchangeable middle class. The top executives at the plants, LSU and the State Capitol brought a lot to this town but also took it away with them when they moved in four years. By the time the boom peaked in the late '70s, Baton Rouge was a rough amalgam of subdivisions that had yet to become neighborhoods, a city that had not yet coalesced into a community. The heady growth transformed this town but produced some vague, ambivalent feelings along the way. You meet a lot of people who have lived here nearly all their lives, who don't intend to live anywhere else, but who confess to an empty feeling, an impersonal attitude toward the hometown they wish they felt more for.

Baton Rouge outgrew its antiquated social structure and business leadership as the city's economy was reorganized around the petro-chemical plants and burgeoning state government. Baton Rouge was a new American industrial city, unfettered by a rigid social and economic order but also lacking a sense of history or a unifying myth. There was nothing to point to—other than smokestacks and Huey's Capitol—and say, that's Baton Rouge. So that's where Billy Cannon and the LSU Tigers came in. Led by Cannon and his dazzling broken-field running, LSU won the national football championship in 1958, and Baton Rouge adopted Tiger football, embodied in Billy Cannon, as its local legend, its homegrown myth, a cause to get drunk on and yell about, something snobbish New Orleans couldn't match. Thereafter Baton Rouge became obsessed with football, the seven home games forming the hub of the social season, a universal bacchanalian celebration of local spirit. It seemed a healthy obsession but really it was a doomed one. That incredible championship season and Cannon's legendary exploits—commemorated each year by the playback on TV of his famous 89-yard Halloween night run against Ole Miss—created a mythical standard, a dreamlike Pigskin Camelot that could never be relived. Playing was not enough. Winning was not enough. Regardless of how successful a year was, when LSU registered its first loss of a season a gloomy funk settled over the town as it realized this wouldn't be *that year* again.

The other problem was what a city in need of myths will overlook to deify a local hero. The myth grew bigger than young Cannon could live up to, but the city hot for a hero ignored any warning signals that Billy was anything less than the all-Baton Rouge role model, proof to a generation that if you studied hard and scored enough touchdowns, you could write your own ticket. Because Billy was a star at Istrouma High, local folks were willing to wink at his 1956 arrest for rolling an LSU professor outside a gay bar downtown. Because Billy was Louisiana's greatest sports hero ever and a successful orthodontist, they laughed off the stories of his gambling losses (word was, when a hot poker game was formed, the gamblers sent a cab for Billy Cannon). Cannon's support was even eagerly sought by candidates despite his helping convicted Teamster boss Ed Partin to organize the city's garbage workers. To his credit, Cannon never tried to hide or smooth over his rough edges—his public did that for him. Cannon's arrest in July came just months before he was to be inducted into the College Football Hall of Fame and on the eve of the 25th anniversary of that championship season. By now, Baton Rougeans had seen enough mediocrity pass through Tiger Stadium to begin finding meaning in other things and to stop taking the athletic feats of 19-year-olds quite so seriously. Waking to a shattered dream and faded myth, most locals took Cannon's fall in stride and with humor. Within days, limited edition fake Billy Cannon $100s were circulating among friends: a photocopied bill with an old football picture of Billy in Ben Franklin's place. Instead of "E Pluribus Unum" it read, "Go to Hell, Ole Miss."

The effects of football mania are still seen in Baton Rouge's political system. Many Tiger football stars found that the name recognition they developed early in life was tailormade for entering politics. Lettering in football became the modern political equivalent of a war record. Former jocks were elected to the Baton Rouge City Council, the school board, the judiciary, finally the mayor's office, occupied now by Pat Screen, formerly LSU's first scrambling quarterback.

Outside of accepting gridiron experience as a qualification for public service, Baton Rougeans had nothing else they could agree on. Baton Rouge grew up not as one community but as three separate and isolated worlds: the newcomer professionals and old families of South Baton Rouge and LSU; the rednecks and union workers of North Baton Rouge and the plants; and the blacks. Since no one trusted the other enough to work together, political control came through playing one group off against the other. By the early '60s, the politically attuned labor unions hooked up with the black leaders to forge an unbeatable coalition. South Baton Rouge, with its fading old families and transient middle management class, couldn't even make a case for electing a Baton Rougean as mayor. Woody Dumas, for 16 years president of the parish council and mayor of the city in the '60s and '70s, commuted to City Hall from his home in Baker, up in Ward Two north of the plants.

While the Chamber of Commerce painted a picture of progress and stability, while football players ran for city council, a new breed of labor-backed politicians were taking over the courthouse and City Hall. The shrewdest and most ambitious among them was a flamboyant, Bible-beating Bakerite named Ossie Brown. His rise to power as district attorney in 1972 after losing a string of elections pointed up the deep divisions and contradictions within a city that didn't know itself very well or the real story behind the people it put in power. With more imagination and pure nerve than shown by anyone before him, Ossie played on those divisions and his own themes of morality and law enforcement to become one of the most powerful politicians in the state. Brown was a colorful, high-powered defense attorney who became a public figure larger than life. Ossie's what you get when you cross a high-sounding Baptist preacher with a fast-talking criminal attorney. He played both parts so well, craved publicity so much, worked so hard to overcome people's suspicions, he seemed to re-create the role of Elmer Gantry in Baton Rouge politics.

The former governor from Pelican Boys State, the drum major from Baker High, the song leader in his Baptist church choir, Ossie started his legal career on a dubious note when he was thrown out of LSU Law School for cheating. After wheedling his way back to get his law degree, Ossie became both a successful defense attorney and a mover in local labor politics. Although he lost in local elections for DA, mayor and congressman, Ossie hustled his way into a bit part in the great national labor drama of the '60s—what to do with Jimmy Hoffa.

After years of pursuit, Robert Kennedy's Justice Department finally put racketeering Teamster leader Jimmy Hoffa in jail on the strength of testimony by Baton Rouge Teamster leader Edward Grady Partin. Hoffa's only chance to get out rested on getting Partin to recant his testimony. In his book *The Rise and Fall of Jimmy Hoffa*, Walter Sheridan, a former investigator for the Justice Department, said that Ossie Brown injected himself into a bizarre scheme to get Mafia boss Carlos Marcello to put up $150,000 to persuade Partin and others to testify that the Justice Department used illegal means to get evidence on Hoffa. Sheridan writes that Ossie had to fight off other aspiring bagmen to be the sole negotiator among all parties involved. Ossie claims to have never read the book, though it contains a long, fascinating passage in which Brown, apparently surreptitiously taped by Partin, tells the Teamster leader of a conversation he and Carlos Marcello had on the problems of getting that much cash in a hurry:

> "The man [Marcello] said they're watching every move he does and if he goes and draws anything out of his bank—he said they're checking him like a hawk. . . . He said, 'What I'm willing to do is this, and if they don't trust me this much, hell, there's no point in doing anything.' He said, 'I'll give you, talking to me, my note on demand for the one hundred and fifty. . . . ' He said, 'That can be attorney's fees.' He said, 'If they can't trust me, there's nothing I can do.' He said, 'What more would they want? I'm not going to lie. I've never reneged on a deal yet. But,' he said, 'I can't do more than that.' He said, 'I'm trying to stay out of this thing. We'll all be in the penitentiary.'"

The payoff fell through, so nothing ever came of the tape recording, but even more strangely, no one even took notice in Baton Rouge when the book was published in 1974. Ossie didn't even have to deny it. The town just wasn't paying attention.

Ossie cut quite a figure in courtrooms and union halls, but Ossie knew the real action was as a public servant. But his entree to power was blocked by his inability to get the black vote. They were one group of Baton Rougeans paying attention to Ossie Brown—they were scared of him. He had already announced his adherence to the ideals of segregation and he didn't help his ethnic gap problem by successfully representing a Klansman accused of murdering Washington Parish's first black sheriff's deputy. After his Klansman trial he doubted he'd ever run for office again. "I could never receive the colored vote, and I couldn't change my feelings to get their vote." Whether or not he changed his feelings, he turned his "colored vote" problem around with his most celebrated legal victory ever—the defense of Sergeant David Mitchell, the first American serviceman tried in the My Lai massacre. When a military panel acquitted the St. Francisville soldier in 1971, Ossie basked in national attention and received absolution in local black churches. Ossie called in his black and redneck coalition chips in the 1972 race against respected and popular South Baton Rouge attorney Frank Foil. Foil had all the good government vibes Bennett Johnston had going for him in the close governor's race the year before. Plus something extra. Foil's campaign got hold of a tape recording of a virulently racist speech Ossie made in Bogalusa while running for Congress in 1968. The tape caused such a reaction in the black churches where it was played, the Foil campaign prepared a radio commercial using the tape to air on the city's black station, WXOK. But Brown got wind of the spot, called black leader Joe Delpit who called Edwin Edwards who called the station owner, his good friend State Senator Mike O'Keefe, and had the spot killed. On the strength of an overwhelming black vote, Brown won the election by less than one percent.

Not unlike other dedicated public servants, Ossie Brown thought his election was a mandate to put his face and name before the public as often as possible. But Ossie was so much better at it, giving freely of his time and energy for charitable causes, especially if there was TV coverage. Ossie became the star of the annual Jerry Lewis MD telethon and a regular pitchman during the "I Care" drug awareness week. He saw his role as not merely the public prosecutor but at the same time the

189

defender of public decency. In fact, it was hard to tell where Ossie Brown Crimefighter left off and Ossie Brown Arbiter of Taste and Morals began. In his second term, after tiring of busting adult bookstores, he escalated his personal war against smut by blocking Monty Python's *The Life of Brian* from playing in Baton Rouge because it was "sacrilegious." His Moral Majority constituency cheered even louder when he pushed through an ordinance outlawing the local sale of roach clips and hash pipes. Ossie even combatted godless communism by smuggling Bibles into the Soviet Union on a tour. But when he went so far as to propose outlawing the sale of cold beer in convenience stores, he backed down when his black and labor supporters raised hell.

Back on the crime front, Ossie Brown compiled an impressive record as DA, notching a conviction rate among the highest in the country, an achievement which helped him be elected president of the National District Attorneys Association. What his sterling record did not show was the high number of cases nol-prossed, reduced or lost between the cracks. It was revealed late in his second term that the state police were sending major narcotics cases to the feds instead of working with Brown's office. One drug agent said that for 10 years Baton Rouge had practically been a "drug dealers' free zone."

Ossie seemed especially incapable of bringing corruption charges against politicians while across town the U.S. attorney was shooting them like fish in a barrel. Before the feds indicted and convicted Gil Dozier of racketeering, Brown presented his investigation to the parish grand jury, which gave the agriculture commissioner a clean bill of health. Shortly thereafter, Dozier's department rented the first floor of a vacant office building owned by Ossie.

Whenever the record of Ossie Brown Crimefighter was criticized, Ossie Brown Public Crusader took over, launching a new moral offensive, be it against roach clips, smut or cold beer, that diverted media coverage and rallied his true believers to the cause. And there was always a new charity telethon around the corner or some grisly crime scene at which he could be televised directing the investigation. Not everyone bought it: a growing number of Baton Rougeans doubted his integrity and resented his moralizing, but his true believers were vocal, his black vote sewn up, his own mouth always in gear and every other attorney in town too intimidated to take him on.

An aggressive and clever district attorney—with his power to investigate or not to investigate, to seek indictments or not to seek indictments—can obstruct justice while making a public show of serving it. Some law enforcement officials believe Ossie Brown did exactly that in the officially unsolved murder of Jim Leslie. When the Shreveport adman was gunned down in the parking lot of the Prince Murat Hotel, it touched off one of the hottest murder investigations ever in the parish with the sheriff's office, the city police and the district attorney actually competing to crack the case first. Or were they? A conspiracy theory quickly developed around Shreveport Public Safety Commissioner George D'Artois, suspected of ordering the killing because Leslie had testified against D'Artois in a public funds scandal in Shreveport. Earlier in his career, Ossie Brown had represented D'Artois, whose own stern law enforcement image covered his involvement with members of the Dixie Mafia. The late Sheriff Al Amiss repeatedly complained that the city police chief and the district attorney were interfering in his investigation. When Amiss got a warrant to arrest a key figure in the plot, Ossie Brown, according to an eyewitness public official, called the suspect at a North Baton Rouge bar to warn him to hide from the sheriff and to call Ossie in the morning. The suspect thanked Ossie for the tip but said the sheriff had just walked in the front door. Amiss claimed to have solved the crime when he went to Shreveport and arrested D'Artois, but back in Baton Rouge, Ossie torpedoed the case by refusing to grant immunity to two key witnesses who could have testified against D'Artois. Brown defended his actions, saying he thought the two witnesses had more to do with the killing than they were telling. D'Artois went free and died of a heart attack within a year. The case was never solved.

When U.S. Attorney Don Beckner reopened the case three years later, he found Ossie Brown at it again, this time intimidating a key federal witness by threatening to indict him in state court. Beckner had to warn Ossie he'd be indicted for obstruction of justice if he didn't stay out of the case. The feds eventually convicted two of the conspirators on a related charge, an unsatisfactory conclusion to one of Baton Rouge's most haunting murder mysteries.

Stories were written. Suspicions were raised. But somehow the questions of Ossie Brown's bungled investigations did not generate as

much publicity as when Ossie shaved his head on a dare to raise a
$34,000 contribution for the Muscular Dystrophy telethon. Politically
Ossie was still top dog in this parish. His tight connection with black
leaders continued to ensure his assistant DAs' elections to vacant
judgeships. Mayor Pat Screen, though a Southsider, was an old law
partner of Ossie's. Ossie's former top assistant David Bourland was now
Screen's top assistant. Edwin Edwards, his old campaign manager from
Pelican Boys State 40 years ago, looked like a good bet to return to the
Mansion. Sheriff Al Amiss was dying, and Ossie was sure to have a hand
in electing his successor. His old nemesis Don Beckner was back in
private practice and the new U.S. attorney Stan Bardwell, though a
Republican, promised a new era of harmony and cooperation with the
district attorney.

By early 1983, Ossie Brown appeared to be coasting not only to
reelection in 1984 but to preeminence in parish politics. Now if he could
just crush that little toad Mike Cannon.

Though no relation to Billy, Mike Cannon represents the flip side of
the Baton Rouge myth. If Billy Cannon stood for everything Baton
Rouge wanted to be, Mike Cannon represents everything it fears it is.
Everyone went to school with a guy like Mike Cannon: far from the
football hero, he was the pudgy but scrappy and hustling waterboy who
sold contraband cigarettes to the players on the side. He was the guy in
the back of the class who made funny faces and imitated Curly and felt
accepted when others laughed at him. Mike could have never made it in
politics in his hometown of Covington, an old-line, blue blood resort
enclave dominated by rich expatriates from New Orleans. More Mike's
style was Baton Rouge, a scrappy town on the make where money and
hustle meant more than pedigree. Fresh out of law school he played his
angles, published the daily legal news, then a real estate listings service,
then a shopper. He broke into politics in 1975 with a bruising campaign
for clerk of court in which he lacerated both his opponent and his
opponent's father, the outgoing clerk, with a deadly indignation and
humor. He may have been unknown and overweight but he knew how
to campaign, tirelessly plugging away, putting up his own yard signs,
knocking on every door he could reach. His capacity for shameless
self-promotion knew no bounds. Through the teeming crowds outside
LSU football games he walked, holding high his yard sign for all to see.

There was no level he would not grovel to for a vote. And classless Baton Rouge loved it, they loved anyone who thought so little of his own pride that he would lie prostrate asking for their vote. And he got it, beating the favorite with a strong showing all over the city: white collar, redneck and black. The last was the most surprising because the black leaders had uniformly backed his opponent. What was first an embarrassment to black leaders turned into a threat when Cannon began hiring—without their advice and consent—more blacks in City Hall than had ever worked there before. The little hustler's success did not go unnoticed in the upper echelon of parish politics. The courthouse was only big enough for one gang—and Mike Cannon didn't belong.

Mike was busy building his own gang in his office, setting up an intricate system of pay raises and promotions based on willingness to work for and contribute to his next campaign. Cannon's mistake was in doing too efficient an organizing job, as it caught the attention of a district attorney in bad need of a good public corruption case to silence his own critics. Ossie sought indictments against Cannon and convicted him of public salary extortion in time for the 1979 elections. He seemed like a sure goner then, a convicted incumbent lucky not to be in jail. Ossie Brown had wounded Mike Cannon, and the black bosses were determined to finish him off. But come election time, Cannon, besides hustle, humor and craftiness, exhibited a magnificent sense of self-pity, breaking up and crying on TV. He went out and put up his own yard signs again, he knocked on more doors, he hired more blacks. And he prevailed. His stunned and frustrated opponent Jimmy Kilshaw gave up on elective politics. "If I can't beat a convicted criminal, I can't beat anyone."

Cannon smiled in response. "I think he's exactly correct."

Baton Rouge reelected Mike Cannon but it was no longer happy with him. Right or wrong he was always in a fight with someone: with Ossie Brown over court records and with Mayor Pat Screen over access to the executive elevators in the Governmental Building. Lawyers continued to complain bitterly about Cannon's high fees and the inefficiencies of his turnover-heavy office. The staid *Morning Advocate* reacted in horror when Cannon and a carload of employees took a long, meandering trip up the Eastern seaboard for a clerks' convention. And all Baton Rouge clucked over the messy divorce fight and property settlement battle that

193

degenerated into a fistfight between Mike and his estranged wife's partner. And the black leaders were getting hungrier for Cannon's minority patronage.

You can get away with murder in Baton Rouge but don't flaunt your penny-ante corruption. The question of Mike Cannon was becoming less a political issue than a matter of taste. The scrappy hustler the city at first so admired had now become an embarrassment. At last the courthouse gang and the country club set had something they could agree on: Mike Cannon had to go.

Early in 1983, an odds-on surefire candidate acceptable to all three elements of Baton Rouge politics began raising money. Sandra Thompson was determinedly beginning her comeback from one of the strangest near misses in Louisiana politics. Perhaps no one else in state politics had risen so fast, come so close and fallen so flat as this engaging woman whom everyone loved to talk about.

It was apparent from the day the young mother started work in the secretarial pool that Sandra Thompson was not long for her clerk-typist civil service designation. A beautiful woman with delicate porcelain skin, exquisite features, ladylike bearing and tenacious ambition, she soon caught the eye of Secretary of State Wade Martin and was within months his executive secretary. Martin placed great confidence in Sandra, an extremely self-assured woman who took easily to dominating office politics. A secretary interviewing for a job in Martin's office was struck by the way Martin repeatedly interrupted the interview to take calls from Sandra, soliciting her opinions and deferring to her judgment in running his office. Her career advanced even more rapidly after she met Edwin Edwards, who stunned insiders by naming her to the cabinet as secretary of the Department of Culture, Recreation and Tourism. Her rise to power did not go unnoticed among the veteran state work force. Sandra made legions of enemies among women in government because of her ability to charm and impress powerful men into giving her the kind of opportunities no woman had gotten so quickly with so few apparent qualifications. Many chose to believe the widespread rumor that it was more than charm that attracted the secretary of state and the governor. Women in the governor's office particularly resented Sandra's rapid rise. Which is interesting when you consider that however Sandra Thompson succeeded in government, it was not any worse than the plotting and scheming of hundreds of ambitious young men who scratched, clawed and stabbed their way up the ladder of success. But a woman's ambitions and manipulations were somehow more offensive and threatening.

Sandra succeeded in the bureaucratic jungle by gaining the attention of powerful men but she failed because of her inability to work with those around her. She had impressed the governor with her ambition but eventually turned him off with her tenacity. "When he wouldn't return her calls, she'd come sit in the outer office," said one aide. The top administrators in her department couldn't stand her and bitterly complained to the governor. To keep peace in his own inner circle, Edwards fired her. "We objected to Sandra so much because she was so unqualified," an Edwards aide remembers. For those who chose to believe the rumors, it was more than that. She was, in their eyes, the girl who got too much.

But power moves weren't enough to stop Sandra Thompson—she bounced back to run for secretary of state in 1979. And she was an instant hit, *the* bright new face on the state scene, with money, charisma, powerful supporters, yes, but also enemies—the most prominent of whom was her former boss's wife, Elaine Edwards. Elaine Edwards did not like Sandra Thompson. Either she believed the rumors or like some of her women friends in government she resented a seemingly unqualified and strikingly attractive woman going so far in a man's world—in *her* man's world. After Thompson led the field, almost winning in the primary, Elaine Edwards publicly endorsed Thompson's runoff opponent Jim Brown, saying he was far, far more qualified than "the other candidate." Louisianians gasped at the announcement. It was not just a political statement, but an intensely personal one, an apparent admission that if no one else believed the rumors about Sandra Thompson and Edwin Edwards, Elaine Edwards did—and she was going to do something about it. Baton Rougeans treated the endorsement as a joke, another chapter in the trashy soap opera they had witnessed for eight years. Some who heard it expressed sympathy for Sandra—it probably would have helped more than hurt had Sandra not found a way to blow it on her own.

Sandra Thompson looked like a shoo-in for the highest office a woman had achieved in state government. She was far ahead of runner-up Jim Brown and she had strong business support to fund her runoff. Then she shocked everyone by endorsing Louis Lambert for governor over Dave Treen. Somehow a desperate Lambert half-sweet-talked, half-scared her into it, warning that if she didn't endorse him, he would see to it her name would not be on one major black ballot in the state. Sandra should have known better, but she fell for Lambert's threat. Her endorsement of Lambert was the shocker of the 1979 race and an obvious, irreparable blunder. Her big business backers like Ed Steimel of LABI dumped her overnight, pumping a lot of money into Jim Brown's campaign, which used it to produce some devastatingly effective ads— one featured a Barbie doll (Sandra), moving mechanically to the music. The public got the point and dropped Sandra.

You have to give the young woman who started off as a secretary her due. She came awfully close to the catbird seat in Louisiana politics. Using the high-profile, low policy secretary of state's post, she could have been a formidable challenger to embattled Lieutenant Governor Bobby Freeman in 1983. From there, it's just a matter of time for the young and the patient. Sooner or later in this state, you figure a governor has to die or go to jail. But instead of challenging Bobby Freeman in 1983, Sandra is sizing up Mike Cannon. For one who had come so close to going so high, running against Mike Cannon for clerk of court was slumming of the rankest sort. Actually it was a clever move, for to win the parishwide race and to control that patronage would position her nicely to run for mayor of Baton Rouge after Pat Screen finishes an expected second term in 1988. She only had to knock off Mike Cannon. And how could that be a problem? His bad press got worse by the day. The big law firms were shoving money at her. All the major black leaders were in her corner. Junior Leaguers were calling to donate their time. Early polls showed her ahead of Cannon 4-1, the courthouse wisdom was she was a lock.

With other candidates jumping in the race as though he was dead, Mike tried to keep a positive light on his bleak political prospects. On visiting one lawyer's office, Cannon downplayed the possibility one of his own top employees, Mary James, would also enter the fray. "I don't think Mary's gonna make the race, she's awfully sick, you know," noted Mike in the tone of a funeral director observing how lifelike the beloved looks. "And her husband's in bad health too. You know, I told them they should take some time and take a trip, you know, before neither one of them can get out of bed." That's Mike, a cheery word for everyone.

His own staff's morale was a problem—they had to wonder how tight their job security was. His office/campaign workers, canvassing door to door, flinched as doors slammed in their faces. One old lady angrily chased Cannon's campaign manager down the street. In a rare display of shared community expression, Baton Rouge was saying it no longer wanted to be embarrassed by Mike Cannon.

As far as his politics went, Ossie Brown had no cares at the start of 1983. His major enemy was on the ropes, without Ossie having to do any punching. Getting rid of Cannon would return order to black patronage and friendly cooperation to the courthouse, the peace and control on all fronts Ossie most desired for his own reelection campaign in 1984.

But all was not so rosy in Ossie Brown's life or in his political world—and as 1983 wore on, both began to unravel. Like Watergate, Ossie's problems started because a cop screwed up and did his job. In August 1982, two policemen patrolling near the LSU campus spotted the brake lights lit on a car parked in an alley behind a bar. Closer inspection revealed two men holding a suspicious-looking white powder. The police arrested Dr. Kraemer Diel, LSU's team dentist, and Glenn D'Spain, son of a multi-millionaire businessman. The car—and, as an investigation later showed, the cocaine—belonged to high-living local oil heir Claude Pennington.

Had justice taken its course, charges could have been filed based on the arrest. But Ossie Brown had his own course in mind. He sent the case to the grand jury, which heard the testimony of Glenn D'Spain but not the arresting officer and eight months later decided not to indict either subject. Sure, some eyebrows were raised in town but it wasn't the first time the child of a prominent citizen appeared to receive special justice. But this was also not to be the first time the U.S. attorney would step in to do the job the district attorney didn't. Stan Bardwell announced he was entering the case. Then everything started to fall apart. Two days later, Pat Screen's top aide David Bourland revealed that an ice cream company owned by himself and Ossie Brown received a $134,000 loan from Glenn D'Spain's father, Jim, the day after the grand jury decided not to indict. Though Bourland said he had signed Brown's name on the loan papers and that the district attorney had instructed him to call off the deal after D'Spain was arrested, the investigation and public attention focused on Ossie Brown.

Baton Rouge could smell a major scandal. Diel and D'Spain were indicted by the federal grand jury in two hours using the same evidence available to the district attorney. Fascinating facts tumbled forth. Claude Pennington, who owned the car and the cocaine involved in the arrest, also had recently invested in Brown's and Bourland's company. Pennington had already been the source of many rumors about drug use and his friendship with Mayor Pat Screen. The investigation began to focus on the question: were Brown and Bourland looking for potential investors on the police blotter? Brown first became interested in the high-spirited D'Spain boy after his arrest in early 1982 for streaking through a sorority house. Shortly after that, Brown and Bourland approached D'Spain's father on buying their troubled ice cream business, which was failing fast and bleeding Brown and Bourland.

As the summer and the investigation wore on, Baton Rouge reveled in the rumors as TV cameras filmed Ossie, both D'Spains, Diel and Pennington coming and going at the federal courthouse.

Ossie's friends didn't exactly leap to his defense. Yet the politicians found it hard to believe that as clever an operator as Ossie Brown would be caught in such a transparent bribe. Edwin Edwards, killing time riding around Houma before a banquet, repeated the politicians' party line. "It's so blatant what Bourland did, I can't believe Ossie knew about it. There's probably an explanation. I just don't think Ossie would do that." After more thought, however, the former governor concedes, "Well, Ossie is a liar. I love him like a brother and I would say the same thing if he were standing here, but he will climb a tree to tell a lie rather than stand on the ground and tell the truth."

Edwards doesn't like to see any public figures getting in trouble—bad precedent. But the summer ordeals of Billy Cannon and Ossie Brown have provided unexpected benefits. Both stories have dominated the front pages and TV news in Baton Rouge since mid-July, relegating DCCL and the governor's race to the status of merely a curious sideshow.

U.S. Attorney John Volz

Louis Charbonnet

Hank Braden

Don Hubbard

Sherman Copelin

Bob d'Hemecourt

Mayor Dutch Morial

Bud Rippoll

Dan Richey

Mayor Tilly Snyder

Ned Randolph

Photos by Natchitoches *Times*

Will the real man please stand up: Natchitoches Sheriff Norm Fletcher (above) and challengers Clarence Noel (top right), Bill Dowden (middle), and Herman Birdwell (below).

Sam Thomas

Gus Mijalis

George Fischer

Joan Duffy

U.S. Attorney Stan Bardwell

Jules LeBlanc at Corporate Square at peak of his financial empire.

Edwin and Marion Edwards embrace at airport near Crowley following the murder of their brother Nolan.

16. The Power of Forgiveness

These are the dog days of August, the uncomfortable peak of a sweltering, humid summer, the hottest in years. The worst part of early August is knowing you still have an unbearably long way to go, a good two months before there are three straight days of crisp autumn weather.

These are the dog days of the Edwards campaign. By this week when Dave Treen officially starts his campaign, the challenger has been in the field two solid years, on the road every day, exhorting, attacking, pushing: pushing his staff, pushing himself, pushing his luck. And it's not working. In fact, he's losing ground. A Joe Walker poll released this week shows Edwards' lead dramatically slipping from a heady 20 point margin in May to 11 points in the first week of August. For the first time, Treen has moved ahead of Edwards among white voters polled.

Edwards is caught in the ebb tide of DCCL and Treen's integrity offensive. There's not much he can do about it, except to ride the flow, but he's fighting it anyway. He's tired and bitter and showing it as he daily mocks Dave Treen's integrity, lashes out at the press and browbeats supporters who nervously hint their concern.

It's not lost on the press. Jack Wardlaw writes in his "Little Man" column in the *Picayune* that Edwards "has lost some of his bounce. He's not his usual good-humored self, even facing friendly audiences. Is he just tired from a strenuous campaign, or is something going wrong?"

"Yeah, I read that," says Edwards in the front seat as Darrell Hunt at the wheel merges onto I-10 heading for New Orleans. "I get it from both sides: you're being too aggressive, you're not aggressive enough, you're too cocky, you're not cocky enough. And all that just goes in one ear and out the other. When I meet the person who has won as many elections as I have, I'll sit down and listen to him."

Edwards was badly shaken by the death of Gene Jones, his constant companion and guardian since 1972 when Jones, then a state trooper, was assigned to the new governor. Gene retired when Edwards left office and was ever at the candidate's side in public. "Gene was my Jonathan," says Edwards in the way that Marion at the funeral eulogized Gene as the biblical warrior who devoted his life to protecting David.

Edwards silently stares out the window as Hunt cruises in the passing lane. He leans forward to turn up the radio, but freezes as the car just ahead in the right lane blows a tire and swerves wildly to the left, with rubber peeling off the back wheel and the hubcap flying off to hit the Olds. Darrell cuts to the right to barely avoid ramming the car as it skids into the grassy median.

"Is he okay?" Edwards twists around to see the other driver getting out of his car unharmed. Yet another close call. Two days before, Edwards at the controls of his plane heading for Shreveport had to quickly dive to avoid a midair collision with another plane. These are hairy days.

Edwards is in the St. Bernard Civic Center only 30 minutes, costarring in a bridal show with white-tuxedoed Eddie Bopp. He quickly changes before leaving and is on his way back toward the expressway ramp and Metairie with a deputy sheriff, his siren blaring and beacon flashing, clearing the road ahead. "I told the sonofabitch not to use his damn siren." Edwards turns up the radio, ever tuned to a country western station, at just the right time. "Listen to this, this is my song":

> *You look like someone I once knew,*
> *But I don't remember loving you.*

The song ends and with it Edwards' brief light mood. Back to lying Dave Treen and his lackey press.

"I know that Paul Hardy was promised his cabinet job to endorse Dave Treen in 1979. I know someone who sat at the table with Hardy. Now it doesn't bother me that they made a deal, even if it is against the law. What bothers me is the press lets him get away with it. The fucking *Times-Picayune* saying it was all wonderful how they all backed Treen. I could prove it was a deal if someone wanted to put up $30,000 or $40,000. Otherwise, it's not worth my while."

"You criticize Treen for not fulfilling promises. Is that lying?"

"It's dishonest. He's dishonest in that he represents he's going to do things that he doesn't do. He makes a commitment and won't fulfill it and then he won't even talk to that person to explain. When I make a commitment I can't fulfill, I give the money back. The press hears about his broken commitments and they say it's just politics, but they don't say that with me. It's because the news profession doesn't view him as a threat."

"And they do you?"

"Oh yeah."

Edwards is opening his East Jefferson campaign headquarters in Metairie, not far from Dave Treen's suburban home. The headquarters consists of a mobile home on a vacant lot at the entrance to Whitney Estates. The Republican legislator for the area, Charlie Lancaster, laughs at the choice of location. "I love it. They're blocking the traffic in the neighborhood and getting everybody mad. He won't get a vote in Whitney Estates." Maybe that's the point. Edwards' East Jeff organizer George Fischer knows their votes will come from working class Kenner or Harahan instead of silk stocking Metairie where they've placed the headquarters. So who cares if the neighbors in Whitney Estates are inconvenienced. They'll vote for Dave Treen anyway. As far as George Fischer's concerned, they can shove it.

Warming up the crowd is radio personality Keith Rush, telling the folks that when callers to his show complain about an acute traffic or flooding problem, the DJ only has to call the Mansion. "And every time, if he didn't get on the phone right away, I get a call back within the hour, and he always says the same thing. 'Keith, are you looking for me?' This time, ladies and gentlemen, Edwin Edwards is looking for us, and here he is . . . "

Edwards bounds onstage to the cheers of 400 and delivers a localized attack on the hometown boy. "Dave Treen won four years ago because this parish gave him a 40,000 vote lead. Is that going to happen again?"

"No!" roars back the crowd.

"Anyone here have drainage problems?"

"Yeah!"

"Well, Dave Treen doesn't know about it. He vetoed a $29 million appropriation to help you get out of the water and mud. You remembered him, but he forgot you. He said he was going to get you jobs. Did anyone here get one?"

"I lost mine," yells the middle-aged woman in the front row.

"He's been governor three and a half years and he hasn't made a decision yet. What can you do with a guy who takes an hour and a half to watch *60 Minutes*?"

"Fire him!"

"And you saw what happened on TV when I challenged him to get out the race if he couldn't prove I had done anything wrong. He turned red. It was the first time in my life I've seen any color in his face."

The crowd is so excited they press on him as he leaves the stage, trying to shake his hand, get his autograph, have a word. The crowd reaction catches the Jefferson Parish sheriff's deputies by surprise—they nervously and quickly move into the crowd to get a close look at everyone who gets near the candidate. Edwards' own people are used to his effect on crowds, but the bad omens of the past week are keeping them on their toes as well.

One of Edwards' three young assistants—Darrell Hunt, Stan Cadow and Sid Moreland—is ever at his side in a crowd, not so much to protect as to keep Edwards in pins or cards or to get someone's name and number to follow up on a request. The three are so attuned to the boss's needs and wants that barely a word is passed among them. He holds out a hand and two "EWE 83" pins are placed in it; he motions with his finger and an assistant is there with a notepad to write down some supporter's information as Edwards moves on to shake the next hand.

Darrell Hunt signed on early in the campaign, returning home from a solar energy business venture in Arizona. The son of a high-powered attorney and lobbyist E.C. Hunt of Lake Charles and the nephew of the late, pioneering Corrections Secretary Elayn Hunt, Darrell may be born to politics but is hardly caught up in it. Through 18 months' solid campaigning the Amherst graduate has not lost touch with the world of the mind, excitedly asking me once, down in some place like Chackbay or Chauvin, "Have you read the latest Doris Lessing book yet?" Or when the boss is shamelessly pulling heartstrings before an audience that doesn't know better, Hunt catches my eye and wipes a fake tear from his cheek.

Stan Cadow is fresh out of college but an old hand at politics, having parlayed his political machine at SLU into a national office with the Association of Student Governments. Cadow started this campaign hating long drives but he soon overcame that as he shatters land speed records racing from one end of I-10 to the other to meet Edwards' plane. Stanley has also developed into the junior Lothario of this campaign. "You see that girl that popped out of the cake at the party? Yeah, well, she knocked on my door at two in the morning."

Sid Moreland, one of the few North Louisiana aides on Edwards' staff, is, like the others, personable and well-dressed, but does a far better job of blending into the background—a quality that will serve him well by campaign's end.

Darrell, Stan and Sid have all learned something about crowd control in this job. How does one part the seas of humanity for the candidate to walk through without offending the faithful? No problem for Stan, who, with the command voice of a state trooper, can make a hole faster than can the Root Hogs. Darrell employs more finesse. "I don't raise my voice, I just say in a normal tone, 'I'm going to vomit, I'm going to vomit' and people move right out the way."

Yet none of these men can fill Gene Jones' shoes, or his holster. Before Edwards even decided what he would do for a bodyguard-driver, Wayne Ray made up his mind for him. The Monroe native and Westbank businessman was an old friend of Gene's, had even worked out patterns the two would run should anyone threaten Edwards. Two days after Gene's funeral, Wayne says, he walked into Edwards' office and announced, "I know I'm totally out of line, but I'm not taking no for an answer. You need me, so I'm staying and you just as soon get used to it." Edwards, said Wayne, didn't want to fight. "Saddle up," said the candidate.

Edwards crisscrosses the city expressways three times today without touching down once in New Orleans. The day ends at a fund raiser at Maurice's Restaurant in Gretna hosted by architect Sergio Slammacelli. The party is remarkable for its lavish spread, every bit as exotic and excessive as the Hilton mermaid spectacular, and for the range of guests, from SOUL leader Sherman Copelin to Mayor Leo Kerner of Lafitte, where, says the mayor, "You don't pay a ticket unless you want to or taxes unless you have to." Apparently the old pirate's spirit still lives down in Barataria.

Edwards goes off in a booth with Copelin—it's getting near that delicate time to agree on all the expenses the Edwards campaign will bear for SOUL's support.

Not far away, sampling the crab claws, a Westbank lawyer doesn't share the enthusiasm of his fellow partygoers. "I guess things are going all right, but I get these bad feelings. Blacks are strong, labor's strong, but I don't see any effort to talk to the white middle class, white collar voters. There's been a lot more of them who moved here since he ran last." His voice trails off as he sizes up the stuffed mushrooms. "Things like this are okay, they raise money, but it's always the same crowd—he hasn't got around to many other people over here. Plus, I'm waiting to see what happens with the pardons issue, but I tell you right now I don't feel good about it."

Fog at the airport has set the Treen campaign back to its usual 30 minutes behind schedule, a consistency that is lost on the Ruston Peach Parade participants standing in the muggy morning air waiting for the governor to arrive and to get the show on the road. The Mindenettes are ready to strut and march with the Minden High Band backing them up, the Homemaker float ("Learn and Lead") is next to a contingent of El Karubah potentates, wearing fezzes and revving their Harleys, as a squadron of jets from Barksdale Air Force Base zooms over and the Peach Queen, in her snug and sequined purple gown, is poured into the back seat of a sky blue Rolls Royce. The Peach Parade is raring to go, but the grand marshal has paused beside a truck plastered with Edwards signs. "I thought this was supposed to be a nonpolitical parade," frowns Treen, who expressly asks that the Treen bumperstickers be taken off the car in which he will be riding. Correction: Dave Treen doesn't ride in parades. No candidate for governor does anymore. Ever since that fool Jimmy Carter walked up Pennsylvania Avenue, no self-respecting politician can claim to be a man of the people unless he hoofs it for the entire parade route. Here's Dave Treen loping down South Trenton Street, darting from one side of the street to the other, shaking hands, patting kids' heads, calling out, "Hi, friends." Much of Ruston is on the sidewalks and responding warmly, clapping, cheering him on. Oh, a discordant note or two: "What you mean my friend?" mutters a state worker after the governor passes. "Edwin Edwards is my friend." Or:

"We've been waiting for you," the mother of a Mindenette smilingly scolds the featured attraction.

Dave Treen is stealing away from the office for a rare full day's campaigning. His staff loves to see him out like this, for he is very good with this kind of crowd. No, he doesn't electrify an audience like Edwin Edwards does or even attract the crush of a crowd that Edwards does at a parish fair. Treen sort of blends in. Here he is on the sidewalk outside the Ruston Civic Center, shaking hands with the ladies in the booths, while others walk past him without even noticing. Somehow it's harder not to notice Edwin Edwards. Treen works a crowd differently, in that he really works it, shaking hands with everyone he has eye contact with, which can make getting the governor to the car and to the next stop on time an advance man's endless nightmare. Edwards can glide down a sidewalk with nods and waves or shake hands through a crowd and there's barely a holdup. Not Treen. He's accepting the gift of an alligator pencil holder while nervous aides hold up traffic at the street crossing.

"Governor, they're holding up the traffic for you."

"Well, they shouldn't do that."

So he hasn't all the right moves down. Many Louisianians appreciate the fact that he is not as glib and smooth as Edwin Edwards. Treen, though he can be as wooden as his name implies when addressing a group, is very friendly and animated one on one. His aides contend that he may not attract crowds to his appearances the way Edwards does, but then the middle class voter is less apt to be lured out by free hotdogs and beer to hear some politician talk. The Treen voter can be resolutely detached, like the lady at the crafts fair who purposefully goes around the governor, who is shaking hands at the door. Not a snub, she says. "I'm already going to vote for him, I don't need to talk to him."

Supporting Dave Treen can be as much a matter of taste as philosophy. At a luncheon hosted by the leading citizens of Lincoln Parish, the daughter of an influential Republican is laughing at one of Edwards' leading local supporters, George Cook, who owns a pawnshop downtown. "You should see it, it has Edwards stickers all over it. We just think it's great, I mean it's so-o-o tacky."

And if only more voters were as serious as young Karl Ulmer, who sees no gray areas in the choice before the voters. "When you go in the voting booth, you know there are only two ways to vote, right or wrong."

Most of the luncheon guests are solidly behind Treen and are confident he'll carry Lincoln Parish as he did in 1979 and most of North Louisiana as he didn't. That was the shocker and residual mystery of Treen's triumphant election night, how North Louisiana conservatives, who would exhibit no trouble voting for Ronald Reagan in 1980, went in droves to Louis Lambert. And if they did it for Lambert . . .

The luncheon guests hope that folks have grown to know and trust Dave Treen, even if he is a Republican. "Why Lambert?" conservative businessman Jack Ritchie repeats the question. "I just don't know the answer to that, though I've asked it many times. You hear people say 'I'm a Democrat,' well, I am too, but I'm also a man."

This time around they feel that Treen has a fighting chance in the rural Bible Belt because now he has a four-year record that can stack up well against Edwin Edwards', especially on the all-important honesty and integrity count. And they're excited to see their candidate ready for battle. "I have never claimed to be more virtuous than anybody," Treen tells the luncheon guests, "but in this campaign I will talk about things that are on the record: like DCCL and my opponent's rip-off retirement. If something in his record needs to be discussed, I will do it."

A short time later the governor is on I-20 on his way to dedicate a park in Arcadia, best known as the site where Bonnie and Clyde were ambushed. Relaxing in the front seat, he takes a few shots of his own at his critics who constantly compare his deliberative style of management to Edwards' faster pace. "Well, what do you want to happen? Do you want to get the job done? Or are you worried about style? If the law gives me a certain number of days to make a decision on a bill, why shouldn't I take that time instead of shooting from the hip? The bottom line is that the job is getting done in a way beneficial to the state of Louisiana. I find it curious that people think Edwards got things done when a lot of the problems were shoved under the rug."

It's taken three years but Dave Treen is growing comfortable with his power, with his politics and with this side of himself he is projecting to the people. It's the image Gus Weill is looking for, Gary Cooper as governor, the strong and resolute silent type who makes no excuses for taking his time but nothing else in dispatching his solemnly sworn duties. This will play in Ruston. Moving from a dead stop, the Treen campaign has slowly picked up steam and now some momentum as it hits the

August campaign kickoff at full stride. The polls are showing some movement, the candidate is showing some life and Edwin Edwards is showing a caustic, negative side of his personality that will lead him into real trouble. What really has the Treen staff brimming with confidence is that their man is ready to take the fight to Edwards with his strongest weapon still in the holster.

The pardon power is the power of kings, the last of the great life-or-death choices still bestowed upon executives in a democracy. Next to granting clemency to a condemned convict, the pardon power is the most impressive of the Louisiana governor's grand arsenal of prerogatives. Hiring and firing and spending millions pale in significance beside the ability to free a prisoner from jail and return him to society.

Edwin Edwards continued a long tradition of Southern governors in making wide use of the pardon power. John McKeithen once brought a convict band onstage with him to sing his rebuttal at a Gridiron show, and then pardoned all the musicians on the spot. Reporters learned later Big John was just joshing, but it seemed like a perfectly natural gesture for a governor to make. It was traditional, even expected of a Louisiana governor, that he pardon most or all of his Mansion staff of trusties and commute dozens if not hundreds of sentences in his final weeks in office. The public attitude toward pardons began changing in the late '70s, especially after Tennessee Governor Ray Blanton's wholesale abuse of the power led to a scandal and a takeoff on "Chattanooga Choo Choo" called "Pardon Me, Ray."

Conservative, tough-on-crime Dave Treen brought a completely different attitude toward pardons with him to office. The steady stream of signed "gold seals," an average of one every working day during Edwards' last term, slowed to just one a month during Treen's first three years. Outside prison walls, the radical shift in policy was barely noticed, except by the Treen research staff. After two years investigating Edwards' pardon record, the black vinyl binders bulged with every conceivable statistic, broken down by crime, by parish, by law firm, and rich anecdotal summaries of the most egregious cases.

Early on, the Republicans knew that if they could just play it right they had one hell of an issue. Certainly better than the two other outrages on which they're basing their attack on Edwards. Edwards' tailor-made

$40,000-a-year retirement is not causing nearly the indignation John Cade hoped for. To the middle class voter, it's just another victimless crime in Louisiana politics. Who's getting hurt except the poor dumb bastard taxpayer, and since no one pays taxes, that must be someone else. The same for DCCL, the victims of which were a relatively few state employees who did not get as good a return on their tax-sheltered investment as could have been provided. Besides, among middle class taxpayers, there's not much sympathy for state workers to start with. And state employees themselves are less concerned about what Edwards did with DCCL than the 10 percent pay hike Edwards is promising. Plus, the issue is so damn confusing few people know what it stands for—literally or politically. "You don't have to worry about DCCL here," Leonard Chabert tells Edwards as they look down on Thibodaux from the helicopter. "Most people think it's part of Nicholls State."

But the pardons issue is different. Everyone can relate to crime, and most citizens at one time or another get enraged over a story of some guilty bastard getting off on a technicality, or of a parolee going right out and knocking off a 7-Eleven, employees included. It's an excellent emotional issue that can be neatly reduced to a score:

EDWARDS 1,181 TREEN 34

Treen and Cade keep the issue under wraps through the summer as they wait for just the right time to launch their pardons offensive. Meanwhile Scott Welch and the research team sharpen and define the issue. The numbers on pardons look so good the researchers can't get enough of them. Edwards' 1,181 pardonees include 124 murderers, 62 rapists, 199 armed robbers and 222 who committed drug-related crimes. Edwards' actions cut more than 4,000 years off total time served, with an average of one criminal a working day being pardoned during Edwards' last four and a half years in office.

You want case histories? Treen research has people stories, such as that of Henry Soto, with a record of 25 arrests, whose sentence was commuted by the Pardon Board and Edwards to time served, over the vehement objections of New Orleans DA Harry Connick, who called the action "totally irresponsible." Edwards said he did it because Representative Eddie Bopp asked him to. Eddie Bopp asked him to because Henry Soto paid him $2,000.

There was Forrest Hammonds, convicted in the 1973 murder of well-known Baton Rouge druggist Billy Middleton, pardoned by Edwards over the howls of protest of the city's pharmacists. When Edwards left the Mansion he took Hammonds with him to be the groundskeeper at his Highland Road mansion.

There was former Monroe Mayor Jack Howard, convicted of unauthorized use of public property and attempted public contract fraud, pardoned by Edwards in a rush job just in time for Howard to run for mayor again in 1976.

Edwards brushes off the rumors of the planned Treen offensive with characteristic insouciance. The Soto pardon, for instance, was no big deal. "At least it's not as bad as the guy I released up in North Louisiana who went out and murdered somebody." That was Leon Roberson, convicted of manslaughter and pardoned by Edwards as a favor to a legislator.

But there's more. To tie a neat bow on the perfect campaign issue is research revealing that the law firm of the governor's executive counsel, Camille Gravel, represented more clients before the Pardon Board than did any other firm (126) and that the governor's brother Nolan represented 14 prisoners before the board.

For his part, Gravel, one of the top defense attorneys in the state, said he mainly represented his former clients before the Pardon Board. Others who came to him "may have thought I would have more influence with the governor." Gravel said the most he ever received for a pardon was $10,000, a few times $5,000 but usually about $1,000. Actually a prisoner doesn't even need a lawyer to go before the Pardon Board. The main thing going for a pardon applicant is the support of a home legislator and the absence of opposition from the home district attorney. Yet it's easy to figure how word can get out at Angola that the path to freedom starts with hiring the governor's brother or executive counsel.

Edwin Edwards knows the big guns are coming. Treen may want to delay discussing the issue, but Edwards, when asked by reporters, is eager to defend his own record by attacking Dave Treen's. Edwards begins pointing out that Mr. Law and Order has pardoned four murderers, two armed robbers, one heroin dealer and has cut loose one criminal whom Edwards had refused to pardon. But the best number going for Edwards is one Treen doesn't plan to mention: 78. That's how many of the 1,181 criminals pardoned ended up back in jail—a recidivism level of only 6.6 percent.

As the Treen research machine methodically churns out its facts, Edwards, true to form, begins to make up some of his own. In a summer interview he claims that Camille Gravel's firm has represented fewer than 25 prisoners before the Pardon Board.

Wrong. According to Pardon Board records, Gravel's firm represented 126 clients, fives times more than the next most active firm.

In the same interview, Edwards states that before leaving office he signed a bill that would forbid the firm of the executive counsel to represent clients before the Pardon Board.

Wrong again. Edwards had a chance to sign House Bill 1000 by Ron Faucheux in 1979, but he vetoed it instead. Dave Treen signed a similar bill in 1980. When later presented with the discrepancy, Edwards is surprised. "I vetoed it? I thought I signed it. I remember in the back of my mind saying, 'Well, I won't be governor anymore, I don't give a damn one way or the other.'"

Edwards' misstatements—consistently nailed by Treen research and thrown back in his face within 24 hours—are helping neither Edwards' credibility nor his impending pardons problem. But he's in no mood to back down. He knows Treen is about to break the pardons issue with a media barrage before the end of August. Edwards resolves to fire first, going into the studio to cut a radio spot blasting Treen for an unpardonable pardon. "And why doesn't Dave Treen tell us about Jarrell Frith? After Dave Treen pardoned him, he was convicted of the attempted rape of a six-year-old girl."

Real wrong. Had he checked his facts he would have learned that Jarrell Frith was not pardoned, he was paroled. Not by Dave Treen's Parole Board, but by Edwin Edwards'. Edwards' crack research team took the information from a story in the *Morning Advocate* that reported the wrong date of Frith's release. Edwards has made factual errors during this campaign but none nearly so serious. Instead of defusing Treen's pardon attack, the flagrant error will only attract more attention to a very damaging issue and to his own sinking credibility. Instead of mining the beach for Dave Treen's assault, Edwards' commercial is about to blow up in his face.

As the tapes go out to radio stations Edwards flies into Alexandria for the Tilly Snyder testimonial at the Civic Center. Edwards works the crowd while Tilly, the ever-present cigar anchoring the scowl on his face, paces up and down behind the empty front table, impatiently waiting to get his show started. While Hunt and Cadow work pin and card duty, Sid Moreland finds that someone has leafletted all the cars near the Civic Center with photocopies of spicy passages from Clyde Vidrine's book. Sid pays some kitchen helpers to gather up the leaflets and as he supervises from the sidewalk, a car pulls up and the driver angrily challenges Moreland.

"What do you think you're doing?"

"Who are you, what are you doing?"

Sid approaches the car as the driver fiddles with something on the seat. When a policeman walks out of the Civic Center, the man speeds away. A police car intercepts him a block away. A sawed-off shotgun is found on the front seat and the driver is taken into custody.

Inside, Edwards laughs at the leaflet and shrugs off the incident. He does his bit for Tilly and flies back to New Orleans that night.

The next morning Edwards is eating breakfast with Darrell Hunt in Edwards' Garden District townhouse as commuters on the Pontchartrain Expressway tuning into WWL hear the familiar Cajun voice. "And why doesn't Dave Treen tell us about Jarrell Frith . . . "

Across the state in Crowley, Nolan Edwards has already seen one appointment before 8:30 when his secretary tells Bubba Wingate that Mr. Edwards will see him now. The young man, who has been sitting quietly in the waiting room, walks into the attorney's office, pulls out a .38 caliber pistol and fires twice, striking Edwards, still sitting in his chair, in the left eye and right cheek. Secretaries in the outer office are frozen in shock, looking at the closed door, as Wingate holds the gun under his chin and shoots again. The lawyers and secretaries rush into a scene of carnage, blood everywhere, Wingate lying on the floor, Nolan slumped over in his chair.

The serenity of the tree-lined courthouse square explodes within minutes as policemen race from their station down the brick-laid sidewalk. Nolan's pulse revives slightly with mouth-to-mouth resuscitation, but by the time Acadian Ambulance gets him to American Legion Hospital, the 52-year-old father of three is dead.

As soon as the ambulance is summoned, two other calls are made in seconds, one to Marion at campaign headquarters in Baton Rouge. The other is answered by Edwin Edwards in his breakfast room. He hangs up the phone and looks across the table. "You're not going to believe this but someone just shot my brother." As the two sit motionless, Wayne Ray, across the river, answers the phone to hear a nervous and excited Marion ordering, "You get my brother! You get my brother to Crowley right now!"

In less than an hour, a helicopter from Baton Rouge and a plane from New Orleans land at the same time at the airfield in Crowley. The two brothers meet on the tarmac and embrace. Edwin learns his little brother is dead. Marion steers him away from the reporters waiting nearby and takes him to his house. Marion tells Edwin what he knows of the killing from the partners at the firm, that Rodney Wingate was an ex-con and a former client of Nolan's, one whom Nolan had helped to receive one of the last pardons that Edwards signed before leaving office in 1980. Since then, Wingate had sued Nolan for malpractice in handling a personal injury case.

Later that afternoon, Edwards walks out to meet reporters assembled on Marion's front lawn. He is aware he had signed his brother's murderer's pardon but notes that even without pardon or parole, Wingate would have completed his three-year prison sentence by late 1982. Edwards says Wingate's lawsuit against Nolan may have been a motive, but lawyers in the firm have told him Wingate could have been mad because Nolan, who had been lending Wingate money, had cut him off.

He tells reporters his brother will be buried the next day at Woodlawn Cemetery "next to my father" and then begins to cry.

Reporters combing Crowley that afternoon hear policemen, politicians and lawyers repeat the view that Nolan was an extremely friendly and popular figure in town and it was not unlike him to remain on good terms even with a fellow who was suing him. He ran his law practice the way his brother ran the governor's office, casually, open to everyone, eager to do favors. Nolan Edwards was one person everyone in Crowley could talk to, but specifically he was the top criminal defense attorney in the parish, the man to see if you were in trouble.

Rodney Wingate had consistently been in trouble since 1975 when he was convicted on three counts of drug dealing. He was able to get out of jail on a work release program, but violated his probation on several occasions and was convicted in 1979 of conspiracy to distribute cocaine. With Nolan Edwards as his attorney, Wingate was sentenced to three years at Angola in December 1979 with immediate eligibility for parole. He was in Angola less than a week before being paroled out. In February, 17 days before leaving office, Edwin Edwards signed the gold seal pardon for Rodney Wingate, restoring his rights of citizenship and the right to bear firearms.

Wingate went to work offshore and when he injured his back, he asked Nolan Edwards to represent him in a suit against two oilfield service companies. Wingate later complained Edwards had failed to file the suit before time limitations expired, and sued Edwards for breach of contract. Inexplicably, Nolan lent Wingate money and they continued being friendly while Wingate sued Nolan's insurers. In a deposition in that suit, Edwards would say, "In all fairness, Rodney and I have kind of a peculiar relationship, a little bit closer than lawyer and client." Wingate dropped the suit in late 1981, but refiled it the day after he was sued by the First National Bank of Crowley for a promissory note he had failed to pay.

What was the basis of this "peculiar relationship"? Why would Nolan Edwards lend money to and receive cordially a man who was suing him for malpractice? The only explanation offered was that Nolan didn't hold grudges—any other answers died with the two men.

The next day, downtown Crowley begins to fill up with cars coming in from around the state. The line of mourners at Geesy-Ferguson Funeral Home goes out the door and around the block. It's a toss-up which is hotter, inside or out. Outside is the unrelenting August sun, but also a breeze from the south; inside the overworked air conditioning can't keep up with the mob of visitors pressing in for their last respects: family members, Crowley friends, Baton Rouge friends, legislators, mayors, sheriffs, casual acquaintances and the curious. Down the street two senior citizens peer at the crowd of strangers on the sidewalks while inside the white-tiled Acadia Cafe, Jules LeBlanc sips a cup of coffee before the services start.

213

Edwin and Marion stand all day by the open casket greeting the steady stream of mourners. Memories float through the funeral home, of Crowley and Marksville. Picking cotton together. Getting caught smoking behind the barn. The time the three young brothers were put on the bus in Marksville to ride to Charity Hospital in New Orleans, have all their tonsils removed and return home that night. Nolan moving in with Edwin and Elaine in Crowley while he finished at Southwestern. The three brothers, reunited in Crowley, forming their own tight social circle with their new friends Edmund Reggie and Billy Broadhurst and their wives, playing cards, talking late into the night, making ice cream and watching movies in the tiny home theater Reggie built in his back yard. Nolan administering the oath of office in French to his brother.

During a break in the line of mourners, Edwards turns to Wayne Ray and sighs, "Wayne, Wayne, now I know how I got elected governor— by Nolan's friends."

At one point, Edwin leads his mother into a private room reserved for the family, as Miss Agnes cries for "my baby." Even with a son who became governor, Miss Agnes felt something special for her youngest. "Nolan would visit Mother every day and have coffee with her," Marion would later remember. "She never heard anything unpleasant from Nolan. Edwin or I would tell her the difficult things, like when we wanted her to move to Baton Rouge." Nolan even kept the faith after Audrey, Marion and Edwin drifted off to the Nazarenes.

Edmund Reggie enters and embraces Edwin. "I have nothing I can say."

"We were just kids, just starting out in life," Reggie would remember. And after standing with his friends, watching as the coffin was finally closed, Reggie was shaken. "It was like closing the door on my childhood."

Not all the mourners can jam into small, sweltering St. Michael's down the street. Just as well, for the 70-year-old church steams with the body heat in the long service. Many of the political mourners wait outside, and the sheriff's sharpshooters watch from nearby rooftops. Standing on the steps, a black man named Jackson from the town of Washington recalls that although Nolan was not directly involved in politics, he watched after his brother's politics in Acadiana. "If we ever had a problem, he'd drop everything and be there right away."

An hour later the doors swing open and the cooler outside air sweeps over the pallbearers and family. Tears stream down Marion's reddened face as the two brothers lead their mother to the limousine and on to the cemetery amid the rice fields south of town.

A TV reporter watches the procession leaving. "It feels very strange. On one hand I feel like I'm intruding terribly, on the other my heart just goes out to the guy." She looks to the cars heading toward the tracks. "But most of all it feels very strange, very unsettling to watch Edwin Edwards cry. I've never seen him show emotion before."

17. On a Roll Again

The line for beer and hotdogs at the Baton Rouge headquarters opening celebration presented a neat profile of the capital city's Republicans: blue-haired little old ladies, eager, earnest collegians and the button-down post-Preppie types that the youngsters are evolving toward. Walking through the crowd, Gus Weill, in a white tropical shirt and puffing the ever-present cigar, is more interested in the huge, fluttering tent shading the whole parking lot. "Circus tents are like political campaigns. You ever think of that? It's the same feeling of carnival, of magic, and the next day it's pulled down and gone. All illusion."

The Treen aide nearby is less interested in the simile than in the dilemma facing his candidate. "We've decided that Nolan's death can't change our strategy. We can't let up. Two weeks from now no one will remember Nolan. We've got to go with our best shot."

The shooting opens up as soon as the governor is introduced. "It's not my temperament to come out swinging like this," but here comes Dave Treen anyway, hitting the ground running after the weekend hiatus, running straight at Edwin Edwards. "You have to be careful about what you hear from the opposition," says Treen, who is "sick and tired of the distortions and falsehoods" from Edwards, particularly the outrageously wrong pardons ad that was pulled from the air last week. Sure, Edwards left Treen an impressive surplus: "14 stinking hazardous waste dumps that we will have to clean up." Sure, Edwards is decisive and moves fast: "He signed his own retirement bill 24 hours after it passed. If leadership means shooting from the hip, he's the better leader. But if leadership means tackling tough problems, then leadership goes to this administration."

216

You have to give the guy credit for not backing off. It's as though nothing has happened since early last week—Treen has picked his campaign up on the same note he left it last Thursday. But the tenor of the campaign has changed and the Treen camp has not yet come to grips with it. People may well forget Nolan Edwards in two weeks but they haven't forgotten him yet. The murder and the bizarre connection to Edwards still hang over this campaign like a low-lying cloud. The pardons issue, about to break on Edwin Edwards like a 10-foot wave, has dissipated into billows. For many, it will be hard to feel anger toward Edwards for his excessive pardons when he has already suffered at the hands of a pardonee. Instead of Edwards' getting blamed as the cause of the pardons problem, he is getting sympathy as one of its victims. And Dave Treen is not winning any points by stepping up his attack. In early August, it was a bitter, fighting mad Edwin Edwards obsessed with attacking the integrity of the upbeat, positive Dave Treen. By late in the month, the roles were reversed.

Peeking in the window of Teen Age Hut, the town kids know there's big doings in Ville Platte tonight. It's stifling hot inside at the makeshift bar next to the kitchen and only a little cooler in the main room where tables and folding chairs for 300 are crammed with police jurors, school board members, sheriff's deputies, ward leaders, black and white, from Ville Platte, Turkey Creek, Mamou and Pine Prairie—all friends of Edwin Edwards paying $25 a ticket to honor him at his first public appearance in Acadiana since burying his brother five days before.

Some true luminaries on hand tonight. During the introductions, Police Juror Gervis LaFleur will evoke the strongest applause with "You've heard about two-time losers and three-time losers. Well, here's a sheriff who went to jail and won—Potch Didier!" These political functions follow a time-honored format and protocol, starting with an interminable invocation, to be delivered tonight by Reverend M. L. Thomas. Reverend Thomas succumbs to the common temptation facing preachers, who, perhaps inspired and awestruck by the sight of so many politicians silent and with heads bowed, drag out the Lord's word as far as they can stretch it.

"We're come callin', Lord, askin', knockin', beseechin', implorin' . . . we're not askin' for too much, but for you to forgive us our iniquities and

217

to cleanse us of sin for those things we have done that we should not have done, or that we haven't done when we should have done them, or ..." You can hear the feet shuffling through the Hut, the tremor of politicians getting restless, like the day of McKeithen's second inauguration when the governor's cousin prayed on and on while scowling Big John, head bowed, snuck furtive peeks at the darkening rain clouds. Big John had to take his oath inside the rotunda and was he steamed.

A sigh of relief accompanies the Amens as the Cajuns squeeze back into their seats or wander back to the bar. The guest of honor is among friends tonight—practically family. Many have been campaigning for Edwin Edwards since the congressional race in 1965. Yet very few approach him at the head table, as though his own subdued, detached demeanor has thrown up a shield around him. After the non-stop running during the past 18 months, it's been a strangely quiet weekend for the Edwards campaign. Darrell Hunt: "He's pulled the curtain down on his emotions. He's been okay today but it's not been easy on him."

Edwards sits expressionless at the front table listlessly holding a fork. Across the room Jason Savoy picks out the first few notes of the familiar Willie Nelson anthem. Edwards' blank expression doesn't change as the Ramblers gradually join in on "On the Road Again," but slowly he begins tapping his fork on the table. The tempo picks up and Edwards taps harder, then he drops the fork, leans back in his chair and begins to clap. Diners in the front rows join in as the poker face begins focusing on individuals in the crowd. The clapping and the music fill the hall. Edwards lifts his hands above his head and the Hut shakes to the beat. He stands and 300 Cajuns stand with him, their expressions as intent as his. Then the music stops and the shield drops—the poker face breaks into a smile and the Cajuns into whooping and hollering. This campaign is on a roll again, Edwin Edwards is back.

At his last Baton Rouge press conference, Edwin Edwards was literally backed up to the wall and snapping at reporters' heated questions on DCCL and Jules LeBlanc—a harsh scene full of recriminations, the nadir of the campaign.

A week after he buried his brother, the mood has totally changed. DCCL seems like years ago—there is not a question about it today— and the pardons issue, about to crest a week ago, has for now subsided.

Edwards seizes the lull for an upbeat offensive, the unveiling of a slick campaign brochure laying out the Edwards platform. The claims and promises are new, but the artwork is the same Bernie Fuchs illustrations that Gus Weill commissioned eight years ago, showing a dynamic Edwin, with a thinner waistline, wider lapels and more hair, walking and talking among his people. Some of his new commitments are as idealized, especially his prescription for the ailing oil and gas industry. "I plan to talk to the decision-makers with these companies and try to get each one of them to drill one extra well," he says, citing the enormous spinoff each time "a drill bit breaks the earth." Edwards is selling hope like it was Hadacol. Or like Ronald Reagan solving the national economy's ills: "If each American company would hire just one extra worker . . . " The oil companies will respond that they are ready to go—"just as soon as Edwin can come up with the $10 million to drill a new well and find a market for the gas," says one executive.

The press conference rolls into better stuff. Edwards is in a good mood, bouncy and positive. Not even a question about his egregious pardons ad snafu gets his back up. "I should be the last person to rely on anything in the *Morning Advocate*," but in shooting from the hip, he says, sometimes you miss. In this instance, "I was a victim of my own petard."

A little stage-managed drama. Ann Davenport hands him the phoned-in results of a Hamilton poll showing a 49-36 Edwards lead. The poll, conducted in the week after Nolan's funeral, indicates Edwards has overcome his dip in the polls following the DCCL report.

A prediction. "Nothing has been as effective as the unfair, unprecedented grand jury report. Other issues will be raised before the election, but none will be as effective as that engineered report."

Some repartee. Brenda Hodge cites his own recent polls that only one-third of his own supporters believe everything he says: "My wife is one of them."

Some tough talk. Asked if LABI's recent endorsement of Treen showed business is more comfortable working with the incumbent: "Yes, but I don't intend to accommodate them."

Some inside gossip. He corrects a reporter who says Bob Hope will be doing a benefit for Dave Treen. "Bob Hope will be appearing for $60,000. I had him four years ago and it only cost $35,000. Bob Hope is a good friend of mine and a great entertainer and I might buy a ticket myself and go. It would be worth $1,000. I won't buy 10 because I don't want the governor to deliver them."

Edwards is his usual overcute self in places, but overall it is the most engaging, least hostile encounter he has had with the press since his first term. The reporters, in respect for his loss, have given Edwards some respite from the previously biting, probing questions and Edwards has responded without the hostility and bitterness that characterized his relations with the press and the negative image he has been projecting on TV. Edwin Edwards is bouncing back from the worst two weeks in his life, he has met the people, he has met the press, now it is time to meet the enemy.

Dave Treen's early August momentum has stalled. The arrest of Billy Cannon and the murder of Nolan Edwards have wiped DCCL from the public consciousness. The Treen camp needs to regain the offensive, to restate the distinction in the public's mind between Dave Treen's integrity and Edwin Edwards' lack thereof. Republican hopes are riding on the September 1 televised debate on public TV. Despite Edwards' insistence that he "called Dave Treen's hand" and prevailed in their earlier encounter, the televised image showed a carping, belligerent Edwards blowing his cool, getting names confused, appearing more guilty than gubernatorial as a composed Dave Treen stood his ground. The first of a series of public TV debates presents Treen with the opportunity to catch Edwards in another display of pique on statewide TV, to face him down on the issues and to nail him on his record.

McAlister Hall on the Tulane campus takes on a pep rally flavor as family, staff and supporters of both sides fill the seats, run through a few impromptu cheers and settle down to moderator Angela Hill's pre-air admonition that hooting, jeering and other natural partisan reactions will only take precious time away from their own candidate. Yeah, sure, Angela.

Both candidates are at their podiums reviewing notes. At least Dave Treen is. He takes these debates very, very seriously, blocking out all appearances for a day and a half before to study his material. Through the course of three televised debates, Treen will devote a full work week to isolated study. Edwards says his preparation consisted of thinking over the debate on his ride down to New Orleans.

Seconds before air time a makeup woman rushes onstage to pat down Edwards' shiny forehead, which Treen partisans greet with a prolonged "Aww-w-w-w-w."

And the show is on. Brenda Hodge of nemesis WBRZ lobs Edwards a hand grenade of a question she and news director John Spain have been working on and rewriting for the past week. "A recent statewide poll shows that a large percentage of the voters do not consider you completely honest. Many questions concerning your honesty apparently stem from numerous investigations of the financial affairs of you or your close associates while you were governor. TEL Enterprises, Tongsun Park and DCCL are examples. In order to prevent such questions concerning your honesty in the future, will you divest yourself of all personal financial dealings while governor and will you refrain from participating in business or financial arrangements involving government and your close friends and associates?"

Well, where does one begin? "First of all the poll doesn't show a large percentage question my honesty. I think the figure is 30 percent, which is a substantial percentage, but the reason for it is I don't play footsie with the press and I don't play footsie with the U.S. attorneys. We're always at each other's throats—you're trying to get me and I'm trying to get them. And up until now I've come out ahead. The point that I would say about that is a simple one: If anybody knows of any reason that I should not be governor based upon any wrongdoing on my part, I think now's a good time to put up or shut up. We've been hearing that for 15 years . . . "

Hodge breaks in. "Governor, excuse me, would you divest yourself of your personal financial holdings? That was the question."

"What personal financial holdings?"

Hodge bulldogs back in and repeats the question word for word.

"Well, young lady [the clear tipoff that Edwin's mad is when he starts calling female reporters "young lady"], I never involve myself with business with government. If I'd done that, I'd be in serious trouble, both politically and legally. . . . Again, the only way I can answer the question is now is the time to put up or shut up. That applies to people watching the program, to this man against whom I'm running and to you in the media. I think it's a very good question and everybody now has the opportunity. I'm fair game. Shoot. Hit if you can. You're not going to do it." He has gone right to the brink of boiling over but holds his cool as his side shatters decorum with a loud cheer and applause.

Treen responds that he has no outside business dealings other than his townhouse in Washington he rents out. "I am not engaged in any financial dealings in the state of Louisiana. That is something I think any chief executive officer ought to be willing to do." Treen's answer is eminently respectable and forgettable. That, of course, is the problem with televised political debate. A debate coach may give Treen more points for logic, factualness and sticking to the question. But his penchant for numbers and percentages is numbing, and his body language distracting. Treen has this problem with his glasses. He looks more handsome with them off but he can't read his numbers that way, so he is constantly jerking them on and off his ears as he talks. An Edwards enthusiast is chortling. "He's going to swallow the damned things before the night is over."

In her next turn, Brenda Hodge takes aim at Treen, asking what he'll do, if reelected, to turn around his disastrous reputation for being inaccessible to the press, the legislators and the public.

Treen demurs—he knows of no time that he flatly didn't respond to the press. "What's important is that the governor take action at an appropriate time and not when a reporter wants it for a news story. But I promise you and all the media that I'll be more accessible, because I won't have anyone campaigning against me for three and a half years when I take office next term." No better way to turn around a tough question—Treen's side has something to cheer about and they do.

The best part of the night is the questions the candidates pose to each other. Here's Treen's chance to put the tough questions straight to the enemy, *mano a mano*, and to rebut his response. Treen poses a very hard question to Edwards on engineering his own special retirement bill, succinctly detailing everything wrong with it. But Edwards neatly parries. "I didn't engineer it. That was done, by the way, by Edgar Mouton, who was your executive counsel [applause] . . . and the four people you rewarded for their endorsement of you benefited far more than I from that very similar provision of the law." A debate coach may question what Paul Hardy's retirement has to do with Edwin Edwards', but in the average viewer's terms, Edwards has turned the attack back to his favorite point—what Treen did to reward the four Democratic equivalents of Benedict Arnold. And he concludes with another stab. "I can't gloss over the fact that the Legislature did it, I signed it. Just like the Legislature provided you with two pay raises and you signed it . . . . "

Treen is booed when he counters, "I think it's an entirely different situation. . . . " He doesn't recover the edge of his attack. Score a missed opportunity for Dave Treen.

Edwards asks Treen when he's going to make a decision on building the long-awaited addition to Charity Hospital. "I've made a decision," answers Treen. "I've made a decision that we are not going to build that tower that was recommended to me that was going to cost $165 million because I feel I was not getting very good advice." He also feels that the state is being abused by a contract Edwards had signed tying the state to using an architectural firm that is a big contributor to Edwards. Treen, instead, will look to renovating and improving the present facility.

Not a bad answer, underscoring Treen's fiscal responsibility and exposing the sweetheart deal Edwards made with his friends, but Edwards' response highlights Treen's inability to make a timely decision. "On January 2, 1981, you said I will decide by January 15. On January 14 you said you'd make your decision by 'next Thursday.' On March 12, 1981, you said you'd do it before the legislative session ends. On December 3, 1981, you said, 'I'll do it by mid-December.' On April 16, 1982, you said it 'will be coming soon, in the near future, even in a few weeks.' On May 5, 1982, you said you were 'taking a hard look at the plan' and would 'make a decision immediately.' [Laughter rolls through the audience as Edwards tears on.] In August of 1982 you announced you wanted a task force to study it and you wanted a report by January 16, 1984. They don't need to do that. I know what I'm going to do with it." It's a devastating rebuttal. Of all things for Edwards to have going for him: research. Well, it sounds like research. When Scott Welch goes back to check the newspaper files, he can't find any comments by Treen about Charity Hospital on half the dates Edwards mentioned. Not that there's much he could do about it.

On the offensive again, Treen lays Edwards' outrageously inaccurate pardons commercial back in the author's lap. "Do you think it ethical to campaign with such a malicious falsehood and distortion?"

It was Treen's toughest question and Edwards' best answer: "Absolutely not. I told you at the time it was called to my attention that

we got the information from a clipping out of the *Morning Advocate*....
I'm probably the last person in the world who ought to rely on
newspaper articles, and as soon as it was called to my attention, I
extended an apology to you because we had acted on bad information.... We were in error. At least when it was called to my attention I
was man enough to say yes, we made a mistake and we did."

Treen should let it go at that. You can't win by pursuing a point when
the other guy is "man enough" to apologize. But Treen does anyway:
"Well, if you really want to correct your error it would seem to me you
would attempt to get to the people that perceived this outrageous ad on
the radio . . . that lie was spread all over and you can't rely on the
statement that it was in a newspaper to defend your position.... If that's
the way that you're going to conduct this campaign, we're going to have
to monitor everything you say a lot more carefully."

Both candidates are bearing down and biting each other's ears with
every question, but Edwards is scoring with the audience not just on his
questions but on his aggressive parrying and counterpunching. Treen
retreats to his integrity issue. "Why should the people believe the things
that you are saying . . . " and quotes an Edwards 1975 campaign promise
of no new taxes and then his proposing a new minerals tax in 1976.

Edwards throws it back in his face. "Well, welcome to the club." He
pulls a clip from his briefing book. "In 1979 look what Dave Treen
said . . . " as he reads Dave Treen's promises of no tax proposals, which
he too broke. The two go on from grappling over who promised what
and who spent what. Even when Treen is right it sounds wrong. He hotly
counters Edwards' claim that Treen raised bonded indebtedness $1.2
billion. "We did not."

"How much did you borrow?"

"$999 million."

"Oh."

Backstage after the debate, both graciously assess the other's
performance. Treen on Edwards: "He was good, he was clever and very
glib." Edwards on Treen: "He did well considering what he had to work
with."

Edwards leaves quickly with Darrell and Stan while Marion and the
rest of the gang bypass the reception in the Tulane library to go eat.
Upstairs in the library, it's a decidedly Tulane crowd, reserved, well-

dressed university types who are as much like Dave Treen in their dress and taste as in their politics. Well-wishers congratulate the governor but John Cade is steamed . . . at Dave Treen. "He passed up a lot of opportunities for a knockout punch. He let him get away with murder." Captain Fact Scott Welch is at his side. "I was writing down all his lies. They were incredible, everything he said. He was lying faster than I could write them down."

Down St. Charles Avenue, at fashionable Stephen & Martin's, a frenetic Edwards celebration is in progress. The Edwards party, all the children, the state coordinators, the inside team, is toasting the victory. Marion is literally dancing from one table to the other. "I love it when he says that he didn't borrow $1.2 billion. 'It was $999 million.' Could you believe he said that? It's like my wife accusing me of running around with five women, and I say, no, only four!"

New Orleans chieftain Bob d'Hemecourt says the debate will be a turning point in the white vote in the city. "My problem was the integrity issue, and we overcame it tonight. We stopped the erosion in its tracks," he says, clinking a glass of wine with Sam LeBlanc. "We met it head on and we turned it around. I feel so good, I feel like the campaign is over tonight."

The Edwards party has something to celebrate. No matter what you say about that debate, it's clear Edwards didn't lose, he didn't blow his cool, and Treen sure didn't nail him to the wall on anything. It will stand as the most lively and cogent of the series of debates.

In the subsequent debates, the only exchange to top tonight's fireworks will come in the third meeting when straight man Treen sets up Edwards. "Why do you continue to talk out of both sides of your mouth?" And Edwards doesn't miss a beat in pointing both fingers to his own head. "So that people like you with nothing between their ears can understand what I say."

WQUE Pulse of the City. Who are you voting for in the governor's race?
    Voice of middle-aged black man: "I'm for Edwin Edwards because he keeps the people off the strike."
    Voice of young female with Preppie inflection: "Well, I'm for Treen because Edwards has just basically admitted, you know, that like he's a

crook and that he's robbed from government."

Clipped, businesslike voice of young professional: "Treen. I saw his commercials that make Edwards out to be a cheap shot con artist and when I saw the debate, Edwards was a cheap shot con artist."

Voice of young male: "Edwards, because dishonesty is better than ineptitude."

Both candidates make it to Morgan City the following Sunday to march in the parade at the Shrimp and Petroleum Festival. The twin foundations of the local economy form an odd combination but since it's tough enough to get to Morgan City even once, the locals do all their celebrating in one. Morgan City is the end of the world, the last patch of dry ground rising out of the delta swamp of the great Atchafalaya River. It's been touch and go for the Corps of Engineers over the past decade to keep the city's head above water, as a newly constructed 10-foot-high concrete seawall atop the levee is recent evidence.

Morgan City has a long history of exploitation, its own. In 1973, as the Mississippi spring floods threatened the New Orleans levee, there was serious discussion of whether, by diverting more of the Mississippi's water into the Atchafalaya, Morgan City would be sacrificed so New Orleans would be spared. Back before anyone found the shrimp or petroleum, this part of St. Mary Parish was a forest of majestic cypress trees rising from the swamp. Lumber companies wiped that out by the turn of the century to build uptown New Orleans. Since then the shrimp have been nearly fished out. In 1947, Kerr-McGee hit the first offshore oil well, touching off the last exploitative wave through Morgan City. The locals prospered from the booming offshore service industry but they've also had to endure hordes of footloose and dangerous transients looking for a quick paycheck and a place to lie low. Celebrated author-murderer Jack Abbott was tracked down at a work camp here. The quality of life has an inverse relationship to the economy. When the oil business slumped, the crime rate dropped dramatically. And local developers were distraught to learn that instead of the new four-lane U.S. 90 making it easier to get to Morgan City, the oil company managers used it as an escape route to go live in and commute from Lafayette.

So the Shrimp and Petroleum Festival resembles an annual hurricane party—the locals can never be sure that either the ravages of nature or the economy won't soon sweep this place out to sea. The celebration's high point is the Sunday parade, complete with floats, marching bands and politicians hurling beads and trinkets. State Senator Tony Guarisco, perched atop the back seat of a Mustang convertible, checks his trinket supply once more before rolltime. "You can vote Communist in Baton Rouge as long as you throw enough plastic beads at people in the parade back home. It's junk but it's your ass if you run out. You can lose a lot of votes in one bad parade. The blacks say you threw it all to the whites and, hey, people take this seriously." Tony keeps an ironic view of hard times in Morgan City. "People are still in a state of apoplexy over the oil industry. I've been warning them if things don't get better soon, they'll have to start melting down their Rolexes."

As soon as Dave Treen shows up, the parade can get under way. Not that Edwin Edwards is in any rush. He's at the back of the parade, signing autographs, kissing drill-bit belles and crustacean queens and taking issue with Dave Treen's latest ad. "He said his income tax cut saved the average taxpayer $500. What he doesn't tell you is that's over four years—it's only $125 a year. For most people his tax cut didn't help much but it's sure been good for me. It's saved me $10,000 a year."

"Just on state taxes?"

"Sure. I paid a half million in taxes in the last three years. Between him and Reagan, I've saved $50,000 a year."

As for Thursday night's debate, that went just fine, despite "Brenda Hodge's cheap shot question." Disagreement here: the only thing cheap about her leadoff question was that he didn't answer it. He said he would have no business dealings with state agencies but he didn't say if he would stay out of all business deals in Louisiana. So let's run it by again: "Governor, if you get reelected and a business opportunity comes along that doesn't involve state contracts or state employees, but it's a deal, say like TEL Enterprises, that would be enhanced by Edwin Edwards' involvement, would you do it?"

"Yes, I would do it. I'm tired of people thinking I'm going to quit living while I am governor. I can't live off the governor's salary. My income taxes are four times more than the governor's salary." (The governor makes $73,000 a year.) "I'm not looking to make any money off the government, I could just stay where I am and do better than that." He smiles as a Cajun cowboy rides by on his horse, with an Edwards bumpersticker on its rump.

"So what's a governor worth?"

"A governor is worth $500,000 a year. It'll never happen. It's one of the anomalies in the public sector. They want the best possible person but they don't want to pay what that person is worth."

The typical twists of Louisiana politics. Dave Treen, whose Louisiana holdings consist of a house in Metairie and a 1972 Olds Cutlass convertible, is being tagged with the deadly label of "rich man's candidate," even though one of the rich men he's helping is populist Edwin Edwards, making a million a year and proud of it. It's a cute little irony that's hardly been noticed in this campaign. But Edwards is taking no chances. The next day, Labor Day, Edwards has an inspiration as he marches arm-in-arm through the rain with Dutch Morial and Vic Bussie at the head of the Solidarity Parade. By the time he reaches the bandstand in Louis Armstrong Park, he has settled on it and tells a wet crowd of hard hats he will not draw his salary as governor until the state's unemployment level subsides to the national level.

It should win him points with the working people and shut off carping questions about his personal finances and future sources of outside income. Edwin Edwards, sharecropper's son, has an angle for everything, including noblesse oblige.

18. A Visit from the Witch Doctors

Forget yard signs, forget billboards and bumperstickers. Throughout New Orleans and on the Westbank, the premier political medium is the shopping bag. Not just any bag; the candidate who finds his or her name on one from Schwegmann's has received what all the TV advertising can't buy: a public benediction from one of the most respected names in the Greater New Orleans area, John G. Schwegmann. The man was far more than a high-volume discount grocer—he was the patron saint of the all-important Little Man, and the more important Little Woman, the New Orleans housewife. Schwegmann captured the heart of New Orleans, going through its stomach by way of its middle class pocketbook. The Roman emperors ruled and placated the masses by providing bread and circuses. It's simpler in gastronomically obsessed New Orleans, where the circus *is* the bread, and the cheese and meat and vegetables and all else that goes into the daily life-giving ritual of "makin' groceries." And making them at the low, low prices that have been the Schwegmann trademark. Schwegmann beat the national chains at bringing discount shopping on a grand scale to New Orleans, which had clung longer than most cities to the fast-disappearing corner grocery store, once as ubiquitous and as symbolic of The City as the corner bar, which is still ubiquitous and doing pretty well, thank you.

Schwegmann is revered not just for offering low prices but for creating them, through his celebrated decade-long crusade to break the Louisiana dairy cartel. State-regulated milk prices had effectively kept cheaper Mississippi milk off New Orleans' store shelves. He fought in the courts and in the Legislature and in the public media to free the New Orleans consumer from her long economic forced marriage to the Louisiana farmer. But the law and the editorial page of the *Times-Picayune* could take him only so far—Schwegmann began putting his message directly on his shopping bags. On them, he editorialized against dock pricing and other anticonsumer practices, and endorsed candidates who espoused his cause. His brown shopping bag epistles, crude and simple though they were, hit home harder than the high-sounding *Picayune*, bypassing the newspaper's masculine province, the living room, the traditional forum for decisions of the hearth, and going into the kitchen, reaching with volume and impact what no man had reached before—touching the New Orleans housewife in her struggle to make ends meet—while providing the passion of New Orleans existence—food—within the hard-pressed working class budgets. Aspiring candidates followed the busy Schwegmann through his grocery aisles petitioning for his endorsement. Indeed, the brown bag blessing of Schwegmann was coveted more than that of the *Times-Picayune.* The *Picayune* is powerful and respected but it has its detractors—Schwegmann's has only satisfied customers. Orleanians and Westbankers swear at one and by the other. Schwegmann, grocer-emperor, took advantage of his enormous popularity and exclusive advertising media to finish a respectable fourth in the 1971 governor's race and then to win election to two terms on the Public Service Commission, where he constantly opposed rate hikes to utility companies and helped hold the important psychological line on the nickel phone call in Louisiana, long after the rest of the nation had gone to a dime. At his retirement in 1981, John Schwegmann was honored as one whose tangible, undeniable contribution to the quality of life of the average Orleanian ranked next to Jean Lafitte's of two centuries past.

Partly in honor of that memory, partly because he knows he'll find a good crowd here, Dave Treen bounds out of the RV in front of the giant Gretna Schwegmann's near the Westbank Expressway. Treen remembers John Schwegmann fondly from 1971 when they were both running for governor—even more fondly from 1979 when Schwegmann gave Treen his shopping bag endorsement in the heated runoff against Louis Lambert. Not that John didn't take some heat for his controversial stand: the store clerks had to keep a set of blank bags to give to black and to union member customers, many of whom refused to carry their groceries home in a bag endorsing a Republican. That won't be a problem this year. When the old man retired in 1981, Treen could have cemented relations with the next generation by appointing John F. Schwegmann to finish his father's unexpired term on the Public Service Commission. Instead, the governor felt he'd get more mileage from an alliance with the up-and-coming Ben and Brod Bagert machine, and named Brod to the post. Only trouble was, the Bagerts, their impressive organization notwithstanding, were no match for John F. Schwegmann's name in the next PSC election. Treen's brave new alliance was short-lived. "A massive political blunder," a Treen aide called it, and the governor knew better than to even ask for the young Schwegmann's endorsement in 1983.

At least the governor has not been barred from Schwegmann stores, for today he's drawing a crowd of shoppers eager for a gubernatorially autographed Dave and Dodie Treen cookbook. "And remember," says Treen as he gives out each one, "the recipe for good government is on the back page." The shoppers are warm to Dave Treen, but then most folks generally are happy when shopping in Schwegmann's. Practically raised in Schwegmann's crammed aisles, they savor the experience of makin' groceries as much as they do that of eating them. That atmosphere spills over and affects the growing crowd outside. One grizzled shopping veteran emerging from the store raises his can of Schwegmann beer in salute to the candidate.

You didn't know about Schwegmann beer? Another brilliant marketing device and subliminally warm association with Schwegmann stores: it's a shopping tradition to pop a six pack in the store and merrily drink your way from produce to pet foods. Studies show people buy more groceries when hungry; obviously John G. knew something of the effects of shopping while getting loaded as well. Having a brew or two or three when makin' groceries at Schwegmann's is just one more of the great New Orleans traditions viewed with shock and horror in other parts of the state.

When John F. Schwegmann followed through on his father's expansion plans outside New Orleans, questions were raised about the importing of the Schwegmann lifestyle along with the stores. When the Schwegmann company applied to rezone a recently purchased tract of land in South Baton Rouge, representatives of the neighboring Jimmy Swaggart World Ministry persuaded the zoning board to specifically forbid the consumption of alcoholic beverages on the premises. When Billy Nungesser hears of the official welcome the Schwegmann way has received in Baton Rouge, he shudders at the barbarism of it all. "A man like that is dangerous." And he didn't mean Schwegmann.

Watching as the TV camera crews set up to interview the governor, Nungesser is concerned about more than just his friend's candidacy today. The Westbank Republican's son, Bill, Jr., is shaking shoppers' hands too in his campaign for the Legislature. As the cameras begin to roll, Nungesser edges nearer and not too gently shoves his son into the camera's view behind the governor. "Cut it out, Daddy," Junior protests, but the paternal nudge has worked—the face of the young candidate will appear over the governor's shoulder on the six o'clock news tonight.

Back in the RV, bumping along to the next stop, the governor disdainfully views construction work progressing on the new, elevated portion of the Westbank Expressway. "A $500 million boondoggle," he mutters at the symbol of West Jefferson legislative clout. Dave Treen of Jefferson Parish hardly sounds like a man campaigning in his own back yard. Because he's across the river from his back yard. The parish lines in the Greater New Orleans area are fiction, geographical niceties. In order to control the port on both sides of the river, the Parish of Orleans has always straddled both banks, as has neighboring Jefferson. But make no mistake, the cultural boundary is that river dividing the East Bank and the West Bank.

They are two different worlds, separate, distinct and apart. East is East. Metairie and Kenner and the rest of the east bank of Jefferson were settled in the great migrations from the city at mid-century. And West is West. Fewer Orleanians crossed the river. The Westbank is for Westbankers—people who grew up here or came in from the country, to build a polyglot blue collar culture that combines the rough and tumble spirit of a port city with the good life of the bayou country.

The Westbank is industry's toolshed—anything you need from hydraulic winches to drilling mud is offered by one of the firms along the Harvey Canal, a veritable industrial Disneyland celebrating man's quest to do it deeper, longer, wider and faster. The Treen RV caravan pulls into Rental Tools, a major oilfield supplier, and Treen shakes hands against a backdrop of five-foot-long, cone-ended, yellow-painted steel reamers, so named because they are used to force broken pipe and other garbage out of oil wells. The governor steps gingerly among the inventory to shake about two dozen hands of employees and managers celebrating the visit with a po-boy and beer break. Political expression takes an odd course on the Westbank. The proprietors of Rental Tools border on the sacrilegious in their views of Jimmy Carter, whose face is the focal point of two paintings on the wall of the warehouse. In one, his features are combined with those of a haloed Jesus Christ. In the other, his smiling teeth are grafted onto the face of a dog. Rental Tools, with its beer-quaffing employees and its special on reamers this week, wins hands down as most surreal campaign stop of the day.

Along the way the motorcade has picked up two high school journalists, one with Marine length hair who confides to Dave Treen, "I aspire to be President of the United States one day. I want to know what motivates you." Treen is touched that this budding megalomaniac looks to him as a role model. As Treen talks about his desire to help people and how public service is the highest calling, the future leader of the Free World interrupts excitedly, "Really! I feel the same way."

The Treen RV weaves through the narrow streets of Algiers, the oldest part of the Westbank and the only part that belongs to Orleans Parish. Billy Nungesser looks across the levee at the skyline of the city. As is typical of their East Bank-West Bank orientation, Dave Treen and Billy Nungesser fail to see eye to eye on many things, especially the biggest deal to hit New Orleans since the Superdome—the World's Fair. Nungesser explains the frustration of trying to get objective economic data on something no one will argue against. "What are the hidden costs, the police protection, the street maintenance, the traffic control?" He's doubly concerned that in the confusion of the opening, fortunes in cash will leave the fairgrounds in brown bags, never reported by operators and concessionaires and escaping fair dues and city sales tax.

He also resents what the city will have to pay "so that 10 guys can get rich," referring to the well-connected businessmen-developers who have the most riding on the fair and who will likely profit from it immensely whether it flops or not. "They're gonna build condos over the public wharves." Billy points across the river to the U.S. Pavilion under construction. "That ain't no risk. You take a blind guy with a first-grade education and he can make seven jillion on that. It's already ruining the city. Look at that skyline." The fresh-sprouted forest of steel, glass and modern architecture has all but swallowed it up. "That's not what makes people want to come to New Orleans."

Treen is hustling to his next ready-made campaign stop, the Algiers foot ferry landing. He takes up his position as the ferry docks and the landing plank comes down and is almost bowled over by determined rush hour pedestrians, few of whom want to shake any politician's hand as they beeline for the cars and bars nearby. Dave manages to shake a fourth of the hands and give away a little literature. The state cop with him is surprised he did that well. "That was a mean-looking crowd," he says as the last of the herd push through the swinging doors.

Bushed from a day's campaigning, Dave Treen has one more boatload of pedestrians to greet before heading on to a party thrown for campaign workers at Blaine Kern's Mardi Gras float barn. From the parking lot at Schwegmann's to the ferry landing at Algiers, Treen has worked each crowd earnestly and received some warm responses from otherwise harried shoppers and pedestrians. Treen's campaign style is not the problem—anyone who hustles the Schwegmann vote or hangs out at ferry landings isn't an unapproachable stuffed shirt. It's his organization that's letting him down. "This state's too big to campaign in shopping centers," sneers Edwin Edwards at Treen's handshaking blitzes. Yet here he is in his home parish, campaigning as though he were a city council candidate trying to find a crowd.

Edwin Edwards doesn't need John Schwegmann's grocery bags to promote him on the Westbank—every other politico of respect and power on the Westbank has shown up for a fund raiser for the former governor at The Columns near the Harvey Tunnel. The $250-a-head crowd is bedecked in everything from sequined gowns to cowboy boots as they pick over an equally bizarre spread of hors d'oeuvres ranging from caviar to hogshead cheese. A country western band whose singer has been poured into a pair of turquoise hotpants belts out "I Can't Stop Loving You."

This classic Edwards fund-raiser speaks as much to the problems of the Treen campaign as to the strength and popularity of Edwards. Practically the entire Westbank legislative delegation is on hand, including Fritz Windhorst and John Alario, who had once been very helpful to Treen. Alario, in fact, was named by the governor to chair the executive committee of the World's Fair. Yet in this election, Alario is

Edwards' Westbank coordinator. "Treen didn't ask me."

Sheriff Harry Lee, the only Chinese-American sheriff in the country, leaps onstage in his cowboy hat and boots after cutting a mean Cotton-Eyed Joe with his wife. Politicians so moved take the mike to relate personal horror stories about Dave Treen, such as Westwego Mayor Ernie Tassin, who says it took the executive council of the Louisiana Municipal Association representing 283 mayors two years to get a 15-minute appointment with Dave Treen. "When Edwin was in, I'd pick up the phone and within an hour he'd get back with me and within two weeks we'd see him at his office or the Mansion."

Edwards is delighted with the turnout and show of official support in Dave Treen's home parish. Again, it's his affinity for the outcasts and the looked-down-upon. Edwards has not snubbed the Westbank, he has cultivated it. "If the rest of the state knew how much we have spent on the Westbank, from one new bridge to the other, we'd have a terrible time explaining it. But you're going to get a lot more in the next eight years." The crowd roars back and the band strikes up more Westbank honkytonk.

You'll meet the most wonderful array of politicians at an Edwards fund-raiser. Especially lesser candidates looking to tap some of Edwards' friends. The price of admission, $250 for this Westbank party, is a worthwhile investment for furthering one's contacts and just being seen in the right places. Now it's hard not to notice Butch Baum, all six foot eight of him, towering over the partyscape, nibbling on hogshead cheese and crackers and advancing his plan to save the American farmer. Back in Baton Rouge, this unlikely candidate for agriculture commissioner is better known as the hardest hustling, most assertive and successful life insurance salesman in modern history. Butch is a pioneer in self-promotion—he works hard, thinks big and advertises the same way, holding down one of the two most prestigious advertising spaces in the city, the south end zone scoreboard in Tiger Stadium.

Butch says he is in this race because he has given so much to charity over the years he can't carry forward any more charitable deductions. So he's blowing the money on himself—$300,000 of it—to campaign against popular incumbent Bob Odom. Butch is well known in Baton Rouge. Not necessarily respected, but well known. Even with $300,000, name recognition is his main obstacle in this race, so Butch is investing heavily in the next best thing, tearing down the good name of his opponent. He has already hit the radio waves with the charge that Bob Odom is supported by organized crime. For supporting facts, Butch drags up the name of Frances Pecora, a past contributor and employee of Odom's who is doing time in federal prison for attempting to bribe a sheriff she had no idea was honest. It's so hard to tell these days. Baum wouldn't be raising negative issues, you understand, if the plight of the Louisiana farmer were not so desperately serious. And what does Butch know about farming? Well, of course he was raised on one . . .

And why isn't Butch running for something closer to his field, like insurance commissioner? That would be unthinkable, because he would have to give up selling insurance—and that's Butch's life. "It took me eight years to be the top salesman in the country and another three to be the tops in the world." Along the way, he went bust once from all his side investments, but that just made him sell harder to come back bigger than ever. Butch campaigns like he sells, one on one, fixing you with his eyes, which you must look up to see, and softly exhorting you with a persistent good ol' boy folksy tone which you don't notice is being used to destroy the character of his opponent. Baum is an irresistible salesman, but he's in the wrong field. He can sell one insurance policy for $1 million, but he can only sell himself to one voter at a time. But in selling that voter he might also sell him some insurance, like a million-dollar policy. And maybe that's the whole point of this campaign. Rather than cut into his income, the campaign has increased it. "Last year I made the million dollar roundtable fifty times over. I may double that this year. I don't just campaign, you know. I'm out selling too." Butch Baum is not going to beat Bob Odom, but he will spread his name across the state as he's already done across Baton Rouge and will make hundreds of valuable contacts in the process. The world's greatest insurance salesman may have unlocked the key to greater sales still—run for office.

It's easy to pick on Treen's campaign style and staff snafus, especially next to Edwards' smooth-running organization with politicians clamoring to get onboard. The governor's own determination to keep up with the demands of being governor while also running for that office, coupled with long-standing dissension and lack of cooperation between the Cade people and the Nungesser people, is causing some rough edges and a flat public campaign. But Treen is not going to win or lose this election on the road. No more than 20 percent of the voters will see either candidate in a live campaign appearance. The battle will be won or lost on TV, both in advertising and news coverage. Advertising is a function of creativity and money. And Edwards is raising a lot more money. Another factor, perhaps more significant than all of the above, looms larger as the sweltering summer melts into the sweltering fall and as the Treen campaign becomes more listless. The governor's problems have less to do with his own campaign style and organization or even Edwin Edwards' superiority on these fronts. Day by day, Dave Treen is being victimized by a new campaign force that, though it was designed for objectivity and information, is beginning to mold the opinion of the electorate more effectively than anything Edwin Edwards can do or pay for.

It's the toughest question Dave Treen has to deal with. Ask him about Edwards' retirement or pardons or latest outrageous distortion and the governor answers forcefully, directly, confidently. But he's not being asked those questions. Instead, every day he has to get up and go out and face that query he can't answer: "Governor, what about your poor showing in the polls?" The smile may stay on his face, chiseled there, but the muscles tighten, his tone becomes defensive. What is he supposed to say? Perhaps Dave Treen may have wished he had some scandal on his record to defend, some alleged blight on his character—anything but having to answer that damned question about the polls again. What do you say to the TV interviewer whose station's own pollster has just solemnly declared that the incumbent governor is trailing his challenger by 13 percentage points, 17 points, 20 points. Pick a number—they're all as hard to explain. Sure, he can cast some doubt on the validity of the polls and explain that his own polls, scientifically more reliable, show a tighter race. But then the next question always is, "Well, Governor, why won't you release your polls?" *Do you have something to hide?* Dave Treen's smile is barely clinging to his pursed lips as he has to explain to this 26-year-old bright-faced reporter jamming a mike at him that his policy is not to release poll results until the proper time, that the only poll that counts is the one when everyone votes on October 22 "and we are confident that if people get the facts . . . "

For the guy on the other side, you don't even need to ask. Edwin Edwards is constantly talking about polls: his own, some newspaper's, some other candidate's, even his opponent's. It doesn't seem to matter which, they all show he's ahead—and that's all he wants folks to remember. He considers polls so important that he interrupts press conferences to receive the results of the latest one, allegedly sharing with reporters the information he has just gotten . . . *and the envelope please.* Instead of an Edwards bumpersticker on his car, he needs one that reads, "Ask Me About My Latest Poll."

How did it ever come to this? Dave Treen and John Cade had so carefully planned the message they would deliver to the people, they had an answer to every campaign issue a reporter could raise, not to mention a clarification for the newest Edwards distortion. But they didn't figure that everyone (that is, everyone who counted, like TV reporters) would seize on the question they just couldn't, or wouldn't dare, answer. The question of polls settled over the campaign like a shrouding fog, obscuring all issues, actions, even the candidates' personalities. Dave Treen, so confident in his record and his qualifications and the rightness of his cause, would later talk of the dread he felt each morning knowing he'd have to go out on the grueling trail where waiting for him was the enemy he could not confront, expose or silence. He had all the information he needed to engage Edwin Edwards, but he was helpless against the polls.

On their own, polls are benign instruments, good excuses for candidates to spend money to find out what they should already know— if they are as in tune with the hopes and desires of the people as they profess to be. Every candidate should take a poll before even thinking hard about running for office—just to learn whether the race is even worth one's bother. Many a courthouse politician who is sure everyone knows him gets a hard blow to his self-image of universality when he learns he has a recognition factor of 12. Then there are those who find through polls they are too well known. In New Orleans, a seafood merchant named Al Scramuzza, who proclaims himself the Seafood King on his ceaseless and terminally tacky TV ads, got back a recognition factor of 80 and a negative factor of 70. Proof, had he only listened, that peddlers of fish are not necessarily fishers of men.

Polls feed the insatiable desire in politicians to know what people think of them. And what will make people like them more. Nothing wrong with that—for potential candidates who know neither themselves nor the people and are willing to change anything about their personalities or their politics to get voters to like them more, polls serve a legitimate function. Candidates get in trouble by relying too heavily on them, but it's hard not to. Their alleged reliability is seductive—from the computer printouts to the margin of error (my favorite polling term, synonymous with confidence factor or con factor, for short), from the choosing of the demographic sample to the objective wording of the question, even to adjusting the inflection of the interviewer's voice, every variable can be covered to assure a scientific survey. And it may all be deadly accurate. The trick is, especially in a political campaign, there is no proving the pollster wrong. If the results of the election don't support the last poll, then the people changed their minds. The pollster can't help that, he's off the hook. As he should be. It's more likely that an experienced professional can be trusted to provide a fairly accurate snapshot of voter attitudes at any given time. The problems invariably come with the candidates' misuse or overuse of the information they receive. Just like pocket calculators are wiping from our memory banks the multiplication tables our elementary school teachers worked so hard to inculcate in us, so polls are dulling if not supplanting politicians' judgment of themselves and the people. The politician who can't make a decision without reading a poll is cheating constituents of the one thing politicians are expected to know: what and how much the people will stand. That in itself is no great public danger. If overreliance on polling lulls the politician into misreading what the people will accept, he or she will find out the hard way. Isolated stupidity is always remediable.

The danger is that in this banner election year for pollsters, they have struck a rich new vein of clients with more money, more influence and more capacity to screw up the whole system than any platoon of politicians could muster. The horror of 1983 is that the media have swallowed the polls. Armed with this newest toy, the media— independent of the candidates' money and manipulations—have become a dominant and destructive force in this election as well as a grave future threat to the American political system.

The main problem editors used to have with polls was their reliability, without realizing the true question mark was their relevance. What's the point of a poll? For the intelligent politician, that's obvious. Candidates don't take polls to see how they're doing. Far more burning questions than that are at stake: *Which issues should I stress? Which voter groups should I target? How should I comb my hair? Can I afford to divorce my wife?* The most important use for the who's ahead question is in raising money: nothing allays a contributor's fears more than a good poll. And nothing will dry up your money supply faster than a bad one.

The media have one overriding use for polls, to feed the public scoreboard mentality: don't bother us with the play-by-play, just give us the score. It's why people read the sports page—it is finite, quantifiable, there are no confusing shades of gray in a score. The temptation to keep score in an election before anyone votes has proved too great for the media in the past decade. Political races are frustratingly hard to report and to follow—how much easier it is, just to let the readers know who's ahead. The problem was that candidates' polls could hardly be trusted. Invariably, trusted professionals using similar techniques and random samples could poll the electorate at the same time and come up with irreconcilable figures. Instead of backing off using polls as news stories, editors and station owners in 1983 went totally the other way, commissioning their own pollsters to periodically sample the electorate and to keep the viewers up with their own independently kept score. In the minds of editors and news directors, that solved the problem. The party line was: *we paid a lot of money for this so it must be true.* Never mind that an independent poll conducted by the Baton Rouge *Morning Advocate* showed Edwards only five points ahead of Treen in August while an independent poll conducted by a statewide consortium of TV stations showed a 14-point Edwards lead. The special irony was that the *Advocate* and WBRZ, a member of the statewide polling consortium, are both owned by the Manship family, whose money was paying for two different polls that wildly disagreed with each other. The glaring contradiction didn't faze the news management of either organization. Both hawked their own polls as though they had a lock on the truth: the TV station led off newscasts with theirs, the newspaper bannered the front page with theirs. And both ignored or buried any others. Did they really believe that no one noticed?

So even if a news organization could make itself and then its readers or viewers believe that its poll was somehow the most reliable, it still could not answer the relevance question. What is the news value of reporting that Edwin Edwards held a 13-point lead in July, four months before the election? Any trend established over six months of a campaign can be turned around in the final two weeks: the time in which most voters—not political junkies and reporters—begin to think seriously about the election. Both the *Advocate* and the *Picayune* looked silly in 1979 when both showed Treen leading Lambert by up to 20 percentage points, only to have the election come down to less than one-half of 1 percent. Either their polls were dead wrong or the voters were so volatile that the polls made no difference. The *Picayune* wisely deduced from the debacle that there was no point in trying to defend or explain the mess: in 1983 they saved face and money by not commissioning independent polls.

But the state's leading TV stations just couldn't resist in 1983. Polls are the perfect electronic toys for the entertainment-oriented TV industry, which has an even harder time than newspapers in reporting political campaigns. Were it merely a matter of the TV polls being contradictory and irrelevant, no one would object to the new toys. But the longer the campaign wore on, the more obvious it was that the TV polls were dangerously if not unethically playing a major role in influencing the conduct of the campaigns and public opinion.

The closest Dave Treen came to leading in the polls occurred after the DCCL grand jury report was released and before Nolan Edwards was shot. Starting in mid-August, Edwards gradually began to pull away until the September installment of the TV station consortium's statewide poll showed Edwards 20 points ahead. Both camps smelled a rout and started to act like it. That TV poll had several important effects.

Some who still harbored doubts about Edwards' honesty admitted to being lulled by the bandwagon effect of his widening lead in the polls—*well, if everyone else thinks he's okay . . .*

It increased the pressure on Treen to put up or shut up: release your own polls or stop criticizing the TV stations' surveys. When John Cade attacked the consortium's poll (conducted by Dr. Ed Renwick of Loyola University) as "grossly distorted," a defensive Yat at Bud Rip's snapped, "Ya hoid dat, he's called da Pope a liar!"

It ignited the Edwards campaign with the big win pep rally fever. Standing in front of the Edwards headquarters on Veterans Highway, a youthful Edwards volunteer, Edwin Roth, described the latest poll as a massive shot in the arm for Edwards' troops even in Treen's back yard. "We're gonna kill him on the Westbank and we could carry over here too." It's full court press time for Edwin Roth. "I mean, if you're gonna beat someone, stomp him, crush him, humiliate him. That way maybe he'll think twice about running against you next time."

It knocked the wind out of the Treen campaign, which was just gathering some steam for a final offensive. Sipping punch at reporter and grand juror Joan Duffy's wedding, a morose John Cade explained what the latest TV poll results have done for him. "We had 8,000 volunteers scheduled to come in to start our phone banks last Monday. After the poll came out on the weekend, only 3,000 showed up."

Precisely because the TV poll was independent, the Edwards campaign was able to directly use it in raising money. "You can't believe the momentum that poll has given us," chirped Marion Edwards, going over his fund-raising list for the day. The independent nature of the poll, the fact that it was paid for by some TV stations that had been among his brother's severest critics, made Marion's job all the more easy . . . and fun.

Marion Edwards is campaigning almost as hard as he is fund-raising, smoothly shifting gears as he leaves a meeting of black preachers in New Orleans—the Nazarene bombshell had them all on their feet, whooping, cheering and praising the Lord and Edwin Edwards—and glides into Metairie, Treen country, for a cocktail party at the home of heavy equipment dealer Tom Beningo and his wife Elaine. It will be a tasteful, sedate affair—hardly Marion's style—but tonight the campaign treasurer is as interested, well, more interested, in raising money.

His older brother is putting his considerable fund-raising skills to the test. The original $5 million budget is a laughable memory, as Edwin Edwards, who can't say no, is agreeing to nearly every possible campaign expenditure and leaving it to Marion to raise the money. The strategy is shifting from winning to winning big and landslides don't come cheap. Along with the budget, Edwin's early pay-as-we-go, cash in advance fund-raising concept has also been dumped. To hell with cash up front. One of the first things Marion did was sell the Beechcraft, bank the cash and lease a plane for the rest of the campaign. Then he went after the contributors. His plan was to ask not for cash but for a minimum $25,000 letter of credit that could be taken to the bank and borrowed against. The potential contributor is told that if Edwards loses, the contributor will have to eat the note, but, as the odds look better every day, if Edwards wins, the contributor may not even have to put down a dime on the obligation.

Marion offers three easy payback plans for anyone interested in joining this Committee of 200:

1) The contributor gets a book of $500 or $1,000 tickets to the periodic Edwards fund-raisers that he can in turn sell to his friends and associates, the money he raises going to pay down his note.

2) Lesser contributions, the measly $1,000 to $5,000 variety, will be deposited in a trust fund and used to pay down the notes.

3) After the campaign is over and presuming it is successful, the net proceeds of one giant postcampaign fund-raiser will go to retire the remainder of the notes.

"At the very most," says Marion as Bill Murphy wheels into the Beningo driveway, "they know they will only have to come up with half the money. And the chances are great they won't have to come up with a dime." That's a hell of an investment: the gratitude of the next governor and recognition as a $25,000 hitter with the excellent prospects of not having to come up with a dime, and even that not until next year.

Elaine Beningo is an excellent hostess, having laid out a wonderful spread in a lovely home with engaging friends. The only difference between this and any other cocktail party in the New Orleans area tonight is that this one is going to get a pep talk from the brother of a candidate for governor. "I am here to bring you the good news that things are going just great in this campaign. It's like the story I heard about the 80-year-old man who went into the confessional . . . " Surely he's got a better class of joke for Metairie suburbanites than what he lays on Cajun police jurors. But no . . . "Father, I'm telling everyone! And I'm telling everybody I can let's win this one and win it big, let's get out and vote for your friend, my brother, our next governor, Edwin Edwards! No. 1 on the ballot!"

Somehow Marion restrains himself from breaking into his leaping reverse windmill clap and yelling "One! One! One!" while the hostess crawls under the dessert table. But Marion stops tastefully short of leading cheers. Actually, he is the life of the party's first·hour, something quaint the later guests could all hear about. But the point of the visit was hardly to swing any cocktail hour votes to his brother, and that becomes evident as Marion is thanking Elaine Beningo at the door for her hospitality. Bill Murphy walks up with the host and says solemnly, "Marion, Tom wants to talk about his pledge to the Committee of 200." Marion grasps his hand warmly, as though he were welcoming a new brother into Sigma Chi. "You'll be hearing from us right away."

Everything's going so well for Edwin Edwards—now if he could just get down a bet. Buckling up for takeoff for Lake Charles where he and Elaine will attend a state police function, he says he's checked Las Vegas but can't find any action. "I have one friend that bet $30,000 3-1. He's betting $90,000 to win $30,000. That's ridiculous."

A reporter mentions running into an old guy in Breaux Bridge who claims he won $6,000 on Treen in 1979 and says he's going to bet on him again.

"You get his name," springs Edwards. "Find me a bet and I'll give you 10 percent." Do journalistic ethics cover that?

You would expect of course that in Louisiana gambling and politics would have to make the link sometime. No better time than election day. Betting on elections is a tradition across the Cajun prairie, as deeply ingrained as cockfighting. To be valid and collectable, an election bet must follow a certain ritual. The most important is the designation of the vault, one person respected by both parties to hold the money. The bet must be written down, with all extenuating circumstances covered, even the death of one of the parties, either to the election or to the bet. You can find action on any reasonably contested election, from police juror to governor. And the fact that you can't find a close to even bet on Treen down there says as much for Treen's chances as the latest ominous poll.

As always when Edwards lands in Lake Charles, Roland Manuel is there to greet him. Roland is a veteran in the Old Guard, a trusted soldier from Edwards' first congressional race. Since then, whatever Edwards has needed in Lake Charles, whether a ride from the airport or campaign coordination for the four-parish southwest corner of the state, Manuel's done it. A huge, powerful man with a thick Cajun accent, Roland

Manuel, by his appearance, his utter fealty to Edwin Edwards and his reputation to go to any length to ensure a massive landslide, is Luca Brasi to Edwin's Godfather.

"Any bets, Roland?"

"Huh," puffs Manuel. "Around here? You kiddin'?"

"How close to 60 percent will I come here?"

"Oh, way over 60 percent. Everyone is solid for you down here." On the way from the airport to the Interstate, we rarely pass a block that hasn't at least one Edwards sign in a yard or in front of a business. "We've got the signs in everywhere, except one neighborhood where some rich people live. We're gonna take Cameron 85 percent, 70-30 in the four-parish area."

Roland's proudest of his fund-raising efforts, pointing out several businesses whose owners bought $1,000 tickets for the parish fund-raiser which he expects to net $50,000 for headquarters.

"You know who I sold a ticket to? Jack Dolan," boasts Manuel.

"Oh yeah?"

"He didn't want to at first, but I told him if he didn't, when the governor got back in, he wouldn't get nuthin'."

Edwards is silent for a moment at the news of Manuel's triumph, then starts speaking in French, probably something to the effect that the asshole in the front seat is a reporter.

Roland gets the message and changes the subject. "We need to call Roland Breaux. He's got these two black women who need to lease a car so they can start hauling in people to register and absentee vote." Of all the election week activities, from canvassing to direct mail, the oldest and still the most effective is hauling. Flat pick them up and take them to the polls, using everybody from sheriff's deputies to the old black women who know the neighborhoods. Marion Edwards swears by it. "By far the most effective political method is to physically get people and bring them to the polls. Nine out of ten people you bring to the polls will vote for you." Damned decent of them.

Turning off the Interstate, Roland says, "I wouldn't bother you with it, but Nolan has always taken care of it in the past."

"Sure," answers Edwards. "Call Shetland and get them a good used car."

Tonight's function is being held far outside town at a camp called

245

Habibi, which is similar to the name of a well-known New Orleans belly dancer whose skills the former governor once admired. "Habibi," Edwards reads the sign as we approach the entrance arch, "that means flower in Lebanese."

"I wouldn't know," Elaine says curtly, "she was your friend."

Greeting state policemen and area supporters inside the hall, the candidate again urges friends to be on the lookout for any action. (Surely the vice squad can find some.) "I'll take two bets, one on the popular vote and one on who carries the most parishes," he tells the group at his table.

Unwisely the reporter butts in, "That's no bet. Even if you lose the election, you know you're going to carry most of the parishes, like Lambert did."

"Fuck you, you're here to report, not give advice."

He stops for a TV interview with Denise Snelling, who notes his little-publicized campaign promise to appoint women to half of his cabinet posts. Even when hewing to the feminist line he can't let a double entendre slip by. "That's what the press release says," he laughs, "more women in high positions."

Minutes later, when officially introduced by the evening's emcee, both Edwards and Elaine are greeted by standing ovations from the troopers and their wives. Edwards returns the gesture with what they want to hear, a promise of a 10 percent pay raise and that "the number one, two, three and four positions in this department will come from your ranks and not be a boatbuilder or hamburger salesman." The troopers are on their feet again, showing as much partisan support on the part of civil servants as the Hatch Act allows. They especially appreciate the derisive reference to their present boss, boatbuilder and Public Safety Secretary Donald Bollinger. As for the hamburger salesman, Edwards shrugs, "I just threw that in." Though barred from active campaigning, state policemen are respected in their communities—in rural parishes they rate higher than deputy sheriffs. And their sentiments are clearly with Edwards, as the polite, lukewarm reception Governor Treen will receive the following evening will further attest. Not only is Edwards promising a future pay raise, but he also gave state policemen whopping salary increases on his way out of office in 1979. The partisan support pleases Edwards, who took pride in helping to build up and professionalize the state police. There was a time state troopers were considered glorified bagmen, running payoffs from the gamblers to the sheriffs to the Mansion. But over the years that has changed. Edwards, in his term, if he needed bagmen, didn't need them in uniform.

19. A Liar and a Scumbag

A chill runs down the newspaper editor's spine as 207 teenagers, the inaugural class of the Louisiana State School for Math, Science and the Arts, march into the Northwestern State University auditorium and stand at their seats to sing the ancient student song "Gaudeamus Igitur."

Selected in competitive tests for juniors and seniors from around the state, they have come to the Natchitoches campus to start Louisiana's first residential high school, a tribute to the commitment to excellence in an educational system that has a hard time keeping up with mediocrity. There is only one other public residential high school like it in the nation, in North Carolina, and Louisiana's will be the larger when it reaches its full complement of 700 students in three years. The concept for Louisiana's high school Harvard belongs to Rep. Jimmy Long and coincidentally helps him solve the problems caused by declining enrollment and empty facilities at Northwestern. One by one, the politicians on the podium dust off their most timeworn cliches and, in the mangled syntax, grammar and pronunciation these students already know better than to use, gush forth with what a "great leap forward" this school represents and how these youngsters, "the best and the brightest," prove yet again that "the youth of today are the leaders of tomorrow."

Governor Treen has a speech prepared, no doubt rhetorically outleaping all the previous great leaps forward, but he sets it aside for a remarkable off-the-cuff talk, a surprise even to his own press people who thought they had heard it all. The governor begins by telling the students, parents and school officials about his own memories of Northwestern, his mother's alma mater. Elizabeth Spier Treen spent only a few years in the classroom after graduating from what was then Louisiana Normal and before beginning to raise a family. But when Dave's older brother Paul was born totally deaf, her greatest teaching challenge began. His mother, the governor tells the hushed audience, was determined her son would not be shunted off into schools for the deaf but would have the same opportunities as hearing youngsters. So after Paul learned sign language, she sent him to public school and tutored him every night and weekend, all the way through Warren Easton High School and four years of Tulane. "I took it for the norm at the time, but when I grew up and looked back on what she did, I gained a profound respect for the teaching profession. And the reason I responded as favorably as I did to Jimmy Long's proposal was that this school would be located here, where my mother learned her skills."

Whew. It is a moving, emotional speech, the stuff of which legends are made: Dave Treen, the Man, the Saga. His speech comes so straight from the heart, he confesses later, he had never told it before. And almost assuredly he never will again. Here is a man, who will be lucky to get one-fifth of the vote of the state's schoolteachers, keeping under wraps a real-life anecdote that shows he understands and appreciates teachers. That one reminiscence gets the point across more effectively than all his statistics on teacher pay raises, the Professional Improvement Program and educational funding.

So he wants to keep his family out of it—pretty weird for a politician but if that's how he wants it, fine. But the school itself belongs in his campaign. Though it's the brainchild of Jimmy Long, the Louisiana School would never have happened without Treen's support and funding. And unlike some roads and bridges that Treen has paid for while Edwards claims the credit, the Louisiana School is all Dave Treen's as far as gubernatorial bragging rights go. And so what if only 207 smart kids will use it this year, while public education struggles beneath its crushing burden. The Louisiana School stands for something so excellent, so innovative, so uncompromisingly superior, so unlike anything else coming out of state education that the mere mention of it brings the loudest applause at the next scheduled stop in Many. Now it's doubtful that a lot of children from Sabine Parish will attend that school, and the same goes for most other Louisiana communities. But just the idea that the school is there, that Louisiana has what only one other state in the Union has and is setting the curve on something other than teenage

249

syphilis is a powerful political message. He should wear the school around him, claim it in every speech and bring the cameras back to make a commercial.

But he won't.

Here and there during the campaign, Dave Treen reveals himself capable of talking about something other than Edwin Edwards' retirement, Edwin Edwards' pardons, Edwin Edwards' DCCL or Edwin Edwards' latest distortion of the truth and record. Once in a while, usually off the beaten track a bit with no cameras around, Dave Treen would actually talk about himself and the good he had done. Really talk about it, with some depth and conviction and feeling, instead of plodding through buzzword accomplishments as a prelude to attacking Edwards some more. And because this positive emphasis was not as important in the overall campaign strategy, it was never shown on the TV spots, so carefully apportioned for blasting away at retirement, DCCL and pardons. John Cade, of course, could cite sound reasoning for the attack strategy: they were still trailing in the polls and with the limited TV money they had raised, the priority was placed on tearing down Edwin Edwards' image instead of projecting Dave Treen's. "When you're behind you attack," explains Cade, as though he were taking a page from the Republican War College field manual. Just like that. It's what's *supposed* to be done—it's the Republican way. But lost in the lofty, pristine logic of their Tuesday strategy sessions, where they clinically allotted so many TV exposures for each point of attack on Edwards, was any attempt, any enthusiasm for telling who Dave Treen was and why people should vote for him. Much of the blame belongs to John Cade, the real media mind behind the campaign, and his inflexibility in viewing the only options as straight black or white, negative or positive, Darth Vader or Pollyanna. With a little imagination, which is what they are paying Gus Weill a princely sum to provide, they could develop—as has Edwards—an effective campaign of distinctions, showing issue by issue how Edwin Edwards screwed this state and Dave Treen is making things right again. There are certainly enough facts to support such a strategy— Edwards has enough to support his—but the innovative approach would use up precious seconds that could be devoted to heaping more moral outrage on Edwin Edwards. Therefore all such suggestions are promptly canned.

That's why the Treen campaign has paid as little attention as possible to potentially its best issue, one where a valid and provocative distinction can be drawn between the two candidates. What could have been an important rallying point for Treen will turn into the great nonissue of 1983: the environment.

Many thought this would be the year the environmental issue would finally surface as a political issue. For years it was carefully avoided. Any politician who voiced ecological concerns was considered either politically irrelevant or dangerous to the hot and blowing petrochemical industry that had offered two generations of farm boys the crack at the good life that a plant worker's paycheck could provide. Most people living near one of the state's burgeoning industrial complexes either accepted or didn't notice the orange tint of the sky and the foul odor of the air. *Ah, sulfur in the morning. It smells like . . . prosperity.*

Ecological awareness increased overnight one summer evening in 1978 when 19-year-old Kirk Jackson released a load of chemicals from his dump truck into Bayou Sorrel, creating an immediate reaction that caused a deadly cloud of vapors to engulf the truck and asphyxiate the young driver. The news rocked the state. Something had come out of the bayou and killed somebody. Like a home chemistry set gone haywire, the southern end of the state, citizens realized, held thousands of industrial cesspools of unknown but potentially deadly content. And those pits, citizens were to discover with some helpful publicity from the EPA, were all over, with more unknown quantities of who-knew-what being illegally and regularly dumped in bayous and rivers, even where there were sources of drinking water.

More revelations changed awareness into alarm. A national cancer research study pinpointed the top ten counties in the country in per capita cancer deaths: five of them were in Louisiana, along the industrial belt of the Mississippi River.

Vast dead zones were found in Lake Pontchartrain, source of big supplies of the state's oysters and shrimp. Pipelines, channel dredging and road projects threatened the marshland estuaries of abundant seafood. Along the coast, continued channelization of rivers and bayous is helping the sea to erode Louisiana's barrier islands.

Drinking water in New Orleans and Jefferson Parish, never good, became an even greater source of concern with reports of illegal or accidental dumping by industries along the river. But leave it to the macabre Orleans sense of humor—speculation arose that whenever Georgia Pacific dumped phenol upstream, the taste of city drinking water actually improved. That minty taste of spring.

During Edwards' first two terms, environmental concerns were a joke—literally. He had a repertoire of one-liners about hippie, kooky ecologists who cared more for the gnu and the caribou than for this country's energy future. That always got a rise out of audiences of oil producers or plant workers. As much as his flippant attitude enraged environmentalists, Edwards moved quickly to disarm them in the 1983 campaign by going hat in hand to the Sierra Club to apologize for past neglect and promise to be a friend of the environment in the future. He told a reporter later his reception was as good as he could have expected. "No one threw a rock."

Treen, with a hideous congressional voting record on the environment, took the matter more seriously, though his and the Legislature's actions didn't always reflect it. Baton Rouge Senator Tommy Hudson bristled with indignation when Treen vetoed his appropriation for a baseline study of the connection between the environment and the state's cancer rate. At the height of Hudson's heated rhetoric, it was discovered that the Senate, in its infinite somnolence, had forgotten to pass the bill to set up the study. Never mind.

To one environmentalist the choice was less than clear. "I will probably hold my nose and vote for Treen in the uncertain hope that an incompetent, principled reactionary will do less harm than a competent amoral opportunist." Now Edwards could accept that. Treen's slight edge among ecologists wouldn't matter unless Treen could translate the distinctions between him and Edwards on the environment into a cutting campaign issue.

The Treen campaign obliges him by barely mentioning the environment as an issue except to boast about his program of land acquisition in the Atchafalaya Basin—a problem few people knew needed solving. But Dave Treen did break through once in a while, as he did in a speech before the Lake Charles group called C.L.E.A.N. The speech and the crowd's reaction were one of the campaign's most upbeat moments, one of Treen's best speeches, perhaps the clearest delineation between Edwards' and Treen's approaches to the environment. And it was largely unreported and unnoticed.

Lake Charles is an unlikely rallying point for the environmental cause. The lake port city at the southwestern edge of the state is home to the huge Cities Service refinery, a big Olin Matheson fertilizer plant and other industrial firms. Lake Charles is a paycheck town with a rough and tumble hardhat mentality, what Baton Rouge would be without the greening influences of LSU or state government. No one raised much hell about pollution here until it became known what a rotten sewer the BFI Willow Springs disposal site had turned out to be. Concern about the site ignited a citizens' movement, led by C.L.E.A.N., that caused the Treen administration to finally order the site closed this year. It was a signal victory for the environmentalists, serving notice that the ecological issue was alive and kicking in the very heart of petrochemical Louisiana.

Into this actively churning atmosphere walks Dave Treen to receive an honorary membership in and endorsement from C.L.E.A.N. No mere band of do-gooders, C.L.E.A.N. boasts some of the city's elected politicians, such as District Attorney Lynn Knapp, who is looking to the police jury race as the next battleground for the newest hot issue in the parish, licensing area salt domes for storage of hazardous wastes. C.L.E.A.N. is feeling its oats, but not getting overconfident. This is still Lake Charles. Says president Shirley Goldsmith, "We've had women who call us to volunteer but they want their names kept secret. They say their husbands work at PPG or Olin Matheson and could lose their jobs if their families get involved with us."

Against this backdrop, Dave Treen has the perfect opportunity to demonstrate his solidarity with the clean earth. He opens to a strong ovation with the state's latest move on the BFI plant in Willow Springs. "After I got the facts and spent some time on it—one of the details Dave Treen immerses himself in—I have decided that we will persist in our closure order." After laying that present on them, he goes on for 30 minutes without notes, ticking off the environmental achievements of his administration, which include:

—forming the Department of Environmental Quality to give full departmental weight to solving ecological problems;

—setting up the Coastal Environmental Protection Fund to save Louisiana's eroding barrier islands;

—starting the Abandoned Hazardous Waste Fund with a first year appropriation to test five of the sites earmarked for federal Superfund cleanup money;

—increasing monitoring of plant discharges along the Mississippi River;

—upping the fines to polluters 10-fold over the Edwards administration;

—starting an aquatic filtration pilot program in Jefferson Parish to improve drinking water;

—putting up $12 million in state money for buying land in the Atchafalaya Basin and $10 million for land in the Tensas.

He closes his remarks to enthusiastic applause with this vision: "I sense we're forming a consensus among people of good will in Louisiana that we are the custodians of this earth charged with keeping and preserving this magnificent state of Louisiana for all who come after us."

The best part follows, a PR man's dream, as the question and answer period turns into one spontaneous testimonial after another from individuals in the audience who alerted the state to water or air pollution or illegal plant discharges and got results. "I never expected any response from the state and I was surprised when I got action," says a man who notified DNR of stream pollution.

He makes a strong impression on the C.L.E.A.N. group, but just on that group. To make a clear distinction between Treen on the environment and Edwards on the environment, he needs to make that same speech more. But he won't. And why not? Because the polls say not to. "The environment only shows up as the sixth most important issue in our polling," says Scott Welch. Shows what a little lack of imagination can do. The Treen camp, religiously following its polls, decides there are no votes in the environment. They're wrong. It's all a matter of how you frame the question. You can ask a voter on a poll what he or she thinks of protecting the environment and you'll get a lukewarm response. But ask about his or her mother dying of cancer and you can evoke some anger, you can create an issue that people can get mad about. Yet another case of Governor Dave Treen making a difference, but candidate Dave Treen not making the point.

It's not that a more positive approach has not been considered—Treen, in fact, has argued for it in the Tuesday strategy sessions he did attend. But shifting gears is not easy, the greatest resistance caused by an absolute obsession shared by Treen and Cade to answer "the lies of

Edwin Edwards." Dave Treen cannot abide Edwin Edwards' "continuous distortions of my record," though there isn't a damned thing he can do to stop him. "Lie" is the operative word in the Treen campaign. I use the word advisedly because Treen and Cade employ it so broadly to include any incorrect statement by Edwards, whether a premeditated untruth, a result of shoddy research or mere overblown campaign rhetoric. Hardly a week went by that a Treen campaign story headline in the *Advocate* or the *Picayune* did not contain the magic three-letter word, as seen by these heads:

TREEN SAYS EDWARDS LIED ABOUT CUTS
TREEN: EDWARDS LIED TO BLACK MINISTERS
TREEN: EDWARDS LYING MACHINE IN HIGH GEAR
TREEN LABELS EDWARDS CAMPAIGN A LYING MACHINE
TREEN CALLS EDWARDS' AD "OUTRAGEOUS AND FALSE"

Unsatisfied with the news coverage, Cade wants to pursue the issue in advertising. "I think I'm going to have to take out a full page ad called 'The Lies of Edwin Edwards.'" Enough already. In their righteousness and obsession with correcting the permanent record, the Treen people don't realize what a bore and a joke their own press releases, seething with anger and outrage, are becoming. Worse yet, they are doggedly trying to prove a point that many people already believe, accept and don't seem to mind. Edwards' own poll shows one-third of those who say they intend to vote for Edwards also agree with the statement "There is something about Edwin Edwards I don't trust."

That's the great failure of Cade's attack strategy, it doesn't answer the question "so what?" Many of Edwards' supporters believe he is a little shady and still very effective as a leader. All along, Treen has failed to show how Edwards' untruths make him less capable a leader. And Treen is also unaware of the damage his truth crusade is causing his own campaign. The more he talks about Edwards the more attention he draws to Edwards, and the more "lies" he rails against, the more a ninny and a nit-picker he makes himself appear to be. It can only be a shallow understanding of human nature that leads Treen and Cade to harp incessantly on another person's being a liar, never realizing that blind adherence to the truth makes ordinary people feel uncomfortable. A frustrated Roy Fletcher can neither believe it nor stop it. "It goes beyond the absurdity of one politician calling another a liar, it's broader than that. People just aren't going to throw stones at someone else for lying. We all do it."

The hopeless integrity crusade ebbs to the point that Treen aides believe Edwards is deliberately making statements Treen would surely label as lies and pounce upon. Edwards laughs as the Treen campaign uses up inordinate time and energy and the patience of supporters, chasing after Edwards' newest lies with all the relentless frustration of a man trying to nail mercury to a table. Each new attack increases Edwards' own immunity. So he doesn't always tell the truth, the whole truth and nothing but the truth. Why should he? If he's a little off, Dave Treen is sure to be right behind to correct him.

At a state meeting of 600 Jaycees at the Airport Sheraton outside New Orleans, Edwards engages in a little role playing. Noting at the start of his speech that Dave Treen turned down the invitation to address the group, Edwards offers to speak on behalf of Governor Treen too. Speaking first for himself, he talks about his efforts to bring more industry to Louisiana. Then raising his right hand for Treen, he responds, "He's a liar."

Speaking for himself, he notes his concern for education. Speaking for Treen, he says, "He's a liar." The Jaycees roar with delight and elect Edwin Edwards governor in their straw poll.

Maybe Treen and Cade should be excused for their unpolitic obsession, sparked as they are by more than a desire to win, by a deeper urge to express moral outrage. Cade's preoccupation leads him into the major loose-lipped faux pas of the campaign. John, who beneath his pressurized stern exterior possesses a good sense of humor and easy rapport with his own staff, has fallen under the bad influence of Scott Welch's and Roy Brightbill's pressroom vocabularies. Late in the campaign, wrapping up a press conference in Alexandria, Cade, feeling relaxed—too relaxed—slips into his staff's youthful vernacular to recount yet another flagrant Edwards distortion. Mutters Cade, "What a scumbag!" As the words leave his tongue and he sees TV reporter Babs Zimmerman's eyes light up, he realizes that he has relaxed in front of the wrong person. The famous scumbag quote is on the wire within hours. The comment makes Cade look more silly than mean. "Scumbag," says a TV station owner. "That's a word my 14-year-old daughter uses . . . to describe her friends." Just to set the record straight, the *Picayune*'s Charlie Hargroder tracks down the accepted definition: "scumbag: *(n)*—used condom."

At Edwards headquarters, the quote evokes more laughs than anything else. Within days a "Scumbags for Edwards" bumpersticker joins the other campaign memorabilia on Sam LeBlanc's office wall. Yet to those farther removed from the action, the quote further denigrates John Cade's image as a proper, principled Republican gentleman. The comment tars him as a petty, bitter gutter fighter bent on character assassination. It's not the case. John Cade is the good soldier, ready to lay down his image and his reputation for the good of his friend and leader Dave Treen. Admirable qualities, but in his earnestness and enthusiasm he is doing more to destroy his own image than Edwin Edwards'.

As for Dave Treen, there seems a deeper reluctance, as suggested in his uneasiness at even mentioning his mother in the context of his education plank, to show the voters his positive, human side. It's a staff joke and not a very funny one. With aide Alphie Hyorth at the wheel of the press bus bringing up the rear of the Treen caravan heading through Opelousas, a reporter remarks how the campaign poster of smiling Dave Treen in shirtsleeves is one of the best photos ever taken of the governor.

"Treen doesn't like it," says Alphie.

"But it looks intimate and friendly."

"That's why he doesn't like it."

Pacing the floor of the control room of WRBT, Roy Fletcher is a bad cross of dead tired and cat nervous. He rubs his eyes and sits back at the board to cue up one more commercial. "We're doing something positive today." He waves the visitor in. "Reelecting Dave Treen is good politics," says the voice on the TV monitor. "Six major newspapers in the state have endorsed his reelection. For example, the Opelousas *Daily World* says, 'Edwin Edwards tiptoes around the law like a burglar...'" Well, it was positive for 15 seconds, anyway.

Fletcher cues up another cassette, this one the official endorsement spot from Henson Moore in Washington. It's one of the very few Dave Treen spots that does not mention Edwin Edwards' name, an indication of how wide a berth the Republican congressman is giving the Democratic candidate for governor, who also happens to reside in the

Sixth District. Henson appears to speak off the cuff, and fairly well, until the ending, *why you should elect Dave Treen.* Elect? Moore makes a face and moans—*Nooo-o-o*—and does it again: *why you should reelect Dave Treen.*

Moore's spot is very interesting—this is the first peep we've heard out of the popular Republican from Baton Rouge since the campaign began. On several occasions, Treen and Moore were in the same town on the same day and did not appear together. When Treen opened his Baton Rouge headquarters, he was introduced by New Orleans Congressman Bob Livingston. Treen was in Baton Rouge the night of the Catholic High Men's Club Barbecue, a *de rigueur* campaign stop for any candidate. Henson Moore was there, Dave Treen wasn't. The distance between the two seems all the more baffling in light of Treen staffers' inability to get any Democratic legislator, any DA, any mayor to come out front for him. There are stories of so much enmity between Moore and John Cade, going back to 1979 when Moore felt that Cade was encouraging Henson to run and then pulled the rug out from under him when Treen finally made up his mind. Actually, Moore's reluctance to help a fellow Republican doesn't go as deep as past resentment. Henson, instead, is thinking more about his future and what may happen if he backs the wrong candidate in this election. Moore started hot and heavy for Dave Treen. At the Republican state convention back in February, Moore rocked the rafters with a burning anti-Edwards speech, rechristening DCCL "the Deceitful and Corrupt Corporation of Louisiana." Shortly afterwards, he received a letter from Edwin Edwards. According to Edwards, no threats were involved. He was merely seeking to establish with Moore what would be considered acceptable partisan support and what would be taken as an act of war. "I told him in the letter I have every respect for his desire to endorse and campaign for Dave Treen but that I will not tolerate any gratuitous attacks on my integrity or saying anything about me that is untrue, especially on those matters which he knows nothing about. To his credit, he called me and wrote me a letter saying that he had been caught up in the partisan spirit of the convention. And that was it. No person reading that letter could interpret it to mean I was warning him not to campaign for Dave Treen." Just the same, Henson Moore, whether out of an abundance of caution or lack of desire to stick his neck out for a sinking cause, artfully practices his disappearing act for the duration of the campaign. What can Edwin Edwards do to Henson Moore? Plenty. Moore has coasted along this far in the heavily Democratic Sixth District precisely because Edwards has not tried to go after him. Were Edwards to find and fund an attractive Democrat to run for Congress every other year, Henson would have to start coming up with a half million dollars for every election just to hold onto his job. Party loyalty goes only so far in this business.

It's been a rough campaign for the mighty Gus Weill organization. After building up a good relationship with the governor to get the account, Weill finds himself dealing far more with John Cade and liking it much less. Gus has pushed all out for Treen, even committing the adman's cardinal sin, crossing the line from paid professional to campaign supporter by speaking for Treen at the big Lafayette rally. But in the final months of the campaign, his ardor cools—it's apparent that the message is exclusively John Cade's medium. The last indignity is the rumor that Cade has fired Weill. It's not true, Roy Fletcher cuts all the TV spots for the Weill agency to the very end.

Still Gus grows more uncomfortable with the situation the longer it drags on. The final straw comes at John McKeithen's reception before the first LSU home game. As Gus describes it, "I was at the party standing near Governor McKeithen when someone I knew from past Edwards campaigns came up to me and told me, 'You'd better get your business straight with Edwin or it will be your ass.' That really stunned me that I would get that kind of threat for doing my job. I later checked with Edwards and found, of course, that was not true, but it left me with a bad feeling about what political campaigns were coming to." And seeing what this campaign was coming to, Gus opts out the only graceful way possible, announcing in late September that once this one is over, his agency will no longer handle political campaigns.

The Treen people take the announcement as a slap in the face, but, at this point, one more indignity hardly seems to matter.

20. "The Healer Is Coming . . ."

Every candidate needs a George Fischer, a general from the old school of ass-kickers and order-barkers, someone who will take a complex, challenging, even risky task and do whatever is necessary to get it done. A few minutes after dawn on the first day of October, the former secretary of the Department of Transportation and Development is making his final inspection on the ultimate road show, a nine-day, 64-parish, 80-stop campaign blitz by Edwin Edwards and his entire entourage. And since it's being done for Edwin Edwards, Fischer knows the unwieldy assemblage of five motorhomes, two helicopters, an airplane and a cast of thousands waiting along the way must operate with perfect timing, effortlessly, and with maximum enthusiasm.

George Fischer was bred for this job, getting firsthand training on grand maneuvers as the young military aide to General Mark Clark. Back home in Jefferson Parish, he amassed his fortune supplying the new suburbanites with the essential of life, gasoline, through his large and successful service stations. Politically he was the peerless bureaucrat, heading at different times the state's two largest agencies, Transportation and Health and Human Resources. As powerful as Fischer was in Edwards' first two terms, he was not power hungry like former Commissioner of Administration Charlie Roemer. Fischer may see himself as a general but he is also a good soldier, with total fealty to his king.

Fischer's leadership style makes him the perfect man for this task and vice versa. Those who have dealt with Fischer describe him as ruthless, demanding, unrelenting, and those were the compliments. The legislators and civil servants who didn't fall into line at attention, went face to face with Fischer. A lobbyist described the ordeal as "getting Fischerized." "At least you know where you stand with George," marveled one legislator. "He's not the kind of guy to stab you in the back, he'll stab you in the chest." Edwards likes Fischer because he is totally loyal and obedient. But only to Edwards. Anyone else who gets in Fischer's way is going to get shoved around. So, to maintain peace and to limit casualties in the campaign, Edwards needed to give Fischer so large, so complex, so challenging, so time-consuming an assignment, and enough warm bodies to order around, that George wouldn't have either the time or the inclination to bull his way into any other aspect of the organization. If the nine-day Motorcade serves no other purpose than to keep George Fischer occupied, it's worth the full effort and investment.

The trip had been planned early in the campaign as a final media and organization blitz, a way for Edwards to get a lot of press attention all over the state and to involve all parish volunteer organizations in one massive dress rehearsal for the big day three Saturdays away. As October dawns Edwards is growing more confident that, barring some unforeseen catastrophe, he will roll to victory on election day. Yet for all the good publicity he stands to gain from the Motorcade, therein also lies the considerable risk that Edwards will be embarrassed by disorganization or disinterest. Nothing is worse for a politician than a perfectly coordinated campaign rally that brings out more organizers and reporters than people. Edwards, ever conscious of "the tides," approaches the marathon blitz with a certain trepidation if not dread. Bone weary and emotionally spent, Edwards feels that the last thing he needs to do in the home stretch is to thrust himself into a 10-speech-a-day rally regimen which can gain him nothing more than what he has but which can reveal, under the glaring lights and blaring bands, pitifully small turnouts and shallowness of support. And there'll be no hiding failure, for this was unabashedly planned and promoted as a media event. And the media could latch onto no hotter story than the man of the people taking his show on the road and flopping.

For his part, Fischer is determined no detail will be left to chance. He sets his team to the task early in the year, mapping out routes all over the state, then sending out teams to drive them and drive them again. Four times they traverse the state, timing every leg, assuming an average speed of 38 miles per hour. Two of Clifford Smith's helicopters are lined up to whisk the candidate and a pool of press members to some remote stops while the caravan lumbers on down the road. An airplane stands by in case of an emergency, and to shuttle back to Baton Rouge daily with TV tapes and departing reporters. No matter if it rains—there are contingency plans for each stop. Supporters with motorhomes are valuable commodities at election time—Fischer lined up six of them, in varying degrees of magnificence (Charlie Boudreaux's $380,000 Bluebird with a horn that plays "On the Road Again" is the lead attraction), to carry Edwards and team. A chartered bus, stocked with food, soft drinks and beer (only for consumption after five—Fischer's rule), complete with driver and two stewardesses, is reserved for the press. Fischer orders that the press corps, to vary in number from six to 30 over the nine days, be waited on hand and foot. Thoroughly uncomfortable reporters who ask will be allowed to fetch their own Cokes. As long as Fischer doesn't find out.

But for all Fischer's planning, he can only do half the job: getting the candidate there. The parish volunteer organizations, 64 of them set up by Sam LeBlanc, are charged with finding a place, hiring a band (as long as it can play "On the Road Again"), lining up the free hotdogs and Cokes—beer and sausage po-boys if they can—and the people. That would be the trick, especially at some rural stops at 2 o'clock on a hot weekday afternoon.

Straining to see through the motorhome's tinted glass windows, Fischer sighs in relief to see 400 Marksvillians cheering Edwin and Elaine, who disembark from a white Cadillac at the courthouse steps. Well begun is half done. Fischer's mind is clicking ahead to the next two stops as he surveys the responsive crowd, the hustling aides in their yellow windbreakers, the local volunteers pouring the Cokes and dishing out the hotdogs—everything is . . . wait a second. Fischer jerks in recognition of something terribly wrong. There in the front of the crowd, the young woman smiling as she holds her tape recorder up to capture the master's voice. Treen volunteers! Fischer has a fit. Infiltrators, provocateurs, along on George Fischer's crowning mission.

He glares hotly at Treen research director Scott Welch, mouthing silent but scabrous salutations at him, shoving yellow jackets to move in and tail the enemy troops.

"What are you doing here?" asks the surprised and delighted reporter.

"We just want to see how many lies are being told to the good people," answers Captain Fact, who, along with Lanny Keller and John Cade's daughter Martha, has drawn the assignment of bird-dogging the caravan to its end, identifying and transmitting back to headquarters all Edwards' lies and misstatements. If Fischer couldn't quite keep his cool, Edwards could—and use it. "There stands Dave Treen's monitor," he tells the Marksville crowd, pointing to Welch. "They're taping everything we say. And if they listen, they may learn something."

The rest of the day will be cat and mouse between the yellow jackets and the Truth Squaders. The press bus horn blows, the caravan loads up and heads out, with the Truth Squad in close pursuit. On to Ville Platte and Eunice and Opelousas, at every stop Edwards introducing "Dave Treen's monitors," which always evokes a good growl from the crowd. Lanny Keller, in the middle of 1,000 Cajuns, and with yellow jackets on his heels, whispers to a reporter, "One time, he's going to say, 'Stone them' and they will."

The idea that Cade would send out Treen volunteers on the Motorcade has completely eluded Fischer, who thought he had prepared for every contingency. And it has terribly frustrated him. A yellow jacket explains, "To George that was dirty tricks, and it's exactly what he wanted to do to Treen, but Edwards wouldn't let him. Then to have it done to him was about more than George could take."

Going back to their van after the Breaux Bridge speech, the Truth Squad members find the air let out of two tires. The yellow jackets have struck again. Captain Fact leaves a local volunteer with the van and leads the squad to their backup car a block away. When the Motorcade pulls into St. Martinville, Welch is waiting at the bandstand, smiling broadly at Fischer. Fischer explains to amused reporters, "I suppose they let the air out of their own tires for the story."

The Truth Squad is just the angle the press, already bored after the first speech, is looking for. The sight of Clancy DuBos of WDSU interviewing Welch finally sets Fischer off. Shoving through the crowd, poking Captain Fact in the chest, he demands, "Can't you take your interviews somewhere else? This is our event, we don't need you here." With Fischer's son Kevin standing three inches behind Welch blocking off any retreat, the general offers an ominous invitation. "You come along if you want. You can have a hotdog or drink a beer, but I can't be responsible for what our people do." Clancy DuBos is wildly signaling for his cameraman to get the confrontation on tape, but Billy Broadhurst and Mike Baer quickly intercede. "No problem, no problem," says Baer, his lawyerly mind filling with visions of assault suits. Broadhurst pulls Welch aside and apologizes for Fischer's temper. "Hey, when this campaign is over, I'll buy you a steak."

"Oh, what he said didn't bother me," says Welch looking over his shoulder, "but his son was standing on my damn foot."

As the first day rolls surprisingly smoothly on, Fischer's initial rage over the Truth Squad mellows. He even concedes a grudging modicum of respect for how they've kept right up with Fischer's schedule (which they have pirated a copy of). Not that he likes them one bit. "I told that boy, that smooth-faced boy," says Fischer of Fact, "that he's gotta live here when it's all over. They're provoking us, and we've gotta take it like men, but any one of our people could punch their lights out. But we can't do that even if that's what they want. But we can only hold our people off until October 22. After that, they could be walking down the street and someone's going to slap them."

Edwards is keeping the Truth Squad busy. As Edwards ticks off the local projects in each parish Treen has vetoed, Keller feverishly checks facts and pecks out press releases challenging Edwards' claims. When Edwards rails about $9 million in projects vetoed in the Opelousas area, Keller can't believe it. "St. Landry Parish groans under the weight of public works projects the Treen administration has built. Per capita, he has spent more money in this parish on public works than any parish in the state." Keller, only on the campaign trail for a week after taking leave from the governor's press office, is appreciating Captain Fact's lament of months past: "The man tells lies faster than we can write them down."

Through New Iberia and Morgan City, where Edwards hauls out one of his favorite targets, Treen's proposed "sin" taxes on beer and cigarettes. "Who drinks beer and smokes cigarettes?" he asks the cheering blue collar crowd. "Dave Treen doesn't drink beer. He drinks Chivas Regal. I don't drink and I don't smoke but I'm not gonna let them tax your beer and cigarettes."

He ends the first long day at Blackham Coliseum in Lafayette, telling 4,000 ecstatic Cajuns, "I understand where you're coming from. I speak your language. I worry for you. I want to do something for you.

I'll never turn my back on you." Blackham rocks.

Queen Sauce Piquante XIV is just leaving the fairgrounds at St. Mary's Church Sunday morning in Raceland as Edwin Edwards is coming in, followed by a massive entourage of yellow jackets, cops, TV cameras, assorted reporters and local politicians. A couple of hundred drift toward the bandstand, though most of the festival goers are up in front of the church, sitting under the spreading oak, feeling the breeze coming off Bayou Lafourche, eating magnificent alligator sauce piquante, and listening to a band that doesn't know how to play "On the Road Again."

Since everyone seems to be having a good time, Edwards lays off cataloguing Dave Treen's vetoes in the area but cites other grave offenses against the people. "When I was governor, I let the state police work these festivals. This year they were taken away from you by Treen and Bollinger. But you wait, next year you'll get them back." He promises to work with the oil and gas industry "to get the trucks rolling again, to get the boats running again, to get the welders working again." He looks forward to the day when "we can go to the Mansion and eat crawfish and boudin and sauce piquante and play bourre."

Fifteen minutes later, Dave Treen leaps onto the same bandstand Edwards has just vacated. While the governor's entourage is much smaller than the contender's, the crowd that gathers around is just as large and just as outnumbered by the folks on the front side of the church eating piquante and listening to the music. Dave Treen may have taken the state troopers away but he promises something the folks in Raceland have never seen and may not know what to do with: foreign tourists. "Next year many people from all over the world who will be coming for the World's Fair will also come to the Sauce Piquante Festival here on Bayou Lafourche. The fair will permit us to showcase Louisiana and we'll get the people here who make the decisions regarding investments and it will get Louisiana moving ahead again." Dave Treen can't throw around the promises like Edwin Edwards does, but he tries his best, in sticking to the facts, to show he's made a difference in these lives, mentioning, for example, the two patrol boats that have been added to monitor dumping along the Mississippi. He closes with a request that even he must know is wishful thinking. "I want every voter, no matter his or her present leanings, to make an informed judgment on October

22 and take every opportunity to learn about the policies and the record of the two candidates." And that's the difference. Edwin Edwards dares these people to hope and to dream. Dave Treen challenges them to study.

By Monday morning, the reporters are noticing something odd about the crowds: they're still there, in numbers almost as strong as on the weekend. In Kaplan and Jennings and Lake Charles and De Quincy and De Ridder. WBRZ's Brenda Hodge begins paying less attention to the speech, and, moving through the audiences, she asks, "Why are you here?" and many answer, "I don't have a job." And Edwin Edwards is telling them what they want to hear. "You give me a job, and I'll help you find a job. After he got his job, 128,000 people lost theirs." The discontented are coming out to hear the man they believe can make a difference. "I'd have a job if we had a decent governor," says the fellow in the workshirt. So powerful is the image of the governor's office that it's believed he can move state government and the state's economy as well. Though some businessmen quietly (very quietly) doubt there is much a governor can do to stimulate hiring, the out-of-work still turn to Edwards—and he doesn't turn them away.

Edwards is promising more than hard work, honesty and good government. He's promising prosperity, jobs, hope, yes, salvation.

That comes out the first day in Ville Platte, at the end of a Horace the Peg-Legged Pig joke. A ridiculous joke, but every audience loves it. Okay, it's about a visitor to a farm who wants to know why the farmer's pig has a peg leg. The farmer says it's Horace, a wonderful pig, that has saved his family on many occasions with great acts of pig heroism. "Don't you ever say anything bad about Horace," says the farmer.

"I wouldn't dream of saying anything bad about him, but why does he have a peg leg?" asks the visitor.

"Well, man, you don't eat a good friend like that all at once. That's what's happening to us," says Edwards as the crowd roars. "We've lost an arm and a leg and an eye and an ear. We're being picked to pieces a little at a time. But don't worry," he raises his hand and bends forward as the cheers of the crowd almost drown him out, "the healer is coming."

The theme pops up again and again as the caravan rolls through the Cajun prairie into the piney hills of Central Louisiana. "Someone is

266

coming," he says, "to deliver you from your despair." It's the evangelist's message with the politician's promise. And the faces in the crowd shine with more than partisan political loyalty. You see it in the eyes of these middle-aged men dressed in work clothes with nowhere to go work, cheering the candidate's promise to get the boats running and the rigs working. You see it in the faces of black women, kids in tow, low-paid state workers afraid the Republican budget knife will cut them off. Edwards gives them a laugh and a memory of better times and a hope those days can come back—unrealistic or not, it is something for worried people to hold onto. "You can sell despair like crazy," says one local candidate, "and you can sell hope on top of that even better." Edwards is selling more than good times around the corner, he is selling salvation in the face of despair.

Edwards finds no more fertile ground for his message than when he rolls into the sandy hills and piney woods of Long country. Standing under a magnolia tree on the courthouse lawn in Winnfield, Reverend Clarence D. Bates entreats the faithful waiting for their candidate, "Hey, are you tired of being starved to death? Get a button and show whose side you're on."

Not having seen the good Reverend Bates since the Pentecostal rally in Tioga, I try to run the morality question by him one more time. "How does Edwards' reputation for womanizing square with the Pentecostals' view of morality?"

The reverend eyes me severely. "Yea, there are many womanizers in this world, but there are not many leaders like this man. We cannot changeth the man, only the Lord can changeth the man . . . "

Okay, okay.

Reverend Bates must interrupt his comparative morality class to climb up the platform erected next to the life-sized statue of Huey to announce the Second Coming, brushing off his best imitation of his old boss Uncle Earl. "I'm glad all you fine people have come out to hear the issues of the day," rasps out Bates, scratching his side. "It shows industry. It shows fortitude. It shows that you've got but three friends in this world: Sears and Roebuck, Jesus Christ and Edwin Edwards!"

This is just the prop Edwin Edwards has been waiting for. Pointing to the statue at his side, Edwards beholds the figure of Huey Long. "Fifty-five years ago a sandy-haired man came down from these sandy hills and started Louisiana on its road to prosperity. I have come back to you today to tell you that which he started 55 years ago will not die as long as you and you and you support people like Edwin Edwards." The cheers and applause start and keep up throughout the speech, with the black woman in the green dress sitting on the lawn chair nodding and clapping, "Uh-hunh, uh-hunh," as the wealthy Edwards deftly ridicules the rich man's candidate. "What's he ever done for you? He cut the income tax and that only helped the rich people like Brother Bates and myself and the sheriff here." One of his favorite and most effective lines, localized for each audience. He especially loves to throw it at a roomful of Rotarians—"Dave Treen's income tax cut only helped wealthy people like you and I"—and they all sit up straight in their chairs, feeling more important.

But lest anyone mistake the difference between the rich candidate and the rich man's candidate, Edwards asks, "When was the last time he was here in Winnfield?"

"He came to the country club once," pipes a voice from the audience.

"You see, if Dave Treen gets reelected, you'll have to join the country club to see him."

Time for his favorite prop. "Where's that letter?" Darrell Hunt immediately holds out a direct mail piece on economic development sent from Treen to businessmen. Edwards holds the letter and the microphone out to a teenager in the front row. "What's the color of Dave Treen's signature?"

"Blue."

"Same color as his blood." The populist audience laughs as loud as it cheers.

Dave Treen may be criticized for waging a negative campaign, but he can't touch Edwin Edwards for dripping sarcasm, but that's Edwards' special gift, to ridicule with humor. He wants to get them mad but also to leave them laughing. "Dave Treen cut the old age pension from $50 to $40. Listen, my momma wouldn't let me come home if I did something like that to poor old widows. . . . He tried to cut the Right to Bite program [which provides free dentures for elderly indigents]. When you're old, all you can do is eat. You don't want to have to eat mush and syrup. But Dave Treen doesn't care. Not only does he want to put the bite on you, he's trying to gum you to death."

His audience roaring approval, Edwards shows no fear as he strides into his most sensitive issue. Since the Motorcade began, the candidate has been wrestling with a suitable explanation for his pardons policy, a process that by degrees has wound him up to his grandest rhetorical excess, to wit: "Dave Treen makes it sound like I go to the penitentiary every few days with the keys and say, 'Here, you go rape someone' and 'Here, you go murder someone.' But that's not the way it works. . . . There may have been some pardons I didn't sign that I should have and some I signed that I shouldn't have, but let me tell you something. The greatest man who ever lived died on the cross to pardon us for all our sins." At the foot of Huey's statue, Clarence Bates shakes his head in admiration—*got to remember that one.*

Now back on the attack, the candidate shifts gears to go after his opponent's sin tax hike proposals. In Morgan City, he warns Treen will make the poor working man pay more for his beer and cigarettes. Deep in the Bible Belt, he switches to lesser vices. "He wants to raise the tax on a pack of snuff. Suppose if you have no teeth, all you can do is dip a little snuff. But if Dave Treen gets elected, you better go buy all the snuff you can." To highlight this outrage he points to the statue at his side. "This man must be rolling over in his grave." Probably so. Laughing.

The Motorcade cuts across North Louisiana. On a helicopter side trip, Edwards visits John McKeithen's law office in Columbia, displaying great tact in not pulling the whole damn muletrain into town at a time when McKeithen is trying to lie low on the governor's race. Big John flirted with Treen in 1982, saying at his own football party in Baton Rouge, "His situation has improved considerably here in the past few months. I can't put my finger on basically why, but there is a consensus that Dave Treen is basically a good man. That counts for a lot here." The Treen people were really hoping to get McKeithen in their corner to help unlock the conservative but stubbornly Democratic North Louisiana country vote. Hiring Gus Weill, McKeithen's longtime friend and advisor, helped at least get the former governor to sit on the fence. As he said in 1982, "I campaigned vigorously for Mr. Lambert in the second primary because he was the Democratic candidate," and in the next election, "I haven't made up my mind what I will do." But the Treen people can't push him any farther. And in the summer, McKeithen slips into neutrality when his son Fox declares for a legislative race.

In the most sparsely settled parishes, the sizes of the crowds surprisingly grow. Over 1,000 greet Edwards at the remote airfield in Mansfield. Now Brenda Hodge is getting new answers to her question of why folks have come. From a group of blacks getting off one of six school buses in Mansfield, a man says, "My juryman told me to come. He came and picked us up."

Things are going well, too well. When his voice cracks in Colfax, reporter Marsha Shuler suggests the unthinkable, "It sounds like he's losing his voice," as the horrified Motorcade staff shudders. A doctor is waiting at the Holidome in Shreveport and tells the candidate no speaking for 18 hours. Alter ego Marion is back in Baton Rouge trying to drum up the last few million. Edwards looks to his legislative allies in the region, Don Kelly and Charles Barham, to step up and speak for him. All he has to do is find them. Mike Baer makes the rounds of Shreveport bars in search of Kelly, who's had enough of the dust, heat and hills and is out carousing at Cowboys when Baer catches up with him that night. "The Boss can't talk. You gotta speak for him first thing in the morning." Kelly winces, putting down his bourbon. "Glad you found me."

Kelly is bright-eyed and sober the next morning and he and Charlie Barham carry the Edwards standard through Farmerville, Springhill and Arcadia. What Democratic legislator wouldn't love to stand in for the Great Pork Barreler, and yet his most effective pinch hitter is daughter Vicki, his ad agent who is more at ease on a Little Theater stage than on the back of a flatbed truck. But she rises to her most challenging role: "Defense of Daddy." Vicki shares her father's flair for rhetorical overkill, blasting Treen's pretensions that the budget is balanced: "If this is the kind of honest governor you want, I'm moving to another state." Or in Shreveport: "Our candidate has lost his voice, but he hasn't lost his hearing. He's here to shake your hand and listen to you and let you know he cares." When she sees the yellow ribbons in the trees of the Claiborne Parish courthouse square, she picks up on the lyric, "Yes, we still want you." But her best line plays off John Cade's "scumbag" remark. "That man's calling my daddy a scumbag. You know that can't be true. If it were, I'd be a scumbagette. And this lady here"—pointing to her surprised mother—"would be a scumbagess." Other than a few forced, hoarse words and some disarming gestures (such as stripping barechested to don a Grambling jersey) the candidate contentedly stands back and beams as daughter commands centerstage. Next to Marion, she is the most involved Edwards in this campaign, more so than her mother and sister Anna, who are often present but in the background, far more so than her brothers, who rarely attend campaign functions. With every stop she evolves more into the ultimate political . . . wife, seizing the candidate's fallen standard. Her zest for the spotlight is appreciated by her father. On the credenza behind the desk in Edwards' campaign office, there is one picture: Vicki's.

The Motorcade's only scheduling snafu occurs when Darrell Hunt calls one morning to wake Edwards at 5:45, though the helicopter isn't there until 7:15, by which time Edwards is bone-tired, half sick and venting wrath on Darrell. It's not unusual for Edwards to lose his temper, but his vile moods pass quickly, purged and forgotten. Not today. Already behind schedule in Clinton, Fischer decides to send Vicki on to Greensburg and take Edwards directly to Amite so he won't miss the start of a parade. Edwards, a morning slow starter, does not notice until he looks down over St. Helena Parish and sees a crowd.

"We were going to let Vicki handle this stop, Governor."

"The hell you are. Get this mother-fuckin' thing down right now, goddamit," he yells, scorching everyone in the copter until he is on the ground, on the bandstand and has interrupted Vicki with an apology to the crowd and a promise to be back.

Edwards' mood is no sunnier when he gets on the press bus for the ride to Franklinton. As the candidate munches on a yellow apple, the reporters quiz him about his newest "hard to believe" statistic on the pardons issue, to wit, that in the last three years, Dave Treen's Pardon *and* Parole boards had let out more prisoners than in Edwards' last three years.

The reporters on the bus immediately take aim at the trial balloon, questioning why he lumps pardons with paroles, since the governor has the final say on pardons and commutations but not on paroles.

But he appointed the Parole Board, answers Edwards. "If he's all that concerned about letting criminals out, why did he let his Parole Board do it?"

"Are you including first offenders?"

"All pardons, paroles and commutations. From whatever source, by whomever is responsible: Santa Claus gifts, Easter bunny presents, all of them—he let out more than me."

"But aren't you raising a new issue with paroles?"

271

"He's the one who raised the issue."

"Governor Treen said nothing about paroles."

"You're gonna let him say what he wants to say?" says a piqued candidate as he slams down his open palm on the Formica table, bringing a groggy press corps to attention but fast—even Bruce Morton from CBS is curiously observing the candidate's seething but controlled confrontation with reporters.

"You're comparing apples to oranges," says Candace Lee.

"I'm comparing apples to apples, I'm including every way you can get someone out of prison early." His eyes flash angrily at Lee, his nemesis from the *Advocate* and DCCL days. The two still have this special chemistry that sets them at each other's throats.

"But your figures don't include the first offenders that get out under provisions of the new constitution."

Wham—the hand comes down on the table. "Young lady"—he's pissed all right—"do you know the meaning of the word 'all'?"

"But you can't include first offenders since they get automatic pardons under the constitution."

"Well, baby doll, you take them out and I will look even better." He bites hard on his apple, then runs through his numbers again, hitting the table a half dozen times for punctuation.

"I just don't understand what numbers you're comparing," challenges Lee.

"And I don't understand why you don't understand. You're imprisoned by your own logic." Edwin Edwards is not so constrained, not even by the facts. Once Mike Baer gets the exact figures later that afternoon, they show the total of pardons, paroles and commutations under each governor for the final three years of both terms: Edwards 2,263, Treen 2,110. His morning statement, adjusted for reality, shows that though the two were close, more prisoners were released from state prisons during Edwards' last three years than during Treen's. Whatever that means—other than that the press statement Edwards released this morning is wrong.

A reporter asks Edwards, "Are you going to revise the press release your office just sent out?"

"No, let Treen do it."

Though he spent the morning jousting with the press, he's back on the bus early in the afternoon, warning Brenda Hodge of the dangers of push-tab tops as he opens her Coke. "I never drink from these things. You can't tell what roaches, bugs, insects and mice have teeteed all over it when you push it into your Coke." He hands her the opened Coke.

"So you're giving it to me?"

"I was hoping maybe I had got you so disgusted, you would let me keep it."

Edwards displays an ambivalent attitude toward Baton Rouge's Channel 2, a situation that confuses his staff and doesn't make Brenda Hodge's job any easier. Since Edwards has reviled owner Doug Manship, refused to place any ads on Channel 2 and threatened a total boycott of the news department, aides naturally assumed they were to freeze out Brenda Hodge too and not even send her press releases and schedules. Family too. Strapping on her seat belt for a helicopter flight, Hodge asks Elaine Edwards if her back, which caused her pain the day before, feels any better this morning.

No reply.

Brenda looks over to Hunt. "Darrell, is my seat empty?"

The games are getting to Brenda, who, knowing that the candidate, whatever his bluster, is not so stupid as to reject free media coverage, pretends the Big Chill is not there. Through the trip, Hodge is trying to report on an issue a day in the race. She plans on using the black voter issue for her Thursday story, but she starts getting nervous when Edwards goes through almost the entire day without mentioning the issue, one of his major topics of days past. With just one stop left before the film plane goes back to Baton Rouge for the day, she grabs Mike Baer. "Tell him I've got to have the black voter speech at the next stop."

Midway through his remarks in Tallulah, Edwards winks at cameraman Abe McGull, who rolls the tape: one black voter speech coming up.

Business is shut down for the day on Columbia Street, the main drag in Bogalusa, for the candidate's appearance. People line the storefront sidewalk as Edwards works the crowd, shaking hands, kissing babies, kissing mothers, barely breaking stride. After one especially wet kiss, he holds out his hand and almost by reflex Stan Cadow puts a handkerchief in it.

Speaking from a temporary podium at a street corner, he reaches further into his rhetorical trickbag. "Dave Treen has criticized me for my pardons. When this campaign is over, I'm gonna write one more pardon.

I'm going to pardon Dave Treen for being a bad governor. I'll pardon him for bankrupting the state. I'll pardon him for putting people out of work." Working the cheers to a crescendo, he closes with the Messiah appeal. "You go from here today and you stop people you see on the street and you tell them that you were here on this day when one came to you and brought you a message of hope for the future. Go from here and tell them one is coming . . . "

Down the street at Goodman's, Mike Baer's father's dress shop, Vicki is choosing the outfit Edwin has promised her. When Edwards enters, the store owner presents him with a woman's purse. "Governor, we want you to have this for your wife."

"My wife? I'll give it to my girlfriend."

"Which one?" asks daughter coyly, checking a new outfit in the mirror.

The Motorcade rolls into St. Tammany Parish, the across-the-lake refuge of rich Orleanians escaping both the city and the suburbs. Though it's a Republican stronghold, a parish Treen expects to carry handily, Edwards has targeted it with three scheduled stops. After days of red clay hills and flat pine forests, the Motorcade rolls into its most scenic stop, at Mandeville, looking out on majestic Lake Pontchartrain.

All but the hardest core repair to the seawall to better experience the balmy, brilliant afternoon and to get away from the 62nd version of the same speech. The Truth Squad, having kept up with the forced march tempo and continuing local hostilities along the way, especially needs a break. Captain Fact, in fact, is losing it, as he seems unable to handle the press's cynical, so-what attitude in the face of Edwards' stream of lies. "He claimed Treen vetoed the sewer project in St. Landry when Treen did no such thing. You may say it's petty, no big deal, well maybe it is when you've heard as many as he's told. But isn't that the whole point? The man is lying. How can you believe the sonofabitch if he says he's going to build a bridge or a road or do anything. Goddamit, if he lies about one thing, he'll lie about anything."

Lanny Keller strolls over to the rescue. "Scott, I'll have to give you a lesson in talking to reporters. Did you know that in print, 'sonofabitch' looks even worse than 'scumbag'?"

But the Captain's not the only one losing it. Onstage, Vicki, spelling daddy late in the day, is straying from any text she's ever followed or

274

invented. Maybe it's that the more sophisticated, less receptive crowd here in Republican country is not responding on cue like they did in the hill country. Complaining of all the slings and arrows her daddy has faced, she says, "I almost wish he didn't run this time, even if I wouldn't have received the 15 percent advertising commission." Drifting deeper into uncharted rhetorical waters, Vicki struggles under the emotional duress of her role. "Yes, my daddy's been controversial and a lot of people have said some mean things about him." Her voice quivering, her eyes watering, her daddy standing next to her, speechless, motionless and very concerned, Vicki fights to control her voice and find a point to make, fast. "And so maybe he has done a few things for himself, but in the interim, he did a lot of good for everyone else."

The crowd, as embarrassed as the speaker, cheers her performance while she regains her poise and a wrapped-tight daddy looks on without a word. A good place for the curtain to fall. In any other political family, Vicki would come down with a sudden but acute case of laryngitis for the rest of the tour. But two stops later, Edwards is at her side as she goes front and center again before 1,000 enthusiasts in Denham Springs, introducing "Your friend, my daddy, our next governor . . . "

"Tell your readers not to worry," Edwards tells Houston *Post* reporter Jim Simon as the press bus rolls out of Zachary the next morning. "I only steal from Louisiana, not from Texas." However, "if we don't get Dave Treen out of office, there won't be anything left to steal." So far the candidate has found the Truth Squad amusing and their attention to detail highly curious and irrelevant. "It never occurred to me they would be so technical. They punch everything I say into a computer. When I said only 18 percent of Treen's appointments were women, he came to pieces, got all uptight, said it was 20 percent." He rolls his eyes. "He's accused me of everything else, he hasn't caught me with a billygoat yet."

To Edwards, Dave Treen's real problems started before he was even elected. "Dave Treen never recovered from the shock of the deal he made in 1979 with the four Democrats. You fellas never recognized that to be as serious as it was in what it did to those four guys but also how it hurt Treen. It was so unlike the image of him. When he appointed those four fellas, it destroyed his aura. Dave Treen set the stage for the erosion of his popularity. He never built on the narrow base he had." Edwards smiles, leafing through the Dave and Dodie cookbook smuggled onto the bus. "Look, this is the difference between Dave Treen and me. Here it says, 'Recipes you can depend on.' If I put out a cookbook, it would say, 'Recipes you can enjoy.' I bet there's no seasoning or spice in this. Here we have Dave and Dodie Chicken. Boil in water. Prior to serving, remove heart."

Edwards staffers vie with each other to show proper homage. But none can touch Bentley Mackay, who chooses ridiculous new costumes, from military uniforms to hard hats, on which to emblazon his campaign stickers and pins. Today he's outdone himself, standing proudly in the Baker K-Mart parking lot next to his freshly painted gold and blue car with Edwards stickers all over. "Well, it needed painting, and if you're going to make a fool of yourself, why not just go all the way. The wife says I have a touch of Alzeimer's—but I say that's the way to go."

Edwards has a special surprise for the crowd and the press—he brings onstage two serious-looking folks, the human sides of Edwards' pardons. Doug and Judy Rogillio's story: "We were sentenced to do 18 years for six counts each of simple burglary. After 18 months in jail, he signed a pardon for parole eligibility, then he signed our pardon after we got out. So we're four of his pardons. We've gone back to prison since, as part of our prison ministry. Because he signed our pardon, we can now work for other people."

It's a good media moment, though he doesn't play it for all he can. It shows he knows how to mix emotions and issues, even when he's on the wrong side of one. Edwards gives us a pardonee couple who have turned to preaching. Treen gives us more numbers.

In a shopping center in Boutte, on U.S. 90, the Truth Squad has arrived and is relaxing in its van, drinking beer, waiting for the circus. Captain Fact, his good humor restored, is working on refining his Edwards imitation. "Dave Treen has *tahrahrized* my people," mugs the Captain, leaning back. "I *cahre* about the schoolteachers and the *lahnchroom* workers." Fact pops me a Coors. "And you know, I've looked it up. There's not a damned thing he can do for lunchroom workers. They don't get supplemental pay. They don't have a retirement system. Oh, but he *cahres*."

On the second to last day of the nine-day ride, staff and press are catching a second wind heading into New Orleans from the Westbank.

An enthusiastic crowd meets Edwards in Westwego near the Huey P. Long Bridge, but the real stunner is to come at nightfall—Louis Roussel is working up the grand finale at the Fair Grounds. The reporters can tell they are in for something as the incoming crowds surge about the buses pulling up to the historic racetrack. Edwards gets out of his motorhome and wades back through the crowd to check on the reporters. "You all right?" he asks Marsha Shuler, and then Bob Mann. "Stay close to me." And he positions them in the center of the flying wedge of police and security guards surrounding the entourage as it plows into the stands, then up a jammed escalator to the temporary stage. The stage is too small for all the politicians and hangers-on piling onto it. This is a job for George Fischer, who places himself at the steps to decide who gets to go onstage and who must grovel with the crowd. Fischer helps Louis Roussel, Jr., Fair Grounds owner and lender of a quarter million, through the crowd and onto the stage. But he denies entry to Louis III, only the heir to the Roussel fortune and a measly $50,000 lender. Little Louis doesn't hear a word of the speech or even look at Edwards the rest of the night, but only glares hotly at Fischer. Fischer, of course, is getting a big kick out of it. Admitted is Senator Mike O'Keefe, one of Edwards' oldest allies who is in deepening trouble in his Senate race. Blocked at the steps is challenger Ben Bagert. "Why's O'Keefe up there and I'm not?" demands Bagert of Mike Baer. "Because Mike's supporting us and you're uncommitted, that's why." But Benny Bagert isn't quitting quite so easily. Even if he hasn't endorsed Edwards, Bagert is not going to stand by while O'Keefe alone gets to bask in the cheers next to King Democrat. So as Edwards speaks Benny stoops low and half-crawls underneath the temporary stage, pushes up on one of the plywood squares and pops onto the stage, arms raised, triumphant. It's that good ol' Jesuit High kick 'em, knee 'em, gouge 'em winning spirit—Benny Bagert will not be denied.

The flimsy stage trembles as Edwards descends, then horrifies his nervous security detail by heading back into the heart of the crowd. Reporter Marsha Shuler finds herself at the head of the flying wedge, right behind the lead cop. "I didn't think I'd be this close to a man tonight," she jokes to mask her growing fear of the excited crowd. "I've never been so scared in my life."

High on a few thousand beers and the soaring Edwards rhetoric, the crowd presses in harder against the security wedge, trying to get close. A woman stretches her arm out, holding a handkerchief, trying to touch Edwards' brow, shiny with perspiration. When the wedge reaches the escalators, there is no movement left, and the crowd surges in tighter.

Then it happens. Wayne Ray, looking nervously at every pair of hands, thinks he sees something, a man reaching into his coat and grabbing an object. Ray doesn't wait to see what he pulls out, as he rams the man with his forearm and body, sending him reeling backwards. Fischer grabs one of Edwards' arms, Billy Broadhurst the other, picking him up off his feet, and yells to the lead cop, "Move it!" The wedge bolts forward. At the head of the wedge, Shuler hears someone say, "He's been stabbed." Looking over her shoulder, she sees a startled look on Edwards' face as he is grabbed and lifted off the ground by his aides. Wayne Ray sees the person he hit collapsing and knocking over everyone behind him on the escalator. "Well, we lost that vote."

In the bar of the Monteleone an hour later, the correspondents tell their latest war story. The reporters felt fear, but for the Edwards aides, it was higher anxiety. The first thought that rushed through Gene Rizzo's mind, the aide who was next to Edwards, was, "Do I like this guy enough to get in the way?" "I was scared of the crowd," says Fischer, "but I'm sure glad we had them. What would Dave Treen have paid for that crowd. If the Truth Squad told the truth, they should hate going home, they'll be gnashing their teeth. I'd hate to bring the message back of the crowds we had. If I were them, I'd mail in the news from Texas."

The frightening experience at the Fair Grounds makes a strong impression on Marsha Shuler, who has been irking Edwards' aides all week by lowballing crowd estimates in her dispatches. (Rolling into Baton Rouge Saturday morning, Edwards offers her a deal. "I'll accept your numbers on crowd size if you accept mine on pardons.") But in her wide eyes tonight, the crowd must have tripled or quadrupled. Taking a security guard's word for it, she pegs attendance at 34,000 in the next day's *Advocate*. That steams Captain Fact, who has yet to give up on combatting Edwards' distortions. "There were no more than 6,000 to 8,000—the grandstands weren't even filled up." At an uptown street party the next day, with a crowd of about 300 (if you count the guys listening from inside Frank's Bar on the corner), Fact and Keller joke within range of Shuler, "Looks like about 50,000 at least, wouldn't you say?"

After dinner, an intrepid band of reporters and regulars stroll out into the Quarter to end the evening at one of the nicest balconies in town— the bar of the Chart Room, overlooking the Pontalba Apartments, the Cabildo, Jackson Square, the ancient hub of Lafitte's New Orleans.

The candidate will start his campaign day the next morning with Mass at the Cathedral. The closest this crew will get to that stop is to walk past the old church in the moonlight. A street minstrel strums his guitar.

"Can you play 'On the Road Again'?" asks Baer.

"No."

"Good."

The next morning before Edwin Edwards Nazarene struts onstage for his last round of preaching salvation Swaggart-style, Edwin Edwards Catholic attends Mass but does not receive Communion. "I didn't have time for confession."

There is tension back in the city. From the second day of the caravan, there had been scattered death threats, the most serious coming in Plaquemine with reports of two men in a pickup truck with shotguns who were supposed to be gunning for Edwards. Then this last day in New Orleans, just as the caravan is pulling away from the Irish Channel block party, the state police get word the two men in the pickup truck have been spotted uptown. Having gone this far with the candidate unscathed, the security team takes no chances. Almost to the last stop in Metairie, the caravan detours to a Baskin-Robbins where Edwards buys ice cream for everyone, even passing out cones to the neighborhood kids. Meanwhile, the state police are combing the Metairie crowd for shotgun-toting rednecks. With an all-clear, Edwards swoops into the last stop, does a Cajun two-step across the stage, hugs newsman Norman Robinson and takes special pride in the crowd of 3,000. "We're right in Dave Treen's back yard. Why, in my back yard, he couldn't get 20 people." Halfway into his speech, a couple of field mice scamper over the toes of spectators who squeal in fear. A startled Edwards spins his head in that direction, but catches himself and doesn't break the tempo of the speech.

Then it's over. Charlie Boudreaux's horn bleats out the theme song one more time and the motorhomes head out Veterans Highway for separate trips home. The Truth Squad and some reporters repair to the nearest darkest hole for cocktails and closing assessments. Captain Fact bristles at the observation that the Treen Truth Squad attracted even more attention to Edwards and underscored the negative nature of the Republican campaign. "We attracted a lot of attention to us by being there and to what we've been saying." Fact also believes the constant presence of the tape recorders may have dampened some even wilder rhetorical excesses of which we all know Edwards is capable. Regardless of effect, for Scott Welch, the Captain, shadowing the Motorcade has been an unforgettable experience. "The high point of the campaign for me, even if I am going to have to go live in Nairobi when it's over."

Lanny Keller too marvels at the scope of the operation and George Fischer's stickling adherence to detail. But so what? Most of those who came out were either partisans or bored and looking for free beer. "I really doubt it had any measurable effect. It all sounds good, but I'd like to see some numbers."

And that seems to be the boys' problem in the Treen camp. In looking for the numbers, they're missing the point. Even if Edwards did not directly sway one new convert of the 100,000 who turned out for the nine days of appearances, the real effect, the real impression was made on the local volunteers who put it all together. The local organizers from Lake Providence to Lake Charles were directly involved in the overall campaign operation in the most personal way, getting their friends out to see Edwin Edwards. In a campaign that relies as heavily on flat moving warm bodies to the polls as it has on TV advertising, the Motorcade was an impressive and successful dry run for the big day, now less than two weeks off.

21. Laches Pas la Patate

As Edwin Edwards' Motorcade, the biggest deal of the campaign, disperses in Metairie, the guests for Dave Treen's biggest deal are just arriving at the Sheraton. Tonight, Bob Hope will add some luster and excitement and $2 million to the governor's campaign coffers, enough to make the final TV buys and pay the last bills. The Treen campaign has pulled out all stops for this one, including turning loose top fund-raiser Billy Nungesser to sell $10,000 tables to industrial buddies on the Westbank and down the bayou. The money's the whole deal, but the Treen campaign is looking for extras too, such as rewarding their bigwig contributors with a special predinner cocktail party where Hope is expected to show. Plus, *USA Today*, hitting the streets Monday with its first official Louisiana edition, wants a picture of Dave and Bob together. But across the lobby glittering with furs and diamonds, the sight of the nervous Treen aide whispering into the walkie-talkie hints that all, once again, is not right on the campaign trail. The aide sidles up to break the bad news to the campaign official. Hope has blown off the cocktail party, *USA Today* and his picture with Dave Treen with one terse message. Explains the aide, "Hope says he's getting paid $60,000 to entertain, not to politick. Then he called for a car and said he's going to eat at Antoine's."

A detached observer can see the Great Man's point of view. He can have fawning Palm Springs Republicans kissing his hand every day of the week, but at his age, how many more chances will he have to eat at Antoine's? Aides nervously check their watches as the dinner, scheduled to begin at 8:30, is delayed to kill more time waiting for the star attraction. John Hill of Gannett, owners of *USA Today,* steams as his deadline comes and goes for the photo of Hope and Treen together. His request, he learns, has been lost in the much more important infighting between the state campaign staff and the New Orleans campaign staff.

The evening drags on. At least they sold enough tickets. And surely if these Republican contributors aren't used to being abused and taken for granted by Cade and company by now, they truly are naive and deserve everything they get. Finally, past 10:30, the big band sound strikes up, two blondes do a few toned-down Las Vegas numbers. The band then plays "Thanks for the Memories" at 11:17 as Hope strides onstage. What Treen gets for $60,000 is a weak B team effort, with only two localized jokes. One about how the state has had only two Republican governors in 100 years and "I knew them both" and a real weak sister about Edwin Edwards being out in the parking lot letting air out of tires. Beyond that it was predictable fare:

—"I had a DeLorean but I had to get rid of it. Every time I drove down the highway it tried to suck up the white line."

—"I heard a guy who was convicted of cocaine possession and sentenced to either 10 years in prison or two years in Congress."

—"You heard about the stolen Carter briefing book. At least Reagan stole the whole book. Some congressmen have been taking pages."

—"In California, homosexuality is legal. I'm getting out before it becomes compulsory."

And that was the best stuff, interspersed with a few songs and worse jokes—it was a real wham bam thank you ma'am affair. Perhaps that's being unfair. John Cade is beaming about the performance. "It was the high point of the campaign for me." And considering the campaign John has had, that's not hard to believe. But it's easy to have been spoiled by the nine-day road tour of a combination rock star/evangelist/stand-up comic who never failed to hit the footlights right on time. Plus, after hearing Hope's puerile routine, even Horace the Peg-Legged Pig sounds good.

If guilt works by association, Edwin Edwards is in rotten company on the evening news October 11—a significant date, the first day of the last two weeks, the time when most voters begin really making up their minds, when both campaigns play their final hands. For many (that is, most) who have not watched one debate, attended one campaign rally and have changed the station whenever a campaign ad has come on, the first image they have of Edwards in these final two weeks is that scene every politician wishes to avoid: being filmed walking out of a federal courthouse. In fact, it's courthouse night on the news. First story. Edwin Edwards appears before the New Orleans federal grand jury investigating bribery in a cocaine case in Houma in which Edwards represented a client against whom charges were dropped.

Second story. Claude Pennington pleads guilty to possession of cocaine as part of the grand jury investigation of bribery charges against Baton Rouge DA Ossie Brown.

Third story. Senate President Michael O'Keefe appeals his conviction to the Fifth Circuit Court of Appeals.

Throw in Ginny Foat, and almost the entire newscast is devoted to public figures walking in and out of courthouses and protesting their innocence on the steps, before the TV cameras.

Edwards shows no emotion other than his practiced pique at being dragged into the simmering cocaine caper involving Terrebonne Parish District Attorney Norval Rhodes. Edwards had received $10,000 for representing one of three young men arrested for cocaine possession. Edwards' client, the son of a wealthy contributor, had charges dropped after one of his friends pled guilty. The immediate suspicion was that Edwards' client got off as part of a deal to appoint Norval Rhodes as head of Wildlife and Fisheries in 1984. That balloon had been floated in January (before the cocaine arrests) and shot down immediately by angry Terrebonne hunters and fishermen, who disliked Norval Rhodes enough as DA to fear what he could have done in Wildlife and Fisheries.When later in the week Rhodes is indicted for lying to the grand jury and Edwards walks away clean, it appears to be a case of Edwards getting bad publicity but nothing more for the bad company he keeps. Just another shadowy episode in the annals of the friends of Edwin Edwards. Compared to other grand jury appearances, it would have hardly registered in the public consciousness without the predictable Treen ad hurriedly produced that demands Edwards answer questions raised by the investigation. The commercial ends with the announcer asking, "Mr. Edwards? Mr. Edwards?"

Reporters groan each time pardons are raised in the campaign. The hoary issue has been beaten into the ground by both Treen and Edwards—each day there is a new approach, a new line of attack, a new statistic, a new interpretation of the old statistics. And both candidates have fallen short. Treen has been long on numbers but very short on explaining the harm that has been done by shortening so many sentences. Similarly, Edwards usually fails to mention the mere 6 percent recidivism rate of his pardonees. But reporters are too close to the campaign to know how it affects the people. As many voters are just beginning to listen, Treen is redoubling his pardons attacks and barely even mentioning DCCL, retirement or, of course, the good Dave Treen has done. In the final televised debate at UNO, Treen directs three straight questions about pardons to Edwards, who parries them almost reflexively. Edwards is confident he has the issue licked with a recent ad signed by 14 district attorneys praising Edwards for being tougher on crime and more cooperative with local police. Edwards could have had more signatories but he carefully excluded those under grand jury investigation: no Ossie Brown, no Norvel Rhodes.

Edwards' using the DAs as a shield ignites Treen all over again, pushing him on to do just what Edwards hoped he would do: attack the DAs. "Political logrolling has reached a new low," a Treen press release reads, "when district attorneys like Harry Connick of New Orleans, John Mamoulides of Jefferson and Nathan Stansbury of Lafayette try to defend Edwards' pardons record." On he goes, taking on each DA with well-aimed shots, singling out cases in which those DAs had publicly opposed some of the pardons Edwards had granted. "Is he the same John Mamoulides who said [of one Edwards' pardonee] 'He is an animal. That man should not be out of prison as far as I'm concerned.'"

When Edwards is confronted with the DAs' apparent hypocrisy in the final debate, he dismisses it as standard political procedure. "It's true they publicly oppose most pardons. It's part of their job. But when any of them contacted me directly and made an issue of a pardon with me, I took their feelings into consideration." In other words, he listened to what they said, not to letters they released to the press. Meanwhile, Treen's public attack on the DAs doesn't hurt Edwards but brings the DAs even more solidly into his corner.

And yet . . . as comfortably and as confidently as Edwards strides into the campaign's final days, as reporters give up even trying to paint scenarios of Treen making it a close race, as the final independent polls show a steady 15 to 17 point Edwards lead, as the threat of an indictment from the Houma cocaine case fades, one last piece of news disrupts the cresting rhythms of Edwards' headquarters. Of all things, a poll would do it. Sure, John Cade leaked Kennedy poll results to the Shreveport *Times* showing a four-point spread but the cat and mouse game Cade has played in releasing poll results discredits Kennedy's stubbornly optimistic numbers. The real thunderbolt comes from, of all places, Edwards' own pollster Bill Hamilton. In his final poll completed a week before the election, Hamilton reports the bottom dropping out of Edwards' lead— it's only a 46 to 42 margin. Could this be, as the Treensters have predicted all along, the turning point caused by the cumulative weight of the integrity attacks, the relentless pardons offensive and the added push of the cocaine grand jury finally undercutting Edwards' support? A spokesman for Hamilton cannot explain the drastic slip from the 11 to 15 point lead they showed through October. Factoring in undecideds, they project Edwards will take 52 to 53 percent of the vote. But with a 4 to 5 point error factor, says the spokesman, "that's a close race to call."

The news rattles the confident Edwards organization. After three years of riding so high, is the floor to fall out in the final week? The numbers don't square with the cresting visible support for the campaign, but this organization that has lived and benefited so much from polls isn't about to dismiss the first one they don't like. The final, strange Hamilton poll may actually be a godsend—the organization moves with even more urgency into the last week's massive direct mail, phone bank and get-out-the-vote blitz. Plus, Edwards has saved a few last surprises.

Before leaving office in 1979, Edwards said he had appointed Pam Harris to chair the Parole Board because "she's the kind of Republican who will give Dave Treen trouble." Here was a perfect example of an Edwards appointee who should have been run off the Parole Board as quickly as possible. Yet she was the beneficiary of the deep split between John Cade and Billy Nungesser in the running of the administration. When she began to fall out of favor with Nungesser, Cade began liking her more—a natural response, to anyone who understood the workings of the Fourth Floor.

285

Though she resigned in 1982, the time bomb kept ticking until Edwards decided to detonate it. In the campaign's final week, he strikes. An indignant Pam Harris appears on a TV commercial claiming to have resigned from the Parole Board because of the undue political pressure exerted by Treen administration officials. In a predictable response, Cade calls Harris "an embittered woman" and tries to set the facts straight, even producing a sworn statement from Harris during her Parole Board tenure stating that no one in the Treen administration ever interceded, even when asked for guidance, in Parole Board decisions. But the public has heard Cade cry lie and distortion so much that his outraged counterclaims are barely noticed. The Harris spot, however, is. It is one of the most talked about issues in the final week and the beauty of it is, it takes the proxy attack to the logical extreme. Here is a Republican appointee attacking the guy who has been doing the attacking for Dave Treen. As dirty as the race has become, Edwards, as is his political and personal habit, has managed to keep his hands clean.

The last place Edwin Edwards has any business going this final week is Houma, where District Attorney Norval Rhodes has just been indicted for lying to the same grand jury Edwards has testified before. Dave Treen's TV ads are still asking what did Edwards do to get the DA to drop the case and was he paid to influence the outcome? "Mr. Edwards, Mr. Edwards . . . "

Then there's the strange Hamilton poll telling Edwards that not all is right and he should be steering clear of those places where things are going wrong. But Edwin Edwards has friends to help and promises to keep. His old buddy Leonard Chabert is in trouble in his state Senate race and Edwards had committed, even before the grand jury questions arose, to spending two days of the last week in Chabert's Lafourche and Terrebonne parishes.

"I've been getting calls on you all day, Leonard," teases Edwards when Chabert meets us at the airport.

"What, what?" demands Chabert.

"They're saying I can't save you, stay away. Chabert will be the stone around your neck."

Chabert grunts. If Edwin Edwards were embarrassed by Leonard Chabert, he would have noticed it many years ago. With his swarthy complexion, stout figure, slicked-back hair and bug eyes, Chabert resembles Luca Brasi even more than Roland Manuel does. And he's far more demanding. Edwards has joked throughout the campaign, "The state can save $40 million a year if Leonard Chabert isn't reelected. The capital outlay budget isn't big enough for all he wants."

Leonard goes back with Edwin to the 1971 race and to the high times thereafter. "Leonard's in Clyde's book," Edwards reminds the reporters. "It really pissed him off when Clyde said he had three whores one night in London."

"Yeah," fumes Chabert, "It was five! Five, dammit!" He pounds the steering wheel of his van. Oh, the depths of Clyde Vidrine's libel, to underestimate Leonard Chabert's capacity for whoring.

Edwards keeps teasing. "I told someone the other day I can't think of what horrible thing I could do to lose this election. But this is it, coming down here to help Chabert."

"You get those tickets for the fight?" Chabert has been talking about the Hagler-Duran fight in Las Vegas since the visit here three months ago.

"Sure do, Leonard, but you can't go. You'll be in the fight of your life that weekend . . . if you make the runoff."

"Sheeeyit."

Pulling into Calvin's Exxon, Chabert says, "You need to drop in and say hello to this guy."

"Oh, this is great, Chabert. I've visited with popes, presidents and heads of state for this, so I can come down here for you and hang around filling stations."

Well, it's a big deal for the folks at Calvin's, and the proprietor proudly presents Edwards with a miniature captain's wheel, mounted on cardboard with "Calvin's Exxon" lettered thereon. "We're going to put this on the mantelpiece at the Mansion." With all the mementos, knickknacks, wood carvings, duck decoys and specious objets d'art presented to Edwin Edwards and promised a place there, it's going to be one crowded mantelpiece . . . *and ugly-y-y.*

There's something about being down the bayou, in this roughest toughest part of the state, that tends to loosen Edwards up even more. "Imagine Dave Treen asking me what I did with my fee in that case. I should have told him I spent it all on girls and booze and cocaine."

Stan Cadow perks up in the back seat. "Is that what we've been snorting?"

"Yeah, whenever I do I get younger and more virile and I attract more Girl Scouts."

It's hard to imagine a candidate less guarded in front of reporters. He almost gives the impression he doesn't mind our being along. But we know better. Take the Earl Long story he tells. "One time Earl Long was riding in the back seat with Camille Gravel and Edmund Reggie at the end of a campaign and old Earl was swearing, 'Man, am I ever tired of kissing ass, but once this election is over, I'm gonna start kicking ass.' Gravel and Reggie chimed in, 'Yeah, that's right.' Then after the election, Reggie said he realized 'Earl was talking about us.'" We all laugh, but later realize Edwin was talking about us too. As well as all the advisors and hangers-on and contributors who think their lousy $25,000 makes them campaign strategists. "Darrell, estimate how many times I've had to bite my tongue and listen to how I should run my campaign."

Hunt leans back. "Well, take all the egos in the campaign and multiply it by five or six, but that's still small compared to the advice we've got on personal security."

But it's the tone of the unwanted advice that bugs Edwards the most. "I wouldn't mind if they phrased it 'I'm not sure why you're doing this, but . . .' Instead they look at you like you're crazy and say, 'What the fuck is the matter with you?'"

A reporter reads aloud a dispatch, John McKeithen's belated and tepid endorsement of Edwards. Halfway through Big John's circumlocutions, the endorsee interrupts, "What he's saying is, 'After carefully studying the polls, I have decided to endorse Edwards.'"

Talk turns to Dave Treen and the observation by the reporters present, after time spent with both candidates, that Treen personally dislikes Edwards. Notes one, "I get the feeling that Treen hates you and that Cade feeds that feeling," and concludes that Treen's attacks on Edwards would be more believable if he were to give Edwards credit for something instead of painting everything as a lie or dishonest act.

Edwards, of course, agrees. "Dave Treen wouldn't give me credit for one altruistic thing. If I did something for senior citizens he'd say I was screwing some old lady."

Reporters note the growing size and fervor of the audiences Edwards has drawn in the last month. "The greater the crowd," says Edwards, looking out of the window, "the closer the cross."

After a rest stop, it's on to the Bayou Centroplex in Galliano, on the banks of Bayou Lafourche. Chabert has planned two bashes on consecutive nights, one in each parish in his district. A good 1,500 are jammed into the Centroplex, a western band is playing, the folks in the kitchen are holding off on serving the sausage dinners until the speaking is done. The crowd is hopped up on beer and country music and thunders applause as Chabert welcomes everyone. Leonard is much in evidence on the walls, as his posters match Edwards' in number and totally outshine them artistically. Leonard has added a new dimension to political posters as well as garish self-promotion. Not only are his posters in full color but they are sequined as well—his tie in gold, his coat in blue. The posters glitter out at you, each an artistic as well as political statement—bold, gripping and brutally tacky. Forget Luca Brasi, Leonard Chabert *is* Liberace.

The Edwards entourage grows onstage. He is here to help not only Chabert but Lieutenant Governor Bobby Freeman as well, who has performed one of the great feats in desperate coattail clutching in this campaign. His TV spots—cleared by Edwards—make the outright proposition to the voters that "Louisiana will soon have a new governor and I will be able to work with him." Shameless, perhaps, but effective, as his polls show he is closing the gap on Jimmy Fitzmorris, who, though he enjoyed commanding leads in the polls throughout the summer, still has the knack for turning easy wins into heartbreaking losses.

The race in Terrebonne and Lafourche is a battle of Chaberts. Leonard's son Marty is running for dad's old House seat against incumbent Murray Hebert. And Leonard faces a pack of strong opponents, including a black and someone else named Chabert. Keeping track of all the Chaberts is becoming a major concern. No wonder he put sequins on his posters.

Bobby Freeman makes an all-out plea for Democratic unity. "The people are crying out for Edwin Edwards, and I am too. We've been a team before, I want to get the team back together for you."

Chabert takes the mike and challenges his rivals to outdo what he has brought to the bayou parishes through his pork barrel pipeline, reminding them of the hospital they built together, the roads, the recreation centers, the water systems. "We built the seawall together—you remember." But under Dave Treen, the pipeline has all but shut down. "Treen vetoed the drainage projects we needed so bad and then he went and gave two million dollars to those flute tooters in the New Orleans Symphony."

With that, the band breaks into the Cajun downstretch anthem, "*Laches pas la patate.*" Don't drop the potato. Back in the days when that's all a Cajun family had to eat some nights, Edwards explains later, holding onto the potato until it gets in the pot took on deep significance. So many people have their hands on Edwin's potato now, he would have a hard time dropping it on his own. Now he's asking this crowd, "my kind of people," to hold on with him. "We just finished a caravan of the state, we went to 64 parishes, I looked at 150,000 to 200,000 people from the Arkansas border to the Gulf of Mexico, from Mississippi to Texas, people just like you, worried about jobs, worried about the education of their children, worried about the budget out of balance, worried about what was going to happen to them tomorrow and let me tell you one thing: they have reason to be worried. But I want you to leave here tonight and go to the Tenth Ward of Lafourche Parish or wherever you're from and say to people that you were here on this night when one came to talk to you, who's served you before, who's just as concerned as you are. Tell them that all these bad things that have happened to us in the last three and a half years will soon be behind us because Edwin Edwards is coming October 22!"

Edwards steps back and the crowd goes wild, screaming, waving posters, then joining in a thundering chant of "One! One! One!" The candidate is mobbed on his way out, a much friendlier mobbing than at the Fair Grounds. Just outside, a nonhearing woman signs a message to Edwards, who signs back. "She said, 'I love you' and I told her I love her too." Very touching. And as the van pulls away he leans back and sighs, "I could have read to them from a Sears and Roebuck catalogue."

Even with free hotdogs, beer, sausage po-boys and door prizes, getting more people to turn out for a political rally than for a high school football game is a supreme organizational and promotional challenge. The biggest crowd to come hear Edwards so far numbered 10,000 in Shreveport in September. On the last Thursday before election day,

Edwards is looking down from the Cajun Field press box at 15,000 cheering, partying faithful waiting for the last campaign rally. Marion had okayed the rally only a few weeks before on one condition: he would not spend a dime on it. Out went the scavenger hunt squad to hustle up everything from a football stadium to 2,000 pounds of sausage (courtesy of Price LeBlanc), even a $1,500 horse as a door prize ("Why don't they just raffle off a seat on the Mineral Board?" drawls the reporter who's seen one rally too many this year). It quickly grew into a superrally, a massive last rally, not just of this campaign, expounds Marion as the press bus loads up for the trip, but "one last hurrah, one last old-fashioned rally to end the last campaign of this kind." The old-fashioned political rally died long before this campaign started, but as a testament to Edwin Edwards' celebrity appeal and staff organization, it's been revived to appeal to the candidate's sense of history and need to have thousands of people screaming for him.

He has what he wants tonight—the crowd, which he has been allowing to build for two hours as the band plays and the aides throw miniature EWE footballs into the stands, now fills up one side of the football stadium. After the harrowing Fair Grounds experience, security is tightly in place as a cordon of police with German shepherds keep the crowd in the stands and off the stage.

Finally a stir in the press box, a buzz in the crowd, then cheers as congressmen, United States senators and four generations of the Edwards family file down the aisle onto the stage. But not Someone. At the insistence of Wayne Ray, Edwards and the ever-present, ever growing entourage go down the elevator and around to the locker room entrance. In a state where political and football manias can be mixed and confused, it's appropriate Edwards would make his last great campaign entrance in a football stadium, under the goalposts. A huge roar goes up as the silver head appears, the band strikes up That Song, Edwin and Elaine begin to walk through the goalposts, but can't let a cheer like that go to waste and break into a run, with the entourage in hot pursuit. They hit the stage clapping and dancing, family members are brushing back tears. Rarely does a crowd get this worked up for a football team, much less for a politician. Maybe only one person besides Edwin Edwards can fully appreciate this scene. There he stands on the stage, looking up in wonder at the faces of Louisiana, with their intense expressions of hope and fervor and great expectations. It's been a long, long time since Russell Long has seen a crowd so moved by one man—maybe 50 years.

In the last month of the campaign Edwards has been so accustomed to giving 10 speeches a day, he's had time to perfect and embellish his total speech, his Full Gospel Campaign Message, and when John Breaux gives Edwards the mike, he lets go.

"I do not bring any message of rancor or hatred or discord. I come to heal the wounds that we have suffered through the last three and a half years. . . . Not a week from Sunday, but on Sunday morning, you will feel that fresh breeze blowing out of the northwest of the state as it ripples through the pine leaves of northwest Louisiana, flows over the central part of our state down into the southern part of Louisiana. It's bringing a fresh new message of a new dawn and a new era and a new government and a new hope and a new aspiration for this state." Even well into his speech he's having a hard time getting over this crowd. "There will never be a time in my life when I will forget this night. I suppose, I suppose"— his voice gets unsteady and he steps back to put his arm around his mother—"there is too much Cajun in me for me to stand here in front of you and hug my mother and not be filled with emotion. And I hope you will forgive me for it 'cause I love you so much and I love this state so much."

Fortunately the maudlin stuff passes and he gets into the full swing of his speech, with the full lean into the crowd, knee bent, hand waving and the spirit moving. "The heart in us are people in Louisiana who understand compassion and who understand the concerns of their peers. I've been there, and you have been there, we've been there. We've seen what it's like. . . . We have been robbed of our inheritance, cheated of our hope and deprived of our aspirations. But I tell you right now, you tell them also that on October 22, just 24 hours from now, someone is coming who is going to heal this state and make things better. You give me, give me the power and the prestige of the governor's office and I'll put it to work for you. There'll be no longer ivory towers and closed mansions and locked doors. There'll be no unanswered telephones. There'll be no people in this state trying to talk to somebody to find out what's happened to them, trying to find out how they can make their lives better. There'll be no longer people desperately looking around for somebody to listen to their problems. The people working for me will be in tune with the needs and desires of the people and we are going to serve the people of Louisiana as we did during the eight years we did that before. That is what you need and deserve, that is what this state can afford, that is what governments are all about. And with your help on Saturday we are going to begin to make all of that possible. Will you help me? Will you help me? We can do it ... I feel it in my bones and it's going to billow and swell until on Saturday at six o'clock when they open the polls, the clang of the sound of the voting machines is going to be so tremendous that all the nation will sit up and take notice that we have come back to life. One more time, I can't hear you, one more time ..."

The press bus leaves before the drawing for the horse, which is just as well, as these reporters have seen enough extravagance, showmanship and demagoguery to fill a stable. Edwards and staff have outdone themselves, not just for the size of the crowd, but for the zeal and intensity that not even free beer and country sausage can inspire. His final appearance completes the evolution from mortal, venal public servant to political and economic messiah. The reporters feel that Edwards has brought the fanaticism to a peak at just the right time. To go on any longer would be to go too far—observes Norman Robinson, "This Messiah bullshit is gonna get him shot."

The governor's race is the great vacuum cleaner, sucking up all the contributions, controversy and even interest from the statewide scene. The only interesting question in the lieutenant governor's race is what to do with poor, poor, pitiful Bobby Freeman, who two months ago was given up for dead but now has finally come up with at least one qualification for keeping his job: slavish and unquestioned fealty to Edwin Edwards. Bobby's big break came by achieving official martyr status after Dave Treen vetoed his entire office's appropriation because Bobby wouldn't accept a cut. His feud with the governor is his badge of honor. The question of his office's budget is in the courts: if Bobby loses there he will lose his staff, though he's had trouble explaining exactly what they do.

Outside of that, the state front is sadly quiet. The attorney general, treasurer and secretary of state have no opposition. The commissioner of elections is just going through the motions. Other than Butch Baum's novel approach to greater insurance sales, there is nothing happening in the agriculture commissioner's race except for this guy going around the state giving out cucuzzi seeds. The usual flock of unknowns is challenging Sherman Bernard for insurance commissioner, but Sherm's not worried. Face florid and hair slightly disheveled as he holds forth at a political cocktail party, Bernard waves off the suggestion that a newcomer in the race is any threat. "Lemmie Walker's nothing but a toot in the wind. A toot in the wind, ya hear me?"

Sherman Bernard is the Rodney Dangerfield of Louisiana politics. No respect. Though he is one of Louisiana's most successful politicians, the odds-on favorite to win his fourth term as insurance commissioner, politicians have yet to take him seriously. Each spring he sends to the House Commerce Committee his package of legislation proposing streamlined reforms for insurance regulation, which is summarily dismissed unread. The past two governors have tried to abolish his office as an elected position. Even within the insurance industry he regulates, the commissioner is often derisively referred to as "the housemover" (his former occupation). The man gets no respect. Not only did his car get towed away from the New Orleans airport, but when Sherman called the security guard "chickenshit," he got arrested. The grandest trophy in his office is a magnificent, mounted blue marlin. His wife caught it.

Is it any wonder they line up every four years to run against Sherman Bernard? But they just can't beat him, the people just won't get rid of him. It could be that Sherman Bernard fulfills a need in the public to have at least one high official they can look down on. In that way Sherman is more than a housemover, more than an insurance commissioner, more than just another rogue politician trying to throw his considerable weight around. To Louisiana, Sherman Bernard is Every-man, and he may be unbeatable.

It's just getting too tough to knock off an entrenched state official. And what's the point? Statewide offices are more often dead ends than stepping-stones—the best way to the governor's office is still through Congress or the PSC. Nor are the positions themselves very powerful since civil service and the centralized power of the governor's office have siphoned off most of their former patronage prerogatives. For a while, secretary of state was the sexy office to run for. You didn't have to do anything controversial and your name was on almost every piece of paper the state sent out. But look at poor Jim Brown, unopposed for a second term but still selling cookbooks to pay campaign debts from his first race.

But were it not for the dearth of politics at this level, Kelly Nix could be in real trouble. If any incumbent appeared to be a likely candidate to get knocked off when this election year started, it was Superintendent of Education Kelly Nix. When we last left Kelly in 1979, he was staggering through a tough reelection campaign against a host of scrappy opponents. Going into debt and campaigning all out in the final weeks, he was pinning his hopes on winning in the primary. When it appeared challenger Tom Clausen might force him into a runoff, Kelly's pique runneth over in just the wrong place, on TV. He told a WBRZ reporter that if the people weren't going to give him the post in the primary, "Then I feel like that song, 'You can take this job and shove it.'" He knew right away it was the wrong thing to say. If there is one thing the people can't abide, it's a politician who feels he or she deserves the office. Nix had to redouble his efforts, eat some crow, borrow some more money to stave off Tom Clausen in a close race.

Then Kelly ran into real trouble. Soon after the election, the U.S. attorney was sniffing at the scent of a warehousing kickback scheme involving high members of the Department of Education. Two of Nix's top aides were convicted and sent to prison, but Kelly escaped as an unindicted co-conspirator. Tarred with the brush of scandal, Nix seemed highly vulnerable to some ambitious good government type challenger. A few trial balloons were floated, but as no one could really work up any excitement for the race, no one showed up at the post except retread Tom Clausen.

Kelly Nix was elated. Clausen had the loser image and was tied closely to labor and teachers. Nix had the clear field for the conservative voter, especially for his tough stance on requiring education graduates to pass the National Teachers Examination before being certified and his highly praised successes in raising requirements for graduation. All Clausen had going for him was good name recognition provided by the all-time best campaign sign of any candidate: the yellow school bus with "Clausen" inscribed thereon. They were still up from the 1979 race, instantly recognizable and very effective in that they did not contain Clausen's face. He didn't have much money to spend or much to say, other than that Nix was crooked and that Clausen would be easier on teachers—not a positive message in a state that barely respects the education establishment.

Late in the campaign Kelly is coasting, running an even more lackluster and underfunded campaign than in 1979. Why not? Clausen is saying nothing new and the voters are showing scant interest. In August, Kelly Nix leads Clausen 52-15 in an *Advocate* poll. And it just seems to get better. Not only is Kelly endorsed by LABI, the powerful business lobby, but he and his old boss Edwin Edwards embrace and trade endorsements on the Motorcade. The only disquieting note in the final weeks is the news of Kelly's daughter being busted for cocaine in Hammond. In a state inured to vice, this drug is starring in a number of political and personal scandals. Next to media-commissioned polls, cocaine is gaining recognition as the most destructive newcomer on the state political scene.

With his opponent basking in the adulation of 15,000 in Lafayette, Dave Treen is planning his own final mass rally (this will make two in his campaign) at the Central Baptist Church gospel sing that Videt Polk has been whipping up as he wages his pulpit campaign through the Bible Belt. For the last two months, defensive Treen aides have scoffed at the big Edwards crowds as meaningless, saying Treen is making as effective a mark with their TV ads on pardons, their direct mail campaign and Dave's good, sincere, one-on-one campaigning at the Winn-Dixie. "We'll turn out the big crowds in the last week," assures press secretary Roy Brightbill. Turn off, perhaps, is a better word, as the low intensity Treen campaign—consistently 40 minutes late throughout the last three months—hits the pressurized demands of the final two weeks and buckles. A fairly decent turnout waits for him to cut the ribbon to open a Lafayette petroleum show, but they've dispersed by the time he shows up. So he goes to a trailer and talks to the milling showgoers over the PA system. His so-called Canal Street parade consists of the governor stopping busy lunchtime traffic, walking the streets of the New Orleans Central Business District, peeving the impatient few who notice him to start with.

But if Dave Treen held onto hope this long, he must have known it was all over when he entered Central Baptist Church in Baton Rouge to find only 150 people, many of them office and campaign staff who felt they were at a wake. No dozens of church choirs and busloads of fundamentalist faithful. The enormous, silent, cresting wave of church-goers cleaving to Dave Treen's moral message, the same folks who are to bring the Bible Belt back to the decent candidate, have evaporated. Dodie Treen is hopping mad and doesn't try to mask her agitation, backing an aide against a pew and demanding to know who's responsible for this disaster. Sadly for Dave Treen, so concerned with the permanent record, the disappointing church rally is his one campaign appearance covered by the New York *Times*, which reports a Treen aide apologizing for the shabby turnout. "It was handled by a real Jim Bob." Indeed it was. Videt Polk has blown it big time.

Down to the final week, so many elections hang on who comes through with what they say they're going to do. And to pay. The Edwards computer is kicking out thousands of checks of $20 to $50 to individual workers, haulers, phoners, canvassers, ballot distributors. Still there are persistent reports that on top of all the money they're claiming to spend, even more Edwards cash is hitting the streets. Blacks in Tangipahoa Parish call Treen headquarters with reports of A. Z. Young's "cash car" making the rounds of the parish, his trunk filled with $10 bills. Coming down to the moment of truth, candidates shell out their last dollars (literally) to Cajun and black leaders with only the hope their "supporters" will conform to Lyndon Johnson's definition of an honest Mexican, "one who stays bought."

And if through a shortage of funds or customer loyalty, a politician is not able to buy or rent the support he needs, the next best thing is to blow the whistle on the corrupt. In Alexandria, Tilly Snyder confides in his viewers the only possible threat to his resounding first primary victory comes "because of cash money accumulated in this area to be spent at the polls and in violation I feel of the so-called campaign practices act. It was prevalent in LeCompte, in Cheneyville and Glenmora where the present senator's people spent a great deal of money two nights before the election. This time we are making preparations to catch some of these people in their own trap. They broke it up over in Leesville. They got into it in Baton Rouge and New Orleans. But for some reason they overlooked it here. We have contacted people today and yesterday in

LeCompte, Cheneyville and Glenmora and we are going to get our hands on some of this money that has been put out down there by Mr. Randolph and some of the other good government associates. This is a clear-cut violation of the law and I want you people to take the money, take the money and call 442-4204 and we will have the proper authorities in touch with you in a few minutes. I have friends tell me they will endeavor to reward you, to reward you well if you will work with us in breaking up this system. . . . That number is 442-4204."

The reporters following Treen settle in for a final dinner and drink together on election eve at Poets. "This campaign ended not with a bang but a whimper," says Bob Mann of the Shreveport *Journal* in assessing the carnage of the final week. A colleague agrees, "I've never seen Dodie so hot as Thursday night at that church." Though also disappointed, Treen mustered one last evangelical hurrah from the pulpit. "The way he described his career in Congress," critiques John LaPlante of the *Advocate*, "all he ever did was vote, study the issues and pray."

With one final show of grit and positive spirit, Captain Fact joins the table and asks if the reporters got Cade's press release saying he was going to sue Pam Harris. "We don't print 'gonna sues,'" says Marsha Shuler. "When he files the suit, we'll run the story."

Coming down to final confessions, the Captain hews to the party line. "No, I think it really is, really is, close enough to go either way." That's worth one last bored, incredulous stare. The Captain looks back to his menu. "Well, maybe it'll rain."

With reporters crowded around the gazebo behind the Edwards home on Highland Road, Marion reviews ground rules for press coverage election night at the Monteleone. The 15th floor suite is only for family and close staff, but the candidate will be down regularly to the press room on the second floor before addressing the masses in the two ballrooms. The casually dressed young man with the red moustache interrupts. "I have a problem with that." Joe Bernstein of *60 Minutes* is looking for something more in the way of spontaneity, which means he's looking at the wrong campaign. *60 Minutes* will want more candid shots of Edwards and his family following the returns, not performing behind a mike at a podium. That's what the local TV stations want too—in fact all are angling to get the split screen facial reaction of both candidates as the projected winner is announced at 8:03. The news director as stage manager. Edwards promises their projections will get nothing more than a poker face from him, while with Treen they won't get past the Mansion's front door.

Edwards appears with Elaine and full family, including all six grandchildren, thanks the press for their coverage (which has turned around remarkably since Nolan's death) and hits Dave Treen one more lick. The issue of the hour is federal poll watchers, all eight of them, the Justice Department is sending into rural Louisiana parishes election day. Compare that to the 300 feds who swarmed into Mississippi in the August election and you have to once again admire Edwards for getting as far as he has with an issue that's no issue at all. Since the UNO debate, Edwards has been challenging Treen to repudiate the poll watchers and to "use his influence with the Republican president to leave us alone and let us conduct our own election." Treen should have done just that (not that it would have stopped the poll watchers) or flat ignored the whole thing. Instead, to Edwards' delight, Treen escalates the nonissue by announcing he will call out the state police if Edwards continues to threaten "physical and legal trouble" for the poll watchers. Now Treen is stuck defending, even protecting, agents of the federal government, whose main interest in is protecting the rights of blacks so they can go vote for Edwards. And who does that alienate? White conservatives, one of the few groups Treen has held onto so far. Edwards does not let that final irony escape, as he paints a horrific vision of a far-reaching conspiracy, tying in the poll watchers with Dave Treen's use of "United States attorneys, federal grand juries, federal agencies, the FBI and other federal agencies throughout the campaign" to influence the election.

With Treen flailing to get out of that paper bag, Edwards entreats his persecuted followers to turn the other cheek. "I say to my voters, 'Pay no attention to them.' I suggest my supporters pass them by, give them a friendly sign of some kind . . . go and vote and then leave." A smiling Sam LeBlanc catches my eye and looks down at his finger, forming the friendly sign of the bird.

Parting shots. NBC's Ken Bode asks for a prediction and Edwards draws a big laugh with "58-42." He will later confess that was a tongue in cheek prediction. When it comes to putting his money where his mouth was—yes, he finally found a bet—he picked himself to win by 150,000 votes, or about a 10-point spread, in Jack Wardlaw's $1 press corps pool.

With the press conference breaking up, Edwards is holding his granddaughter as he chats with Bode. The playful smile on his face as he looks into the baby's eyes belies the icy tone in his voice as he talks about Dave Treen. "I wouldn't mind if Treen were claiming that I am stealing the election just like he says I'm stealing everything else in the state. But he won't admit that he has called the feds in, which in fact he did. He may not believe it, but he's not the only honest person in Louisiana." When it's all over and the dust has settled, there will come a time to settle accounts. "Say if the Democrats win the White House next year and we have an aggressive U.S. attorney like Billy Broadhurst. Then it could be time to investigate the investigators."

Staff, friends and hangers-on outnumber reporters at this final press conference, each bidding for a moment alone with the candidate. Leaning back on the swing, impeccably dressed and characteristically melancholy, Darrell Hunt is amused at how the entourage and the army of supporters have swelled in the last weeks. "You get down to the end of the campaign and we start having all these people coming out for us, acting like they've really been with us all along, our 'good friends.' Man, the definition of a friend in politics is strange indeed."

The heated rush of a campaign's end often crowds out a dispassionate observer like Darrell Hunt. The reserved, cerebral Hunt better matched the candidate's own existential qualities during the lonely days of plane trips and car rides to fish fries and smoke-filled rooms, when it was loose and easy, few reporters, no cameras, no platoons of "good friends" competing to lead cheers. Now as the glare of campaign's end illuminates every move and mood of the candidate, as new advisors with their own agenda and advice push into the spotlight, Darrell retreats farther into the shadows.

Ken Bode, NBC film crew in tow, pauses at the swing to thank Darrell for his help.

"And by the way, Ken," Darrell remembers, "I really am not cynical."

"Oh yeah," answers Bode, "then what are you?"

"At this point, my real feelings are so beyond anyone else's perceptions . . . "

"Then let's just say you're not innocent."

"You're right there," Darrell looks down, smiling, "I am not innocent."

Sam LeBlanc grabs Bode. "I've got all that stuff in my office you wanted to film."

"The bumpersticker too?"

"Got it. 'Scumbags for Edwards.'"

Edwards is moving about shaking hands with reporters, a final farewell. Sure, he'll see these guys tomorrow. If he wins, he'll see them during the transition, he'll see them next year weekly if not daily, in press conferences or in off-the-cuff conversations in the Senate chamber. He'll see them for years to come. But he'll no longer be the candidate, the private citizen, the lone operator on the road with Darrell and maybe a reporter along, on their way to a Cajun barbecue. The longest campaign is coming to an end as his good friends and future instruments of power crowd in for their place in the inner or outer circle. The campaign, the old campaign, with its constant travel and shopworn speeches, but also with its informal air and loose bullshit, has all but disappeared now. The access, to a degree, will still be there, but it will be more controlled, regimented, watched over by the new and the old palace guard. Edwards feels it and it probably feels good, knowing, like Uncle Earl on his way back to power, that he can soon kick the asses that he used to kiss. The longest campaign is ending, the circle is closing, and Edwin Edwards is shaking hands and saying goodbye to the people he'll see again tomorrow . . . from a distance.

22. One for the Zipper

Dawn on Saturday, October 22. A fresh, cool wind is indeed blowing in from the north across the piney woods to the Gulf, bringing . . . rain. Election workers for all candidates have been up and out since four in the morning, putting up even more yard signs on all the illegal public places they didn't put them during the campaign. And the voters are getting up too, most of them far earlier this Saturday morning than on most workdays. They've heard the stories of massive turnouts and many have the same idea. Vote early and avoid the lines. So many with that idea, in fact, that there are lines at the polls at six. This after a record absentee vote in the three weeks prior.

The debate goes on in this country between voting on Tuesday or Saturday. Since Louisianians vote on both days, Saturday for state and local, Tuesday for federal, the comparison shows Saturdays draw the biggest turnouts. Carter-Reagan was a hot election in this state, but a greater percentage (and much higher numbers due to intense registration drives in 1983) turned out for Edwards-Treen. It's more convenient. Folks have all day to vote on Saturday, they're not crammed in lines at eight at night, trying to get in their vote after work, as they did in the last presidential election, with many deserting the polls after the networks projected Reagan the winner.

"I want a piece of this one," says the LSU grad student whose idea of beating the rush is to rise at eight for a vegetarian omelet at Louie's as fortification for standing in line at the polls. "For two years now we've been bombarded with more political bullshit than I've ever seen. Everyone I've talked to just can't wait to vote. You feel like you've been living it, like you're a part of it."

Down on 13th Street, the teenage girls waiting in the street outside St. Francis Xavier School are a part of it too. At $20 for the day, they race each other to get their printed ballots of Joe Delpit or rival splinter groups or some prominent preacher into the hands of each voter getting out of his or her car. Those who don't have cars have transportation— from the black neighborhoods of New Orleans to rural Cajun wards in Acadiana, the haulers are out in force, making repeated trips in station wagons, vans and farther in the outback, the old school buses still roll.

The big TV stations can play with their exit polls and projections, but if you want to follow what's really happening on election day, tune in to the black radio station in your hometown for an earful. You've heard of remote broadcasts from shopping malls and car dealerships, how about a WXOK remote broadcast from the political headquarters of an enterprising minor candidate in Baton Rouge, Mr. Alvin Johnson, who has invited various white politicians to make personal appeals for the black vote. After a string of sheriff's candidates make their pitches, there comes a news flash from Sandra Thompson's headquarters that bogus ballots bearing Pearl George's name are being circulated in Eden Park endorsing Mike Cannon. The announcement stresses that Pearl George is strongly supporting Sandra Thompson and any Pearl George ballots endorsing anyone else are bogus, counterfeit and just one more desperate dirty trick by Sandra's opponents to steal the election. No one has to say it, but it sounds like a Mike Cannon job through and through: high quality printing, widespread distribution, deadly effectiveness.

Traditionally, the major gubernatorial candidates gather in New Orleans on election day, if for no other reason than it's the only place where decent bars and restaurants are still open after all the ballots are counted.

The Edwards contingent has taken over several floors of the Monteleone in the Quarter, while the Treen forces are camped at the Royal Sonesta around the corner. Dave Treen, however, has defied tradition by returning to Baton Rouge after voting this morning in Metairie to sweat out the returns at the Mansion. Treen forces remain split right down to election day. Cade and the state headquarters staff are at the Baton Rouge Hilton; Nungesser and the New Orleans contingent are in the Quarter.

The major difference between Democrats and Republicans on

election day is that Republicans stay at their headquarters and perform something called ballot security, taking phone calls about allegations of fraud at polling places. Democrats are on the streets, hauling in the votes and engaging in other practices that cause those Republican phones to ring. At the Monteleone, Mike Baer has just returned from the Operating Engineers Hall, where Senator Nat Kiefer has been directing the Edwards forces on the streets, with reports of enormously heavy voting. "Some precincts had up to 50 percent turnout by 10 a.m. It's unbelievable." That's all Marion Edwards needs to hear as he and Bob d'Hemecourt leave the hotel to check the action on the streets. He feels a big victory in his bones and heady confidence that his post-election day fund-raiser will be a smash success. "They're gonna be lined up from here to Grand Isle. It'll cost 'em $100,000 to see Edwin and $50,000 to see me."

Edwin Edwards is already acting like he's governor, as he is 30 minutes late for his election day press conference. There's not much to say, gone even is the saber-rattling over the poll watchers who have been discarded as an issue no longer needed. He's relaxed and playful as he leans against the wall in the hotel corridor after the conference. A reporter has seen the latest bumpersticker: "We won one for the Zipper."

"You mean you're going to hold me to just one?"

In his suite on the 15th floor, he eats a grape and watches the bank of three TV sets for the evening's returns. All that's on at this time is a football game, a Tarzan movie and a Treen commercial filmed at the Governor's Mansion. "Tsk, tsk," mocks the candidate, "look at Dave Treen using the taxpayers' electricity to film his spot. I bet Gus Weill's even flicking his cigar ashes on the carpet." He gets a kick out of the commercial. "Treen should have taken my offer to not spend any money on advertising. They thought that they could outraise and outspend us and were they ever sadly mistaken."

Out on the streets, d'Hemecourt and Marion get out of the car in front of the two-story modern building next to the expressway on North Claiborne. The SOUL headquarters itself is down in the Ninth Ward, but Edwards has turned over this building to the black political organization for the all-out get-out-the-vote effort. "We never leave the place unattended," says d'Hemecourt. "We had to decide whether to hide the place or to decorate it." Their decision is obvious, as the full-color Edwards posters cover every inch of the glass front building. The New Orleans coordinator points out the two diesel generators in a steel cage at the corner of the building. "Standby power just in case someone wants to try something funny." It's obviously not Republicans they're worried about. Election day is serious business in New Orleans. SOUL is taking nothing for granted, especially after their unprecedented press conference in late September when they endorsed Edwards, Senator Hank Braden and later strongly opposed Mayor Morial's unlimited terms amendment.

SOUL leaders Don Hubbard and Sherman Copelin lead the tour of the buzzing complex. As we enter, a young man in SOUL t-shirt and tennis shoes pushes his way through the door, drops off a large box full of computer punch cards and bolts back out to his double-parked car and is off. The runners, explains the businesslike Copelin, are bringing in the names of everyone who has voted so far today. The 114 runners crisscross the city, making regular trips to 300 of the 400 precincts, the ones with substantial numbers of black voters. A worker in each precinct has a box with a punch card for each black voter in that precinct. As the voting commissioner calls out the voter's name, the SOUL worker pulls that card and puts it in the box that the runner comes to get every hour or 90 minutes to return to headquarters. In the SOUL building, dozens of workers in SOUL t-shirts are keying in the names into computer terminals, which then spit out the exception report, an updated list of every black who has not voted in that precinct. That information is fed into the computerized phone bank that keeps calling the voters during the day with taped get-out-to-vote messages.

It's apparent SOUL has married the paternal streetwise operation of the black organization with the most advanced electioneering computer technology. Fifteen years of fighting the street wars both with and against the City Hall machine, matched with all the modern advances of phone banks and computer technology and the money that Marion Edwards has raised, has produced probably one of the most effective election machines in the state. Copelin says SOUL has 2,000 people working election day to turn out the 121,000 registered black voters in the city.

Copelin and Hubbard walk us through rooms of computer terminals and long lines of telephones both manned and linked to computer dialing machines. Copelin punches up some of the different taped messages, some carrying the voices of different black legislators around the city, some geared to different times of day. "Here's the one we start using at five o'clock: 'Hello, this is Edwin Edwards. The polls will soon be closing. You have only a few minutes left to vote. Please get out and vote for me.'" Some even double as weather reports, as one tape warns, "It is raining outside, you may want to take an umbrella to the polls . . . "

Hubbard turns the corner to reveal his favorite part of the operation. "These are my messy people," he says, pointing to ten callers busy on the phones. "They spike rumors, they spread rumors, they put out our side of the story. Whenever something would happen during the campaign, say if some black preacher or Louis Charbonnet has just come out for Treen, they get on the phones and start telling people why. We just snowed them under." I flash back to Treen supporter Anna Johnson complaining about the mysterious flood of phone calls through the Ninth Ward, warning that a vote for Treen was a vote for Reagan.

"They also tell the people not to talk to pollsters, don't talk to whitie. It screws up their polling."

What do you care if pollsters talk to blacks?

"Hey, we'll take care of the blacks."

And the blacks are taking care of Edwin Edwards. SOUL is turning out a huge black vote in the city, reversing the traditional pattern of higher percentage turnouts among whites. And Edwin Edwards is taking care of SOUL. His campaign finance reports list no payments to SOUL, since the group requested all individuals and invoices be paid directly. An Edwards spokesman estimates the total at $75,000. But informed sources in New Orleans, piecing together all reported payments to and purchases on behalf of Copelin and Hubbard and companies they own, peg that figure at closer to $750,000. All perfectly legal—and incredibly lucrative. Any wonder Sherman and Don are called the Gold Dust Twins?

Is it worth it? Well, consider that the same sum spent producing and airing TV commercials would provide about three good statewide buys that might or might not win over undecided voters. The SOUL money is spent on a sure thing—physically registering and bringing to the polls thousands of voters who might otherwise not vote. And this campaign will show that once at the polls the delivered voter will vote for Edwards at a rate closer to 99 out of 100 than to 9 out of 10. Then consider all the time, money and effort Dave Treen and John Cade spent courting the black vote in hopes of capturing just 15 percent, hopes that are crumbling in the face of nearly unanimous organized black support for Edwards. And the unprecedented numbers in which the blacks are turning out are running up the score.

Later John Cade will say he saw it coming. "We were polling 15 percent among blacks during the summer, but they all came off us in September," recalling a black preacher in Alexandria who said he was for Treen in June but had turned against him by September. "'Dave Treen is a fine man,' he told me, 'but can you honestly tell me that Dave Treen's election would not help Ronald Reagan?' I couldn't," shrugged Cade.

As impressive as the SOUL operation is in the governor's race, it is matched in local races by the pure clout and muscle of Dutch Morial's City Hall organization. While the black groups present a united front in the governor's election, they are pitted in bitter street battles in the local races. SOUL has split sheets with the mayor, coming out for Hank Braden against Morial's man Dennis Bagneris and, says Copelin, "We are violently opposed to the unlimited terms." While SOUL has spread its net across the city, Dutch is concentrating his forces in the Braden-Bagneris senatorial race, swamping the allied forces of SOUL and Braden's COUP. The SOUL tour completed, d'Hemecourt wheels back down Canal to the Quarter. "Three o'clock," he notes. "We should know in a few minutes."

"I promise I won't tell anyone but the Boss," Mike Baer pleads and angles to get the results of one of the exit polls from a reporter. "Of course I won't tell any other reporters. You know I wouldn't. Okay, what you got? [Pause] That's unbelievable! Thanks!" Baer hangs up and yells through the press room, "58-40!"

Within minutes the projected final score has rippled through the entire hotel and half the French Quarter. At 3:15 in the afternoon, the party is on. Down in the hotel bar just off the lobby, the Edwards supporters are streaming in from all over the state. Some have the freshly minted EWE 87 buttons, one has the "Vicki for Lieutenant Governor" sticker, all have the news.

The afternoon celebration is too much to take. After a year at the elbow of this campaign, it's time to get away. Out on the streets, the sun is reflecting off the morning rain puddles in the mess of city sidewalk work. Already into October and the heat that has sat atop this campaign since April has burned through the wet morning chill and brought the clinging mugginess with it. The oyster bar around the corner is just far enough away from the jubilation. Oh hell, an Edwards aide at the bar. But apparently he's escaping the same thing as he stares into his beer. "You work for three years and you know in three minutes," he says of the news stations' announced intention to declare the winner at 8:03 p.m. Now with the news leaked at 3:15, there's not even the suspense of waiting until dark. We sit, we drink, we swallow oysters, we console each other on how the miracles of modern science are destroying the politics we grew up with. It's not enough that the media polls kept a running score on the election before it was even held. Now once the voters go to the polls, we aren't even allowed the queasiness in the stomach, the suspense of waiting and wondering those delicious few hours during which the returns trickle in. We're robbed of the mystery of the verdict of the people. The loser is given no hope, the winner is allowed no suspense, no frightened first impressions of early returns, no slow unfolding of the voting patterns, no anguished fear of betrayal waiting for the black vote to roll in, no phone reports from the provinces telling which way the key parishes went and which clerks of court haven't let go of their returns. By their restraints of time and broadcasters' timidity, TV does a lousy job of reporting the issues and personalities at stake in an election. But not content to just leave it alone, TV inflicts its incessant polls on the people and strips what's left of the suspense of election day with their unwanted and unneeded projections. A melancholy end to a fun campaign. At least *dem ersters* were good.

With the drama blown out of the evening, the only thing left to pass for excitement is the maneuvering of the TV stations to get into Edwards' suite to catch his reaction as the projection flashes across the screen. Typical showbiz gimmickry: competing TV news directors decree they should get a split screen of Edwards and Treen receiving the news of the projection. Treen has the good sense to tell TV to forget it, while Edwards says he won't crack any expression until he gets the word from

Sam LeBlanc's selected precincts at nine.

Wayne Ray and the state police have sealed off the 15th floor. Still, the reporters set about pulling any string to get into Edwards' suite for an early comment. Brenda Hodge goes to Mike Baer, Alec Gifford to Wayne Ray, Clancy DuBos to Bob d'Hemecourt, all to no avail. Norman Robinson is discovered tiptoeing down the hall of the 15th floor, having snuck in by the stairway, and is escorted out again. When the big moment finally comes at 8:03, the camera is jostled and doesn't even properly focus on Edwards, who is looking the other way. And so it goes, a misadventure in irrelevance.

Down in the ballroom, the TV reporters are grasping for anyone to interview, as the candidate remains in his suite. They talk to Marion, to Broadhurst, to LeBlanc. Finally Brenda Hodge ropes in Vicki and asks a throwaway question about her own ambitions. Vicki is dead serious. "Some people have talked to me about running for lieutenant governor and I'd have to give it serious consideration." Hodge is stunned. A staffer nearby has had enough. "They need to put that girl in a political detox center."

Between eight and nine, Edwin and an unusually small entourage slip out the back entrance for dinner at La Louisiane. Going downstairs to check for news, aide Sid Moreland encounters the parking lot attendant watching returns on his small screen Sony.

"The governor's upstairs—can you keep us up on the returns every ten minutes?"

"You mean Governor Edwards? Here, you take him this TV." Edwards orders dinner with the Sony as a centerpiece. Wayne Ray comes over. Treen's trying to get in touch, can he call you here?

Vicki erupts, "Hell no, Daddy, don't talk to that asshole after everything he said about you." Edwards rolls his eyes and walks across the room to the phone as conversation at every table halts. Edwards listens, thanks Treen for the congratulations, allows as how Treen had his share of bad luck but that is the way it goes in the business. He agrees to work with Treen during the transition, thanks him again for his call and hangs up. As he turns, dinner napkins from all over the room fly into the air as diners, in on a piece of history, let go of their cool.

Back in the hotel, Edwards descends to the cheering faithful and the TV cameras and claims his victory. He congratulates Dave Treen's supporters, except for one. "This campaign will send a message that Louisiana doesn't like dirty politics practiced in this campaign. They tried to indict me, they called me names, they spread rumors about me that were untrue and malicious, but I am glad to have had the jury of the greatest people in the world. Now that he has got that message, John Cade can go back to Alexandria and shovel fertilizer with the guy he got out of prison. He has spread his fertilizer over the airwaves, let him go back and shovel the real stuff."

With the phalanx of family, both by blood and politics, backing him up on the stage, Edwards thanks all and singles out one. Calling Vicki in from the flank, he lavishes rare praise on her. "Others expressed some doubts about Vicki early in the campaign. But I know from which loins she comes and had full faith in her. Poor baby, she couldn't resist sticking the pin in Gus Weill."

For a change of pace, it's down the street to the Treen party, if you can call it that—it more resembles a wake with a lugubrious Billy Nungesser mourning the passing of power. Billy the realist knew what was coming for Dave Treen. Their own Kennedy poll, which had been so out of sync with other pollsters all along, began tracking the overwhelming movement to Edwards in the final week. "It was like getting run over by a truck." But Billy's real sadness tonight stems from his son's heartbreaking third-place finish in the Algiers House race. The elder Nungesser could see his own days in state government numbered, but he wanted badly to leave behind a seed to grow. But it is not to be.

Three hours after congratulating Edwards privately, Dave Treen finally goes to the Baton Rouge Hilton to thank his disheartened faithful and to announce that at this late hour he won't be able to make it to New Orleans. As for immediate plans: "I hope to get a couple of days' rest—maybe in Las Vegas. Sometimes I think I should have spent a little more time out there."

The Treen troops nonetheless are proud of their reluctant warrior and the class he displays in his concession speech. The Republicans in this state, ever short on victories, can always fall back on class. And they can always feel superior in that regard over Democrats. A morose young Republican groans as the TV cameras switch back to the celebration at the Monteleone. "I can't believe how tacky Edwards was with Cade. Oh yes I can, he's such a sleaze." Actually, Edwards' comments on Cade, though not really necessary, are fairly reserved, considering the names John has called Edwards during the campaign.

Not that Cade has many defenders even back at Republican headquarters. "I'll tell you why we lost," says Republican National Committeewoman Ginny Martinez angrily. "Because Dave Treen wasn't the candidate. John Cade became the candidate." To his credit, Dave Treen defends "the much maligned John Cade, my campaign chairman," to the many Republicans waiting to take John out and shoot him. Treen reasserts one more time it was he who was calling the shots. Too bad so many of them landed right in the foot.

So strong is the Edwards tide, with a margin hovering at 60 percent, that it is pulling Lieutenant Governor Bobby Freeman along to a 47-40 percent lead over Jimmy Fitzmorris. Sherman Bernard, with his overwhelming uninsured motorists vote, will be in a perfunctory runoff against Republican Dave Brennan.

"Whoa, that's gotta be a mistake," whistles the shocked reporter as the Education results flash on the screen. Kelly Nix, considered an easy winner two weeks ago, is getting blown out by Tom Clausen. How do you explain that? "I can explain it," says a grimly smiling Republican. "Clausen got the teachers, he got labor and probably a good black vote, but Clausen won because every Treen person I know voted for him. Nix may be conservative and Clausen is just terrible, but Kelly pissed us all off when he wrapped himself around Edwards. That's what killed him." Plus his daughter's drug bust couldn't have helped. You can just hear voices through the hills: *If the man can't control his own daughter, do we want him lookin' after our chirren?*

The good ol' boys aren't faring well in the sheriffs' races. Incumbent Ed Layrisson is crushing Frank Edwards' comeback bid in Tangipahoa. And up in Natchitoches Parish, Sheriff Norm Fletcher is pulling over 60 percent of the vote in whipping a whole slew of real men.

Getting the news in Washington, D.C., Russell Long is doubtless pleased to learn that: 1) Edwin Edwards won and 2) Dan Richey lost. The libertarian light has gone out in the state Senate and in Concordia Parish, as the darling of the Liberty Lobby has been vanquished by Bill Atkins, despite his being labeled the dupe of the International Big Spender Conspiracy and of the corrupting pinball machine operators of

America. Russell's cousin Gillis is no less happy with news out of Alexandria that not only has his former congressional challenger Ned Randolph been forced into a runoff, but wild man Tilly Snyder, getting to be something of an embarrassment for Gillis, ran last. Garnering less than 40 percent of the vote, front-running Randolph is in sad shape for a runoff against newcomer Joe McPherson, who has strong labor support. Up in Shreveport, creationist Bill Keith trails black challenger Gregory Tarver. Two mischievous New Orleans area legislators wire Keith their condolences. "Sorry to hear how your race has evolved . . . "

Down the bayou, Leonard Chabert may be able to see the Hagler-Duran fight after all. Though forced into a runoff, he has a wide lead. Son Marty can make the trip too, as he comes up short in his race to inherit his dad's old House seat.

In the Baton Rouge clerk's race, Sandra Thompson, at one point leading in the polls 4-1, limps into a lead with 28 percent of the vote. And with a late surge from the black boxes, the discredited incumbent Mike Cannon has barely edged into second place. The bogus Pearl George ballots (who could have done that?) undoubtedly aided Cannon in capturing a slim 300 vote lead over the third-place finisher.

Down in The City, Dutch Morial is dancing. By the hard work of SOUL, plus just about every white vote in the city, the mayor's unlimited terms amendment has been crushed. He didn't even keep it close. But Dutch worry? He won the big one, kicking old nemesis Hank Braden out of his Senate seat and away from any rivalry with Dutch as the city's premier boss politician. Morial has only a couple of dissident black legislators left to crush in the runoff: Louis Charbonnet, who supported Dave Treen, and Nick Connor, who, much worse, opposed the Dutchman in his last race for mayor.

Out on the Lakefront, Mike O'Keefe has finally received his verdict from the people. Even with the staunch support of Edwin Edwards, Dutch Morial and labor boss Victor Bussie, former Senate President Mike O'Keefe was so desperate the final week that his people were pushing anyone who just couldn't vote for a convicted felon to vote for Republican Anna Lundberg, just to take votes away from front-running Benny Bagert and force a runoff. A good byzantine try, but not even close—Bagert rolls to a stunning majority over the field of four. Not only does he sweep the white neighborhoods of the Lakefront and Midcity, but he also cuts deeply into O'Keefe's black support. Mike may have had the mayor and the major black leaders on his side, but Bagert had nearly every black preacher with him. And he did what most white pols wouldn't dare, he tirelessly worked the black neighborhoods door to door. The size of Bagert's victory in the face of allied Democratic kingmaker opposition is another indication of the new force in Louisiana politics. The Bagert campaign with its synthesis of the tried and true tools of machine organizational politics and the new world of high campaign tech should serve as the model for the independent urban candidate of the future. Yet as excellent as was his organization, the Boy Wonder went the last 10 percent on his pure, raw, overgrown punk nerve.

Across town, they are dancing at Bud Rip's. The legendary bartender has edged into a slim lead over incumbent Eddie Bopp. Comeback kid Rick Tonry finishes last.

Up on the 15th floor, the best efforts of Wayne Ray and the state police are crumbling before the tide of Edwin Edwards' many "close personal friends" landing in waves off the elevator and petitioning for admittance to the candidate's suite. It's like this with every election party. Edwards doesn't want to exclude anyone, so there is no respite from the mobs for the family and inner circle. All these folks think they are in the inner circle or that "Edwin wants us here." And he probably does, or wouldn't dare say otherwise. Although treasurer Marion can rate every supporter's importance according to dollars contributed, to the candidate a vote is a vote is a vote. Edwin never has been willing to exclude or to rank any supporter. Basically, he orders his political world the same way Earl Long did: he is on the top level, no one is on the second level and everyone else is on the third. And most of them are showing up on the 15th floor.

Even in the jammed celebration suite, champagne corks popping with each percentage point gained, Edwin Edwards is the quiet center in the storm—quiet and withdrawn and not altogether well. The past weeks have been grueling, as he has met every demand of the staff, the press and the public to be the total candidate. And now as the total victor, winning perhaps the last hard race he'll ever have to run, he stands in the corner of the room, by his mother and his wife, and appears to draw ever more into himself as "close friends" crowd in even closer.

The only way to clear this room is to take everyone down with him for one more appearance before the throngs and then to come back up and absolutely shut down the 15th floor. He takes Nolan's widow on his arm and tells the cameras and crowds below, "No one had a better brother than I had in Nolan and no one had a better wife than he had in Eleanor." Three and a half years' work done, next on Edwards' agenda is a two-day hunting trip with Wayne Ray to get away from it all. But he doesn't get that far. Home to Highland Road on Sunday he collapses into bed with a raging fever and barely moves for two days.

Sherman Copelin feels so good this Sunday morning he might even go to church. He and A. Z. Young stand outside the Monteleone's wrecked ballroom, flipping through the morning papers, beaming about the monolithic black vote—about 94 percent for Edwards, 97 percent in New Orleans—and laughing over the poor fools who were going to deliver Dave Treen's 15 percent black vote. "I think I'll go to Prophet Abernathy's church this morning, sit in the front pew and just smi-i-l-le up at him," says Copelin of Treen's leading black man of the cloth.

Aides, contributors, parish coordinators and reporters trickle in from breakfast or straight from bed. Scattered around the ballroom, reading over the returns, the campaign cognoscenti can't help but gape at how the massive victory is broken down into its elements. Edwards took every parish in the state except for narrow Treen wins in his home Jefferson and conservative St. Tammany across the lake. In only seven other parishes, mostly urban, did the incumbent get over 40 percent of the vote. Edwards carried 24 parishes, mostly rural, by more than 70 percent of the vote. In two of the small parishes where the federal poll watchers came in, Edwards topped 80 percent. Though he swamped Treen in Acadiana, his heaviest percentages—79 to 81 percent—came from five rural, mainly black, strongly labor parishes around Baton Rouge. As for pure numbers, New Orleans weighed in for Edwards with a 53,000 vote margin and nearly 65 percent. The black box vote totals were astronomical, even comical. In several boxes, some of the also-rans finished ahead of the governor. At Greenville School in North Baton Rouge, Edwards got 860 votes to Treen's 2. Edwards received more votes than any candidate for any election in the history of the state. When the last few country boxes came in Monday morning, he broke the mythical million. The final body count:

Edwards—1,002,589—62 percent
Treen—585,385—36 percent
7 also-rans—21,209—1.3 percent.

After four years in office, Dave Treen did worse than when he first ran against Edwards as a largely unknown private citizen and token Republican challenger in 1972. He only lost that one 57-43 percent.

The other big losers election night, though their electronic wizardry disguised it, were the exit pollsters. They were flat wrong. They predicted an 18-20 point Edwards win. Edwards won by 26 percent, clearly outside the acceptable 3-4 percent margin of error. With such a blowout, the discrepancy was barely noticed—but numbers are numbers and theirs were clearly off. And these were polls conducted *after* people voted. The witch doctors can't explain this one away as a last minute shift in the mood of the voters. Had it been a closer race, they would have been keenly embarrassed. Instead they were merely wrong. Politics 1, Witch Doctors 0.

There is, of course, no shortage of theories to explain the overwhelming landslide. One must start with the built-in, immense popularity of Edwards, who, with a few correctible exceptions, ran a flawless campaign that mixed equal parts personality, opportunity, hi tech, low talk and flesh-pressing politicking—and was funded with great sacks of money. From the beginning he was close to unbeatable, but he could not have achieved the unprecedented landslide without a lot of help from his enemies. As Harnett Kane wrote of Huey Long, "His enemies made him by their puerile tactics." In his own post mortem at the Mansion on Monday, Treen ticks off his own reasons for his poor showing, ranging from Democratic dominance to his own lackluster efforts at public relations. That explains why he lost, but the reason he was humiliated— the answer many fence-sitters cited for why they could not bring themselves to vote for the incumbent—is Treen's incessantly negative attacks that totally overshadowed any attempt to project the positive aspects of his administration. In the campaign's final three months, we saw Dave Treen's image as a dull but honest good guy deteriorate into a nattering nabob of negativism, to borrow a phrase from another big-time Republican loser.

Sure, maybe Treen needed to attack to make up lost ground. But he and Cade did that so stridently and clumsily that when they weren't playing into Edwards' hands they were turning off the electorate in droves. The Treen braintrust hoped to cast the voters' decision as a choice between an honest governor and a flashy crook. But given the immense personal power attached to this office, most voters viewed the decision not on a political or a moral basis but on a psychological one. It was a matter of winners and losers, survivors and chumps. Whom did the voters choose to identify with: the solid, respectable type who works hard, plays by the rules, tries to do good and in the end gets screwed, or the self-confident, self-assured man of the world who breaks what rules he can't make work for himself and gets what he goes after?

The people didn't stop liking Dave Treen, they stopped respecting him. Many good Democrats who voted for Treen in 1979 earnestly wanted him to succeed, to show that he could grasp firmly the reins of power and run state government firmly and fairly. If that meant playing a little hardball partisan politics, the folks were up for it. But Dave Treen wasn't. Armed with little more than stamina and good intentions and saddled with a divided and disoriented staff, Treen showed that he couldn't or wouldn't lower himself to the world of politics in order to succeed in it. All along, he preferred being right to being governor—he got what he asked for.

Ossie Brown

Mike Cannon

Sandra Thompson

Leonard Chabert

Scott Welch, Captain Fact

John Hill

Sid Moreland

What Dave Treen wouldn't do for a vote....

At the final rally in Lafayette.

On the press bus.

When Edwards lost his voice, Vicki rose to speak for "your friend, my daddy, our next governor . . ."

Crowds of passion: Edwards revs up the masses at the Fair Grounds, then is hustled out following a scary incident in the packed crowd. (below right)

Edwards and aides Wayne Ray (above) and Darrell Hunt (below).

Commissioner of Administration Stephanie Alexander

When a magazine asked state celebrities who would portray them in a movie, Edwards responded: Errol Flynn.

Father and daughter dance in Palace of Versailles.

The governor-elect in Paris: "I thought, when I was born, that I was destined to be a king."

Governor Edwards hams it up at the Alexandria Gridiron Show following the controversy over his remarks on the death and resurrection of Christ.

23. "I'm the Lesser of Two Evils"

The Baton Rouge Republican leader is relaxing in his back yard with his family when he notices someone is standing on his carport. The figure moves closer. It's Mike Cannon, who doesn't want to disturb the fellow at home except to impart one brief message. "I'm the lesser of two evils."

The runoff elections are mostly mopping-up operations. For the only remaining drama worthy of Louisiana politics, there is Baton Rouge, where the governor's election has been only a prelude to the main event—an all-out, vicious, bitter and dirty gutter fight between the most unlikely of contestants: Mike Cannon, stripped of his honor and his good name, and Sandra Thompson, who is about to lose what's left of hers.

The Baton Rouge clerk's race is significant not in the office itself or even in the vileness of personal attacks—the Natchitoches sheriff's race holds no peer there—but in its lessons about sheer exploitation and defense of a seemingly indefensible position. The contrast between the two could not be more perfect: Mike Cannon, tried and convicted, the caricature of the fast-talking, slippery carnival hawker; and Sandra Thompson, the porcelain-featured, establishment-backed darling of reform. And there are similarities. Cannon's enemies range from the local bar association to the daily newspapers to the black bosses to the parish's top politicians, including the mayor and the district attorney. Sandra, though she can't match that enemies list, has made her share of foes along the way, especially among women in state government who feel she got more than she deserved and that she stepped over plenty of bodies along the way. That she has done nothing essentially different to advance her political career than have scores of ambitious young men does not overcome for Thompson the gaping double standard and ingrained sexism (ingrained more deeply than racism) in Louisiana politics that demands that a woman in government be not just competent but outstanding, above reproach, warm and courteous and not too aggressive or good looking.

The textbook of politics says that any incumbent who can't garner 40 percent of the vote in the primary is dead in the water, he need not even carry on. By that rule, incumbent Mike Cannon, with only 27 percent of the vote, has no business even showing his face. Sandra, though she only received 28 percent after starting with a wide lead in the polls, has the best shot at getting the votes of the other two primary candidates, who also ran hard against Cannon's image and record. With momentum and money, she should be able to easily beat Mike Cannon, whose back is to the wall and whose campaign treasury is empty.

Mike Cannon appears to be a political basket case. But though he may be out of everything else, from credibility to money, he does possess an active imagination and an innate grasp of politics far more highly developed than other politicians his age who have dulled their instincts with slavish reliance on polls and media posturing. Next to his old nemesis Ossie Brown, Mike Cannon may have the highest negative ratings of any Baton Rouge politician, but Mike always sees to it that before the campaign's end his opponents' negatives are higher than his. That is his special gift.

Plus Cannon is one of the parish's most underrated personal campaigners. That's part of his disarming political style: he doesn't push himself on people, he doesn't glad-hand and bluster. Instead of table-hopping through political functions, Cannon will plant himself at one picnic table, relax and follow the conversation, until everyone there is comfortable with him. He is very good at giving the impression he has nothing in the world better to do than to sit here to get to know these fine people. If time is a factor, he goes directly to those he knows can help him and lies prostrate at their feet until they're too embarrassed to do anything but give in. That treatment works well for Cannon on local Republican leaders. They have no use for Sandra Thompson to start with, still remembering her surprising endorsement of Louis Lambert in 1979. Plus, Cannon has something they badly want: some kind of entree into the black community to save their Republican sheriff candidate,

Elmer Litchfield, from getting the Dave Treen treatment in the black and labor boxes. Making the rounds of more leading Republicans' back yards, the embattled incumbent secures one end of the political spectrum and begins working his way back toward the other. For the past year he's been working tirelessly for the blessing of Edwin Edwards in the most subtle and unobtrusive ways. When Edwards assembled 3,000 extras on the Capitol steps in May to form the backdrop for his Gandhi spot, one of those little dots on the screen was Mike Cannon, sitting silently in the sun, paying homage just and due. His girlfriend, Cathy Broussard, took leave from the clerk's office to work in Edwards' campaign. Despite his past falling-out with Sandra Thompson, Edwards cannot go against his credo of not getting involved in a local race without a very strong reason. Yet another member of his family, who has even less use for Sandra Thompson, does.

Elaine Edwards, who made it clear in 1979 that she would endorse even Bonzo over Sandra Thompson, refueled the old memories and rumors by sticking it to Sandra one more time and telling the press that she and her children were endorsing Mike Cannon. "I just think Mike has done a good job. It's as simple as that."

As simple as that, Mike Cannon has managed to get both the parish Republican leadership and the Edwards family in his corner on his way to building the kind of coalition Earl Long would be proud of. And he isn't through. Cannon redoubles his efforts to hold and increase his black support in defiance of the unified opposition of the so-called black leaders.

Yet, even with his clever political alliances, his support from Elaine Edwards, the blacks and the Republicans, his own hustle and shameless self-pity, Mike Cannon knows he cannot win this race without Sandra Thompson's help. He knows her vulnerabilities, but he can't appear to publicly exploit them. That would make him look mean as well as disreputable. No, this is a job for Sandra Thompson, one that only she in the past has proven herself capable of.

Throughout her career Sandra Thompson has been depicted as a Barbie doll, Pinocchio and a shrill mouse. No other candidate in Louisiana politics over the past decade has been portrayed with such a creative and wide array of demeaning images. With some justification, Thompson is beginning to feel ganged up on. And like any

319

self-respecting though not necessarily wise politician, she starts shooting back. People expect low blows out of Mike Cannon, but Thompson's slashing back—that old double standard again—goes against the grain of her ladylike image. Already the two have printing presses working, matching flyer against flyer. There are flyers and there are hate sheets— mall shoppers find versions of both affixed to their windshields. Both candidates disavow the hate sheets which delve into vile rumors, half-truths and untruths about each other. The flyers are more comical, engaging in the old political art of damning by comparing. Here's the candidates' flyers' interpretation of each's educational qualifications:

CANNON FLYER

MIKE CANNON:	**SANDRA THOMPSON:**
LSU Business Adm. degree, 1968	Attended Northeast Louisiana State
LSU Law School, J. D., 1971	College; attended Southeastern
Fellow of the Institute of Court	Louisiana College; attended
Management, 1983	Louisiana State University;
	Attended Southern University.
	Has not earned a degree.

THOMPSON FLYER

MIKE CANNON:	**SANDRA THOMPSON:**
Law degree. Suspended by the	Will earn B.A. in Government (3.5
Louisiana Supreme Court on	grade-point average) in May, before
recommendation of the Louisiana	taking office in July.
Bar Association.	

It becomes obvious political theater to arrange debates between Cannon and Thompson, knowing full fireworks and low personal attacks will ensue. It's a bad trap for Sandra to wander into, fighting Cannon on his own ground. Sandra would be wise to say she will let Mr. Cannon's criminal record and his running feuds with other parish officials speak for themselves and to keep her campaign on a higher plane. But Sandra is too tenacious to back off. In public debate, Cannon does a better job of sticking to his qualifications and Thompson's lack thereof, while Thompson slips into more cutting attacks, often bringing up Cannon's divorce suit and his fight with his wife and her partner over their old business. In parrying those attacks, Cannon is able to dip into his flawless self-pity routine (he even cried once on TV over all the terrible things Ossie Brown was doing to him). Cannon also makes full use of his past battles with District Attorney Ossie Brown, now beset by rumors that the federal grand jury is about to indict him on the cocaine and ice cream case. Cannon hints darkly at the danger of losing the independence of the clerk's office to the evil political empire of the district attorney and implies Sandra will be co-opted and controlled by same.

Sandra Thompson, in her frustration, is making the same mistake as Dave Treen, waging a negative campaign to drive home a point most voters already accept—playing into the hands of the human tar baby, who's just begging her to hit him again, hit him again, until her once-lily-white hands are as dirty as his, and worse, she's entangled in a fight she can't win. That awful chemistry between them is highlighted in an exchange before one group in which Cannon charges that Thompson's ads mislead the reader by saying he is involved in several personal lawsuits without saying that he is the plaintiff.

Thompson: "We didn't say which way . . . "

Cannon: "You admit, that's a little tricky, right?"

Thompson: "Mr. Cannon, I'll admit that everything you've put out about me has been misleading . . . "

Cannon: "You're pretty smooth."

Thompson: "I have to give you the all-time record for being smooth."

Cannon: "No ma'am."

Rule of thumb: in any acrimonious exchange, the loser is the one who talks the most. Count the words.

In another debate, Cannon wisely shuts up and lets Thompson dig herself in deeper.

"If you think back over the past two terms, there have been a lot of probably very good, qualified people who would have run for clerk of court but they're so frightened by the kinds of campaign tactics that Mr. Cannon is so well known for, they decided not to run. He is *well known* throughout this parish and when I started talking about running, everybody said, 'Let me warn you, when he gets through with you . . . ' In fact, he sent us little threatening statements through other people. 'Mr. Cannon wants you to know you won't even hold up your head in East Baton Rouge Parish when he gets through with you. Your children are going to be embarrassed to go to school.' These are the facts, I'm telling you, the man, the kind of tactics that he uses against his opponents . . .

We need to get that kind of man out of office so that we can run positive campaigns in the future."

With only two weeks to go before the runoff, Thompson, not satisfied with the damage she has done herself in public debates, self-inflicts her ultimate weapon. It's a radio ad meant to ridicule Cannon in the same way the Barbie doll, Pinocchio and mice ads have ridiculed her. In the ad, a voice poses hard questions to Mike Cannon on the state of the clerk's office, to which an animal sound responds, "Ribbit."

Mike Cannon a frog. How clever. The ads are an instant hit with the public always appreciative of creative new ways to engage in political-personal attacks. Sandra receives many compliments on the ads from supporters who are glad to see her giving Mike Cannon his due. What she is really giving him is the election.

Cannon and his ad consultant Pat Wallace pounce on the ads, seeing the opportunity to combat bitter humor with a droll response. The greatest favor a candidate can do for an opponent is to create a joke ad that can be turned back on the jokester. Within days, a series of well-written ads appear featuring a Lewis Carroll-like illustration of a well-dressed frog, condescendingly answering Sandra and making her appear to be hysterical and naive. They are clever, pointedly funny ads that show Mike Cannon can take a joke and convincingly dispose of his opponent's charges. Both Sandra's frog ads and Mike's frog ads are the talk of the town, and the momentum begins to shift back to Cannon.

No matter how bad off a candidate is or how deep in debt, it's expected he or she throw a victory party on election night to thank workers and to sweat out the returns together. Bobby Freeman is hailing his victory at the Capitol House, while down in New Orleans, Bud Rippoll conveniently greets well-wishers from behind his own bar. Sandra Thompson has reserved the Hilton ballroom. And Mike Cannon . . . as usual, he's at the office, hosting his subdued, traditional party, while his office staff receives the returns and voting machine keys from the election commissioners. Cannon's on the phone with Pat Wallace as he watches the returns flash on the screen during the TV movie *Mommie Dearest.*

Thompson edges into a narrow lead on the early returns, but as Cannon checks each box that comes in he grows more cautiously confident to see he is carrying the black boxes strongly and still holding onto 40 percent of the vote in the white neighborhoods. It's a question of whose people get out to vote. New results flash up every five minutes but in between it's rather strange watching emotionally drained and tense politicians and workers, hanging on the political life-or-death decision of the voters, gazing anxiously as Faye Dunaway brandishes a coat hanger at a little girl. "Kinda looks like Sandra and me," says Cannon, looking up from his tally sheets.

Then the big move. The black vote starts rolling in, Cannon bolts to a 500 vote lead. Workers cheer as Cannon slumps back in his chair, one hand holding the phone, the other pawing at the air. "C'mon, my people, c'mon." And here they come. With each new crawl across the screen, Cannon's slim lead builds, cheers ring out, the frog cake is cut. The final returns showing Cannon's 2,000 vote lead appear at the bottom of the screen during the scene where Faye Dunaway/Joan Crawford is laid out in the coffin. "That's Sandra all right—dead." Enter the TV cameras. No split screen debate tonight, it's all Mike. "I may look like a frog, but I feel like a prince tonight."

Cannon's ally Elmer Litchfield wins his election to become Louisiana's only Republican sheriff. Up in Shreveport, black challenger Gregory Tarver is polishing off scientific creationist Bill Keith while in Alexandria, Victor Bussie's hard work has paid off in the thumping end to Ned Randolph's Senate tenure. In New Orleans, Dutch Morial has exacted his revenge, snuffing out both Louis Charbonnet and Nick Connor, replacing them with safer, more loyal blacks. And at Bud Rip's bar, a bouffant mama is raising her bottle of Dixie beer in celebration of Bywater's favorite bartender. "Who dat say dey gonna beat Bud Rip?" It's hard to tell if the crowd is happier over Bud's long-awaited success or his newly announced intention to hold onto the place while serving in the Legislature.

But the election story tonight is in Baton Rouge, where Mike Cannon has engineered a brilliant comeback from the political dead. Though he is no more popular than when the race began, according to his game plan and with a lot of help from his opponent, Sandra Thompson is less so. In going against the grain of the voters' determination to turn out all those brushed by scandal, Mike Cannon has made an important point about Louisiana and American politics. His victory proves that you can be

323

disliked and discredited, tried and convicted, fat and ugly, with your own sordid life story laid bare to the world, you can have the city's press firmly against you and its most powerful politicians out to get you, you can be underfinanced and politically isolated and have an attractive, dynamic woman hell bent to beat you. But if you keep your cool and your sense of humor and if you play your politics right, you can beat the whole damned world amassed against you. And that's what makes this country great.

24. The New Deal

They begin their days together, when Edmund Reggie picks up Marion in Crowley and then stops at Billy Broadhurst's and sets off to Baton Rouge. Crossing the Atchafalaya Swamp, they talk about people and jobs, making or breaking the hopes and plans of the hundreds who want to be a part if not own of piece of the new administration of Edwin Edwards. Officially, Edwards' brother and his two longtime friends are members of the executive committee of the transition team. In reality, they are the shadow cabinet, trusted draftsmen connecting the broad strokes of the grand design by the Great Architect. The three have been with Edwards since the first race for the Crowley City Council 30 years before. They are still his chief operatives, meeting with him first thing at the transition office (formerly state headquarters) on Silverside Lane and reviewing the order of the day. Marion is primarily concerned with retiring the $4.3 million in $25,000 and $50,000 notes given by members of the Committee of 200. Broadhurst and Reggie are screening the major appointments to executive positions, the boards and commissions, as well as planning the first legislative package with another veteran confidant Camille Gravel. Another executive committee member, Ann Davenport, though not returning to her old job as executive secretary, is overseeing the hiring and training of a new Fourth Floor staff to work as smoothly as the one Davenport oversaw four years ago.

The governor-elect has promised a new kind of state administration, different from the previous one or, for that matter, the one before that: open, fresh, clean, responsive, responsible, attracting only the best and the brightest and ever the equal opportunity employer. For all the freshness and newness, Edwards still likes things to work. Hence, the job of the old hands, to set the new faces in place and have them ready for a running start March 12.

The change in atmosphere from the old campaign office to the new transition office is apparent from the first step inside the door where the visitor is now met by a couple of state policemen and Kermit Richard, the official greeter who knows who needs to be specially cared for. Everyone else is sent down the hall for a visitor's badge. Upstairs, the once supercharged but relaxed atmosphere has settled to a dignified rush. Even Gus Mijalis, whose casual swagger and easygoing good humor epitomized the former tone of the campaign of friends, appears positively buttoned-down and elegant peering over his glasses with a bundle of important papers in hand. Aides who two months ago were setting up drivers and country western bands and campaign contributors are now immersed in weightier tasks, setting a new government in motion, and not just any government, but a new political order, "a hallmark against which all future administrations will be judged," as the office inspirational has it.

The generator of all this dare-to-be-greatness looks around for a spare room to chat with his visitor. Interviewing Edmund Reggie is like throwing paper airplanes into a fan—he greets each question with a windstorm of enthusiasm followed by gusts of tangential thoughts and spontaneous observations. As good as Reggie's b.s. is, he is merely the animator for the Great Architect. "Edwin gives us a real sense of direction. He has the composite in his mind, he sees the complete picture. And the amazing thing is that after eight years in office and four years running for it, he's coming up with the freshest, most far-reaching, most innovative ideas I've ever heard to move the state forward. He keeps telling us to not be afraid to reach higher, to do something progressive, to go farther than the accepted limits of what state government can do."

The recurring theme is that Louisiana will see a different kind of administration. How different? "Well, last time we had Clyde Vidrine, so we have to guard against that." The difference this time, says Reggie, will be in the people. "We are putting together a cabinet and subcabinet with people who would be attractive to private industry. Edwin sold them on coming in on state pay and at salaries that won't be increased. And not because someone is the son of a contributor. Edwin's coming in without a single commitment. That's one blessing of raising and spending $13 million. He had all the money to run with. Now he doesn't have to use the state treasury to pay off any promises."

Reggie disappears down the hall and returns with his "precepts of understanding" all major appointees must commit to: no salary increases for the foreseeable future, decreasing the number of employees in each department, giving Edwards in January a comprehensive plan to realistically reduce departmental expenses without reducing legislatively mandated programs. "If they can't say they'll do a better job for less, they're not the people we're looking for. That's the test."

Also, he reads on, no spouse, relative or children will be hired by or have any business with an official's department. And all will observe an open door policy, meeting the public and returning all phone calls on the day they are received. "The governor does that himself. If he does that for the whole state, then every secretary in every office will do the same. There will be no more kingdoms. . . . We'll all respond in the same way to the public. Edwin is so against bureaucratic arrogance."

Reggie whips up his rhetoric in a grand crescendo. "I am staggered and amazed by the enthusiasm of the man and by the fresh, imaginative ideas he wants implemented. He's more full of ideas than he was in 1972." Time will tell what Edwin and Edmund are full of, but the transition staff at least, getting the full Reggie treatment, can't help but be believers.

The aide looks around one time and confides, "I tell you what pisses me off is the way he's been so damned nice to some people who did nothing for us." Within the heady atmosphere of the victors' camp, some loyalists, though conceding Edwards does a fine job of taking care of his friends, still can't understand his reluctance to punish his enemies. It was much more fun during the campaign when Edwards gave no quarter, finding, even funding, candidates to run against and pin down Treen supporters. But his massive landslide has allowed him the luxury of granting political pardons. "There is not a vindictive bone in his body," says Judge Reggie. Not many stupid ones either. Edwards knows when and with whom to make peace—as long as the vanquished come bearing the olive branch. Yet sometimes absolution is not his to give. When asked at a press conference if any of Treen's black appointees will be kept on, Edwards refers the question to the back of the room where Dorothy Mae Taylor and Sherman Copelin are sternly shaking their heads in unison.

Rapprochement takes many forms. Following tradition, *Advocate* publisher Doug Manship hosts a dinner party at the City Club for Edwards and the newspaper's editors, at which the two old enemies toast and joke with each other. Manship will tell friends, "I don't know why he wants the job," but he extends his editorial good will and will ultimately endorse Edwards' $1 billion tax package.

Stranger than that, while Anna Edwards is planning the inauguration she receives a call from John Spain, archfiend news director of Channel 2, the very man who sent John Camp after Edwin Edwards. Spain just wants to offer Anna any assistance in media coordination, credentials, pool coverage, anything he can do to help. The press corps gawks as Spain assumes all press coordination chores for the politician who had publicly reviled him a few short weeks before. Either Spain or Spain's boss Manship has decided that eight years is a long time for a cold war and that a fresh start is in order.

Edwards is breaking important new ground for women and blacks in government by making good on his promise of a balanced administration top to bottom. Stephanie Alexander is a far cry from the wily, ambitious and imprisoned Charlie Roemer as commissioner of administration, and pediatrician and hospital administrator Dr. Sandra Robinson offers a style and an approach to the state's largest department, Health and Human Resources, that are light-years distant from those of Edwards' last DHHR head, whip-cracking George Fischer. But Edwards' most surprising top appointment is neither female nor black, rather a white guy named Ron Faucheux as secretary of commerce.

In New Orleans that news shakes City Hall where Dutch Morial, having vanquished or tamed all rivals for his sovereignty in the city, and who has also always received appropriate reverence and a wide berth from candidate Edwin Edwards, is now humiliated by Edwards' awarding a plum cabinet post to Faucheux, Morial's bitter opponent in the racially spiked mayoral race of 1982 and a prominent figure in Dutch's hall of black candles. Slain by Dutch, Faucheux's career was in a heap, alongside any citywide ambitions of other white candidates in black-dominated, Dutch-ruled New Orleans. Faucheux had stalked the lieutenant governor's race but decided not to run. And therein lay his reward. As a favor to his staunch labor ally Victor Bussie, Edwards had talked Faucheux out of the lieutenant governor's race with the lure of the future cabinet job, thus taking a lot of pressure off embattled incumbent Bobby Freeman, who was both labor's candidate and their insurance policy should something untoward happen to Edwards. Some Edwards staffers were at first surprised and disgruntled because of Faucheux's minor contribution to the campaign, but later nodded with respect and approval when they got the full picture. "It was a clever case," says one, "of Edwin letting labor borrow on his assets." It was also the opportunity for Edwards to send a clear message to Dutch Morial. Candidate Edwards had bowed and scraped to humor Dutch, to keep him out of the governor's race, to keep the black vote united, even catching a lot of flak for endorsing Morial's unlimited terms. Throughout the campaign, Edwin Edwards showed Mayor Morial the utmost respect and honor. But now Edwin Edwards, coming to power, is letting Boss Dutch know who's really boss.

Through his appointment process, Edwards is keeping another promise, to invite public comment or criticism before announced appointments are finalized. Every release of proposed appointments bears the curious disclaimer, "Any person knowing just reasons why any such persons should not be so appointed is asked to speak now or forever hold his peace." Edwards completes nearly all of his cabinet appointments— that is, all the blacks and women he's going to name—in time for *60 Minutes* to film them for the upcoming show. So complete is Edwards' demographic mix, it's getting to be a joke. He introduces his new secretary of the Department of Culture, Recreation and Tourism as a Cherokee Indian, even though Noelle LeBlanc's Indian ancestor preceded generations of New Orleans uptown society. No matter, an Indian's an Indian on the vita. At one point Edwards even introduces his new director of the office of veterans' affairs, a handicapped black Republican, who turns out to be everything Edwards could ask for, except a veteran. His name is quietly withdrawn. During that same show and tell for the cameras, at which black and female faces far outnumber one lonely white guy, an irreverent aide pokes a reporter and asks, "Where's the Jew?"

Edwards achieves peace on his own terms with the state press corps but doesn't presume the good will carries beyond the border. That's the way it's always been. Even at the height of his popularity in his first two terms, Edwards and his Cajun rogue image played to bad reviews in the Eastern press. Even on his best behavior, he's been snubbed, as when he approached the podium at the 1976 Democratic National Convention to second the nomination of Jerry Brown and the networks switched to commercials. Visiting journalists in the 1983 campaign couldn't resist the easy cliche of the cocky politician-king who dazzles his subjects with corruption and excess. But Edwards' remarkable landslide could not be denied. On election night, *USA Today* was planning a story for the Monday edition, and NBC's Ken Bode had been in to prepare a report for the Sunday news show. Then late election night, half a world away, a terrorist drove a loaded truck bomb into the Marine barracks in Beirut, sending shock waves through the nation's press for the next weeks, wiping out all else from news budgets, burying the Edwards victory in the rubble of that disaster.

When the *60 Minutes* piece aired in early December, it fell in neatly with the pack. The 13-minute segment ignored the immensity of the Edwards victory and the appointment of his balanced cabinet to home in on the 12-year-old allegations of Clyde Vidrine. There's Clyde and an embittered Lewis Johnson interviewed on camera by Ed Bradley, who feigns civics textbook incredulity at the idea that a governor would actually appoint a large contributor to an important state job. The report focused on the 1971 money angle, especially Edwards' disputing the claimed amount of Jerome Glazer's contributions—"My version is it was $45,000. I think Clyde skimmed $30,000 from the money." That kind of talk was just too sexy for producer Joe Bernstein to pass up—so it forms the meat of the show. It may have been more interesting to try to explain how Edwards was twice overwhelmingly reelected after those allegations first surfaced. That, the story leaves you to assume, is because Louisianians are ignorant and hopelessly duped by Edwards' cult of personality. The truncated, unbalanced report raises more questions than it answers and though it does no new damage to Edwards' already tarnished reputation, the show does manage to insult the state as a whole and to deepen the national misunderstandings of Louisianians' approach to government.

330

Edwards' final campaign finance report weighs in at 20 pounds for 1,867 pages, listing over 10,000 contributors and over 19,000 individuals who received a check from the Edwards campaign. That includes the thousands of part-time workers receiving $20 to $50 for canvassing, taking people to the polls, telephoning. Edwards wheels the documents across the parking lot to the Ethics Commission office to make a point that the law's requirements are a "particularly silly exercise in good government" and call for his "taking a long look at the campaign finance law." In practical terms, he questions how "one person who receives a $20 check for working on election day can alter the course of the election or history and we don't need to keep track of every check."

A gaggle of candidates who have just filed their reports wait outside in the parking lot for Edwards to finish his media event. Among them is Butch Baum, who ran a respectable but not respectable enough second to Agriculture Commissioner Bob Odom's landslide. Well, it was all a good experience for Butch, who made a lot of new friends and contacts. But only one thing bothers him about the election. "Well, what really disappoints me is how poorly I did here in Baton Rouge. Odom beat me 80,000-27,000 right here in my home. You know, I just couldn't figure it and it got me a little mad. So I went back through my records and did you know that in the past 15 years I have donated $1,653,000 to charities here. And the sons of bitches wouldn't even vote for me," says Butch looking off in hurt disgust. "But I guess it worked out all right. I've saved $25,000 since the election. When the charities call me now, I just tell 'em, *Call Bob Odom!*"

"Your Worship," the governor-elect greets Archbishop Philip Hannan in the Little Capitol's dining room. Edwards is back already to his old Mansion tradition of breaking bread at noon with everyone from legislators to out-of-state journalists to the reigning Arkansas Pork Queen. The afternoon appointments follow. It's the same idea in a scaled-down version during the transition. Today's lineup includes the good archbishop who has driven up from New Orleans, press secretary-designate Meg Curtis, Wayne Ray, Marion and Thibodaux contributor C. O. Calogne, about to be appointed to the Mineral Board.

After the archbishop says grace, he expresses his own gratitude that the governor-elect is on board to help him talk some sense into the

331

Italians dealing with the World's Fair. Seems the archbishop, having been guaranteed one of Michelangelo's sculptures for the Vatican Pavilion of the World's Fair, is now running into thorny problems with the Italian government, which apparently is using the sculpture as a pawn in its ongoing domestic political crisis. Seems the Italian government, which has final say on the movement of the Vatican's precious artworks, has reneged on its earlier agreement with the archbishop and now says it can't possibly send the priceless sculpture for fear of breakage. The Italians have offered to send another sculpture, but you don't rise to archbishop in the Catholic church without knowing how to play politics. "I told them what I am going to do," says the archbishop, unfolding his napkin. "The entire pavilion is designed with the spot for the Michelangelo as the focal point. I told them we will simply leave the pedestal empty with a card explaining the absence of the Michelangelo. Then we'll let them explain."

Edwards compliments the prelate on his grasp of the jugular. The archbishop's confession seems to relax the governor-elect into treating his excellency to a spate of his latest ethnic jokes. And since the subject is Italians, "Did you know the Italian Army recently held maneuvers for the Third World War? They spent three week practicing this"— Edwards puts his hands up over his head. The archbishop smiles politely into his salad. But just in case he didn't catch that one, "Do you know why the new Italian Navy has glass-bottomed boats? So they can see the old Italian Navy."

Edwards especially loves telling Italian jokes to Italians. "This is all in your honor, C.O.," he nods to his contractor friend.

"Governor," protests Calogne, "as long as you've known me, you continue to think I'm Italian. I'm a descendant of a French prince."

"C.O., the only thing worse than an Italian is one who won't admit it."

At this point the archbishop might consider putting Edwards on that empty pedestal in the Vatican Pavilion to do his Italian routine. Instead, the prelate diplomatically shifts the conversation to Project Harvest, the ambitious humanitarian effort to get surplus food at the market and from restaurants into the hands of the urban needy. Edwards follows the discussion with interest, then interjects a question. "Did you hear about the Italian girl that says, 'Mama, Mama, I'ma preg-a-nant.' 'Don't worry,' says her mother, 'maybe it's not yours.'"

A good comic knows how far he can ride a gag, but of course Edwards can't let the routine end without "What's black and blue and floats in the river? A Cajun who tells Italian jokes."

The luncheon guests sigh in relief, but the host is on a roll. After the Italian jokes, can the pope jokes be far behind? Did his worship hear the one about the Pope sending 300 septic tanks to his native Poland? "He got a telegram back that said, 'Have the tanks. As soon as we learn how to drive them, we'll attack the Russians.'"

Okay, the archbishop chuckles at that one. What else is he going to do? Edwards and Hannan have been friends for years—the archbishop has presided at all the Edwards kids' weddings. He understands Edwards' distaste for boring formalities. And a big part of it may well be that Edwards, having spent three years being uncharacteristically nice to everyone ("I'll even be nice to reporters," he said during the campaign in Morgan City, "and when I get back in, I'm gonna be a real son of a bitch."), is getting back to his old self again. Edwards, who escaped the lower class with a straight shot to the upper class, doesn't truck with middle class morality and convention. And the son of Boboy Edwards doesn't kiss rings of Catholic archbishops. Nor does Philip Hannan, who understands the prerogatives and uses of power, expect him to, as the two skilled politicians disappear into Edwards' office to plot the next move against the unsuspecting bureaucrats in Rome.

Marion would like to sell about 20 more seats on the plane. "We don't have to, but it will be nice." Nice indeed. So far the Paris fund-raiser will gross $5 to $5.5 million and will net $4 to $4.2 million to pay off the notes secured by the letters of credit from the Committee of 200. The campaign treasurer is rightly proud of himself for having conceived, implemented and sold this spectacular fund-raiser, the capstone of the most expensive campaign in the history of American state politics. He considered a rerun of the 1972 trip to Mexico City and South America, but Marion knew the monstrous debt would require an even more magnificent promotion. And what could be more logical than a return to the homeland, the source of Louisiana politics' grand excesses?

With two jumbo jets almost filled, Marion's main task now is fighting a rearguard action against everyone trying to scramble aboard for the $2,100 special deal that the press and legislators are getting. Marion is on the phone to a friend of Bob Odom, explaining that the press reports were wrong, that not all state officials get the reduced price, only legislators. He is only selling $10,000 tickets, but, well, look, "I can raise $5,000 if he can raise $5,000. . . . Yes, someone gave me $5,000 to help someone who needs it to be able to go, so if you can get that $5,000 . . . "

"Sherman Bernard wants to go too," says Mike Baer, cupping his hand over his phone.

"Same deal," says Marion, cupping his hand over his.

Sam Thomas, a coordinator of the trip, says every effort has been made to accommodate travelers, including their E-Z credit terms: "$2,100 down and five payments of $2,000. We all know it's not how much that counts but what are the terms," he laughs going out the door.

Marion says it's been tough holding the line, but it's been held. "By the time this trip is over, I will have raised more than what Jefferson paid for Louisiana in 1803. That was $15 million. By the time this trip is over, I will have raised $17 million [$13 million for the campaign and $4 million to repay the amounts raised by letters of credit]." And you don't beat Napoleon's take by selling at-cost tickets. "Look, no one's getting a free ride. Everyone's got to pay. The governor, his ticket is paid for. Same for my family, my wife. Everyone is paid for," although some very thoughtful wealthy contributors and industries paid for tickets for Edwards to use or give away.

Baer puts down the phone in triumph. "Got him! He and his wife are going. $20,000."

Marion has cast his net wide, asking many who did not contribute to the campaign but who now are looking for some way to get on the bandwagon after the parade has passed. "Some Treen supporters have even called us and asked if Republicans can come along," laughs Judge Reggie. No problem at all, this is an equal opportunity scam.

Many were asked. Like the lobbyists who opened their mail to find two artfully designed tickets to the Paris fund-raiser and the letter instructing that a $20,000 check be returned because Governor Edwards knows you will want to go along. And it did no good to ditch the invite, for it was followed up by a phone call a week later from a campaign aide inquiring if the check was in the mail yet. "I've never seen the squeeze on lobbyists like this before," says the veteran. "You have to admire the way they have organized this." Lobbyists are the perfect target for a postelection fund-raiser. The private organizations that work for private companies do their business with the Legislature and with the regulatory boards, representing their clients as would a lawyer. Their unofficial, privately funded role in state government leaves them open for an appeal of this sort, with the ever so slight suggestion of an offer you can't refuse. It's not merely a question of one's clients getting roughed up in the Legislature or the bureaucracy, it's a matter of being left out of the action. Many of the state's boards and commissions have by tradition or law included representatives from several of the different industries and interest groups that are overseen by the boards. In many cases, complains the lobbyist trying to be objective, "it's lousy government, fox in the henhouse stuff," but it's ingrained in the system and no lobbyist can afford to have his people left off a board. The Edwards team knows the system as well as anyone, says the lobbyist. "They know what you want. They have systematically put together all the boards and commissions and who they know wants input to what selections. There are people in government for 40 years who don't know that, but the Edwards people do." And they hope to capitalize on the lobbyists' self-interest by encouraging them to buy tickets or to get their clients to pony up. "It's the smartest thing I've ever seen," says the lobbyist, "I'm still shocked at how sophisticated it is."

Yet, despite a good effort by Marion's sales team, few lobbyists sign up for the trip. Their entertainment expense accounts just go so far. The greater concern among lobbyists is the fear that Edwards and company are moving in on their turf. You just have to look at the new lobbying organizations being formed. George Fischer, having played no role in the transition, has formed a lobbying company along with his old aide (and Edwards' old press secretary) Jim Harris. Marion Edwards has gone into public affairs/lobbying, taking a vice president's post at Freeport-McMoRan, a giant company with sulfur plants and oil and gas interests in Louisiana. Ann Davenport and Vicki's husband Larry Cormier have formed a lobbying group and are already handling some legislators' fund-raisers.

Davenport, Cormier, Fischer and Harris all held posts in prior administrations. This time they're back in the action but not on the state payroll, so they don't have to worry about all the disclosure requirements and nagging ethics rules that have come to make state service a real drag for the governor's connected friends. This time around, Edwards can take care of his friends at arm's length, without the state having to pay for it, at least not directly. The parallel world of lobbyists, of private firms paid by private companies to inform and influence legislators, boards and bureaucrats, operates free of the strictures of state service. The combination of the lobbyists' freedom and access and the governor's friendship can work in ways smoothly subtle but devastatingly effective. Say your company or industry association has some important legislation coming up this session—now, who's your lobbyist again?

Before Dave Treen can gracefully leave office, there is the final untidy business of calling a special session to cure the impending deficit whose existence Treen downplayed when not denying it during the campaign. His cool, reasoned remarks to the opening joint session are hailed by many as his most impressive address as governor. "Yeah, just like MacArthur," breezes one legislator, "he saves his best speech for last."

But it won't be enough. House members are impressed by the lame duck governor's speech but stop dead in their tracks at Treen's request to reimpose the state income tax rates he cut three years before. Faced with legislative intransigence, Treen swallows hard and calls in the old master to whip the boys into shape. Showing up in blue jeans and windbreaker, Edwards casually moves to take charge of the special session, encouraging and cajoling the legislators, some of whom are lame ducks themselves, to start wiping out the major initiatives of the Treen administration. Not only is the full income tax reimposed, retroactive to cover 1983, but the congressional lines are redrawn in the Orleans area to create a majority black congressional district and to cut away 80 percent of Republican Bob Livingston's neighboring district. Also, the Legislature suspends creation of Treen's Department of Environmental Quality, a measure Treen will ignore anyway.

"It's the lemming Legislature," the sardonic reporter labels it. "It's so funny, I mean these guys won't go to the bathroom without calling Edwards. In the House, they're so-o-o upset at the idea of electing Joe Delpit Speaker pro tem," she says of Edwards' choice of the black Baton Rouge representative for the No. 2 leadership post, "but they won't dare vote against him." She's right, they don't.

On the Senate side, the solons have adjourned for the day after waving through the entire Edwards-Treen corrective package with barely a dissenting vote. Relaxing on the side of the chamber are two former Young Turks of the Senate, Tommy Hudson and Tony Guarisco. Entering their third terms, neither is that young anymore and Hudson, for one, has changed nationality. Turks don't get elected to Senate leadership positions and Hudson is campaigning hard for Senate president pro tem. But Guarisco's flame still burns brightly for lost causes and new conspiracies to alert the world against. "Did you see they're installing missiles at the White House and any plane that comes close gets destroyed, no questions asked?" Hudson, the frequent visitor to Washington, is looking at Guarisco like he just fell off the onion truck. "Oh sure, Hudson," Guarisco continues, "you probably think it's great. Look at you, I bet you're a part of it."

"Tony, have you ever seen an aviation map of D.C.? They've got this black rectangle from the Capitol to the White House with the warning that any plane that strays into that air space gets blown away. That's nothing new."

"Yeah, well, now they're gonna do it with missiles," huffs Guarisco. "That's Reagan for you."

"Guarisco's our Spartacus." Hudson pats his old roommate on the back. "On the very first vote, the Edwards people are looking to see who will come out against them and here's Tony in the back lighting a match to his foot."

Guarisco holds both arms behind his back. "They're gonna lash me to that pillar. I'll have to eat heavier before the regular session starts so that I'll last a few days longer."

John Hill passes by and asks Hudson, "Has Edwin told you who you'll be voting for for pro tem?"

"I just sent my ballot to him," smiles the candidate, doing his lemming imitation. "Now, John, you're so cynical. Don't take that to mean I'm going to let Edwards tell me what to do. No, he's just going to go ahead and do it."

At Tour D'Argent, after a day of touring Paris, playfully posing with fur-draped models from the House of Revillon, signing a cultural and trade agreement with government officials at the Chamber of Deputies and having a private audience with President Francois Mitterand,

337

Edwin Edwards sidles over to Bob Courtney near the TV cameras and asks, "Heard anything on Ossie Brown?"

That Edwin Resplendent, triumphant in Paris, the touring statesman with his bulging entourage of 600, could even bother to worry over the Baton Rouge DA's impending indictment suggests the governor-elect's mind is not all on his trip. So how is his royal tour going?

"Oh, I've done just what Marion told me to do. I've been good, I've gone to all the functions and smiled at people and shook hands, but tell you the truth, I want to get the fuck out of here and go home."

Anyone who would raise a toast in Paris and say, "I was destined, I thought, when I was born, to be a king, and tonight I can be," can't be expected to tolerate long separations from his people. The royalty theme is carried to the limits of good taste and beyond, especially the little lapel pins with the profile of Edwards and the inscription "Sun King." Whenever the awe-inspiring events crammed into each day—from laying a wreath at the tomb of France's unknown soldier to Edwards' induction into the Society of Beaujolais—got to be just too overwhelming, Edwin could be counted on to puncture the pomp and pageantry. After waiters in 17th-century garb bearing candelabras led the gawking 600 through the Palace of Versailles and served them *Saumon Marine a l'Aneth Sauce Moutarde Brune*, Edwards tablehops and poses for pictures wearing a waiter's periwig. And when it came to wisecracks, the king of repartee could not have had better set-ups. Exiting Notre Dame Cathedral, Edwards is greeted by a Louisiana nun, now living in France, who jokes, "Governor, I'm going to give you a French kiss."

"Okay, Sister, just don't let me get in the habit."

He even provides CBS with the perfect closing line for its story. Asked the most important thing he got out of the trip, he can't resist. "Five million dollars."

Finally the governor-elect is able to relax and have some back-home kind of fun: shooting craps at Monte Carlo. With its dome of stained glass and its gold-leaf, the 19th-century gaming room at the Monte Carlo Casino is not exactly Harrah's, so Edwards tries to impart some continental manners to his rowdy buddy Gus Mijalis. "Don't holler if you don't have the number, dummy," Edwards yells at his exuberant friend.

"That's me, a nine! A nine!" Mijalis shouts back.

338

"You can holler, you can holler," yells Edwards.

The biggest news of the trip—a banner headline in the *Morning Advocate*—comes an hour later when Louisiana's most famous gambler finishes a $15,000 run. To hell with decorum, the governor-elect slaps the table and instructs the dealer, "Give me my money. Give me my money. Give me a wheelbarrow for my money."

Organizers Marion Edwards and Sam Thomas are dubbed the generals of the trip. They keep the tour moving—campaign style. When 100 more of the Louisianians than expected show up for a night at the Lido, Marion slips the *maitre d'* $1,000 and seats appear from nowhere.

Daughter Vicki commands her share of attention on the trip. She even makes the network news, displaying her barefoot-in-the-bayou charm in responding to the reporter's question "Did you pay $10,000 to come on the trip?"

"Hell, no, I'm the governor's daughter."

She makes some head-turning entrances as well. When she walks into the gaming room in Monte Carlo in a stunning black and gold gown with a gold-glittered, black ostrich plume swooping back over her ear, reporter Jack Wardlaw observes, "Looks like tonight's entertainment is going to be Vicki singing *Carmen*."

Time and *People* are along for the ride to capture *The Beverly Hillbillies Go to Paris* spirit of the occasion. Most of the travelers, though, are not new to Paris or insensitive to her charms. Nita Thomas, walking through Versailles' Hall of Mirrors, where the chandeliers are dimmed to candlelight level, is enthralled. "I feel like Cinderella going to the ball. It is like a fairy tale." On the whole, the supporting cast of 600 acquit themselves quite well. "On their best behavior" is the term most often used to describe their comportment. Still they can't resist a little silliness. At dinner at Le Train Bleu, all are minding their manners until legislators Jesse Deen and LaLa Lalonde climb atop the center table to have their picture taken next to the brass rooster atop the decoration. A reporter gasps to Representative Clyde Kimball, who laughs it off. "Hell, I'll probably take it home with me," says Clyde, as he slips an ashtray into his pocket. On the ride back to the hotel, the merrymaking legislators sing "Jolie Blonde" and then, of course, "You Are My Sunshine" as the bus rolls down the moonlit Champs Elysees.

"How about a Dave Treen letter opener, still left over from the inauguration?" Lanny Keller is handing out mementos to reporters on the governor's last day at the office. But there's a catch. "You have to take one of his boring books, too." They've been left over since Treen was in Congress. Boxes of files are still being hauled downstairs but the pace for some staff members has in fact quickened this last day. Ray Lamonica breaks his hurried stride to explain, "There's so much left to do. You can't have something signed by one secretary and by another governor. Everything started by this administration has to be finished here." And today. For Treen will spend Friday in New Orleans doing TV interviews and will go home that night to his condo on the golf course at Beau Chene, the picturesque St. Tammany development where he and Dodie will eventually build.

Treen welcomes reporters into the high-ceilinged, dark wood office, the old Court of Appeals library, designed with intimidation in mind. Treen is in good spirits if not particularly good form—his voice is going fast as he croaks out answers to the final formula questions for the wire service and the TV reporters.

If you had it all to do over again . . .

"I would not make any different decisions, but I would probably try to find someone who was an expert on TV projection to get across the idea to the public what a warm, sensitive, hilarious, witty person I really am."

That's odd since at a party you're so relaxed and make everyone feel so comfortable.

"Yes, I know, but it just seems that in press conferences, I don't know, I look too serious, too stiff, but it is sort of an adversarial relationship."

What will you be thinking about when you walk out of this office the last time tonight?

"I really can't answer what I'll feel like. This office really hasn't done what I thought it could do in terms of ego inflation. It's a nice office, nice-looking, but I associate it with all the burdens of the job. I've never had a chance to sit on the sofa over there and look around the office and enjoy it."

And leaving the Mansion?

"We left with mixed feelings. Dodie and I were both surprised that we didn't feel sadder about leaving it. But we had a very nice weekend

340

alone, just the two of us, in the condo. It was very nice."

The governor looks forward to another nice weekend playing golf, then returning to Baton Rouge for the inauguration. If all that goes as quickly as he hopes, "I can still tee off in the afternoon and get in 18 holes."

He interrupts so Robyn Eckings can do some cutaways for her public TV interview. While Robyn re-asks her questions for the tape, Treen throws in joke answers that sound more appropriate than his on-the-record comments.

Do you blame anyone for your defeat?

"Four hundred thousand voters."

Then there are the little readjustments to normal, mortal existence outside the power and glory of office. "I'll have to get used to carrying my car keys and wallet again," he says, thumbing through his modest Member of Congress billfold. For transportation there's the 1971 Cutlass convertible—indeed it is the real Treen family car, not a prop kept around to look good on financial disclosure reports. At the end of the day, however, Billy Nungesser presents his friend with the keys to a new Cadillac, a going-away present from some of his friends and supporters.

Leaving the governor to toil and grind through his final hours in power (let the record show that Dave Treen finally left his office at 2:30 a.m., March 9), the reporters take the gold-door governor's elevator to the basement. "I couldn't help but feel sad seeing him there," says one. "He is such a nice guy and I don't think people ever understood him." No, they didn't, but neither did Treen show us much of himself to understand. Dave Treen remained to the end his own man, refusing to allow the demands of power and politics to push him onto the public stage to display his charm and project the correct image of the sincere public servant getting the job done. The people didn't need to see an actor, a stand-up comic or a self-assured power broker: Dave Treen, the man, was impressive and likable enough to form a better personal bond with the people. But he was too imprisoned by that office which he never had enjoyed to project the real Dave Treen to the people of this state who want more than a public servant as governor, who want a personality who shows he is a leader and knows how to use the awesome powers

341

granted him by the voters. To have projected that image, even the correct image, would have required Treen to give over a part of his life for public consumption. And that, Dave Treen, an intensely private man thrust into an intensely public life, was not ready to do. The really successful politicians readily and completely give over their private lives to their public. They live onstage, never shrinking from the camera's eye, revealing a carefully concocted and constrained persona or, like Edwin Edwards, letting it all—or most of it—hang out for the amazement and entertainment of the public.

In a way, you have to admire the public man who refuses to go public with his life. Just as many appreciate the fact that Dave Treen was not adept at politics and would rather be right than governor. We admire and respect those people, but history shows we don't elect them. And if by some chance we do, we get rid of them at the first opportunity. It's no putdown of the gifted politicians or the people—it's a matter of electing the right person for the right job. Treen had something to contribute to public service. His talent was to study an issue, pick it apart, hear the conflicting arguments, ignore the outside pressures and decide what was right. He was not meant to be the one with the vision, the dream, the one to gather his resources and set his course and to move a constituency toward his goal. By his style and character, he was a judge and not a leader. Dave Treen could not have been a better person, but because of who he was he could not have been in a worse job.

The Reverend Clarence D. Bates died in early February and was honored in a raucous, free-wheeling and joyous memorial service at the Greater First Pentecostal Church in Alexandria. Sister Vesta Mangun led the congregation in singing "I'll Fly Away" as mourners were swept away in homage to the colorful ward-heeling preacher, Uncle Earl's old state trooper, Edwin Edwards' staunchest defender and Central Louisiana's most creative political moralist. His work on this earth done, he'll be sorely missed, but in a way old Clarence, though never one to shrink from any seemingly irreconcilable contradiction between faith and politics, nevertheless is probably relieved and happy to receive his final reward before having to rise to his greatest challenge: explaining the newest outrage to emanate from Edwin Edwards' lips.

25. The Last Hayride

Inconceivably, it rains on the coronation of the Sun King, and Edwin Edwards is sworn into office—in English by his son Steven, in French by his brother Marion—in the House chamber instead of on the grandstand built on the Capitol steps. But far more serious storms are brewing this day. As she promised Edwards in the tabernacle in Tioga in July, Sister Vesta Mangun sings at the inauguration but she is none too happy about it. The wife of Louisiana's leading Pentecostal preacher will later tell church members she sang to give glory to God but it irks her that glory to Edwin Edwards comes with the deal. While Catholic bishops say Mass and Protestant preachers pray, the new governor finds himself caught in a raging firestorm. Edwin Edwards, who started his first term with questions raised about his gambling trips and TEL Enterprises, starts his third term embroiled in a hotter controversy: the death and resurrection of Jesus Christ. Talk about a whole new tone.

Edwards, celebrated for his penchant for saying the darnedest things, stepped in it good this time in a remarkable, spontaneous interview with his friend Stanley Tiner, editor of the Shreveport *Journal*, in which he wandered into political never-never land by revealing his innermost and highly provocative thoughts about religion. For all the hard times he's had with the press over the years, it's fitting and ironic that he would catch the most heat for saying something to one of his few friends in the business. He stumbled into it with Tiner, explaining the presence in his bathroom of Tocqueville's *Democracy in America,* the Bible and the latest issue of *Playboy.* Downhill from there as Edwards, the born Catholic, born-again Nazarene, reconverted Catholic and favorite of the Pentecostals, espoused beliefs that set him at odds with every church he's ever belonged to.

343

"My religion is my relationship with other people," he said in the copy-righted interview appearing in the *Journal* a week before the inaugura-tion. "I feel comfortable with anybody's image of his God, if my conscience is at ease with relations with other people. I don't have any fear of facing your concept of God or your neighbor's concept or the Hindu's concept of his God or the Arab's concept of his God, if I am able to live my life in good conscience not doing violence to someone else."

"Are you a Christian?" asked Tiner.

"Yes."

But then the litmus test. "Do you believe Jesus died on the cross, was buried and resurrected?"

"No. I think Jesus died, but I don't believe he came back to life be-cause that's too much against natural law. I'm not going around preach-ing this, but he may have swooned, passed out or almost died, and when he was taken down, with superhuman strength, after a period of time he may have revived himself and come back to life. . . . I cannot embrace the idea that a person literally, actually died and then came back to life. . . . I certainly believe there was a Jesus, as a historical character, who molded his life by design or by accident to fit precepts of the prophets as to who the Messiah was to be."

Edwards, who said his transition from "absolute faith to one of analy-tical dissection" took place at about age 30 (which would place him in Crowley at the start of his political career), said he prays to God "for wisdom, peace, knowledge and understanding" and that he believes in a hereafter, certainly a heaven, but "I'm not quite sure there is a hell."

"Where will Edwin Edwards be in the afterworld?"

"If I'm to be consistent with my own self-analysis, using a strict interpretation of the Bible, I think I'm going to have a hard time making it, just as will most people I know."

For Edwards, a big believer in the bottom line as well as natural law, the comments are almost as bad as being "caught in bed with a dead girl or a live boy." Though barely noticed in New Orleans or Acadiana, the interview sets off a firestorm of rage and condemnation in North and Central Louisiana. The letters pour in to the editorial pages in Shreveport, Alexandria and Baton Rouge seething with righteous indignation and betrayal. "Monday should have been a day of mourning for all Christians in Louisiana," writes Rick V. Moore of Alexandria. "Because on Monday, Edwin Edwards was sworn into office, a man who claims to be a

Christian and yet doesn't believe that Jesus Christ rose from the dead (If that didn't happen, there would be no point to Christianity)." Quoting Romans 10:9, Mrs. Patricia Williams of Baton Rouge writes, "'That if thou ... believe in thine heart that God hath raised him from the dead, thou shalt be saved.' Apart from belief in Jesus' resurrection, no one can be saved. Tell Mr. Edwards, yes, I believe that there is a hell, I grant him that many will be spending eternity there, sad to say, but *Hell is no joke.*"

Edwards receives some support from unexpected places, such as some reporters and columnists and even a few preachers who note that Edwards' statements counter the suspicion that he only cynically uses his dual faiths to appeal to the broadest possible range of Catholics and Protestants. He shows he takes his religious beliefs seriously enough to question and analyze them instead of accepting them blindly. And to let those dangerous ideas spill out of his gut indicates the seriousness of his search for faith that a garden variety politician would do all he could to squelch.

As well as renewing his refreshing unpredictability and spontaneity, Edwards' ill-advised remarks reveal a deeper side of himself, giving clues to what makes the man tick. Reporters who laughed off Edwards' messianic message that developed over the last months of the campaign begin reviewing his words in the new context: *The healer is coming... Go and tell all whom you meet that someone is coming to cure the ills of this state and to take care of you... The greater the crowd the closer the cross.* It all seemed then to be a grand rhetorical joke, Edwin surprising even himself with what he could say and get away with. But maybe he wasn't joking—the more outrageous his messianic claims, the more the crowds' wild responses egged him on. Perhaps he was witnessing, revealing his own moral spark that drives him so relentlessly. To apply natural law to what happened to Christ on the cross in one way challenges his divinity and in another reveals the incredible potential inherent in a human who possesses enough brains, energy, vision and *chutzpah*. It may say that if Christ were not *the* Messiah there may be room for more. And that anyone who dares to live his dreams can achieve all the wealth, fame and power he seeks and bring economic and social salvation to his people and, of course, his disciples. Is this what really drives Edwin Edwards, the Healer, the Sun King? That we'll never know, for Edwards quickly slams shut his metaphysical window in defense against the angry backlash that mars his reascension to power. In the torrent of phone calls and letters pouring into his office—as much heat as he's caught for saying or doing anything—Edwards regrets ever opening his mouth on a subject "humanity has been debating for 2,000 years." And he chows down his words quicker than any political gaffe he has uttered. "What I failed to properly point out clearly," he tells a group of Louisiana Catholic bishops, "was that natural law is an obstacle that is overcome by my faith in God and my personal belief in the Scripture, which teaches that Jesus was the God-man who was sent to this world to redeem mankind." Just to set the record straight, "I accept on faith that the death and resurrection of Jesus actually took place because I accept the Bible as the inspired word of God and without the death and resurrection of Jesus, his divinity could not be fully established. . . . To the extent that I erred or was misunderstood, I apologize and ask for forgiveness and understanding from everyone of all faiths."

But absolution comes easier in the confessional than in the brush arbor. Though Brother Mangun accepted Edwards' recantation and apology and even tried to lay a little of the blame on the press, resentment and alienation still run deep through the Pentecostals, who have long considered Edwin Edwards one of them. A common feeling expressed by many of the brethren is that on Edwards' next trip to Tioga *he'll have to go in the altar before he steps into the pulpit.* To "go in the altar," explains my Pentecostal guide, means to lie prostrate at the foot of the altar before the congregation and to beg forgiveness for one's sins. That'll be the day.

Edwards is beaten up pretty badly by the whole affair, and it will take time for the wounds to heal. Next to even opening his mouth on the subject, Edwards probably most regrets not having Clarence Bates around to put it all in perspective.

He leans against the clerk's desk in the nearly empty Senate chamber, dressed in his usual lobbying uniform of windbreaker, blue jeans and oversized belt buckle with "Edwin" inscribed thereon. "Thank you, Sammy, I've already eaten," the new governor turns down the Senate President's invitation to dine, as he would prefer to be alone with his public, as represented by a handful of reporters and TV cameras setting up for interviews at the tail end of this special session.

Edwin Edwards doesn't want to go through another week like this again. Having just "gone in the altar" with his public apology to "everyone of all faiths," he has ridden a wild rollercoaster of a special session testing both the heights and limits of his power and succeeded in passing the largest tax package in the history of the state—and now he's sorry he did.

One week after the inauguration, he welcomed the Legislature to the New Order, appearing before them somber and determined, wearing reading glasses even, to lay out his massive $1.1 billion "economic development" package (as far as clever new euphemisms for "tax" go, Reagan's "revenue enhancements" pale in comparison). He laced his statesmanlike address with horror stories of impending drastic cuts in human services ("many too unspeakable to even mention") and veiled threats ("you can't get run over if you're on the train"). The Big Train analogy set the tone of the first three days as the House rushed through half of the taxes, barely slowing down. Things were moving so fast at one point Baton Rouge Representative Jewel Newman went before the Channel 2 cameras to explain why he voted for the gasoline tax, which had not yet been brought up for a vote. Even the leading obstructionists in Edwards' eyes, the editorial writers of the *Times-Picayune* and the *Morning Advocate*, fell into line endorsing nearly his entire package. And Doug Manship personally instructed Channel 2 to make available public service time to carry the governor's message. Conservatives' cries of what's the big rush were lost in the din of the voting machine bells ringing up another Edwards tax vote victory. Of course everyone knew what the rush was. Better to go into special session and pass taxes in March than to wait until the regular session starts April 16, the worst day of the year to even mention the word "tax."

Among those already flattened by the Big Train were Dutch Morial and a pack of lesser mayors who were seen wandering the halls in search of a sympathetic ear. Dutch, though careful not to criticize the wisdom and good faith of the governor, had received a commitment from Edwards not to seek a state sales tax, since Morial was planning to ask New Orleans voters for another cent on the sales tax to run the city. Many other mayors, planning the same move, found themselves on the rails alongside Dutch, as the state sales tax was the first to roll through. Dutch was not even able to convene a breakfast meeting of the New Orleans delegation to plot a counter strategy, citing the lack of a convenient meeting place. Now come on, Dutch, everyone knows it's infinitely harder to find a good breakfast in Baton Rouge than in New Orleans, but the real reason he can't get the city delegation together is that half of them don't care to hear what he has to say. It's a telling indication that although Dutch has vanquished his foes and reigns supreme in the city, his power in the State Capitol has ebbed lower than any New Orleans mayor's in the last half century. In a city he has helped to polarize into black and white, Morial controls only half, albeit the dominant half, making him far less influential than a Moon Landrieu or a Chep Morrison or a Bob Maestri, who could lead the entire delegation. Also, the city's white flight to the suburbs is reflected in New Orleans' waning legislative power. The jailed president of the Senate Mike O'Keefe of New Orleans is replaced by Sammy Nunez of neighboring St. Bernard Parish. Speaker of the House John Hainkel of New Orleans is replaced by John Alario of the Westbank. Mayor Dutch Morial now rules a fiefdom divided within itself and with its tax base now tightly hemmed in. Just in case he missed the point on the Faucheux appointment, Edwin Edwards has just delivered Lesson 2 on who's the new Boss of Orleans.

Midway through the week, Edwin's spell wears thin as the combined efforts of conservatives, business lobbyists and scared legislators derail the big train at the $720 million mark. Remarkably, the business interests, who were supposed to have been vanquished by labor and Edwards, escape the taxing session almost unscathed, while the biggest taxes—sales, gasoline and entertainment—hit the poor and working classes hardest. Edwards and legislative friends breezed into the special session only to find a far better organized and effective business lobby than he has ever had to contend with. Worse still, nearly every dollar of the new taxes so painfully raised must go to cover this year's gaping deficit and to keep up with built-in budget increases, leaving little if anything for his promised pay raise for state employees, the biotech research center, drainage program and economic development package. He's talked the Legislature into passing part of his massive tax package but he didn't get enough, he claims, to give the people anything for their money. "That's what I told them," he says, cheerlessly looking out over the quiet chamber. "If we do this, let's do it well, do it effectively, let's get the show on the road. If not, let's all retrench and head for the bunkers. Now we're in a Catch-22, we're halfway in both categories."

The last place Edwin Edwards feels like being this Holy Thursday is on the federal courthouse steps. But he comes today not to appear before a grand jury but to show his support for his friend Ossie Brown, who is waiting for his trial jury to return. The governor stays only briefly, going off with Ossie in the courthouse foyer for a quiet conversation. Ossie returns to his vigil on the steps. He's been through this kind of agonizing wait before, as a crack defense attorney and as district attorney. Except those other times he was getting paid for it. Now he's the one paying—in legal fees, personal anguish and eroding popularity. The past 10 months have been private and public torture for him as the federal investigation dragged on, indictments came down and he stood trial.

U.S. Attorney Stan Bardwell, who began investigating Brown shortly after the Justice Department decided not to indict Edwin Edwards, also waits to hear from the jury that has been deliberating since the night before. The extortion case against Brown and former mayor's aide David Bourland all boils down to the government's presentation and Ossie Brown's credibility. Bardwell ignored suggestions that he bring in an experienced prosecutor from John Volz's office in New Orleans, going to trial instead with two inexperienced assistants against Brown's and Bourland's phalanx of top-flight defense attorneys. "This was a story that needed to be told," Bardwell would say after the jury heard the government's witnesses: millionaire Jim D'Spain, who testified about his son's cocaine arrest and his subsequent $134,000 loan to Brown's and Bourland's ice cream company; millionaire Claude Pennington, who stated he paid an intermediary $10,000, which he assumed was going to Brown, to keep his name out of the cocaine bust; assistant district attorney Richard Chaffin, who said Brown instructed him to steer the grand jury clear of indicting the two cocaine suspects; and District Judge Donovan Parker, who testified Ossie Brown asked him to quash evidence against one of the suspects. But the most important witness was Brown himself, who took the stand for five hours and in excruciating detail—including constant references to his family—told his side of the story, insisting the loan was consummated without his knowledge and against his specific instructions, and denying he interfered in any way with the grand jury investigation.

And now the wait. Brown, like Edwards last year, finds himself pursued by the U.S. government as his campaign for reelection begins.

Ossie already has two announced opponents, with even stronger ones waiting in the wings and on the jury's verdict. If he's found guilty he's gone. But if he's acquitted, the potentially stronger challengers will stay out of the race and Ossie will be very hard to beat.

Ossie masks his nervousness by clowning and joking with reporters, attorneys and office workers sweating out the vigil on the steps with him. At three o'clock word comes the jury has reached a partial verdict that has been sealed pending the completion of their deliberations. Brown disappears. Reporters alert their stations to stand by for a live cutaway. They wait some more.

Two hours later, in Judge Frank Polozola's crowded courtroom, Ossie Brown buries his face in his hands and sobs uncontrollably. Co-defendant Bourland and their attorneys cry openly too along with family and friends, who are making such a ruckus, the bailiff cannot restore order. Brown and Bourland have been found not guilty on all counts. Bardwell and his young assistants sit in stony silence as spectators mob Ossie Brown.

Downstairs, the local TV stations cut into the network news to announce the verdict and to focus the cameras on the courthouse doors to await Ossie Brown's exit from the gates of hell. Minutes later, friends and supporters practically carry Brown through the doors and to the waiting battery of microphones and cameras. In the street, two men in a pickup truck slow down to shout, "Shoulda hung him," and moments later a man wheels his convertible into the post office parking lot and yells, "We'll get you next time." But the taunts, if noticed, are ignored by Brown, who is brushing off even reporters' questions to deliver his message directly to his supporters and the people of East Baton Rouge Parish listening at home.

"So many people have been standing by me through this, and let me say this: I am a Christian. And I prayed from the word Go that God would bring me through this. Through Faye and the kids we suffered a lot. God has prevailed and I'm here to tell you today I'm stronger in my faith in God than ever before. I'm going to let my life be what I ought to let it be for Him. And people can ridicule me. People can make fun of me in the press and criticize me for my stands on morals and decency, but I'm going to do my job as God gives me the wisdom to do that job. And I prayed, 'Lord, if you want me to be district attorney for six more years, you exonerate me in this case. If it's not your will, then let me be found guilty.' God has given me that answer. So come Monday, I want everybody to know, I am running for reelection . . .''

The door to the governor's den opens and out comes a delegation of legislators as the next group waits in the dining room to be called. Edwin Edwards is back to the standard operating procedure he's most comfortable with: working at home. In fact, he's barely been to his imposing office in the Capitol since his predecessor departed there early on the morning of March 9. And as expected, there's been an even greater change in priorities in the gubernatorial appointment schedule. Every afternoon the governor is in town during the session is legislators' time. After lunch, Edwards blocks out the rest of the day to "hear confession," as a New Orleans ward boss once described it. If a legislator has something on his mind, a request or need for guidance, he only has to show up, put his name on the list, get a chocolate chip cookie or glass of iced tea from the kitchen and wait his turn. The governor stays until his waiting room is empty.

Directing traffic and answering the phone from the small anteroom next to the den is the governor's new executive assistant, Sid Moreland. The youngest and least noticed of Edwards' former campaign aides, Moreland has followed his personal motto of "Stay low, stay long" into his demanding but exciting new job. "It happened kind of fast," drawls the 23-year-old from Ruston. Darrell Hunt needed a break after two years at Edwards' beck and call, and now works for Stephanie Alexander in the Division of Administration. Stan Cadow is in Intergovernmental Relations. And Wayne Ray, originally slotted for the executive assistant's post, opted not to go on the state payroll where conflicts could arise with his outside business interests. That left to Sid the job of relaying the governor's messages, scheduling appointments and briefing him on requests.

There are always requests, especially from legislators, each of whom seems to represent a district with unique and crying needs. The inveterate favor granter that he is, Edwards would love to accede to all their pleas, or at least those of legislators who stood with the governor in the past, painful taxing session. But Edwin Edwards faces a baffling new problem. As much as he would like to reward the tax hikers' cooperation, the new money raised has all gone to shore up the state's tottering finances. Edwards instead has had to go back to the Legislature to announce there won't be money even for employees' pay raises unless the legislators make more deep and unpopular cuts in the proposed state budget. In his first administration, his severance tax increase allowed him to decrease personal taxes while offering more state services. Now on his second coming, he has had to raise personal taxes and begin cutting services. The savings his office has proposed include some of the same cutbacks for which he beat Dave Treen over the head so relentlessly during the campaign. Ironically, Edwards has the power and know-how to enact the same cuts that Dave Treen had to back away from. Indeed, an unprecedented and revolting predicament.

The door opens again, legislators exit, leaving the governor to sit at his desk by the bay window and look out toward Capitol Lake. The new realities have had their effect already. Shortly after taking office, he agreed with a reporter's observation that he appeared to be more serious this time around. "These are serious times. I'm scared to death. With conditions as they are, I don't want to make quips that a year from now will come back to haunt me. Things today don't lend themselves to the solutions of the '60s and the '70s." Finally, sadly, after generations of Louisianians using other people's money—whether from the Spanish fleet or Standard Oil—to finance the state's first-provider populist traditions, Edwin Edwards finds himself having to go to the people—the little people even—for enough money just to keep the state solvent while having to defer his promises of economic salvation and deliverance. And a year from now, or four years from now, what will there to be to show for it? What then will he say to his own question that Dave Treen could never answer: "Where has all the money gone?"

He may try to point to a more effective, efficient state government led by Judge Reggie's legions of the best and the brightest. He will undergo the character-building exercise—until now unheard of in this state—of painfully cutting the budget and having to listen to the cries of the constituency he promised to deliver from uncaring Republican hands. He will juggle some of his ambitious great leaps forward into smaller hops. He may even give his blessing to the mounting pressure for a state lottery (he can't offend the hard-shells any more than he has already). But even with all that, he knows the odds run strongly against any government satisfying its taxpayers their money is well spent. The problem Edwin Edwards now faces is that people realize more than ever that it is their money being spent, that gradually the old Louisiana apathy—*it's not our money*—will turn into the same wary, antitax sentiment and resentful distrust most state governments feel from the people.

Wisely Edwards has buffered himself. The poor devils in the Legislature who listened to him and voted for his taxes will be the first to feel the rage. Then local mayors and parish councils, cut off from easier sales tax hikes, will have to make the first moves on the sacrosanct tradition of miniscule residential property taxes. Assuming he can stay clear of the U.S. attorneys and the preachers through four years, he should be able to win a historic fourth term. But the tougher question he may face is, why bother?

Having nothing more to look forward to than employee layoffs and dreams deferred, Edwards may be spared terminal boredom only by the high anxiety of watching the state totter on the precipice. For he knows Louisiana is running out of time. The 21st century, the federal government and the American economic system are closing in on this state. Without a drastic and unprecedented shifting of its tax base and upgrading of its education system, the state is doomed to a slough of wretchedness once the oil companies suck it dry and pull up their rigs and leave. The specialized, technical jobs that are left won't be available to Louisiana kids finishing high school with what was once a perfectly adequate sixth-grade education. To prevent that, to provide any kind of future—even far more modest than the grand designs he envisions—will require not just the overhaul of the entire tax base and school system but first Louisianians' whole attitude toward self-government. Our free and easy, banana republic, oil sheikdom days are numbered. Louisiana can either do what it has to do to become a mainstream American state or it can struggle to keep up with Mississippi. Dave Treen, though he knew the right direction, couldn't steer the state onto that path—he too closely represented what Louisiana needs to become. Edwin Edwards was elected because he represents what Louisiana is—*un de nous autres*—and now he must sell his followers not just on his vision but the painful steps needed to get there.

A prerequisite is a cleaner administration that holds the trust of the people whose money he's spending and keeps the ever vigilant U.S. attorneys at bay. And he knows, as hard as he may try, it can still all go to hell in his hands.

For no one's totally pulled it off yet. The state's past heroes hadn't the chance to achieve their visions' full potentials. Lafitte was exiled. Huey was shot. Uncle Earl was driven crazy. But for Edwin Edwards, who works just within the law and lives on the cool side of passion, it may be his fortune, or his curse, to live out his destiny and to see to what ends his dreams come.

Index

John Maginnis is a native Louisianian who has been covering state politics since 1972. He currently writes a statewide syndicated newspaper column and is editor and publisher of *Gris Gris* in Baton Rouge.

Cover photo by Harold Baquet/Zone One.